Praise for Manda Collins's delicious Regency novels . . .

HOW TO ROMANCE A RAKE

"With her trademark wit and charm, Manda Collins has penned a deeply romantic and emotionally satisfying story in *How to Romance a Rake*. Her heroine is plucky and tremendously appealing, and I cheered for her well-earned happily-ever-after."

—Vanessa Kelly, award-winning author
of *Sex and the Single Earl*

"Collins's second installment of the Ugly Duckling trilogy is both a lovely, sensitive romance and a taut thriller. Collins brings a dashing hero and a wounded wallflower together in the type of love story readers take to heart. With compassion and perception, she delves into the issues faced by those who survive physical and emotional trauma. Brava to Collins!"

—*RT Book Reviews*, 4 stars

"Absolutely delightful, *How to Romance a Rake* is an emotion-packed, passionate historical romance."

—*Romance Junkies*, 5 stars, Blue Ribbon Review

"*How to Romance a Rake* is a wonderfully moving story about two damaged people coming together to form a unique bond. Manda Collins is now on my auto-buy list, and I can't wait for the final book in this series."

—*Rakehell, Where Regency Lives*

MORE . . .

"How to Romance a Rake is a wonderful story. It is the sort of story that warms the heart and reaffirms the notion that love conquers all. Books like *How to Romance a Rake* are why I read romance."

—*Romance Novel News*

"The passion sizzles in this book, and while Collins delves into deeply emotional issues, she also infuses her stories with plenty of humor along with a terrific secondary cast. *How to Romance a Rake* is going straight to my keeper shelf. I highly recommend it!"

—*Romance Dish*

HOW TO DANCE WITH A DUKE

"Sexy, thrilling, and romantic—whether she's writing of the mysteries of the heart or of the shady underworld of Egyptian relic smuggling, Manda Collins makes her Regency world a place any reader would want to dwell." —*USA Today* bestselling author Kieran Kramer

"A fast-paced, adventurous love story that will enthrall readers. Her dynamic characters, a murder, and passion combine with the perfect amount of lively repartee."

—*RT Book Reviews*

"If Manda Collins keeps writing novels like [this], she is sure to become a bestseller."

—*Romance Junkies,* Blue Ribbon Review

"A vivid reminder of why I love historical romances . . . an excellent debut by Manda Collins that has me desperate for the next book in this trilogy."

—*Night Owl Romance,* Top Pick

"Manda Collins is a sparkling new voice in romantic fiction. Her smart, witty storytelling will keep readers turning pages."
—Toni Blake

"A splendid read, well written and fun."
—*Romance Reader*

"Written with intelligence, wit, and compassion, *How to Dance with a Duke* is a book that should put Manda Collins on the radar of historical romance readers everywhere."
—*Romance Dish*

"A refreshing and fun debut spiced with just the right amount of mystery."
—*Rakehell*

"Warmth, wit, and delicious chemistry shine through every page . . . With a heroine to root for and a hero to die for, *How to Dance with a Duke* is a romance to remember."
—Bestselling author Julie Anne Long

"Manda Collins writes sexy and smart historical romance, with a big dash of fun. Romance readers will adore *How to Dance with a Duke*!"
—Vanessa Kelly, named one of *Booklist*'s "New Stars of Historical Romance"

"Regency lovers have a new author to add to their dance cards! Manda Collins heats up the ballroom and writes romance to melt even the frostiest duke's heart. With sparkling Regency wit, a dash of mystery, and just the right amount of steam, *How to Dance with a Duke* is an enchanting debut, sure to sweep readers off their feet!"
—Tessa Dare, named one of *Booklist*'s "New Stars of Historical Romance"

Also by Manda Collins

How to Dance with a Duke
How to Romance a Rake
How to Entice an Earl

Why Dukes Say I Do

Manda Collins

St. Martin's Paperbacks

This is a work of fiction. All of the characters, organizations, and events portrayed in this novel are either products of the author's imagination or are used fictitiously.

WHY DUKES SAY I DO

Copyright © 2013 by Manda Collins.

For information address St. Martin's Press, 175 Fifth Avenue, New York, NY 10010.

ISBN: 978-1-250-02383-4

Printed in the United States of America

St. Martin's Paperbacks edition / August 2013

St. Martin's Paperbacks are published by St. Martin's Press, 175 Fifth Avenue, New York, NY 10010.

10 9 8 7 6 5 4 3 2 1

For my sister, Jessie. I'm so proud of you I can't stand it.

Acknowledgments

As always I'd like to thank my fabulous and insightful editor, Holly Blanck, for her continued awesomeness and patience with my absent-minded artistic ways; my lovely and talented agent extraordinaire, Holly Root; everyone at St. Martin's Press who works behind the scenes to ensure that my books come out looking gorgeous; my Kiss and Thrill sisters, Amy, Sarah, Diana, Krista, Lena, Gwen, Sharon, and Rachel; Janga, Julianne, Santa, Lindsey, Terri, and the Vano group for continued support; my family; and last but not least, my readers, without whom none of this would be worth it.

Prologue

"Your Grace," Lady Isabella Wharton coaxed, from the other side of the Ormonde library, "really, you must put the knife down. Whatever will your grandmama think?"

But the Duke of Ormonde, accustomed to ignoring his family's dictates, didn't lower the knife at his wife's throat. "Who gives a hang what that old bat thinks?" he demanded, his red-rimmed eyes devoid of conscience, his normally handsome visage turned ugly with anger. "She's the one who made me marry this miserable bitch. And look where that's gotten me."

As the miserable bitch in question was Isabella's younger sister, she could hardly be expected to agree with him. Perdita, the younger daughter of the Earl of Ramsden, had married the young Duke of Ormonde in a ceremony that had rivaled the royal wedding a decade before. Isabella had been hopeful that her sister's marriage would be successful where hers had failed. Yet here they were now, a few years later, and the groom was threatening the bride with a knife. Hardly the stuff dreams were made of.

"Won't you let me go, dearest?" Perdita asked, her voice surprisingly calm as she held her chin up higher to escape the prick of the blade. A ringlet of her auburn curls brushed the knife's edge as she trembled in her husband's arms. "You know you don't mean me any harm."

"Put the knife down, Your Grace," the fourth member of their mad party, Mrs. Georgina Mowbray, whose husband had also been less than ideal, said, her brisk tone honed through years following the drum. Her petite stature suggested a daintiness that the blonde's determination belied. "Killing your wife will not make you feel any better."

The sisters had befriended the army widow when they'd all three been on the same committee for the Ladies Charitable Society to which they belonged. Perdita had come to the meeting with a bruise on her face and a nonsensical story about falling into a door, and Georgie had guessed the truth of the situation at once. When she'd revealed her own history with the celebrated war hero who had been her husband—a history in which the hero had battered his own wife in every possible way before dying in glory on the battlefield—the three women had forged an unshakeable bond.

"She wouldn't be able to leave me," the duke said with the twisted logic that only madmen and drunkards could understand. "She was fine before the two of you got hold of her with your lies about me."

Isabella nearly screamed in frustration. This was her fault. All her fault. Because Perdita could hardly leave her husband—the laws were made by men and, as such, stacked in their own favor when it came to things like wives, who were little more than property in the eyes of the law—the three ladies had thought they might be able

to approach the duke in such a way that he would agree
to treat Perdita with the dignity she deserved as his wife.
The idea was laughable now, of course, but Isabella had
not known the extent of the duke's madness at the time.
Her own husband had been a brute, but he'd been fairly
easy to understand. Ormonde's possessive nature coupled
with his brutality was far more dangerous than Wharton
had ever been, she saw now.

"I would never leave you," Perdita said, her voice
trembling a little as her strength began to flag. "You know
I love you."

Isabella could see her sister was nearing the breaking
point. She exchanged a look with Georgie to see if she'd
noticed.

She had.

Wordlessly Georgie glanced down at her left hand,
which held her reticule. With her other hand she formed
a pistol with her thumb and forefinger. Oh god, Isabella
thought. She's brought her gun.

When their friend had first informed the sisters that
she carried a small pistol with her wherever she went,
they'd been both fascinated and slightly frightened.
Neither of them had ever had anything to do with fire-
arms. Their father had hunted of course. As did their
husbands. But it was hardly something that the sisters
had been interested in. To Isabella's mind it was rather
revolting to think of animals chased and killed solely
for sport. But Georgie had been matter-of-fact about the
weapon. Following the army, she'd often found herself in
situations where her safety was in question. The pistol
was a practical means of ensuring that safety. Her father,
also an army man, had taught Georgie how to use it, and
when she'd married he'd given her the ladies' weapon as

a gift. Fortunately for Perdita, Georgie had come for their
meeting with Ormonde today ready to ensure all of
their safety.

Swallowing, Isabella realized that if Georgie was to
get the gun out of her reticule, she'd need to distract Ormonde's attention away from her.

"Ormonde," she began; then, deciding that she might
need to seem more familiar, she used his given name.
"Gervase, we aren't here to take Perdita away from
you. We simply wish for you to perhaps be a bit gentler
with her."

"Why?" the duke demanded, his eyes suspicious. "She's
not gentle with me. She scratched my face earlier. Damn
her." He gripped Perdita tighter, and she whimpered.

The nail marks on his cheek bore testament to his
tale, but like any abuser he saw the failing as hers, not
his, conveniently forgetting that he'd been trying to
rape her at the time. Isabella knew that if she and Georgie
didn't get her sister out of his arms and out of his house
soon, he would do worse still.

Needing to make him loosen his grip, she decided to
improvise. "You should be gentle with her because she
might be carrying the next Duke of Ormonde." It wasn't
true. Not that she knew of anyway, but since one of the
failings that Ormonde laid at Perdita's door was her failure to give him an heir, Isabella guessed that he might
be convinced to let her go if he thought he might be en-
dangering his child.

She risked stepping forward as she watched the revelation sink in. "There, now," she said, "you don't wish to
harm your heir, do you?"

But she'd miscalculated. Rather than being transported with joy, Ormonde instead became angry. "What? Is

this true?" he asked, turning Perdita in his arms so that he could look her in the face. "You lied to me?" he demanded, the knife trapped between Perdita's arm and Ormonde's fist while he began to shake her. "You lying bitch! You told me it wasn't possible!" he cried.

"No!" Isabella shouted, rushing forward to pull him away from her sister. "Stop it! Stop it!"

Then several things happened at once.

Surprised by the deadweight of Isabella on his back, Ormonde let go of Perdita and stumbled backward, taking Isabella with him.

Georgie, realizing that she had a clear shot at last, slipped out her pistol and took aim. The shot hit the duke in the shoulder.

At almost the same time, the knife, which had been held between Perdita's body and Ormonde's hand, fell to the floor, followed close behind by the duke, who had been thrown off balance by Isabella's death grip.

Thus it was that the sixth Duke of Ormonde, husband of Perdita, brother-in-law of Lady Isabella Wharton, and of no particular relation to Mrs. Georgina Mowbray, came to be both stabbed and shot.

Though a duke, he was but human. No one was ever quite sure which wound was the fatal one.

But he was dead, nonetheless.

One

One year later

"Υou cannot simply insist I travel to the wilds of Yorkshire to fetch your errant grandson, Godmama," Lady
Isabella Wharton said with a nervous laugh. "It is the
height of the season. I have social obligations."

"Yes," the Dowager Duchess of Ormonde said
acerbically, "you are no doubt expected at one of Lucifer
Dinsmore's gatherings where the ladies dampen their
petticoats and the gentlemen wear Roman togas."

"That was one party, Godmama," Isabella protested.
"And the gentlemen wore robes like the Hellfire Club.
Not togas."

With her dark auburn hair, her voluptuous figure, and
an exquisite sense of style, Isabella was in demand among
the more liberal-minded hostesses of the *ton*. She was
always to be counted upon to add intrigue to an evening's
entertainment. The fact that she was a widow whose
husband had died famously in a duel only added to her
mystique.

"That is beside the point, Bella," the dowager huffed,
"and you well know it. Your social schedule is filled with
frivolity and scandal and little else. It will do you good

to get away from the scoundrels and rakes who buzz around you like so many bees. Yorkshire is lovely this time of year."

If the old woman had been there at all, Isabella would eat her hat.

"Then why do you not go there to persuade the new duke yourself?" Isabella asked peevishly. It was just like her godmother to pawn off such an unpleasant task on her. She'd always disapproved of Isabella and her popularity.

"Because the boy will refuse to see me!" the duchess said, thumping her ebony walking stick on the floor for emphasis. "He must be made to see his duty to the family. And as he will not see me, then he will need to be persuaded by someone else. Someone with the ability to wrap young men about her little finger."

Isabella choked on her tea. "You mean me to seduce him into coming to London?" It was true that she had a way with gentlemen, but as her marriage proved, she was not a miracle worker. If the duke wished to remain in Yorkshire rather than come to London and take up his role as head of the family, then she had no great faith in her power to persuade him otherwise. Besides, as her sister and Georgina Mowbray could attest, Isabella had a poor record when it came to persuading Dukes of Ormonde to do what she wished.

"Don't be absurd," the old woman said, waving a beringed hand in dismissal. "I mean for you to cast a few lures. That hardly constitutes seduction. He must be bored silly with the provincial women of York."

Isabella bit back a sigh. Since receiving the heavily embossed notecard earlier in the week she'd been dreading this encounter with her godmother. It wasn't that Isabella was not fond of the old girl. The duchess had served as a surrogate parent to Isabella and her sister, Perdita, since their mother's death when they were children. Their father, being a typical gentleman of his class, was not up to the task.

And when the dowager's other grandson, Gervase, also a duke, had fallen in love with Perdita on sight, and their subsequent marriage made both sisters true members of the Ormonde family, they'd all been pleased as punch. The duke's bad treatment of Perdita, which the dowager still denied even after his death during an attack on his wife, had soured Isabella's relationship with the matriarch. And she was hardly in a position to take orders from her anymore. She was a grown woman and had endured her own abusive marriage for long enough to appreciate her freedom to such a degree that she resented anyone—especially someone who called her sister a liar—who tried to curb it.

"Perhaps the new duke has his reasons for refusing to come to London," Isabella said mildly. She had said her peace about the late duke to the dowager. She knew there was nothing she could say to sway the old woman's opinion and she'd decided to stop trying. She had come here today as a courtesy, but the dowager's attempt to manipulate her was tiresome. "You did, after all, cut off his father without a cent. That has a way of dampening one's familial feelings."

As did accusations of murder, she thought to herself. The dowager had kept the circumstances of Gervase's death secret solely because she did not wish the family to be wreathed in scandal along with the funeral crepe. That did not stop her from haranguing Perdita in private. Which was ironic considering that Isabella and Georgina, if one was technical about the matter, were the ones responsible for the duke's death.

"My late husband cut Phillip off," the duchess said crossly, referring to the present, reluctant duke's father. "And I spent a great deal of time attempting to dissuade him from doing so. For the little good it did me."

Isabella looked up from picking at a thread on her primrose morning gown. "You did?" she asked, surprised despite herself. "I never knew that."

The dowager's cheeks turned pink beneath the old-fashioned powder she insisted on wearing. "He was my son, Isabella. I hardly wished for him to be thrust out into the world without two pennies to rub together. Much less to never see my first grandchild. Ormonde was as stubborn as they come, however. And when he made his decision, I could do little more than go along with it."

Which perhaps explained why the dowager had clung so tightly to the notion that Gervase could do no wrong. Deprived of her first grandson, the dowager had taken the one she had access to and tried to mold him into the sort of man her husband would not dare cast off. Unfortunately, she'd also molded him into a selfish, haughty brute of a man who had beaten his young wife black-and-blue on more than one occasion. And because he'd been told by the grandmother who all but raised him that he was always right, he'd been unable to see what he did as wrong.

"I didn't know," Isabella said, feeling a bit sorry for the old woman despite herself. "It must have been dreadful for you."

"It was," the dowager said. "But I endured it. And I refuse to endure another separation in the family. Trevor needs to come to London to take up the business of the dukedom. He cannot simply ignore his family obligations by remaining in some provincial Yorkshire hamlet to

play at being a gentleman farmer. He is the Duke of Ormonde and must be made to behave as such."

The old woman pounded her walking stick on the
floor for emphasis.

"I am hardly the best person to preach proper behavior, Godmama," Isabella said, still not ready to accept
the dowager's orders. She was in no mood for travel.
Besides, there was the matter of her reputation. "Indeed,
I am perhaps the worst person to fetch him if you wish
your grandson to arrive in London scandal-free."

"I care not what his reputation will be," the duchess
said firmly. "I simply want him to be *here*."

She glanced up at the portrait of her husband and
sons that hung above the fireplace in her sitting room. "I
am getting no younger, Isabella," she said, her sharp eyes
softening as she turned them back toward her goddaugh-
ter. "But I hope that before I go to join my dear boys I
am able to meet the grandson who was kept from me.
Please, Isabella. Say that you will go get him for me."

Isabella was moved in spite of herself. The dowager
was a difficult woman. But she'd truly loved the despicable Gervase. And despite that love she'd done what she
could to ensure that the true story of how he'd died never
got out. She might have seen to it that all three women
present that day were prosecuted for his death. Instead
she'd hidden the truth. That in and of itself was enough
to make Isabella grateful to her.

But the dowager's next words destroyed any goodwill
Isabella had harbored for her.

"If you do not go," she said, her eyes narrowed, "I will
see to it that your sister's match with Coniston comes to
nothing."

Damn her.

Isabella might have known that the old woman would find it impossible to simply let Isabella make the decision herself. Unable to wait, she'd decided to use the one bit of good to come out of Gervase's death—Perdita's proposed match with the Earl of Coniston—as leverage against her sister.

"You almost had me," she said, shaking her head. "Really, Duchess, it was quite splendidly done. If only you'd waited."

The dowager did Isabella the courtesy of not misunderstanding her. "I had to make sure you would do as I asked."

"I was almost ready to capitulate," Isabella said coldly. "But you couldn't resist threatening Perdita. Could you?"

"It was not a matter of threatening your sister," the dowager said. "It was a matter of using the right tool to make you do what I wished. And you have always been ready to do whatever it takes to protect your sister, have you not?"

Indeed, Isabella had always been protective of her sister. Not only because they'd lost their parents at an early age but also because Perdita's sweet nature made her more vulnerable than most to the darker elements of the world. Like Gervase. And his grandmother.

"I suppose this means you still refuse to go to Yorkshire on my behalf?"

"On the contrary," Isabella said. "Now I have no choice. Just as you wished."

The Earl of Coniston was not, perhaps, as handsome or as polished as the Duke of Ormonde had been, but he'd managed to woo Perdita with his affable good nature and even temper. And Isabella would do nothing that would endanger her sister's engagement. Even if it meant leaving London in the middle of the season and persuading a man with no intention of taking up his position as duke to return to town with her. And the dowager knew it.

"Sadly, it is blackmail," the duchess said without a trace of remorse, "but needs must when the devil drives. Besides, as I told you before, it will do you good to get up to Yorkshire this time of year."

"I'll be taking one of the Ormonde traveling carriages," Isabella said curtly. If the duchess was going to force her upon this fool's errand, then she may as well be comfortable on the journey. "And I wish you to set up an account for me at Madame Celeste's for when I return."

The duchess, knowing she'd won, inclined her head to indicate her assent. "I do apologize for having gone about the business in such a havey-cavey manner, Isabella," she said. "But you know how important family is to me. Especially now that Gervase is gone."

Still cursing her own naïveté, Isabella rose. "If I'm to make an early start, I suppose I'd better be off."

Not bothering to say her good-byes, she stormed out of the dowager's sitting room and hurried downstairs to retrieve her hat and pelisse.

Trevor Carey, Duke of Ormonde, pulled his hat down lower over his face to keep out the rain as he guided his horse toward home. His shoulders were already beginning to ache from the effort of helping haul William Easter's cart back up the banks of the swollen Nettledale River. Yorkshire in spring was given to rain, but this year had been a particularly wet one, which had proved to be more than the normally serene Nettledale—and the ancient bridge over it—could handle. Will had decided to risk the bridge, and as a result the cart had slipped over the edge and into the drink.

It had taken six men and nearly four hours to retrieve the cart, which had been loaded down with goods from York for Easter's village shop. Thankfully, the bed of the cart hadn't been submerged, so most of the stock was salvageable. But Easter had broken an arm and had been banged up quite a bit. A small price to pay, Trevor thought, considering a cracked skull might have ended with Easter drowning in the river. Now he was exhausted and wet and starving and wanted nothing more than a hot bath and a bowl of Mrs. Tillotson's stew.

Peering up ahead through the twilight rain, he cursed at the realization that the dark shadow he'd been watching was not a stand of trees but a carriage tilted at an awkward angle.

Did no one have the good sense to stay in on a day like this?

As he approached the large carriage, which had been built for comfort rather than agility, Trevor heard a woman's voice coming from the interior of the vehicle.

"Liston, stop fidgeting. You will do yourself some further injury." The voice was a refined one—doubtless of some lady who was passing through town on her way to one of the neighboring estates. She had the sound of one who was accustomed to giving orders and having them followed. But it was clear from her aggrieved tone that the fidgety Liston was not an obedient servant.

"But Lady Wharton," he heard a man's voice say, "I shouldn't be in here with you. 'Tain't right for me to share the interior of the carriage with ye like I was puttin' on airs."

"Don't be absurd," came the abrupt reply. "You were

injured when the carriage crashed. It's not as if you are
in any fit state to . . ." Trevor bit back a smile at her ab-
breviated words. "That is to say, you are injured and it
would be foolish for you to catch your death out in the
rain all for the sake of my reputation. Which, as you well
know, is not what it might have been in any event."

Reaching the listing vehicle, Trevor saw that the axle
of the right front wheel was broken. The carriage horses,
their heads bowed under the desultory rainfall, whick-
ered at the approach of Trevor and his mount, Beowulf.

The occupants of the carriage must have heard him
approach, for the lady's voice rang out into the night.
"Hello? Hello, out there! I warn you, do not attempt to
harm us. My. . . . my husband has a pistol!"

As if she'd nudged him into adding the words, her
companion shouted as well, "Aye! I'm armed and dangerous!"

Dismounting, the duke left Bey under the cover of a
large elm tree and approached the carriage. "I mean you
no harm," he said loudly. "I've just come from the village
and wish to offer my assistance."

There was a long silence in which Trevor imagined
the haughty lady and her groom silently argued whether
to accept his help. Then, as he watched, the carriage door
opened slowly.

Stepping forward, he peered into the carriage and
saw a lady huddled against the squabs of the interior,
her pelisse and shawl clutched tightly around her. Her
companion was a man of middle years, whose wan face
and arm clutched tightly to his chest indicated that he was
the injured Liston.

"We were on our way to Nettlefield House when
something happened to the carriage wheel," the lady

said, her lips tight. Were it not for her cool expression, Trevor was quite convinced that she would have been among the most beautiful women he'd ever seen. Even in the dimness of the interior carriage lamps, her dark hair gleamed mahogany in sharp contrast to her porcelain complexion. Her figure, what he could see of it, was buxom. Perhaps more so than fashionable, but he had never been much of one for fashion. He liked a woman with a bit of substance. "My coachman and outriders have gone on ahead to the house to fetch help," she went on. "I assure you we will be quite well, though I thank you for stopping."

"Are you expected at Nettlefield House?" he asked, racking his brain to remember if either of his sisters had told him they were expecting friends sometime soon. He was about to go on, to explain that he was the master of the house, when she interjected.

"I'm sure I don't know what business it is of yours," she said, waving her hand dismissively. "Unless you are the Duke of Ormonde, which you clearly are not"—she looked him up and down, obviously rejecting the idea out of hand—"then I really would appreciate your assistance in getting us on our way. My man here is injured, as you can plainly see."

Trevor bit his lip, fighting the urge to laugh aloud at her cutting remarks. Though he was technically the duke, he took no pleasure in the title. Clearly, this Lady Wharton was some sort of social climber who had come to Nettlefield in search of the new duke to beg some favor of him. There hadn't been many who were willing to travel such great lengths to win his favor, but there had been enough that he recognized a supplicant when he saw one.

If she was expecting him to be a dim-witted yokel, however, then he'd give her one.

"Aye," he said slowly, tugging his forelock in a sign of obeisance, "I can see yer man is hurt bad-like. Bu' won't do ye no good iffen ye catch the death o' cold yerself, beggin' yer pardon, m'lady."

"Just what I been trying to tell 'er," the unfortunate Liston said with a nod.

"Help'll be on its way soon enow," Trevor went on guilelessly, paying no heed to Lady Isabella's pursed lips. "I thin' it would be best iffen ye come up wi' me on Bessie."

Lady Isabella's brows drew together. "Bessie?" she asked querulously.

"Aye," Trevor said with an agreeable nod, getting into his role. "Bessie are t'best horse in all Yorkshire an' make no mistake. She'll carry you up wi' me no trouble a'tall."

The lady's nostrils flared. "Is there some reason why she might have had trouble?" she asked silkily.

"Well, ye're no li'l slip of a thing," Trevor said, widening his eyes innocently. "Beggin' yer pardon, milady."

He could all but see the steam coming from her ears. And yet she didn't raise a fuss as he thought she might. Instead, she looked back at Liston.

"Will you be well if I leave you here, Liston?" she asked the injured man. "I would send you away with this . . . this person if I thought you might ride with him without doing yourself a further injury."

Trevor felt a pang of conscience at seeing her genuine concern for her servant. Still she had not yet proved herself to be anything other than what she seemed. A prickly society lady who had come to Nettlefield to prey upon the dukedom of Ormonde. Doubtless she had some sort of charity to fund. Or a sibling who needed schooling.

"Aye, milady," Liston said, his pale face determined. "I don't want you out here catching your death simply because I was too foolish to keep meself from taking a bit of a tumble. Go wi' this fellow and get to the house. Jemison and Jeffries will be here with someone from Nettlefield before ye know it."

"If that's the case," she said, looking uncertain, "then perhaps I shouldn't—"

But Trevor was tired from his earlier labors and the rain was beginning to come down harder. "Come, milady," he said firmly, dropping his guise of happy farmer for a moment. "Let's get ye up to Nettlefield House. I know the master would have me head for keepin' ye out here this long."

With a grim nod Lady Isabella buttoned up her pelisse and donned the cloak that lay spread out behind her on the carriage seat, pulling the hood up over her carefully dressed hair.

Trevor offered her his hand, and though she glanced quizzically up at him, she took it and allowed him to assist her from the carriage. Fortunately, she'd worn heavy boots for the journey, because the ground was a soggy, muddy mess. To his surprise, she was taller than he'd supposed, her nose almost aligned with his own when she stepped out next to him. Their eyes locked for one heart-stopping moment, before she colored up and looked away.

Well, he thought with an inward grin. Perhaps the prickly London lady was less prickly than he'd at first surmised. He felt his body respond to her nearness in

the automatic way it always did when confronted with a
pretty girl. But there was something about this one that
felt different. Which clearly meant that he'd been awake
for far too long. He needed to get this chit back to Nettlefield so that he could reveal his true identity and send her
back on her way. He didn't like forcing a woman out onto
the road so soon after her arrival, but if she'd come unin-
vited to beg or, worse, at his grandmother's behest then
there was no reason for him to feel any sympathy for her.

Didn't stop him from feeling a churl, though.

"Up ye go," he told her, gripping her around her trim
waist and lifting her to sit sideways across Bey's saddle.
Without further ceremony he put his foot in the stirrup
and mounted up behind her, slipping a protective arm
around her waist to hold her steady.

It was a surprisingly intimate situation between strang-
ers, and Trevor tried to steel himself against responding
further to her nearness. But it was impossible to ignore
her lavender-scented hair and the more natural, primal
scents of female sweat and something that he knew instinctively was simply her.

Directing Bey into motion with a touch of his heel to
the horse's flank, he clenched his jaw and tried to ignore
her. Which proved impossible given the way that her
reluctance to hold on to him put them both in danger of
falling. They might be atop the same horse, but Lady Isabella kept herself as far away from his body as possible.

"I won't bite," he said, unable to hide his amusement
at her diffident grip. Ignoring her protest, he held on to
her more tightly. "Unless you wish it, of course."

He waited for an outraged gasp, but she had no doubt
decided to ignore him. A few moments later, however,

she said, "It's funny. You sound like an unschooled peasant one minute, and then the next your voice has a distinctly upper-class accent."

Caught out, Trevor thought with a frown. "I don't suppose you'd believe that I received lessons from the local vicar?" he asked.

"Not for a moment," she said grimly.

"Well, then, Lady Wharton," he said calmly, "I'm afraid that I've misled you a bit."

"Rather more than a bit, I think," she said sharply. "Though I suppose the lack of proper introduction excuses you, under the circumstances . . ."—she paused deliberately—"Your Grace."

"I do not use the title, as you would know if you'd done any sort of investigation at all." He kept his gaze on the road ahead of them.

He felt her head shake against his chest. "I would not have believed it if I had not seen it with my own eyes," she said. "I knew of course that you had been raised in the country and had some sort of foolish notion about refusing to take up your responsibilities, but I thought that it was an exaggeration. But it's true."

"You and I both know that it's not possible for me to give up the title completely," Trevor said reasonably. "And I fear that my grandmother's tale of my refusal to take up my responsibilities is, like much of her talk, an exaggeration. I consult regularly with the stewards and secretaries of the duchy; I simply do not choose to go to London or to set myself up in grandeur at the ducal estate."

"So you choose to remain here in Yorkshire playing at the role of gentleman farmer," Lady Isabella said with a shudder. "I cannot say that I understand your position, because I do not."

"I choose to remain here in Yorkshire because it is my home," he said stiffly. "I have a responsibility to the people of Nettlefield and I intend to remain here, dukedom or no dukedom.

"Now," he went on, "what brings you to Yorkshire, my lady? Are you perhaps a distant cousin in need of a loan? A young widow whose son wishes to attend Eton? Or did you come at my grandmother's behest to *persuade* me to come down to London?"

She did him the courtesy of not misunderstanding him.

"The latter," she said calmly, as if he hadn't just accused her of being a toady. "Your grandmother has need of you in London. She is quite ill."

"Bollocks," he said, not bothering to guard his language. "She has need of my position because she does not have enough power on her own as the dowager. And if she's ill then I'll eat my hat. She sent you here to lure me with your looks—which are quite splendid by the way—back to town so that she can direct me as she sees fit. Which will not happen while there is breath in my body."

"Oh dear," Lady Isabella murmured. "You are quite averse to the notion, aren't you?"

"I am indeed, so you may return to London at once and inform Her Grace that I have no intention of dancing to her tune."

"I can hardly do so at the moment, given the state of her traveling carriage," Lady Isabella said calmly. "I hope you do not mean to refuse me accommodation, *Your Grace*." She put special emphasis on his title. "Rustic though I suppose it must be."

"I can hardly do so and continue to call myself a gentleman," Trevor returned. Though he'd like to, just to prove a point to his grandmother. But the punishment would be for Lady Isabella, not the dowager. Which would be fruitless. "And fear not. I believe you will find Nettlefield up to your, no doubt, exacting standards."

They rode along in silence until finally they reached the lane leading to the manor. It was full dark now and visibility was such that only the front step was illuminated in the gloom. Even so, the house was not an unimpressive sight. Nettlefield had been built sometime in the seventeenth century by a prosperous squire whose descendent had sold the property off some two hundred years later to Trevor's father, who had been in search of a place to settle his young family. The façade was grayed with age and weather and rather dour, but it was home.

"Your Grace," Templeton, his butler, said from the top step, "we had begun to fear you'd met with some misadventure."

Dismounting and reaching up to lower Lady Isabella to the ground, Trevor was pleased to see her mouth agape. Rustic accommodation indeed, he thought wryly.

"Templeton, see that the blue room is readied for our guest," he told the butler, offering Isabella his arm as he led her up the steps. "Lady Isabella Wharton will be our guest for a few days before she returns to London."

If Templeton thought there was anything untoward about the fact that his master had returned home with a strange lady on his arm, the older man didn't mention it.

"Of course, Your Grace," the butler said, bowing to their guest as they moved into the hallway. "Lady Wharton, may I offer you a warm welcome and offer my assistance should you need anything during your stay?"

"Please have Mrs. Templeton send a tea tray into the sitting room," Trevor said, assisting Isabella to remove

her cloak and handing it to a waiting maid who seemed
to have appeared from nowhere.

He was leading Isabella toward the stairs when a
whirling dervish in the form of his sister Belinda came
bolting into the hallway. "Trevor! Thank goodness you've
returned! Flossie is about to give birth and I fear that
she simply won't rest until she sees you!"

Two

Today was obviously the day for Isabella to find her preconceived notions upended at every turn.

First the fellow she assumed was a common laborer turned out to be the Duke of Ormonde. Then the house she'd expected to have all the elegance and appointments of a shepherd's cottage turned out to be a sturdily built manor house. Now the duke himself turned out to be married to someone appallingly named Flossie, and if that weren't bad enough, she was about to give birth to their child. For all Isabella knew, this young woman who had just burst onto the scene was his child as well.

Isabella rubbed her forehead between her brows, though it did nothing to assuage her burgeoning headache.

But, despite the news that he was about to become a father, the duke merely shrugged. "I will be up directly, Bel, though you know my opinion about Flossie's affection for me. She could not possibly care less whether I'm in the room with her or not. That is, I fear, a notion entirely of your own making." He turned to Isabella, and she felt suddenly diffident under his gaze. "I wish you to meet our guest."

The young girl had seemed about to argue with him over the unfortunate Flossie, but she stopped when she realized that the duke was not alone.

"Lady Isabella Wharton," he said, "may I present my youngest sister, Belinda."

Isabella felt herself being subjected to the same scrutiny the duke had given her when he'd first come upon her on the roadside. Only now her gown was more rumpled, her hair was falling from its pins, and in general she felt a fright. Not that she cared what a provincial young lady who hadn't even made her come-out thought of her, Isabella reminded herself.

Straightening her spine, she subjected young Belinda to her own scrutiny.

Belinda's hair was the same deep russet as her brother's, and it had obviously not been dressed by anyone with skill at the task. Her gown, three years out of fashion, was a passable shade of deep green but was hardly anything to boast about. It was serviceable and nothing more. But it was the young lady's eyes that were her best feature. They were not unlike the duke's. A startling blue that reminded Isabella of the spring sky.

"Lady Wharton," Belinda said eagerly, "how lovely to see you! You've come just in time to see the kittens."

Momentarily startled by the non sequitur, Isabella glanced at her host, who shrugged. "Flossie was perhaps waiting for an audience."

Pieces snapped into place in Isabella's mind. "Ah, the unfortunate Flossie," she said.

"She loves Trevor most of all," Belinda said, tucking her arm into Isabella's, completely unfazed by her most standoffish manner. "He pretends not to care," the young lady confided, "but I know he loves her, too.

How can he not when she is altogether the best cat imaginable?"

Isabella paused when she felt the duke's hand on her arm. "Just a minute, Bel," he said, not unkindly. "Lady Wharton has had a rather trying day. I think she'd probably rather forego a visit to Flossie's bedside for now."

Belinda paused, and Isabella paused along with her, looking to the duke for guidance. "Oh dear," Belinda said, turning to Isabella in alarm. "I am sorry. I didn't think. Of course you won't wish to see Flossie now."

"It's no matter, Bel," the duke said to his sister, squeezing her hand. "I'm sure Lady Wharton does not mind." His blue gaze spoke more loudly than his voice.

"Certainly not," Isabella said quickly. "And I should very much like to see the kittens tomorrow."

Relief shone in the young lady's eyes. "Thank you, Lady Wharton," she said gratefully. "Trevor, I must get back to Flossie. You will come up and see her before you retire for the night, won't you?"

The duke nodded. "Of course."

When Belinda had gone, Trevor led Isabella up the stairs. She followed along, though she knew that showing her to her room was an office that a footman or maid should perform. Clearly the duke had much to learn about being ducal.

"Belinda is my youngest sister," he said, leading Isabella down a rather well-appointed hallway. "She is convinced that her cat holds me in great affection."

Isabella could hear the amusement in his tone even as a thread of steel sounded behind it. "I realize that you will be returning to London quite soon," he said, "but I would appreciate it if you would not subject my sisters to your reason for being here."

Isabella, who had been trying her best not to notice how strong his arm felt beneath her hand, glanced over. "Why ever not?" she asked, realizing that her fatigue had dulled her intelligence. Of course his sisters would be a means of convincing him to return to London with her.

"I think you know why not," he said fiercely. "They have no concept of what life as sisters to the Duke of Ormonde would be like. Whereas now they enjoy a rather easy existence in the country, a trip to London and exposure to its excesses would change their lives irrevocably."

"Don't you think they should be able to make that choice for themselves?" Isabella demanded, as they paused before an open door.

"They are thirteen and seventeen," the duke said, his expression hard. "They are too young to make that decision for themselves. As their guardian, it is up to me to decide what's best for them. And for now, I choose to remain in the country."

Deciding that this battle was one that she'd best fight when she was in her full faculties, Isabella gave an inscrutable nod. It could mean anything, she decided.

"I will leave you to your rest," he said with a slight bow. "I hope you will be comfortable here during your stay."

Leaving her to the care of her waiting maid, the duke departed. And for the first time in hours, Isabella relaxed.

"Sanders," she told her maid, "I would like a bath, I think. And then bed."

"Very good, my lady," the efficient woman said, unfastening Isabella's gown. She'd only been with Isabella for a month or so, but she was quite good at her position. "Oh, my lady?"

"Yes?" Isabella asked, sighing with pleasure as Sanders loosened the ties of her corset.

"I found a note in your case while I was unpacking your things," the maid said, folding the discarded gown over her arm. "It's there on the writing desk. I thought perhaps the young duchess sent it with you."

Frowning, Isabella stepped over to the desk in her stocking feet and pulled the robe she'd donned against the spring chill tighter around her. The note was lying flat on the desk, right where Sanders had said it would be. Her name was scrawled in an unfamiliar hand across the folded page. Rather than being sealed, the letter had been neatly folded into a rectangle, the end flap tucked in to form a makeshift closure.

It was probably something the dowager had dictated to her maid, Isabella thought with a sigh. Why couldn't she simply leave her to the business of bringing back Ormonde without overseeing every tiny detail?

Snatching up the page, she unfolded and unfolded and unfolded until the message was visible in the lamplight.

The words made the tiny hairs on the nape of her neck rise.

I know what you did last season.

Biting back a cry and grateful that Sanders had left to hurry the footmen with her bath, Isabella crumpled the page into a ball and tossed it into the fire.

If only that would erase the words from her mind as well.

His guest settled into her bedchamber, Trevor allowed himself to relax for the first time since learning who Lady Isabella was and why she'd come.

Settled into a hot bath, he leaned a weary head back against the edge of the tub while he listened to his valet, Jennings, putter around the dressing room next door. Contrary to what Lady Isabella might think, Trevor did not live an entirely rustic existence in Yorkshire. His father had been a gentleman, a duke's son, and had not given up the comforts of his former existence entirely. He had simply chosen not to embrace the more frivolous customs of the aristocracy. He had also chosen not to return to the family estate in Sussex or mingle with the beau monde in London. That did not mean that his household in Yorkshire was barbaric. Far from it. When he had purchased the Nettlefield estate, he had set about making it the most elegant home in the county. And once the farms had begun to produce a profit, his wife had begun to fill its rooms with the finest furniture from York and a surprisingly eclectic collection of art and antiquities, in addition to the pieces that had come with the estate itself. As a result, Nettlefield truly was the most elegant house in the county.

Trevor, however, had grown up not caring a whit about such things. While his father had played at being the country gentleman, Trevor had spent much of his time at the side of the estate's steward, Brooks, and learned all he could about the most modern methods of farming and animal husbandry. He spent his days visiting the tenants, ensuring that their homes were sound, and in general seeing to it that those activities his father was too elegant for were performed. He had never considered that the dukedom was something he need worry over. Certainly his father had never paid it much attention, and once he was gone Trevor had given it the same consideration.

Now, of course, the three men who had been between himself and the title were gone and Trevor found himself the head of a family that had turned its back on his father when he dared to marry for love instead of for monetary gain. Well, he'd be damned if he'd reward the Ormonde clan with his leadership. He would stay here in Yorkshire farming and go about his business and they could go to the devil. True, the local gentry and families of wealth would never let him forget his new position, but he had never been much for society—even the local variety—so he simply avoided them as much as he could. When his sisters were of age, he would worry about that. He didn't wish for his eschewing of the title to have a negative effect on Eleanor's and Belinda's marriage chances, of course, but he wouldn't have to consider that for some years.

Still, thanks to his grandmother's machinations, he was burdened with the presence of the all-too-attractive Lady Isabella Wharton beneath his roof. Surely there must be some way to send the woman packing, to convince her that remaining in the country was a fool's errand. He held his breath and ducked his head down under the water, then let the rivulets stream down his face as he rested the back of his head against the edge of the tub. He wondered what his unwanted guest thought of the Careys' modern conveniences. She had likely assumed that the family bathed once a week in a tub near the kitchen fire. He laughed softly at the notion.

But the thought sparked an idea.

The key to getting rid of Lady Isabella was not to do her bidding, he decided. It was to offer her a bargain.

The more he considered the notion, the more he liked it. It would serve his grandmother right if her highborn surrogate failed solely because of her inability to endure the country life. After all, the dowager expected Trevor and his sisters to endure all the ridiculous hardships of life in the city. Why not prove to her that it was not so very easy for a leopard to change its spots? He had his doubts about whether the dowager would last for more than a few days in the country. It was hardly a stretch to think the same would hold true for the town-bred lady she'd sent in her stead.

Pleased with his scheme, Trevor relaxed into his steaming bath and made plans for the next day.

Despite her fatigue, the anonymous note meant Isabella had some difficulty settling down to sleep. As a result, the next morning found her fighting back an unladylike yawn as she made her way downstairs.

In the light of day the note seemed far less ominous than it had before. Obviously whoever had put it in her bag had intended to play some sort of cruel joke on her. Maybe it was the work of the dowager, who wanted to remind Isabella that the circumstances of Gervase's death were easy enough to reveal should she fail in her quest to bring Ormonde back to London. Regardless, she was here now and no amount of intimidation would make Isabella forget her real reason for being here: Perdita's happiness.

Fortunately for her purposes the dowager's carriage had suffered a great deal of damage in last night's accident, so there would be no returning to London for several days. This would give Isabella the time she needed to persuade the duke to come to London.

Or so she hoped.

She found the breakfast room with the help of a maid and was helping herself to toast and kippers when she heard a slight gasp behind her. Turning, she saw a young lady a few years older than Belinda standing in the doorway, her eyes wide and a look of unfettered delight on her pretty face.

"You are much more beautiful than Bel said," she blurted out, dropping into a hasty curtsy at Isabella's single raised brow. "I am Miss Eleanor Carey," she said by way of introduction. "And you must be Lady Isabella Wharton."

Carrying her plate to the table and nodding to the footman that she would like tea, Isabella waited for the girl to take a seat opposite her. She was not surprised to find the duke's other sister to be as rag mannered as the younger Belinda, but she was startled by the young lady's beauty. Surely Ormonde didn't mean to waste this child on some yeoman farmer when she could make a wonderful match in London?

"I am," she said, taking a small bite of toast. "I wonder, Miss Carey, that you are not in the schoolroom at this hour. Surely you have a governess to occupy your time." It was a question but also a judgment. If she did have a governess, then the woman was hardly worth her salt if the girl's casual manner was anything to go by.

"Oh, we don't have a governess at the moment," Eleanor said, eyeing the details of Isabella's gown and coiffure with interest. "They keep falling in love with Trevor, so we have a hard time keeping one. When Miss Timms, the last one, declared her love for him, Trevor decided that we could go without one for a bit."

Isabella had little difficulty imagining such a thing, but it was hardly a logical response for him to dispense with a governess altogether. Clearly his sisters were in need of some sort of social guidance, or Eleanor wouldn't be introducing herself to guests and Belinda wouldn't be accosting him about kittens. Perhaps while she was here she might prevail upon him to allow her to choose someone for the girls when she returned to London.

"Is that sleeve the latest fashion in London?" Eleanor asked candidly, her wistful gaze on Isabella's gown. "We are sadly out of fashion here in Yorkshire, I fear, though the local seamstress, Mrs. Winters, does try to copy styles from *La Belle Assemblée*."

Remembering what it had been like to be seventeen and desperate for news of the outside world, Isabella said, "I purchased this gown only last month from Madame Celeste. And she assured me that this sleeve was what every lady in Paris is wearing. Perhaps I can make some sketches for you to take with you the next time you visit Mrs. Winters? Before I go back to London, I mean."

Eleanor clapped her hands. "That would be wonderful! I do know that Mrs. Winters tries her best, but I fear there is something sadly provincial about her work."

Uncomfortable at the girl's worshipful expression, Isabella decided to change the subject. "If you no longer have a governess to instruct you, how do you occupy yourself?" Surely the duke did not allow his sisters to run wild about the countryside. Even in the country it was frowned upon to allow girls who were not yet out to simply do as they pleased.

"Oh, on most days Belinda and I go to the Felshams' for lessons with their daughters. But they are in London for the season just now, so we are left to our own devices." Eleanor shrugged. "I practice the pianoforte.

Some days Bel and I set up our easels in the garden and paint. I do try to ensure that she doesn't run too wild. After all, we do not wish to develop a reputation. Since Mama died, I feel a certain responsibility to her. Though I know Trevor tries his best, he is a gentleman and hardly one to train one in ladylike behavior."

After Eleanor's earlier enthusiasms, this rather practical speech struck Isabella as surprisingly grown-up for such a young lady.

"How long has it been since your mother's death?" Isabella asked quietly, putting her teacup down.

"Seven years," Eleanor said. "Bel doesn't remember her really; she was too young. But I do and I know she would not like it if we caused talk in the village. She was quite proud. Especially since Papa was a duke's son."

Touched suddenly by the girl's determination to do her mother proud, Isabella made a decision. "Perhaps while I am here I can help you girls by telling you about how things are done in London. After all, you will be making your debut one of these seasons and you would not wish to be completely green when you get to London."

"That would be lovely." The somber mood gone as quickly as it had come on, Eleanor beamed once more. "I cannot tell you how pleased I am that you have come. I fear that Nettlefield is sometimes rather dull, and Trevor cares little for social niceties. He is a good brother, but a dismal duke. He doesn't even really like to be called by his title. Can you imagine?"

Isabella could not imagine, but she knew that the duke's reluctance to accept his title was the least of their worries.

They were forestalled from further discussion by the

appearance of Templeton in the doorway of the breakfast room.

"Lady Wharton," he said gravely, "several of the neighborhood ladies have called and wish to know if you are receiving visitors.

She looked at Eleanor, who shrugged. A habit that Isabella would need to warn her about.

"It is a small neighborhood," the young lady said. "They probably learned about your accident from the servants and word spread. You cannot blame them for being curious. We get very little excitement here."

Lovely, Isabella thought. I am reduced to being an entertainment for rural gawkers. "Perhaps you will come with me to meet them?" she asked Eleanor, thinking that this would be a good opportunity to judge how the girl's manners were when she wasn't overcome with curiosity.

Clearly the invitation was unexpected, because Eleanor's eyes widened before she visibly squared her shoulders and rose elegantly from the breakfast table. "I would be delighted to perform the introductions," she said with a gravity that almost made Isabella laugh. But she didn't. A girl's amour propre at that age was quite fragile. And there was no reason to mock Eleanor for behaving with dignity. If it seemed a bit stilted after her earlier frankness and unabashed enthusiasm, well, she could work on developing an easier manner the more that such introductions became commonplace for her.

Following the girl from the breakfast room, Isabella prepared herself to be scrutinized within an inch of her life.

Three

*R*efusing to be diverted from his daily routine by the presence of Lady Isabella in his household, Trevor went for his usual ride the next morning and followed it up with a visit to his friend Sir Lucien Blakemore's estate, where he was scheduled to look over a pair of leaders for his new curricle. He might not choose to cut a dash in town or attempt reckless races from London to Bath, but he could not deny a certain weakness for a well-sprung, fast equipage.

"I hear you've got a rather attractive visitor at Nettlefield," Lucien said as the two men shared a drink after Trevor's purchase of the horses. "My valet had the news from the tweeny whose sister works in your kitchen," he explained wryly.

Trevor's lips twisted in a wry smile. "Glad to hear the gossip is traveling as quickly as ever through the village." He was hardly surprised, but he had hoped for Lady Isabella to be on her way back to London before the village learned of her presenc. It was bad enough that she'd met his sisters. If the local ladies got hold of her she would tell them her reason for being at Nettlefield, and he had no wish for the collective wisdom of the village to be put to work devising reasons for him to fully accept his position as the Duke of Ormonde.

His father had made that decision for him long ago when he'd chosen to remain in Yorkshire and marry Trevor's mother against the old duke's wishes. If the old duke was worried about the succession then he should have thought beyond his own vanity and into the future. It was hardly Trevor's fault that his uncle and cousin had died so young. He had no sense of loyalty to the Ormonde family at all. Especially after the way they'd cut off his father. Trevor would do his duty to the estate itself, because he knew that the people who worked for it had not chosen to cut off his father, but he would be damned if he'd go up to London and parade himself before the *ton* when he despised everything about the Ormonde family.

"So," Lucien prompted, "tell me about her, this mysterious Lady Isabella Wharton who arrived in the night."

Trevor rolled his eyes. "You make it sound like a Minerva Press novel." He frowned. "Trust me, she is not the stuff heroines are made from."

"Well, what stuff is she made from?" Lucien prodded. "There is little enough to amuse me here in the wilds of Yorkshire. I have never had your knack for animal husbandry or crop management. I am a shallow sort of fellow, I fear, and must needs get my entertainment from gossip."

It was hardly an accurate assessment, Trevor thought. Luce was an excellent landowner and had ably managed his own lands since his father's death when they were in their teens. But it was true enough that little of note happened in their tiny village, so he told him about Lady Isabella and her reason for descending upon Nettlefield in the dark of night.

"But you do not say anything about the lady's appearance, man," Lucien pointed out. "Please tell me that she is at least more pleasant to look at than Lucy Fenwick at The Curdled Pig." Lucy was known village-wide as an able barmaid but hardly attractive.

"Oh, she's beautiful if it comes to that," Trevor said ruefully. "In fact, I don't know that I've ever seen anyone lovelier."

"Even prettier than the Misses Sprinkle?" Lucien asked, both brows raised. The Misses Sprinkle were known far and wide as the great beauties of the county. And enjoyed the attentions of every man within a twenty-five-mile radius as a result. Both were a bit young for Trevor and Luce, however, and were, to both men's sincere regret, as dumb as posts.

"Considerably," Trevor confirmed. "Not least because she appears to be able to maintain more than one thought within her mind simultaneously."

"Interesting," Lucien said, taking a sip of coffee. "So you are naturally going to try to make the lady return to London at once."

"It's hardly as simple as that, Luce," Trevor protested. "She is here for one reason and one reason only. To convince me to return to London and take my place as Ormonde. Which is something I will never, ever do. It's not just a matter of stubbornness on my part. You know what the old duke did to my parents."

"Of course I do," his friend conceded. "But both your parents and the old duke are gone now. And there is a family there who is in need of your guidance."

"I sincerely doubt that any of them are feeling my absence with any degree of discomfort. I manage the estates from here, and see to it that the dependents upon the estate are seen to. What more can they want?"

"Your presence, man," Lucien said firmly. "I know you think that a dukedom without a duke can rub along just fine, but you know as well as I do that an absence like that will open the door to pretenders and usurpers. The dowager herself is not going to live forever. And there was something untoward about the young duke's death. How often does a man fall on a knife?"

"Well, the dowager can damn well deal with the dukedom on her own without my help. And my cousin's death, whether it was untoward or not, has nothing to do with me." He shook his head. "I know you think I'm being a fool about this, Blakemore," he said, "but I cannot simply ignore the years of rancor between my father and his family. It would be disloyal to his memory. And aside from that, I don't wish to expose the girls to that world. Can you imagine the sort of damage the venality of the *ton* could do to someone as sensitive as Bel?"

"She's a bit young for making her debut," Blakemore said practically. "I should imagine that she'd remain in the schoolroom for several years yet. But it might do her some good to mix with girls of her own social station for a change. She can hardly run tame in the village until she's ready to marry."

"You know what I mean," Trevor said. Though he did concede that Bel needed some sort of civilizing influence. "I am in the market for another governess," he said, keeping the subject, albeit tangentially.

"Again?" Blakemore shook his head pityingly. "You're too damned nice to them. You realize that, right?"

"I treat them with kindness and civility if that's what

you mean," Trevor said haughtily. "It is hardly my fault that they mistake it for finer feelings."

"Trev," the other man said in exasperation, "they are governesses. They are unaccustomed to kindness. You have never gotten the knack of polite indifference that is necessary to interact with females of a certain station."

"I have no difficulty with Mrs. Templeton or the maids," Trevor argued.

"That is because you've known them since you were in short coats," his friend said. "Governesses begin life as ladies for the most part, and through some unhappy circumstance find themselves working in the households of what were once their peers. It's a damned uncomfortable situation."

"How do you know so much about it?" Trevor demanded.

"I read," Blakemore said with a shrug. "And I knew a lady once who was forced by circumstance to go into the profession. It is not an easy life. Even in a household where the gentlemen behave as gentlemen."

"Hmm. I suppose you're right that I should perhaps work on cultivating distance. But now you make me feel like a churl for hiring one at all."

"Don't be a nodcock. They need the work, after all. But what they do not need is for you to treat them as equals."

"I don't suppose you know of anyone who is looking for such a position."

Blakemore snorted. "I'm not an employment agency, man. Though perhaps you might ask your guest if she knows of anyone. Most ladies know at least someone who is looking for a position or who has recently lost their governess."

"Good point," Trevor said approvingly. "Perhaps I can find a way for Lady Wharton's visit to be useful before I send her packing."

"Do not send her away before I am able to come make her acquaintance," Blakemore said. "I am currently in need of a bit of dalliance, and a young, attractive widow might be an excellent prospect."

A jolt of annoyance shot through Trevor as he pictured Lady Isabella in an embrace with his friend.

Blakemore's mouth dropped open. "Did you just growl?" he demanded, his eyes wide.

"Of course not," Trevor said, though he suspected that he had in fact emitted such a sound.

Blakemore's eyes narrowed suspiciously. "Are you certain? Because if you have some claim on the lady I will leave her alone."

"Perhaps that would be for the best."

"Because you want her for yourself?"

A silence fell between them.

"Blakemore," Trevor said, rising from his chair.

"Yes?"

"Shut up."

To Isabella's surprise, the tidy sitting room of Nettlefield House was filled with no fewer than five ladies when she and Eleanor arrived. Excellent, she thought. I'm to be examined like a moth-eaten lion in the zoo. She was suddenly struck by the wish to do something vulgar, like pick her teeth or belch. Something that would set their provincial minds on edge.

"Lady Wharton," said a woman with excessively styled blond curls, who seemed to be the leader of the group, curtsying with just the right amount of deference. "It is an honor to welcome you to Nettledale. It is not often that we are graced with someone of your social standing."

Isabella took in the older woman's elegantly cut gown and mentally pronounced her to be a social climber. The woman's next words confirmed the assessment.

"My husband, Mr. Humphrey Palmer, is one of the duke's closest friends. Indeed I cannot think of a day that's passed in the last few months when they were not much in one another's company."

Behind that lady's back, Eleanor's eyes widened and she frowned to indicate that such was not the case.

"Indeed? How fortunate for him," Isabella said, careful to keep her smile polite but not overly inviting. She gestured to the other ladies with her hand, and Mrs. Palmer seemed to need the reminder that they were there. "I hope you will introduce me to your friends."

Mrs. Palmer tittered. "Oh, of course. How silly of me." But her smile was empty of any real self-deprecation. Turning to her companions, she began introducing them. "Miss Fanny Edgerton," she said, indicating an elderly lady with a severe expression, who offered a tight smile. Isabella had met many iterations of her type over the years, none of them pleasant. Still, Miss Edgerton seemed to disapprove of Mrs. Palmer, so that was a point in her favor. Isabella offered the old woman a smile and was rewarded with a grudging nod.

"And, this is Mrs. Green, the wife of our local squire," Mrs. Palmer said with pursed lips. It was easy to see why Mrs. Palmer would be jealous. Mrs. Green was quite pretty, with wide blue eyes and shining red curls. But it was her youth and vivacity that the older woman must find most annoying. She could buy as many pretty gowns as she wished, but nothing would bring back the blush of youth. "Mrs. Green was fortunate enough to meet our squire when he visited Brighton last summer. It was quite the whirlwind romance. We were quite surprised that he married so soon after the first Mrs. Green's death."

Not batting an eye at the matron's ungenerous words, Mrs. Green gave Isabella a warm smile. "Welcome to the neighborhood, Lady Wharton. I will be more than happy to offer you a cup of tea if you will be in residence long enough for such things. We are quite proud of our little corner of Yorkshire." She glanced sideways at Mrs. Palmer. "Even one so lately arrived like me."

Strangely touched by the young woman's generosity, Isabella smiled back. "I do not know how long it will take for my carriage to be repaired, but if I do stay more than a few days I should like that." She might regret the decision later, but it was difficult to remain unmoved in the face of such a good-spirited welcome. Even from someone she'd never encounter in town. "Thank you."

The invitation was echoed by the other ladies, though whether it sprang from genuine welcome or from a desire to compete with Mrs. Green Isabella could not say. She was so accustomed to the cool civility of town manners, however, that the easy welcome came as a refreshing change.

Next she was presented to Lady Penelope Frith and her sister Mrs. Leonie Kilmarten. Both ladies were widows of a certain age, and it was clear from Mrs. Palmer's introduction that they were influential in the neighborhood. "It was Lady Penelope and Mrs. Kilmarten who first welcomed me into the village when I married my own dear husband," Mrs. Palmer said glacially. So much for the warmth, Isabella thought. However, the chill seemed reserved for the sisters, so perhaps she shouldn't be so sensitive. There was clearly some sort of rivalry among the women. Lady Penelope's title probably did not help matters.

"Lady Wharton," Lady Penelope said with the haughty tones that only someone born into the aristocracy could manage, "I believe I am acquainted with your godmother, the Dowager Duchess of Ormonde." She glanced round the room, as if getting the others' attention, "She is the grandmother of our dear duke, you know," she said, as if Isabella were unaware of the fact.

"Are you indeed, Lady Penelope?" Isabella asked coolly. This was the sort of provincial posturing she'd expected. Fortunately for her sake, she'd been taught at the knee of the most condescending of them all. "I believe my godmother is acquainted with a great many people," she continued, furrowing her brow just a smidgeon to affect puzzlement. "She has never mentioned you, I'm afraid."

But Lady Penelope was not cowed. "Dear me," she said, arching one narrow brow, refusing to acknowledge the slight. "The old dear can hardly be expected to remember everyone, I suppose."

"Quite," Isabella returned, preparing to move on.

Lady Penelope, however, was not finished. "We were quite good friends when I lived in London with my dear, dear Alfred. I hope you will remember me to her when you see her next."

"I shall endeavor to do so," Isabella said without much enthusiasm. She knew well enough that the dowager was approached by countless social climbers and hangers-on on a day-to-day basis. Just the sort of person the duke had thought Isabella to be last evening. She sincerely doubted that an elderly widow living in the wilds of Yorkshire would be worth the dowager's notice. Still, she would mention Lady Penelope. If for no other reason than to see her godmother rack her brains trying to remember how she knew her. The dowager despised it when she forgot things.

Realizing that the ladies would stand about posturing socially forever without some distraction, Isabella turned to Eleanor. "Perhaps you should ring for some refreshments for your guests, Miss Eleanor."

The girl blushed but seemed grateful to have guidance. It was clear that she had no notion of how to handle a parade of callers, much less callers who were intent upon staying as long as they could possibly manage.

They chatted amiably while they waited for the arrival of the tray, and once it did, a bit of the tension in the room dissipated. Nothing like a shared cup of tea to calm things among a group of feuding ladies.

She had just begun to pour when Mrs. Kilmarten, as bold and demanding as her sister, asked the question Isabella had been expecting from the first.

"What brings you to Yorkshire, Lady Wharton?"

The words hung in the air above the tea table for a moment as the ladies watched Isabella avidly for some response.

It would serve them, and the duke, right if she lied and said that she was the duke's betrothed and she'd come up to Yorkshire to marry him at last. She enjoyed imagining the varying degrees of horror they'd evince in the face of such a shocking revelation. Small country villages were marvelous for generating scandal, she thought wryly.

Instead, however, she kept somewhat closer to the truth. "Well, Mrs. Kilmarten," she said, taking a fortifying sip of tea, "I was sent on a very important errand by the Dowager Duchess of Ormonde."

Isabella debated telling them the whole truth: that she'd been sent to convince the duke to take up his duties. What better impetus for the duke to take up his responsibilities than to escape the haranguing of the neighborhood ladies? She would certainly think twice before running that gauntlet. Even so, she did not wish to say it before Eleanor, who was an innocent party in the matter. So she said instead, "The dowager would like for the duke to attend her birthday celebration next month at the family town house in London."

It was true enough that the dowager would like for him to attend her birthday celebration. The fact that she would wish him to do so after being presented at court as the new Duke of Ormonde and taking up his seat in the House of Lords was beside the point. At least that's what Isabella told herself.

Despite Isabella's wish to protect the girl, however, Eleanor was intrigued by Isabella's prevarication. "I should very much like to visit London to celebrate my grandmother's birthday," the girl said, her eyes alight. "We have yet to meet her, you know. And I feel sure that she notices the slight. I know I should if I were a grandmother who had never met my grandchildren."

Before Isabella could address that misguided notion of the dowager's sentimentality, a male voice sounded from the doorway. "As you well know, Eleanor," Ormonde said, "we are not on speaking terms with our grandmother. And the dukedom does not change the matter."

He stepped into the room, looking virile and masculine and completely foreign in the room of ladies and tea and biscuits. Isabella was quite sure that every woman in the room—even the elderly ones—sat up straighter and mentally smoothed her hair as he gave a slight bow. "Ladies," Ormonde said, his voice deep and with just a thread of humor in it. "I trust you have been keeping our guest entertained."

"Of course, Your Grace," Mrs. Palmer said with a fatuous smile. "We could not allow her to think us complete savages here in Yorkshire. A lady of such status is such an infrequent sight in these parts. We are quite honored by her presence."

"I feel sure Lady Wharton appreciates your condescension," Ormonde said with a quirked brow at Isabella. "She doubtless was starving for civilized company after her ordeal on the road yesterday."

"You are right, of course, Your Grace," Isabella said with an answering raised brow. "I vow I cannot go above four hours without some sort of socialization. Otherwise I grow intensely bored. So much so that it is quite difficult to pass an evening alone."

At her provocative words the duke's mouth thinned. "Indeed, Lady Wharton? I hope that you will not find us to be too tame here. Perhaps it would be best if you returned to London sooner rather than later. We would not wish you to expire from dullness. Or lack of . . . companionship."

The word hung in the air between them.

Mrs. Green, missing the subtext of their words, tittered. "Lady Wharton has just arrived, Your Grace. I pray you, do not send her back to London before we've had a chance to winkle the latest styles from her. I fear that the village dressmaker is sadly behind the times, and I for one am in desperate need of a new frock."

"You are lovely, as always, Mrs. Green," Ormonde said, though his eyes never left Isabella's. "I feel sure, however, that Lady Wharton would be happy enough to offer you her fashion advice. She is nothing if not full of opinions."

Beastly man, Isabella fumed. How dare he ruin her pleasant visit?

"I should be happy to tell you about all the latest styles, Mrs. Green," Isabella said, deliberately turning her attention away from the duke, who was soon descended upon by one of the other village ladies.

The assembled company passed the rest of the half hour discussing fashion. And before the visitors left, each of them had extended invitations to Isabella and Eleanor to come to tea later in the week.

When the last guest had gone and Eleanor had excused herself to find out what Belinda was up to, Isabella and Ormonde were left alone together. The silence between them might have been awkward, but oddly it was not. Indeed it felt strangely companionable. Which was not a restful thought at all. Wishing to escape the sensation, Isabella made her way to the doorway and tried to excuse herself.

Before she could get the words out, however, Ormonde touched her on the arm. The connection sent a jolt of awareness through her body.

"Stay a moment, please," the duke said, snatching his hand back as if touching her had affected him as much as it had her. A ludicrous notion, Isabella told herself. "I wish to discuss something with you," he continued.

With a nod she stepped back into the chamber, stopping before the fireplace. "How may I assist you, Your Grace?" she asked politely. Why was it so difficult to have anything like a normal conversation with the man? she wondered. Though he was hardly her biggest fan, given that she was here to try to convince him to do something he did not wish to do, his quarrel was with his grandmother, not with her. In fairness, though, she admitted that he might have made the situation much more uncomfortable than it already was. He would have been well within his rights to send her packing instead of welcoming her into his home.

Clasping his hands behind his back, the duke paced a little before the windows overlooking the front drive of the country house. He was dressed for riding, which Isabella assumed meant that he'd spent the morning on horseback. She wondered briefly if he had a suitable mount for her. She did not often get the chance to ride, but being in the country would allow her to get in a good gallop.

Ralph had not liked for her to ride as a general rule. He considered it unladylike for a woman to ride as Isabella did—with her whole being. And so he'd forbidden it. Since his death, she hadn't purchased a mount to replace her beloved Sookey, whom Ralph had sold without Isabella's knowledge. While she was in the country, though, perhaps she could become accustomed to the saddle again. She may as well make the most of the visit, since Ormonde was proving to be resistant to her wiles.

There was no question of failure in her quest to bring him back to London, of course. She refused to allow her sister's match with Coniston to be jeopardized. Perdita had already been through hell with Gervase. She deserved some happiness and Isabella was going to ensure that she got it.

"There are actually two matters I wish to discuss," the duke said, interrupting Isabella's thoughts. His russet hair glinted in the morning sun, giving him the appearance of an angel in a halo. Isabella didn't find the illusion at all amusing.

"First of all," Ormonde said, "it looks as if it will take upwards of a week to repair the duchess's carriage. The local blacksmith is away in York visiting his ailing mother and will not be back before a sennight at least."

Before she could protest he continued, his eyes serious, "Both of our coachmen have looked at the damage and have concluded that the damage was deliberate."

Isabella felt her chest constrict.

"Deliberate?" she asked, feeling like an echo. "You mean someone damaged it on purpose?"

Ormonde nodded. Isabella did not like the gravity in his expression. It smacked too much of concern, which she most assuredly did not want.

"Can you think of a reason someone might wish to harm you?"

I know what you did last season.

The words of the note echoed in Isabella's consciousness. But surely the carriage breaking had nothing to do with the silly message. If she were a betting woman she'd lay odds that the dowager herself had sabotaged the carriage in order to give Isabella a better chance at persuading the duke to come back to London with her.

With a nod she said as much to the duke. "So you see,

Your Grace, it was likely just your grandmother's ploy to see to it that I am here long enough to convince you to return to London with me."

Ormonde frowned. "Lady Wharton, I think you misunderstand me. The damage to the carriage wasn't a bit of tampering to make the vehicle unable to continue on. This was the sort of damage that if it had occurred on any other stretch of road could have killed you or one of the servants riding with you."

Her hard-won poise fading, Isabella's hand rose to her throat.

His gaze concerned, the duke stepped forward and touched her lightly on the arm. "I do not mean to frighten you," he said, "but it is apparent to me that whoever did this wanted to do you or someone else in your party grievous harm."

Gone was the frisson of awareness that came whenever they touched and in its place was cold, hard fear. Isabella fought back a shiver.

"If you think of anyone with a reason to wish you harm," he said firmly, "let me know at once. You were lucky we've had so much rain of late, because the mud cushioned what might have otherwise been a more dangerous fall."

Isabella nodded. With some difficulty she managed to impose some calm upon herself. Wishing more than anything to change the subject so that she would not seem so vulnerable, she asked, "There was something else you wished to speak of?"

His brow still furrowed, the duke took a moment to realize what she was asking. At the reminder he flushed. "Oh yes. It has been pointed out to me that it is perhaps unwise for me to allow Eleanor and Belinda to continue to carry on left to their own devices without some kind of female guidance."

Surprise made Isabella's eyes widen. Of all the things she might have expected him to say, it wasn't this. "I am in agreement with this assessment," she said carefully. She could tell just from her brief acquaintance with his sisters that they desperately needed some kind of guidance. "Surely you are not asking me to act as your sisters' governess, Your Grace? For I can assure you that I have no such qualifications. I am quite abysmal at the pianoforte and I have no gift at all for recitations."

He laughed. It was the first time she'd heard him do so and she was charmed in spite of herself.

"No!" he said, running a nervous hand over his mussed hair. He was clearly out of his element talking about such things. But the fact that he cared enough to approach someone he had no reason to trust said much for his affection for his sisters. "I would not presume upon your good nature in such a way. I would, however, presume upon you to help me find a suitable governess. If that is at all agreeable to you."

She was strangely flattered that he trusted her opinion. Then again, it wasn't as if he had much choice in the matter, she thought, remembering the way the neighborhood ladies had fawned over him that morning.

"Of course I will assist you," she said more warmly than she'd intended. But, she thought, better to seem more eager than not eager enough. "You do know, however, that Eleanor is nearly ready to make her come-out."

His good humor fled at her words. "Not yet, surely," he said. "I believe many young ladies do not make their debuts until they are a bit older."

"Only if some event prevents them from doing so," Isabella said firmly. "Unless there is a death in the family, or some sort of financial difficulty that prevents it, forcing a young lady to make her debut at an advanced age merely serves to put her behind the rest of her peers. I realize that you do not wish to take up your role as the duke, but if your reticence prevents your sisters from taking their own rightful positions in society, Your Grace, you are being unfair to them."

He looked as if he would argue, but she held up a staying hand. "I have no wish to be unkind, or to use your sisters as a means of luring you to London. But surely you can see that your actions affect them."

"But Eleanor is only seventeen. That is far too young for her to be on the town."

"But not too young for her to begin attending neighborhood parties and the like," Isabella said. "Like it or not, Your Grace, she is almost grown and by preventing her from leaving the nest you will only hamper her chances at happiness."

"What a coil," he muttered, looking as if he'd like to tug on his hair in frustration. If he didn't care about his sisters one way or the other he'd have told Isabella to go hang, so his obvious dismay was a point in both their favors. His because it meant he was a kind guardian and hers because it meant that he might be persuaded to go up to London on his sisters' behalf.

She said she did not wish to use his sisters to lure him up to London. That did not mean she would not do so if she must. Besides, she truly did believe that having their brother accept his rightful position would be good for Eleanor and Belinda.

"In any event," Isabella went on, "I will write to my

sister in London and ask her if she will put the word out that you are seeking a governess. I imagine that any governess in need of a position would leap at the chance to work for the Duke of Ormonde."

"Thank you," he said, still looking somewhat hunted.

"And, Lady Wharton," he continued, "I do realize that my decisions affect them. It simply had not occurred to me that by refusing to go to London I was hampering their social welfare. I still think of them as children, I suppose."

It would take a bit of time, Isabella supposed, for him to begin thinking of his sisters as young ladies. Perhaps she could do him some good while she while she was here, in addition to doing the dowager's bidding.

"I understand, Your Grace," she said, smiling at him. "I have a younger sister, too."

Trevor found himself reluctant to ruin their unusual amity by broaching the topic of the bargain, but he knew that he would be doing Lady Isabella a great disservice were he to let her continue on with the idea that they were now at some kind of peace. Far from it.

"There is one further item I wish to discuss with you, my lady," he said just as she was rising from her chair. "It will take but a moment." Feeling like the veriest clod, he took out the sheet of foolscap on which he'd jotted down his list of items for her to accomplish before he'd agree to come to London.

Looking surprised, Lady Isabella nonetheless remained seated and inclined her head to indicate that she was listening.

Trevor cleared his throat. "I realize that you came

here not at your own whim," he said, "but because my grandmother has for whatever reason chosen you to be her emissary."

"Yes." Her dark hair shone in the light from the windows, and Trevor found himself wondering what it would look like when loosed from its elegant chignon.

Realizing the direction of his thoughts, he mentally shook himself and returned to the subject at hand. "Lady Wharton," he said firmly, "I have decided that I will go with you to London."

Her eyes widened, and to his discomfort she smiled. It was the first real show of genuine warmth he'd seen from her since her arrival last evening. "Your Grace," she said with relief, "that is wonderful news!"

He felt like a churl to crush her enthusiasm. But crush it he must.

"I will not go without a concession on your part," he said firmly.

She frowned. "I don't understand."

He gave in to the impulse to run a hand through his hair. "You must allow me to show you just what it is we do here at Nettlefield House. It is not an insignificant amount of work to run an estate such as this. And if my grandmother cannot bestir herself to come here and demand my presence in London herself, the least I can do is impress upon her emissary its importance in my life."

A flash of annoyance crossed her eyes but was quickly masked with an expression of patience. "Your Grace, I have no doubt that your feelings for this place run deep, but I am hardly the best person to convey that emotion to the Dowager Duchess of Ormonde. I have spent very little time in the country myself, and have no notion what it takes to run an estate of this size. The only opinion I

could possibly convey on the subject to your grandmother is that you appear to be attached to the place.
And you can do that yourself in a letter if you wish."

Trevor crossed his arms over his chest and surveyed
her from head to toe. She certainly was not the picture
of a country lady. But he had little doubt that she could
convince the dowager to leave him in peace if she set
her mind to it. Since he could not convince his grandmother himself, he would see to it that Lady Isabella did.
The more he considered the matter, the more he was
certain he was choosing the right course.

"But why bother with a letter when I can have my
very own personal champion?" he asked with a tilt of
his head. "Once you have seen the farm in all its glory, I
am certain you will agree to plead my case to the dowager. Namely that the running of this estate is far more
important than swanning about town in fancy clothes to
attend foolish entertainments."

She was vexed. It was obvious from the way her bosom rose and fell with her frustrated breathing. Then,
she seemed to come to some decision within herself. "Is
that what you think this is about, Your Grace? The dowager wishing for you to buy a new wardrobe and accompany her to soirees and balls?"

"The thought did cross my mind," he said with a
frown. "Do you mean to say that she does not wish for
me to do those things? Along with finding some young
lady with an enormous dowry to wed and get an heir on
as quickly as possible?"

Realizing what he'd just said, he raised a hand in
apology. "Your pardon, Lady Wharton," he said. "It's
just that I cannot help but feel wrongly done by when
my grandmother has not bothered in the twenty-eight

years of my existence to even seek me out. She washed her hands of my parents years ago, and her sudden interest coincides awfully with my cousin's death."

Isabella looked as if she might like to argue but instead gave a short nod. "I do not deny that it looks suspicious. But I can assure you that she has long felt the loss of your father from the family circle. Even so, it does not matter what reason she has for wishing you to come take up your rightful place as head of the family. The fact that she is your elderly relation ought to be reason enough for you to abide by her wishes."

"Even though she has not abided by my own or my family's wishes for some twenty years?" he demanded. "That seems a very unbalanced form of familial affection, my lady."

"It might," she agreed, "but that is neither here nor there. This is my side of the arrangement. If I agree with you that your endeavors here are important enough to keep you from visiting the Ormonde estates in person, then I will tell the dowager so. But either way, you must come to London with me without argument."

"So," he said with a laugh, "you get your way no matter what happens? You drive a hard bargain, my lady."

"I have my orders from the dowager," she said coolly. "Now, do we have a bargain?"

Trevor knew that she could simply make up her mind to disagree with him no matter what she thought of the estate. But he somehow doubted she would do that. There was something about her that spoke of integrity. She might have lied to him about the purpose of her visit or made excuses for his grandmother, but she had not. Lady Isabella might have her faults, but lying wasn't one of them. At least he hoped not.

By having her shadow him about the estate for the next week he would get what he'd been wanting for years: a witness to see that his father's hard work on the Yorkshire estate had not been the waste of time his family had assured him it would be.

That the dowager herself would know how wrong she'd been.

Short of bringing his grandmother herself to Nettlefield House, Lady Isabella was the next best thing.

"You have my word," he said, offering his hand to her in a gesture of good faith. She hesitated for the barest second before giving him her hand. Neither of them was wearing gloves and the brief feel of skin on skin sent a jolt through him that had nothing to do with honor and everything to do with lust.

Her eyes widened in surprise—perhaps she felt the jolt, too—and met his before she pulled her hand back and let it fall to her side.

"Well then," she said briskly, not meeting his eyes. "We have an agreement. How long do you suppose it will take you to show me the workings of the estate? A few days? Might we be able to leave for London at the end of the week?"

It was Tuesday now, but Trevor had no intention of leaving the estate at all, much less at the end of the week. "Oh, I should think it will need more than a few days," he told her. "And of course there's the matter of your damaged carriage. No, I think a week at least. Possibly two."

"But that's—," she began to protest before he interrupted her.

"I really must insist, Lady Wharton, that you let me show you the estate on my own terms. Not all of the elements I wish to show you will be available this week. Sheepshearing, for instance, doesn't begin until next week."

"Sheepshearing?" Her voice was a high-pitched squeak. "I am hardly the most appropriate judge of how best to shear a sheep, Your Grace. Indeed, I think I might comfortably take your word for it in that case."

Trevor managed to keep his expression serious for all of two minutes before she caught on.

"You're joking," she said with a shake of her head. She put her hands on her hips. "Really, Your Grace, was that altogether necessary?"

He shrugged. "Perhaps not, but you must allow that it was amusing."

"For you, perhaps," she said huffily. Then, to his surprise, she softened. "Your Grace, do not think that I do not appreciate the reluctance you feel for joining the rest of your family in London. I do understand what it is like to be estranged from one's family. But I have my own reasons for being here and I hope that you will not make my chore here any more difficult than it needs to be."

He wasn't sure how he knew, but Trevor sensed that it had taken a great deal for her to admit to understanding his plight. "Thank you, my lady. I hope that we will be able to rub along well enough together.

"Which reminds me," he continued, removing the list of tasks he'd written out for her and handing them over.

"What's this?"

"I have written out a list of the things I think you should see to fully understand how much work it takes to oversee an estate like this." He felt like a schoolboy proffering his first love note. An actual blush was stealing into his cheeks. Gad. "You need not accompany me for all of these, but I do not think you can get a true feeling for the estate without at least knowing about these things."

She didn't unfold the paper but instead clutched it in her hand as if it were a lifeline keeping her from being carried away into the open sea.

"Thank you, Your Grace," she said with a slight curtsy. "I will look at this list later, after I have spoken with my maid about our extended stay here. Might I assume that we won't begin our tour until tomorrow?"

Grateful for her cool tones, Trevor nodded. "Yes, tomorrow. Now, if you will excuse me, I must go see to some estate business." Feeling rather like a coward, he hurried off to his study, where he might reflect upon the bargain he'd just made.

Four

$\mathcal{A}$s soon as she reached her bedchamber, Isabella unfolded the page the duke had given her and began reading through the list of tasks he would require of her before he would consider making the trip to London.

She might have known from the first that it wouldn't be as simple as requesting his presence in London and having him accompany her back to town. He was the grandson of the Dowager Duchess of Ormond, after all. It was foolish to imagine that the tendency toward manipulating others would have skipped his generation.

But when Isabella read the list, she wondered if he might have gotten a dose of insanity as well. Not only did the man expect her to visit the tenant farms with him, assist him on a visit to the weavers' cottages, and sit beside him as he performed the duties of local magistrate; he also wanted her to accompany him to a doubtless provincial dinner party at the home of the local squire. She was, it seemed, to get an up-close view of life as a local farmer, whether she liked it or not.

What would she wear, for goodness' sake? These were hardly the sort of events Madame Celeste designed

Isabella's gowns for. Though, now she thought of it, Madame Celeste must fashion some gowns for practical use. Surely not every gently bred lady who visited her establishment was in search of a ball gown.

Isabella felt quite out of her element. As she was sure the duke wished her to be. It was clear enough to her that he thought her just as frivolous as every other member of the *ton*. Perhaps it was her turn to show him that not all London ladies were so disagreeable as the dowager. Indeed, she'd need to prove that to him if she wished to convince him to return to London with her.

Failure was not an option.

After all, if she didn't come back to London with him by her side the dowager would see to it that Perdita's marriage to Coniston was well and truly stopped. And Isabella of all people knew how important it was to her sister to make that match work. No, no matter how much she might wish to throw the list of tasks back in the duke's face, she had to see to it that she performed each and every task to his satisfaction.

When she was finished, he'd be begging her to take him up to London.

Her plan roughly sketched out in her mind, she decided to work on the other tasks the duke had asked for her to assist him with.

After a brief chat with Templeton, who agreed to send a notice to the Yorkshire papers advertising for a governess, and penning a letter to Perdita asking her to inquire among their friends for likely candidates, Isabella found herself in the unusual position of having nothing to do.

When she was in London she could always find ways to amuse herself. Reading or visiting friends or shopping.

Her tour of the estate did not begin until tomorrow. And she felt strangely at loose ends here in this unfamiliar country house. Her previous visits to country houses had been for house parties. Which were, as a general rule, brimming with opportunities for amusement.

She was debating the wisdom of donning a walking dress and indulging in a hearty country walk when a knock sounded on her bedchamber door. Watching as Sanders opened it, Isabella was surprised but pleased to see Eleanor and Belinda.

"Hello, Lady Wharton," Belinda said with a careful curtsy. "We thought perhaps you might wish to join us for an outdoor artistic endeavor. Though Eleanor says you probably won't, as you are much too elegant for such a thing."

"Belinda," Eleanor hissed, "that was not what I said—"

Isabella watched with a pang in her chest as Eleanor's pale complexion turned rosy. Could she and Perdita ever have been so young? she wondered. It was hard to remember it. And yet there was something familiar about these two sisters, something that made Isabella want to shield them from the hurts and embarrassments that awaited them in the world outside their little village.

Giving in to the impulse to put the girl at ease, Isabella broke into her protest. "I would love to join you. Just let me change into something more suitable."

The surprise and pleasure in the girls' faces told Isabella she'd done the right thing. Inviting them into her chamber, she asked Sanders to bring her the green sprig muslin and stepped behind the screen in the dressing room to change.

"I am so glad you thought to ask me," she called over the screen. "I was debating whether to go to the library, but I didn't wish to disturb your brother."

"Oh, he doesn't spend much time in there during the day," Belinda said loudly, as if Isabella were in another room. "He spends most days in the estate office."

Waiting for the maid to finish buttoning her gown, Isabella frowned. "Doesn't he have an estate agent for that sort of thing?"

"No," Eleanor said. "Papa preferred to do things himself and Trevor does as well."

Her gown finally fastened, Isabella stepped out from behind the screen to find Eleanor fingering the silk of one of the gowns neatly hanging in the open wardrobe. When she saw Isabella she snatched her hand back as if she'd been swatted.

Oblivious to their guest's emergence, Belinda was seated at the dressing table powdering her nose with Isabella's enormous powder puff.

"It's all right," Isabella told Eleanor. "You can touch them. They're just clothes."

"They're lovely clothes," the girl said mournfully. "I don't think I shall ever have anything so fine."

"Of course you will," Isabella said automatically. It was impossible not to feel for the girl. After all, she was of an age that she should be being outfitted with a new wardrobe and preparing for the excitement of her first season. Instead she was stuck here in the country. And if their guests that morning were any indication, there was little enough to recommend the local society hereabouts. "Why shouldn't you?"

"For one thing," Eleanor said glumly, "Trevor would

never let me wear something so daring. He doesn't even like it when I wear my hair up. Though I have tried to tell him that I am no longer a child."

"Like me," Belinda said matter-of-factly. "She thinks it's ever so lowering to be childish. But I think it's lovely."

Isabella suppressed a laugh. "Why is that?"

"Because I don't have to do grown-up things. Like dress for dinner and visit with those horrid ladies from the village. I'd much rather spend my time with Flossie and her kittens."

"That's because you are still a child, Belinda," her sister said haughtily. "You'll understand when you're my age."

"I doubt it," Belinda said, spinning around on the vanity stool.

"Your brother is likely right about that particular gown," Isabella said, indicating the deep blue silk that Eleanor was admiring. "But there's no reason why you shouldn't be able to try one of the others. Sanders is quite handy with a needle. I'm a good bit taller than you, but otherwise we are of a size, I think. She should be able to alter it to fit."

Whirling, Eleanor stared at Isabella, her eyes wide. "Do you mean it? I should love that above all things! And do you suppose she would dress my hair for me?"

Feeling like a fairy godmother, Isabella grinned. "I think that could be arranged."

"But what about our painting?" Belinda demanded. "I know precisely what vista I wish to capture."

Both Eleanor and Isabella turned guiltily to the younger girl.

"What if I promise that we will spend tomorrow

painting outdoors?" Isabella asked, seeing Eleanor's guilty look. Clearly she'd forgotten about the original reason for going to Isabella's rooms.

Belinda heaved a sigh. "I suppose that would be acceptable. But only if you both agree to the location I choose for our expedition."

Suspecting that she would regret the promise, Isabella did so anyway. As did Eleanor.

"Thank you, Bel." She gave her sister an impulsive hug. "You are a good sister."

"I am an excellent sister," the younger girl said with asperity. "Now, let's look at these gowns."

The three began sorting through Isabella's wardrobe, searching for which gowns best suited Eleanor's fair hair and skin. And more than once Isabella had to steer her away from gowns that were either far too immodest or far too daring in color for so young a lady. Isabella would hardly miss the gowns, given that she bought far more each season than she could ever wear, but even she knew that there were some risks that young ladies should steer clear of. Especially while buried in the country. What might pass for fashionable in London could sometimes be seen as inappropriate among the more sedate fashions of a country village.

Finally they settled on three dresses that were modest enough to keep from scandalizing the local ladies but fashionable enough to suit the inclinations of Eleanor to throw off her childhood frocks and dress her age. The first was a primrose muslin that Isabella had never quite felt right wearing. It seemed far too young for a widow, and when she saw Eleanor in it she knew that she'd been right. Its puffed sleeves and sweetheart neckline were perfection on the younger lady, and Isabella was pleased to note that it looked far better on Eleanor than it ever had on her.

"This one, definitely," she pronounced as the girl spun before the mirror. "It needs only to be hemmed a bit and it will be just right for you."

"You look like a fairy princess, Ellie!" Belinda, who had not been particularly interested in their quest for gowns, had slowly been won over as she saw her sister's excitement over the clothes. Now Belinda clapped her hands with glee at Eleanor's transformation. "You will have a dozen beaux before the week is out," she pronounced, unconsciously mimicking *a ton* matron bent on marrying off her daughter.

"Perhaps not the week, oh ancient one," Isabella said with a laugh, "but by the end of the summer, certainly."

"Do you really think so?" Eleanor asked, her eyes alight with excitement.

Isabella remembered what it was like to be a motherless girl at this age, and she could only guess how difficult it was to have no female relatives about to guide Eleanor. She wished that she could do more in her short visit.

"I do think so," she said aloud. "I predict you will have at least one beau. Now, let's see what the pink sarcenet looks like. It was always a bit too short for me, so it may not need as much alteration."

"Lady Wharton," Belinda asked, "do you have any sisters of your own?"

Startled, Isabella turned to look at the girl. "I do indeed. How did you guess?"

To Isabella's amusement, she shrugged. The child was as world-weary as an elderly matron. "I don't know," Belinda said, a tiny furrow between her brows. "You just seem sisterly."

Helping Eleanor out of the sprig muslin, Isabella nodded. "I have one sister. She's actually your cousin by marriage. She was married to the late duke."

"Before he died?"

Thinking back to the disastrous night of the Ormonde ball, Isabella repressed a shudder. "Yes," she said after a moment. "She's a lovely person. I hope that one day you'll be able to meet her."

"Not likely," Eleanor said, her ebullience at the gowns dampening slightly. "Trevor will never let us go to London. Certainly not while he's still the duke. He hates London."

"I hate it, too," Belinda said, loyalty to her brother stiffening her backbone.

"You don't even know what it's like," Eleanor argued. "You just hate it because you wouldn't be able to run wild there like you do here."

"I do not run wild," Belinda retorted. "I am a free spirit."

Eleanor rolled her eyes. "You're a hoyden."

"I am not!"

"Girls, girls!" Isabella held up a silencing hand. "Enough! This is not how well-bred young ladies behave. When we have a difference of opinion, we maintain our composure and discuss the matter like rational beings."

Though they looked as if they'd like to argue, Eleanor and Belinda nodded and to Isabella's surprise said, "Yes, Lady Wharton."

Not wishing to look her gift horse in the mouth, Isabella nodded. "Thank you. Now, let's fasten this gown and see how it looks."

When it was secured, Eleanor twirled before the looking glass. As Isabella had predicted, the gown was only a little long, which would mean that it would need the least alteration.

"I think it looks quite well on you, Eleanor," she pronounced. She handed the other two gowns to Sanders and instructed her to take them in and helped Eleanor to remove the pink gown so that she might wear it to dinner that evening.

"I can't wait to see what Trevor says," Belinda said with relish. "He's going to be so surprised. I think you should wear your hair up, too, Ellie."

But Isabella wasn't so sure. "I do not wish to antagonize your brother," she began. "If he's going to be annoyed by this, then we shouldn't do it." She was a great proponent of the adage about catching more flies with honey than with vinegar. Lending gowns to Eleanor was honey. Helping her put up her hair—a style he disliked for her to wear—might be closer to vinegar than Isabella was willing to go.

The girls had no such problem, however.

"He needs to be made to see reason, Lady Wharton," Eleanor said firmly. "If Trevor continues to hide me in the country and treat me as a schoolgirl he'll never see me as the adult I am. And I am an adult. Almost."

Sighing inwardly, Isabella couldn't help but agree. Sometimes men needed to have their comfortable existence jostled a bit to see what was right in front of them. And like it or not, his sister was a young lady now and deserved to be treated as one.

Which meant allowing her to dress and behave like a young lady.

The very fact that she was allowed to have dinner outside the schoolroom was indication enough that he didn't see her as being in the same cohort as Belinda.

Perhaps seeing Eleanor dressed like a lady would give him the nudge he needed to start letting her move in society as a young lady and not a child.

"All right," she told Eleanor, handing her the pink gown and a pair of slippers to match. "Now I suggest you lie down for a bit before dinner so that you're rested for your family debut."

Eleanor nodded and to Isabella's surprise pulled her into an impulsive hug. "Thank you," she told her. "It's easy to see you have a sister. I hope she knows how lucky she is."

Thinking of Perdita and what she might endure if Isabella did not succeed at her appointed task in Yorkshire, Isabella hugged the girl back. And prayed that the Duke of Ormonde would be better than his predecessor and do the right thing by her sister.

Trevor spent the rest of the afternoon going over the accounts, trying to figure out where he'd get the money for repairs to the tenant roofs before winter. It was times like this when he felt the pull of the dukedom . . . or at least the dukedom's coffers. But he had promised his father that he would never use money from the Ormonde family at the Yorkshire farm. He had never until recently been tempted to do so. But a poor harvest last year had left him with less funding than he was accustomed to using at the home farm.

Even so, he was scrupulous about keeping the Ormonde funds and the Nettlefield funds separate. Unbeknownst to the dowager, he had been corresponding with the duke's personal secretary for some months and had been making many of the decisions regarding the

Ormonde House estates. Trevor might not wish to mix with the Ormonde family or take up his role as the duke, but he could hardly let the tenants and the army of servants employed by the Ormonde estate go to rack and ruin over a grudge they had nothing to do with. It wasn't their fault his late grandparents had been so full of their own importance they'd cut Trevor's family out of their lives.

No, he would do his best by the people of the estates, but as far as he was concerned the dowager and the rest of the upper-class hangers-on who flitted about the dukedom could go to the devil.

The memory of the frisson of attraction he'd felt when Lady Wharton had given him her hand that afternoon came unbidden to his mind's eye. But ruthlessly he repressed the feeling the memory inspired in him. He had no obligation to Lady Wharton. The sooner she realized that, the better.

Thus it was that he dressed for dinner in a less than salubrious mood. Looking down at his coat of blue superfine and fawn breeches, he wondered when he'd paid more than a passing thought to his attire.

Fashion had never been one of his favorite subjects. Even in his salad days—though he did recall a time when his shirt points had been ridiculously high—he'd been more interested in horses than the cut of his coats. Allowing his valet to stab a pin into the froth of his neckcloth, Trevor bit back a sigh. Surely he was beyond all this fashion nonsense by now.

Wasn't he?

The question dogged him as he headed downstairs to the drawing room.

It was only due to their current houseguest that they

were even observing the custom of drinks before dinner. As a general rule, he and his sisters dined *en famille* with little ceremony. He knew that the girls should be dining in the nursery or the schoolroom, but it was one of the few times during the week that he actually saw them. The farms and estate kept him busy, and when there was a governess in residence the girls had their studies. But while he was willing to alter their normal routine because of their guest, he was not willing to send the girls back to the schoolroom. If Lady Wharton objected to his sisters' presence at table, then she would simply have to endure her displeasure in silence.

When he reached the drawing room, he found that Lady Wharton was already there. She was at the window gazing out at the view of the back garden. He took a moment to watch her without interruption.

Tonight, she was wearing what he secretly referred to as a gut puncher, for the feeling it inspired in him. The gown was a bluish green, the shade of a robin's egg. It was cool and elegant and hugged her every delicious curve. He might have resigned himself to her presence in his household for the next week or more, but he hadn't quite managed to steel his body against its reaction to her. Perhaps he'd have done better to send her packing at once, he reflected. At least then he wouldn't have to endure the constant state of arousal he'd suffered with since her arrival.

He knew the moment she realized he was behind her because her relaxed stance became deathly still.

Like a doe sensing a hunter.

"Your Grace," she said before turning. Her gown was just as gut punching from the front as it was from the back. The fabric of her bodice revealed as much of her breasts as it concealed, and Trevor had to admit to himself that they were exquisite.

Her dark hair was arranged in a much looser style than the neat chignon she wore during the day. Tonight curly wisps hung down on either side of her face to caress the skin of her long neck, almost as if they'd come loose during some exerting activity. He longed to slip his hands into her silken locks and finish the job of tousling her coiffure completely.

If he didn't expect his sisters any moment he might have tried his luck, but they were coming any moment, and besides that, he needed to get Lady Wharton on his side regarding the estate before anything could happen between them.

Which sounded, he thought to himself, as if he would allow something to happen after they went to London. Which was foolishness itself. The Lady Isabella Whartons of the world were not made for him. He might bear the title of Duke of Ormonde, but that was in name only. In person and spirit he was a country farmer who wished for nothing more than a life tending his crops and seeing to it that his tenants were well cared for. Someone like Lady Wharton could never understand that. And, in truth, she didn't need to. Let her go back to London and find some fancy town lord to sweep her off her feet.

He must have been quiet for too long, because the object of his rumination said, "I don't believe I've seen you dressed so formally before, Your Grace. It looks quite well on you."

Trevor listened carefully for a tone of condescension in her words, but try as he might he could find none. Perhaps she was simply making conversation. Even so, he could not keep the edge of annoyance from his voice.

"I am not a savage, madam," he said, moving to stand with his shoulder against the mantle. He allowed himself to survey her from head to toe. "Nor are you, it would seem. I would mention the formality of your gown, but that would not be polite."

"Touché," she said, acknowledging her own gaffe. "I apologize for my frankness. I am simply having difficulty reconciling your grandmother's description of you with the man before me. I think perhaps the intelligence she received about you was not quite correct in its assessment."

He was hardly surprised to hear that his grandmother had such low expectations of him. She was, if he remembered her correctly, wholly taken up with the pomp and circumstance of her elevated status. It was hardly surprising to learn she assumed he was just as countrified as she was sophisticated. "I suppose my grandmother led you to think that we lived in the barn with the livestock?"

"Something like that," Lady Isabella acknowledged with a warm smile. "Though I think she probably thought you had different stalls from them at the very least. Even provincials have their standards."

Startled by her unexpected humor, Trevor couldn't help but laugh. "I hadn't expected that," he admitted with a rueful smile.

"What?" she asked, moving to the sideboard to pour him a glass of brandy. "That I possessed a sense of humor or that I had the ability to laugh at all. I do so often, I assure you. I find it is the only recourse one has sometimes for dealing with life's more absurd occurrences."

Taking the drink from her, he reflected that her icy beauty was warmed considerably by something as simple as a smile. She was elegantly beautiful when in repose, but when animated with good humor she was breathtaking. He wondered fleetingly why such a woman was ostensibly unattached. The men in London must be blind or in possession of very thin skin.

"You are quite right about laughter," he said, gesturing to her with his brandy glass. "I often see some of the lowest, most unlucky people in my position as local magistrate, but you would be amazed to see the number of poor souls who manage to soldier on solely because they can find the bright side of things."

"Ah yes," she said, nodding. "I believe you wish, as part of my education, to have me sit in on one of your sessions as magistrate. I must confess that I'm quite fascinated by that part of your requirements. It is somewhat lowering to admit it, but I am an avid reader of Minerva Press novels, and someone is always being brought up before the magistrates in them. I hope you won't mind if I gawk terribly."

Trevor might have expected her to admit to many things, but wishing to attend the quarter sessions solely to satisfy vulgar curiosity was not one of them.

"Really?" he asked, a bit dumbstruck. "I would never have guessed it of you. You don't seem like the sort would who enjoy such . . ." He searched his vocabulary for a descriptor that would be accurate without being insulting.

"Such low forms of entertainment?" she asked with a laugh. At his surprise she shook her head with good-humored derision. "I can hardly be a fan of the genre without having heard all of the myriad ways in which they are denigrated by those who have never even bothered to read one."

He gulped a mouthful of brandy. Blinking back tears

as the scorching liquid ran down his throat, Trevor coughed a bit before replying. "I suppose that's right," he said. "I've never read one, though I know Eleanor borrows them quite frequently from other girls in the neighborhood. My own reading is rather duller than yours, I fear."

"Let me guess," she said, eyeing him thoughtfully. "Treatises on agricultural practice?" she said, placing a provocative finger at the corner of her mouth.

He felt his eyes drawn to her lips, though he managed to answer her. "Guilty as charged, my lady," he said ruefully. "And seed catalogs."

"I thought as much," she said with mock disappointment. "I am quite scandalized, Your Grace. You really must reform yourself if you wish to find any young lady willing to—"

Isabella stopped, realizing what she'd just been about to say. What on earth was she thinking, to say such a thing to the man? It was entirely improper, no matter how easily they'd been getting on this afternoon. He was not her brother, that she might tease him about such matters without fear of reprisal.

She was saved from continuing by a cleared throat from the doorway. Turning, she saw Belinda enter the room and cross to address her brother.

"Trevor," his younger sister told him, bounding toward him in the enthusiastic stride that said as much about her age as her attire. "We've a surprise for you, so you must close your eyes."

Raising a brow, he looked at Isabella. She wondered

whether she and his sisters might not have made a mistake by surprising him with Eleanor's new gown. Sometimes men preferred to learn of changes gradually rather than all at once.

"I'm sure that's not necessary, Belinda," she said quickly, slipping an arm around the younger girl's shoulder. "I'm sure your surprise does not need such fanfare as all that. You will make your brother wonder just what you've been up to."

She squeezed Belinda's shoulder in a warning gesture, but clearly the girl had no notion of what the move meant.

"Of course it does, silly," Belinda responded, slipping out of Isabella's hold and stepping closer to her brother. "Now close your eyes, Trevor," she said, reaching up to cover his eyes with her fingers.

With one last puzzled look for Isabella, Trevor allowed himself to be blindfolded by his sister's small hands. "There," he said. "Now what?"

Isabella heard the shushing sound of satin brushing against itself and looked up to see Eleanor entering the room. She looked as fresh as a spring flower in the gown. Isabella had never looked half as good in it, for the color was far better suited to Eleanor's coloring. It was far more demure than the gowns being worn this season by girls of a similar age, and Isabella felt a pang of relief when she realized that the duke could have no objection to the gown. In the half hour since she'd left the girls upstairs she'd been afraid that her original assessment had been wrong.

"Open them," Belinda said to her brother as she removed her hands from his eyes.

Isabella watched with some trepidation as the duke opened his eyes and took in his sister's attire. His expression, far from the warm, good-humored one that Isabella had seen only a few moments ago, was instead shuttered.

"Eleanor," he said sharply, "what are you wearing? Where did you get that gown?"

Perhaps thinking his concern was where she'd acquired the gown, Eleanor dropped into a curtsy. "Good evening, Trevor. Lady Wharton had her maid make over this gown for me so that I might have something to wear that isn't utterly provincial. Don't you like it?"

Isabella could have shaken the girl for her exaggeration. She had not said anything about giving Eleanor the gown to ward off provincialism. She might have known a seventeen-year-old would find it impossible to inform her brother of the situation without editorializing a bit. Even so, barring the provincialism remark, the gown itself was hardly objectionable.

"I am so thankful that we have Lady Wharton to save us from provincialism," Trevor said acidly to his sister, his eyes dark with anger as they bore into Isabella's. "I fear, however, that you will need to return the gown from whence it came. It is entirely inappropriate for a girl of your age. I suggest you go upstairs and change at once."

As soon as the words left his mouth Isabella knew he'd taken the wrong approach to the matter. Eleanor's jaw clenched and her eyes shot daggers at her brother. She was well and truly offended and was not going to back down from this fight without lashing out first. Isabella cringed at the thought. She certainly hadn't expected her gift to cause so much unhappiness. The opposite, in fact.

"You are so horrid," Eleanor said in a histrionic tone. "And I will not have you dictating to me what I may and may not wear. I am no longer a schoolgirl to be ordered about like that. Lady Wharton was only trying to be nice and you are being awful to her and to me!"

"I think Ellie looks beautiful," Belinda said, stepping up next to her sister, the two of them forming a solid wall of opposition. "Just like Lady Wharton!"

"Girls, I appreciate your defense of me," Isabella began, "but I really do not think—"

"I think you've thought quite enough for one evening," the duke said darkly. "Now, Eleanor, I asked you to go change you gown. So, go."

The girl looked as if she'd like to continue arguing, but when she looked to Isabella with a question in her eyes Isabella nodded for her to go upstairs. Looking angry and red-faced and utterly heartbroken, the girl left the room in a huff, followed close behind by Belinda, whose small back was ramrod straight as she hurried from the room.

"Well," Isabella said calmly, "that went well."

The duke looked at her with a glare. "It might have gone a bit better if you'd kept your nose out of my business." He crossed his arms over his chest, looking as unapproachable as he'd ever done.

"Oh, come, Your Grace," Isabella said with just as much starch as she could muster. "It's as plain as a pikestaff that Eleanor is in desperate need of female guidance. And when she asked to look through my wardrobe I thought it was harmless enough. The gown fits her perfectly well and I have seen young ladies of the *ton* dressed far more provocatively in town this year."

"But that's just it," he said bitingly. "We aren't in

town. We are in Yorkshire, where a gown like that one could spell disaster for my sister's social chances in the neighborhood."

But, if he was hoping to sway her with that argument, Isabella was quite prepared to disabuse him of the notion. "Perhaps it is not right for country entertainments," she conceded, "but if that is the case then she might just as well wear it in London when she makes her come-out."

"She isn't going to London to make her come-out," the duke said haughtily. "She doesn't need to. There are any number of young ladies and young gentlemen here in Yorkshire to provide her with entertainments."

"Your Grace," Isabella said patiently, "if you go to London to take up your responsibilities as duke, which you have assured me you will do so long as I follow you about the estate for the next week or so, then you will need to bring your sisters with you. And coming with you will mean, for Eleanor, making her debut. It is perfectly ridiculous for the sister of a duke to be buried in the country for the rest of her life simply because her brother is too stubborn to let her mix with the society to which she is entitled."

His jaw, which had already been clenched, got tighter as Isabella watched her words sink in. A pulse thundered at his temple.

"I have never expected that my sisters would be forced to mix with the family members who shunned them their whole lives," he said curtly.

He looked so alone standing there with his arms crossed and his face as still as a stone. Isabella could not help it. She stepped forward and touched him on the upper arm. It was just a light touch, but she felt the muscle beneath his coat and shirt leap to attention. She could feel the warmth of his body through his clothes, and she had to swallow before she could speak.

"Your sisters need not mix with your family in London," she said quietly. "For that matter, you need not spend a great deal of time with them. You could hire another house besides Ormonde House and keep your sisters there. Your grandmother will not bestir herself to visit them there if you do so. She is self-important enough to demand that they be brought to her, but you need not obey her. Truly, I think having you go up to London would be enough to satisfy her for a long while."

At Isabella's words the duke seemed to lose some of the tension in his body.

"I suppose that is true," he said grudgingly. "I had not considered letting another house in town. Whenever my father ever spoke of town it was of Ormonde House. I suppose I had begun to conflate London and Ormonde House into one and the same."

"They are not," Isabella assured him. "Believe me. I managed all season to avoid the dowager. Until she summoned me to order me here, that is. But you must know that you are the duke. You can order her about. Not the other way around."

At that he laughed. "I do know that," he said ruefully. "I am not such a milksop that I think an old woman powerful enough to make me dance to her bidding."

Isabella looked him up and down. "Your Grace," she said finally, "I do not think anyone would ever accuse you of lacking in courage."

A spark of fire kindled in his eyes and Isabella felt a thrum of desire pulse between them. No, she thought to herself, he was as masculine a man as she'd ever seen.

"Thank you for that," the duke said, the deep timbre of his voice sending a chill up her spine.

Isabella swallowed and blinked to bring herself back under control. She wasn't sure, but she might have swooned a bit. Clearing her throat, she said, "Now, Your Grace, what of Eleanor's gown? Surely it is not so objectionable as all that. I daresay some of the ladies in the neighborhood have seen more fashionable gowns than that. And much more scandalous ones, I assure you."

The duke thrust both his hands into his hair. "I suppose you are right," he said finally. "It is but a gown. I simply wasn't expecting to see . . . that is to say, my sister is becoming quite the—" He broke off with a shake of his head.

"I understand you perfectly," Isabella said, biting back a smile. "Your sister is growing up and you do not like to admit such a thing. It is perfectly understandable."

"It is?" he demanded, his brows knitted together. "A few minutes ago I was a churlish beast who behaved without any kind of logic."

She waved away his complaint. "Do not be foolish. That was your sister speaking in the heat of the moment. She will recover herself soon enough. She is finding this growing-up business just as difficult as you, I assure you."

"Do you think so?" he asked, surprise evident in his expression.

"Absolutely," Isabella said, leading him into the dining room. "Though you might find her a bit easier to deal with if you change how you treat her. She is nearly grown and you treat her as if she is as young as Belinda."

"She isn't so much older than Belinda," he said defensively.

"There is a vast ocean of difference between thirteen and seventeen," Isabella said. "And well you know it. You simply wish there were not. It won't be long before she has beaux. I wouldn't be surprised if she weren't already smitten with some country swain."

He gulped down his brandy at the thought. "You don't think . . ." He glanced warily at Isabella.

"No," she said, much to his relief. "I don't. But you should prepare yourself for the day. You cannot keep her in the schoolroom forever."

"I can try," he said, pacing over to the window.

"You know that's not a rational plan," Isabella said, employing the kind of rational tone women universally used to soothe men into doing their bidding.

"Come," she said, placing her hand on his arm. "Let's go in to dinner. I'll have Cook send your sisters something in their rooms."

With a sigh he turned and allowed her to lead him to the dining room.

"How did you come to be so knowledgeable about the whims of young ladies?" Trevor asked, after they had finished their meal and had retired to the drawing room, where Isabella could have tea and he could enjoy a brandy.

The meal itself had been more pleasant than he could have imagined. He'd expected Isabella to be incapable of conversing about anything but the latest on-dit, but she had proved knowledgeable on a variety of topics, including, to his great surprise, the glamorous world of crop rotation. She'd explained it away, saying that her father had been fond of agricultural talk despite making his home in London. She had, she said, absorbed the information over the course of many years listening to him drone on about it.

Now they had wandered into talk that was more to her taste. Seated in the wing chair across from him, she sipped her tea politely, but it was her eyes that told the real story. They flared with emotion as she warmed to her subject. Trevor wondered how many men in London had been just as intrigued by her as he was.

"I once was a young lady," she said now, in response to his question. "And though I suspect many young men are bewildered by the workings of a young lady's mind, I believe ladies in general are much less difficult to understand than we are given credit for."

Her eyes sparkled as she continued, "We are not so thoroughly inscrutable, are we, Your Grace?"

He laughed at her flirtatious tone. He could well imagine her twisting the males of the *ton* around her little finger with that tiny bit of vocal inflection. "Perhaps not thoroughly," he admitted. "But even you must agree that a great deal of the misunderstandings between our two sexes come about because of a purposeful attempt on the part of females to pull the wool over our male eyes."

"Ah," she said with a sad smile, "but that is because men have all the power. What are we ladies to do but use the wiles that God gave us to ensure that we are able to meet our own needs?"

"Surely that is for the men in your life to provide," Trevor said, wondering when Isabella had first learned that the men in her life were not to be trusted. He found himself re-evaluating his opinion of her. Perhaps he'd judged her a bit too harshly to begin with. The thought bothered him for some reason. He had always thought himself to be a fair man, but maybe he was as guilty of leaping to conclusions as he'd accused her of doing with him.

"Not all men are as honorable as you are, Your Grace," Isabella said taking a sip of tea. "It sounds to me as if your father took his responsibilities to your mother, and you and your sisters, quite seriously. But you must know that not all men are cut from the same cloth. Look at your grandfather, for example. He cut off his son and his wife and children without a by-your-leave. Unfortunately, that is the rule rather than the exception. At least from my own experience."

"What of your father?" Trevor asked before he could stop himself. It was really none of his business, but sitting here in the drawing room of his country house, talking with a beautiful woman while the candles around them burned down, he felt a kind of intimacy with her that made such a question seem less impertinent than it would in the light of day.

And if he were honest with himself, he was just plain curious.

"My father," Isabella began, relaxing into the sofa as she pondered the question. "My father was an earl whose estates were so impoverished that he talked of nothing from the time I turned fourteen but how my sister and I should marry wealthy peers. And when we made our come-outs, we did."

Trevor tried to imagine what it would be like to bear the weight of an entire estate's financial stability on his shoulders. In a way, he knew just what it felt like. But

she was right enough when she spoke of the differences
between men and women. It had been his own choice to
take of the responsibility of Nettlefield. Isabella hadn't
been given a choice. How resentful she must have been.

"So that is how you came to marry Wharton?" he
asked.

"That is how I came to marry Wharton," she said, her
voice matter-of-fact. "He was fifteen years my senior and
married me at his own father's behest. So neither of us
came to the marriage through our own choice. Foolish
me, I thought that would mean he'd understand my
reluctance to . . ."

She paused, coloring a bit. "Well, let us just say my
general reluctance. He was not as understanding as I
would have wished, however. He felt his own frustration at
the situation but was not quite able to understand my own.

"Perdita and I thought that she was to be the luckier
one," Isabella went on, clutching her teacup between her
hands. "After all, she was to marry the young, handsome,
virile Duke of Ormonde." She laughed bitterly. "We were
wrong about that, too."

Even buried away in the country, Trevor had heard
tales of the young duke's wildness. There had been men-
tions of his cousin in the gossip pages of the *Times* and
he'd told himself that he'd done the right thing by staying away from his family. Especially since mixing with
the late duke would have meant exposing Trevor's sisters
to his wildness.

He hadn't thought to extend his sympathies to the fellow's young wife, however. It simply hadn't occurred to
him. He'd assumed that anyone who was foolish enough
to marry a man with that sort of reputation deserved
whatever she got. Now, imagining Eleanor or Belinda in

such a situation, he knew better. Perhaps he'd been wrong to shirk his familial duty. The thought pained him.

Still, he could see that Isabella was reluctant to speak more about his cousin, so he changed the subject.

"How long were you married before . . . ?" He couldn't quite figure out how to phrase the question. And he wanted desperately to know that she had not been trapped in an unhappy marriage for very long.

"Before my husband was so kind as to shuffle off this mortal coil?" Isabella asked with a laugh. "He died in a duel defending the honor of his mistress just shy of my twenty-fifth birthday. We'd been married for seven years."

Seven years, Trevor thought. Long enough for the brute to leave a mark upon her. Long enough for him to beat the spirit out of her. And yet, here she sat. Head held high. Proud. Resilient.

No, he'd been wrong about her, he thought. At least in this aspect. She might be just as obsessed with town frivolities and the like, but she was not the shallow puppet he'd thought upon their first meeting. He might not seek her out as a potential bride for himself, but he was no longer so loath to trust her judgment when it came to his sisters. Perhaps not fully—he might never trust someone else entirely with their care—but certainly when it came to matters of attire and social niceties.

He was lost in thought and, if the truth be told, watching her with a bit too much intensity when she stood. Trevor scrambled to his feet, the movement bringing their faces dangerously close to each other.

"I hope you will remember my little morality tale the next time you wonder why women are so keen to manipulate the world around them, Your Grace," she said, her only outward sign of awareness of his proximity the slight blush in her cheeks. "When so little of your life is under your own control you'll take hold of whatever bit of strength you have."

"Then what is it that you control?" he asked suddenly, remembering her reason for coming to Nettlefield in the first place. Surely someone who had so lately thrown off the shackles of marriage would be reluctant to be ruled by another woman. "If the dowager has some hold over you, then what do you have hold of?"

Isabella laughed. "Haven't you figured it out by now, Your Grace?"

"Stop," he said, suddenly hating to hear the deference for his hated title after they'd spoken so frankly. "Call me Trevor."

He was surprised to see her eyes widen at the request. But she nodded. "Trevor, then."

She said his name again, as if the permission to do so made her wish to do so as much as she could. "Trevor, there is only one thing I have absolute power over." She leaned forward and he could smell the light lavender of her hair and feel the heat of her body so close to his as she whispered into his ear. "Myself."

Without another word she left the chamber, leaving him aching and wanting nothing more than to follow her up the stairs.

Five

*I*sabella went downstairs the next morning still feeling like a fool for revealing so much of her personal history to the duke. Or Trevor, as he'd insisted she call him.

It hadn't been her intention to tell him the tale of how she and Perdita had come to be married to such brutes, but seeing how befuddled he'd been by Eleanor's response to his dictates regarding her wardrobe, Isabella had felt it necessary to warn him just how vulnerable his sisters would be if he weren't there to look after them. She supposed it was only natural for someone who'd been raised in the country as he had been to assume that most husbands and fathers were as honorable as his own father had been, but someone had to point out to him that the world was not as cheery as his country upbringing had led him to believe.

Of course he wasn't quite so naïve as she painted him. She knew that. He'd been to university, and as a landowner he'd doubtless seen things among his tenants that would make her hair curl. But even so, his lack of understanding when it came to women and their precarious position in the world had prompted her to inform

him that far from being the sheltered flowers he assumed them to be, most women were forced to do what
they could to protect themselves from the careless control that the men in their lives exercised over them. It
was one thing to remain ignorant because no one had
ever told him otherwise, but it was something else altogether to refuse to see the truths right before his eyes.

She hoped that her little talk had impressed upon him
the importance of choosing his sisters' husbands with
great care, rather than frightened him away from allowing the girls to go to London altogether. Only after she'd
climbed into bed had she realized that the latter was a
real possibility. After all, if they remained in the country he could allow his sisters to choose their husbands
from among the young men of the local gentry whom
Trevor had likely known all their lives. London offered
a whole *ton* full of fortune hunters, social climbers, and
otherwise nefarious men who wished nothing more than
to marry the sister of a duke not because of her sweet
personality or even her beauty, but solely because of
what such a match could do for his own standing.

Putting it that way, Isabella wasn't so keen on Eleanor and Belinda going up to London herself.

But at least with her guidance, in addition to Trevor's
watchful eye, the girls would be protected from the worst
of the lot. And Isabella was surprised to find herself
looking forward to showing the Carey sisters just how to
navigate the treacherous waters of the beau monde. Not
that she would have much to do with them once she returned to London, she reminded herself. She was here
to persuade the duke and that was all. She had her own
life to get back to in London.

This resolution in her mind, she stepped into the breakfast room to find it unoccupied. Telling herself that she was relieved rather than disappointed, she saw that next to her place at the table were two letters. One was from Perdita, clearly sent by special messenger.

It was the other that gave her pause.

It could not be from the dowager. That lady's correspondence was all but trimmed in gold to mark her elevated position. This was a simple missive. The paper was rather fine, but the lack of markings on it—with the exception of Isabella's name—indicated that it had also not come through the Royal Mail.

With what she considered a laudable sense of control, she opened Perdita's letter first, only to discover that it was another plea for Isabella to reconsider her decision to bow to the dowager's wishes. As always, her sister was willing to sacrifice herself on the altar of sibling affection. But Isabella had had enough of watching her sister pay the price for Gervase's sins. And if Isabella could manage to convince the duke to return to London, then she could see to it that neither she nor Perdita was ever under the thumb of the dowager again. And she could do so with a clear conscience, because she had seen enough of Trevor Carey's character to know that he would die before he let his grandmother dictate to him as she had done to his predecessor.

Folding the note, Isabella moved on to the other letter. Using her knife to break the seal—which was just as nondescript as the rest of it—she unfolded it. She scanned the words and realized several things at once. Whoever had written the message had intended it to cause her great mental harm. To instill fear.

The carriage accident was just the beginning. I know what you did last season and I will punish all of you.

At first she thought the words had been written in brown ink, but she uttered a little gasp when she realized that it was instead blood.

It was positively gothic.

And utterly terrifying.

She knew from what Trevor had told her that the carriage crash was no accident, but to see it put into writing, perhaps by the very person who had tampered with the wheel, was chilling.

Someone with the intention of doing Isabella bodily harm had purposely weakened the vehicle, putting not only her but also everyone else in the carriage at risk, other innocents who had nothing to do with Gervase's death. Someone who was willing to put anyone unlucky enough to be in Isabella's company at risk right along with her.

To her shame, tears sprang into her eyes. Whenever she was truly angry it happened. And this . . . this person infuriated her. What right had he to play god? Gervase had died through his own brutality. Neither she nor Perdita nor Georgina was responsible for his temper that night. They had not lured him into putting the knife to Perdita's throat. Georgina would not have been forced to use her pistol if he hadn't threatened Perdita's life.

But whoever this monster was, he thought that they were responsible. And he was willing to risk the lives of good, loyal, hardworking servants in his vendetta against Isabella.

She had to warn Perdita.

Shaking, she pushed her chair back from the table and snatched up the letters. Wiping her eyes, she hurried to the doorway, only to slam into the solid chest of Trevor.

"Your Grace," she said, hoping she had dashed away most of her tears. "I, that is . . . Trevor. My apologies, I was in a hurry and did not—"

"Not at all, Lady Wharton," he said, gripping her arms for longer than was strictly proper. "I hope you are not unwell. I had hoped to visit the tenant cottages after luncheon."

Desperate to be away from him, she considered taking the excuse he offered but shook her head. "That would be agreeable," she said, trying to make her voice sound as cheerful as possible. To her own ear it sounded false, but he didn't seem to notice. "I was simply rushing off to write a reply to my sister," she said, holding up the letters. "Is there a writing desk that I might use?"

She could feel his gaze on her, seeing more than she wanted him to. But he let her go and said mildly, "Of course. You may use my mother's sitting room. There are paper and ink in her desk. I believe Eleanor uses them for her own correspondence at times."

Nodding, Isabella pushed past him and hurried off in the direction of the sitting room, feeling his gaze upon her as she went.

Pensive, Trevor served himself from the sideboard and took his place at the breakfast table.

Isabella had been lying. Of that he was positive. Something in those letters had overset her; he wanted to know what.

Her confession last night of just how she'd ended up

married to Wharton had confirmed to Trevor that she was in need of someone to look after her. When he thought of how her father had chosen to marry her off to a man so many years her senior solely for the benefit of his own coffers, Trevor felt his hands clenching into involuntary fists—as if he could pummel a dead man. He might not have spent his formative years moving among the *ton,* but he knew that such men existed. He'd seen enough evidence of such selfishness here among the gentry of Yorkshire. Even so, he had been appalled to hear just how mercenary Isabella's father had been. No wonder she was so concerned over his sisters.

He had no intention of allowing either of them to marry without him thoroughly investigating the man in question, but Isabella had no way of knowing that. She was used to the way that the men she'd been around her whole life treated the women under their protection.

She had proved herself in the past few days to be a strong woman. Some might call her cold, but he had not been around her for more than a few hours before he realized that her coolness was a façade. A posture she adopted so that those around her would take her seriously. It was not unlike what his mother had done when she mixed with those members of the surrounding neighborhood who thought his father had married beneath him. She'd once confided to Trevor that when she took tea with the squire's wife she would often pretend that she was a queen, dining with her subjects. Not to say that she thought of herself that way as a general rule. But something about fixing that posture in her mind would give her strength. And would make others see her as something stronger than a farmer's daughter.

It was this sort of posturing that Trevor saw in Lady

Wharton. For whatever reason, she had decided that in order to get what she wanted she would need to appear strong. This morning that façade had slipped and when he saw her hurrying toward him he'd seen tears in her eyes. It might, he told himself, have something to do with the dowager's attempt to lure him to London. But he thought it must be more personal than that.

Swallowing his tea, he considered the wisdom of asking her outright, then dismissed the notion. She would not take kindly to his prying into her affairs. No more than he would if their situations were reversed. But he disliked the idea of Isabella being upset. He told himself it was because she was a guest in his home, but he knew deep down there was more to it than that. He did not dare to ask what that more might be.

For now, he would wait to see if she would confide in him.

Perhaps when he told her of his plans to take his sisters shopping in York she would tell him.

Then again, perhaps she would not.

One thing he'd learned about Lady Wharton was that she would do things when she was ready and not one moment before.

Rising from the table, he set off to find Eleanor and tell her of their proposed trip.

"My tree looks like a blob of green," Belinda said glumly, daubing paint onto the paper with her brush.

Once she'd finished her letter to Perdita, Isabella had gone in search of the Carey sisters and proposed that they spend the morning painting in the garden. The threatening letter had left her with a pang of fear in her stomach, but there was little she could do about it now. Rather than stew about it, she would lose herself in a few hours of activity.

She had found the painting supplies in the girls' mother's sitting room and, since it was too soon for Perdita to have sent any prospective governesses their way, she had decided that she would take up the duties of the position for now and divert both herself and the young ladies for the rest of the morning.

"No, it doesn't look like a blob," she said automatically to Belinda, though her tree did rather resemble a green blob. "Here," Isabella instructed. "Do not put so much paint on your brush. It might take a bit for you to get used to the brushstrokes, but you'll get there."

"Like this," Eleanor demonstrated for her sister. "It's not difficult once you get the knack of it."

"That's easy for you to say," Belinda retorted. "You've done this hundreds of times."

"I can't help it if you chose to stay home every time I went to the Greens' to paint with Mary and Susan," Eleanor said with a shrug.

"You know I cannot abide Mary Green, Ellie." Belinda leaned sideways to look at how her sister was holding her brush. "She puts on such airs."

Before Eleanor could respond, they heard a call from the doors leading out into the garden. To Isabella's amusement, it was the Green sisters.

"Lovely," Belinda said with a roll of her eyes. "Just when I was beginning to enjoy painting."

"Hush, Bel," Eleanor said with a hiss. "They'll hear you."

But it was obvious to Isabella, at least, that Belinda could not possibly have cared less. She wondered if

Perdita had ever felt so much annoyance over Isabella's friends. Then chided herself. Of course she had. It was the lot of younger sisters everywhere.

Eleanor gave her sister a stern look before the Greens reached them.

"Darlings," Mary Green said with a languid drawl that Isabella had to admit *was* rather affected. Mary was a pretty enough girl, but her bored expression, no doubt cultivated to give herself what she thought to be an air of sophistication, just made her look sleepy. "How lovely to see you out here enjoying the beauties of nature."

She kissed the air on either side of Eleanor's cheeks, and when she tried to do the same to Belinda the younger girl gave her a glower that would have done the dowager proud. Isabella would gauge Mary's age to be somewhere around Eleanor's. Mary's sister appeared to be slightly older.

"Lady Wharton," Mary said when Eleanor had presented the newcomers to Isabella, offering her a perfectly correct curtsy, "I have heard so much about you. What a delight it is to finally make your acquaintance."

Isabella returned the greeting with absent cordiality as she helped Belinda with the grip of her paintbrush. She may not have remembered Perdita's dislike of her own friends, but she remembered quite clearly what it had been like to have a younger sister hanging on her every words with them, so she tried to occupy Belinda in an effort to free Eleanor to speak to her friends in some degree of privacy.

Mary Green had no such desire for a comfortable coze, however. Instead, she addressed all of them. "I am so pleased to find you all here," she said, her eyes alight with pleasure, "for just this morning I have heard from

Mrs. Palmer that she, too, has a guest from London. And
she is planning a ball in his honor!"

"A ball!" Susan Green echoed, clapping her hands
together, for the first time since their arrival showing
any sort of animation. "Can you possibly imagine?"

"And I feel sure you know the man, Lady Wharton,"
Mary continued, as if she were an old and dear friend of
Isabella's rather than an acquaintance of approximately
three minutes. "His name is Sir Lionel Thistleback and
he says he was a close personal friend of your dear departed husband."

Isabella had been prepared to hear that this august
personage from London was someone with whom she
had a passing acquaintance, but to learn that he was her
husband's most intimate crony was the outside of enough.
Not only did she loathe Sir Lionel, but he in turn loathed
her also. For him to spread tales of their previous acquaintance among the people of the village of Nettledean
was despicable, mostly because it stemmed from not a
pleasant nostalgia but a wish to ingratiate himself with
the neighborhood at her expense. The idea that anyone
would think she approved of a man like Thistleback was
repugnant. And she was prevented by good manners
from saying anything of the sort. He'd tied her hands,
the toad.

To the girls, however, she said none of what she was
thinking. "I do know him a little," she said, inclining
her head but revealing nothing more of the true relationship between them.

"Do you think my brother might be persuaded to allow me to attend the ball?" Eleanor asked, her eyes
alight with excitement. She gripped Isabella's arm and

turned a pleading gaze on her. "He won't listen to me, Lady Wharton," she said quickly, "but he might be persuaded by you. He listens to you."

Aware of Mary and Susan Green's avid gazes on her, Isabella smiled at Eleanor. It was her fondest wish that Eleanor never make Thistleback's acquaintance. But she supposed that a country ball where Eleanor's brother was in attendance might be the safest location for such a meeting. Besides, Isabella had little doubt that Thistleback was in the process of seducing some local widow and would pay little enough attention to a girl of Eleanor's age. "I do not know where you got the notion that your brother hears anything I have to say, Eleanor," she said. "But I will try to persuade him. It is a country ball, after all. And I think the social niceties are not quite so rigid as they are in town."

"I have heard that you have a great deal of influence over the duke, Lady Wharton." Mary's knowing little smile was coy. "He has spoken of nothing but you since your arrival at Nettlefield."

"I hardly think that the duke spends his days jaunting about the countryside regaling anyone who will listen with tales of my wonder." Isabella was torn between amusement at the girl's exaggeration and a pang of longing. After all, if the duke were really so inclined to do whatever she wished he'd pack his bags today and head off to London to kneel at the feet of his grandmother. She knew, however, that this was not the case.

It was one of the rare occasions when she found herself wishing gossip were true.

But it was Belinda who punctured Mary's tale. "You are just trying to make yourself sound important, Mary

Green! If my brother is so influenced by Lady Wharton, then why was he shouting at her last evening?"

Before Isabella could comment, Eleanor cut in, looking daggers at her sister, "Don't be absurd, Bel. Trevor was simply arguing his point."

"I fear the duke was a bit overset when he learned that I'd loaned one of my gowns to Eleanor," Isabella said with a laugh, trying to dispel any suspicions the Green sisters might have about her interactions with him, argumentative or otherwise. "It was a tempest in a teapot. And Belinda, you should apologize to Mary for insulting her. That was not well done of you."

Mary brushed off the apology, however. "I have known Belinda since she was in leading strings," she said cheerfully, as if she were decades older than the girl. "Tell me about the gown, Eleanor. Was it from Madame Celeste's?"

How the girl knew which modiste she used Isabella would never know. Clearly the gossip network in Nettlefield was more robust than she'd given it credit for.

"May I see it?" Mary continued, her sophisticated pose dropping for a moment in her excitement.

"Me, too," Susan added, grasping Eleanor's arm. "Is it as beautiful as Lady Wharton's other gowns?"

"More," Eleanor confirmed. Turning to Isabella, she asked, "Is it alright if I go show Mary and Susan my gown?"

Isabella was touched that the girl thought to ask her permission at all. She was not in any position of authority over her. But she nodded to her. "Don't forget to show them the slippers as well. The gown doesn't work without them."

With an eager nod, Eleanor hurried with her friends

to the house, Belinda and Isabella watching them as they went.

"I'm sorry for telling them about Trevor and the yelling," Belinda said, turning back to her painting. "I was so annoyed with Mary for pretending that she knows what Trevor thinks about things. She just likes to talk about him because he's a duke."

Isabella looked at the younger girl and was pleased to see she'd done a better job with the tree on the opposite side from the green blob. "I'm afraid most people are that way," she said, speaking of Mary. "Once it becomes known that your brother has agreed to take up his role as the duke, you'll find all of you will become the subject of gossip."

"I won't need to bother with that," Belinda said firmly, "because I don't intend to ever leave Yorkshire. I will stay here and help Mr. Woods in the stables and ignore the silly ladies of the village." Mr. Woods was Trevor's very patient head groom, who let Belinda run tame in the stables.

"Even if your brother decides to go to London?" Isabella asked, loath to tell the girl that she would likely not be allowed to remain in Yorkshire. "I think he might wish for you to go with him. There are many things in London that I think you would enjoy."

Belinda scoffed. "What could the city possibly offer that the country does not?"

So Isabella spent the next hour painting companionably with a thirteen-year-old, regaling her with stories of Astley's Ampitheatre and Rotten Row and ices at Gunter's. By the time they'd packed up their brushes and paints and directed a footman to retrieve their canvases

and easels, Belinda was less suspicious of the city, but
she was still not reconciled to life as a duke's sister.

Unfortunately, Isabella thought, when the dowager
got hold of the Carey sisters Belinda would have little
choice in the matter.

Six

Trevor broached the subject of a trip to York at the luncheon table and was met with distracted enthusiasm. "What's this?" he demanded of Eleanor, somewhat deflated. "I thought you would be pleased at the notion,"

"I believe your sisters are quite pleased." Isabella gave both Eleanor and Belinda speaking looks. "But I'm afraid Miss Mary Green brought news that Mrs. Palmer is planning a ball, and that has quite eclipsed the glamour of a prospected trip to York. Though I believe Eleanor would be quite pleased to visit the dressmaker there."

"A ball?" Trevor asked, puzzled. "Eleanor is too young to attend a ball."

Now Isabella turned a speaking look on him. And he was not pleased to note it said, *Quiet, you imbecile!* He cleared his throat. "That is to say, I had not supposed Eleanor was interested in attending balls."

Isabella's expression said he was doing better but would still not be winning any Brother of the Year awards.

"I believe seventeen is an acceptable age for a young lady to attend a country ball," Isabella said. "I was sixteen when I attended a harvest ball with my school friend Elizabeth Stride, now the Countess of Cleverdon. It was excellent practice for my come-out the next year."

"Please, Trevor," Eleanor said, her eyes at their most plaintive. "I do not know what I'll do if you say no. Mary Green will make me feel like the veriest child if you say I mayn't go. Please?"

Only Belinda was content to eat her luncheon without weighing in on the conversation. Though Trevor thought he noticed a judgmental tone in the way she consumed her peas. Was ever a man more outnumbered than he?

"I suppose if Lady Wharton, who knows far more than I do about young ladies, says that it would be all right—," Trevor began, only to be cut off by cheers from Eleanor.

"Thank you, Trevor," she said, throwing her arms around him. "You are the best brother in the world. And I would simply *adore* a trip to York! There are so many things I must get now to go with my gown. I simply *must* have a new pair of gloves and new slippers as well. When may we go?"

They settled on a day later in the week for the trip to York and then both Eleanor and Belinda—who had by this time finished her judgmental peas—left to make a list of the things Eleanor simply *must* have.

Which left Trevor alone at the table with Isabella.

She seemed to have moved past whatever bad news had brought her to tears at breakfast. Of course prospective balls and the like had a way of distracting one.

"That was well done of you," she said, her blue eyes shining with wry amusement. "I'm sorry your proposed trip to York was overshadowed by the Palmer ball. On any other day, your suggestion would have been the belle of the ball. So to speak."

"Palmer told me that his wife had a guest from London and was planning an entertainment. I should have anticipated a ball." Trevor did not mention that Palmer had also mentioned the fact that Sir Lionel Thistleback had been a great friend of Lord Wharton. He wondered what her own reaction to the news had been. She showed no sign of disturbance, but then she was quite adept at hiding her feelings when she wished to.

He would like to know what had been in the letters she'd received that morning. Could one of them have mentioned Thistleback's arrival? They were hardly on such comfortable terms that he could freely ask her. And the truth of it was that it was none of his affair.

"I believe it is customary for hostesses to celebrate their guests with large entertainments," she said, making no mention of her connection to Thistleback. "And I do think your sister will benefit from the experience. It will certainly make her more comfortable when she makes her debut. If, that is, you intend to allow her to make her bows before society."

"I am still considering it," Trevor said, laying his fork down on his plate to signal he'd finished. "Though I will admit that before your arrival I was much more set against the idea than I am now. I wonder if you knew when you made this trip that you'd become an advocate for my sisters. Could it be that you are growing fond of them?"

If it were possible, she sat up straighter. "I am not a block of wood, Your Grace," she said tersely. "I am quite capable of fondness. And I believe your sisters could do with a bit of guidance from a woman. I lost my mother at a young age, too, so I suppose I understand Eleanor's position."

"I did not suggest that you are without feeling, Isabella," he said, using her Christian name but not caring if she was annoyed by it. "But simply that I believe your intended purpose for making this journey has been complicated by the presence of my sisters. I have no doubt that the dowager would tell you to use my sisters against me. I hope that your affection for them will prevent that from happening."

"Like it or not, Your Grace," Isabella said her expression carefully blank, "your sisters need their family. You have plenty of female relatives in London who would be more than happy to step in and assist you as I have done. I will not be here forever. And for their sakes I hope that you will bring them to London as soon as you are able. If that opinion means that I am using your sisters against you—as you put it—then so be it. I believe that you have done an admirable job of raising them on your own. I simply think that at their age, they need their female relatives."

"Like the dowager?" Trevor demanded, unwilling to let Isabella dismiss the matter that easily. "It's clear she forced you to come here against your will. Would you wish my sisters into the same position?"

That surprised her. He could see it in the wideness of her eyes.

"My reasons for coming here are my own," Isabella said curtly. "I came at the behest of my godmother, who I will admit is a difficult woman to get along with. But your sisters would be around other female relatives in London as well."

"Do you include yourself in their number, madam?" He knew he was being an ass but was unable to keep from arguing with her. He hadn't much considered that his own reluctance to go up to London would have deleterious effects on his sisters, and Isabella's words stung.

Her eyes flashed, and he was oddly pleased to see that she was riled into annoyance. "As I am only related to you by marriage, Your Grace," she said, her dark brows furrowed in temper, "I do not include myself among their number. Perdita, my sister and your late cousin's widow, would be more than happy to sponsor Eleanor and Belinda. I merely offer this advice as a friend, but I can see that you do not count me as such."

"I do not generally count ladies who have ulterior motives attached to their friendship as close friends," Trevor said, trying to put some distance between them. If he let himself he would find himself relying on Isabella far more than was safe. The more he remembered her real reasons for being in Yorkshire, the easier it would be for him to resist her charms. And he could no longer deny the fact that he did indeed find her charming.

"If you are still amenable to our agreement, Lady Wharton," he said, rising from the table. "we will depart for our visit to the tenant farms in half an hour. I suggest you change into riding clothes."

He left the room, trying and failing to forget the flash of hurt he'd seen in her eyes before she masked the look with an angry glare.

Despite her pique at the duke's harsh words, Isabella hurried upstairs to change into her bright blue riding habit for her tour of the tenant farms. She changed as quickly as she could, and finally setting her hat atop her dark curls at a rakish angle, she went downstairs to find her host waiting for her at the foot of the stairs, his riding crop beating a sharp tattoo against his boot.

To her surprise, she saw a flash of admiration in his eyes before he quickly masked it, saying, "I've chosen a sweet-tempered mare for you to ride while you're here," as he and Isabella made their way down the front steps and toward the stables. "After assessing your seat today, if I think you can handle it, and should you wish for something more spirited, I will consider it."

Isabella would have liked to argue, but she could not. "That is perfectly agreeable to me, Your Grace," she said, following him to the paddock where a pretty little gray waited patiently, already bridled and fitted out with a sidesaddle.

The horse nickered as Isabella moved to her side and gave her a good scratch on the nose and crooned softly in her ear. "What a lovely girl you are," Isabella said, rubbing the mare's neck, which was the color of the summer sky at dusk. "What's her name?"

"This is Dolly," Trevor said, watching in bemusement as Isabella made friends with her mount. "She's got spirit for all that she's easy to handle. I think you'll be pleased with her."

"Of course I shall," Isabella said, more to the horse than to Trevor. "Will you help me mount, Your Grace?"

Turning, she found to her amusement that she'd caught the duke admiring her backside. He had the good grace to flush, but that was his only acknowledgment of his wrongdoing. Instead he silently crouched and made a stirrup of his hands, boosting her up into the saddle.

His own mount, a sleek bay who was eager to be on

his way, stood restlessly as a waiting groom held tightly to his reins. Having seen Isabella safely atop Dolly, Trevor swung up into his own saddle, and they made their way toward the bridle path leading to the farms.

"You are a strong rider, I see," he said after some minutes of quiet between them. "I would have thought a lady used to London life would be less self-assured on horseback."

"We do have several parks, Your Grace," Isabella said sardonically. Really, did the man think they walked everywhere in town? "It is even possible to gallop if one arises early enough to evade the tabbies. My father had me in the saddle almost as soon as I could walk. Perdita and I both, actually."

"That is good to hear," the duke said. "My sisters have also ridden from a young age. I suppose it was foolish for me to suppose town life was so very different from the country. It is simply that my parents made such a great show of proving we missed out on nothing by remaining in the country that I never thought to doubt them."

Isabella steered Dolly around a fallen log and frowned. "Did you never go to London when you were at Oxford?" she asked, more than a little perplexed at the notion. "I know any number of young gentlemen get up to mischief in town when they are supposed to be immersed in their studies."

"Once or twice," Trevor allowed. "I stayed with friends a few times, but never long enough to really get a good feel for what town life was all about. Mostly I found it loud and crowded. I much prefer this." He waved at the open countryside around them, which Isabella was forced to admit did give one a feeling of vastness that London did not. "I like being able to look out my window and see mile after mile of rolling hills."

"There is something wild and wonderful about the land here," she admitted to him. "But what of entertainment? What of society? Do you never long for conversation with your peers?"

"You speak as if there is no one to be found here for miles and miles," Trevor said with a laugh. "I have any number of friends from among the local gentry. Indeed, I believe you met some of the local ladies already."

Isabella gave him a look that indicated that she rested her case.

"Oh, come," he said with a laugh. "They are not so bad. Though I do admit that some of them are rather . . ."

"Provincial?" Isabella asked sweetly.

"You are merely annoyed because they came to determine your intentions." Trevor slowed his mount as they came closer to a group of cottages ranged prettily along a country lane.

"My intentions," she said softly, tugging on the reins to bring Dolly to a halt, "are the least of their concerns. They came to warn me off, because they consider you to be their personal property."

"What can I say?" Trevor said with a grin as he dismounted before a tidy little cottage. "They are concerned for my welfare."

Before Isabella could respond, a plump woman appeared in the doorway of the cottage. "Good afternoon, Your Grace." Then seeing Isabella, she added, "Yer Ladyship."

"Good afternoon," Isabella returned. She felt nervous, though she wasn't quite sure why. There was something about the woman's assessing gaze that made Isabella feel as if she was being sized up and found wanting.

"Jimmy," the matron said to a lad of around seven who peeked out from behind her, "go and hold His Grace's horses."

Silently the boy slipped out from behind her and took the reins from Trevor.

"Good afternoon, Mrs. Jones," the duke said to the woman before turning to lift Isabella down. Isabella fought a shiver as she felt his strong hands grasp her around the waist and slide her inch by slow inch down the front of his body. By the time her feet touched the ground she was breathless. The duke, curse him, did not seem to be affected in the least.

"Mrs. Mary Jones," he said to the woman as he handed off Dolly's reins to Jimmy and another boy who had slunk wordlessly from inside the house, "may I present Lady Isabella Wharton? She is visiting my sisters and me for the next couple of weeks. I promised her that I would show her around the estate while she is here. She is quite interested in how we do things here in the country."

If the woman found his explanation for Isabella's presence at his side odd, she did not say so. "Welcome, Your Ladyship. I hope you will come in for a cuppa tea. My girls and I were just about to have some ourselves. And you as well, Your Grace, of course."

"Thank you, Mrs. Jones," Isabella said, following her into the thatched-roofed cottage, which was smaller than her bedchamber in London. Trevor followed close behind, so close she could feel him brush against her as he ducked beneath the low sill of the doorway.

At a worn but clean kitchen table, three girls in varying degrees of age stood and offered curtsies to the newcomers. When Isabella neared the table she saw that they had been working on their letters.

"My Mary has been teaching Lizzie and Rose here their letters," Mrs. Jones said with an air of pride. "I made sure the chickens and the pigs was fed first, mind you, but my Joe and me know it's important for them to be able to read and cipher, too."

"And you do remember, don't you, Mrs. Jones," Trevor said, seeing to it that Isabella was seated before he took his own seat, "that the girls are welcome to attend the village school as soon as they are able?"

The woman placed three chipped but clean mugs on the table along with a small pitcher of milk and an even smaller bowl of sugar. Isabella knew without being told that she and Trevor were being presented with what was likely a very dear supply of tea and sugar. But she also knew that to refuse Mrs. Jones's hospitality would be a grave insult. So Isabella assured the woman that she did not care for much sugar and sipped at her tea.

"I do thank you, Your Grace," Mrs. Jones said to the duke. "But we simply cannot spare them just now. It was hard enough to let Mary go last year. For now, we'll make do with her teaching the littler girls when she's got a moment."

"Is the school something that has been here long?" Isabella asked, intrigued that the duke would offer his tenants' children a means by which they might remove themselves from the countryside he seemed to hold so dear. "I had heard of schools being operated by churches and the like in London, but it had never occurred to me that a country village might also benefit from such an endeavor."

"I hardly think it in my best interest to keep my tenants and their children in complete ignorance," Trevor said dryly. "Indeed, I have found that such instruction makes for not only more engaged tenants but also more ambitious ones. It does me no harm for them to learn to read and write and manage their own funds when necessary."

"I know my girls are ever so grateful for it, Your Grace," Mrs. Jones said with sincerity as she poured her own mug of tea. "Should something happen where they cannot stay on here on the estate, knowing their letters and numbers could see to it that they could get a position in a shop in York or Manchester."

Isabella sipped her tea thoughtfully. She wasn't sure what she'd expected of the duke's interactions with his tenants, but somehow she had not expected this sort of concern for their welfare on or off his land. "I think it's an admirable notion," she said, smiling at her hostess.

Any further conversation was forestalled by a hectic cry from the other side of a curtained alcove. Mrs. Jones stood. "It's the little one awake from his nap. If you'll pardon me, my lady, I'll just go get him settled."

"Do bring him out for a visit," Trevor said with more relish than Isabella would have expected. "We men must stick up for one another, after all."

To her amazement, when the housewife emerged carrying a pink-cheeked toddler with golden curls the duke reached out to take the lad in his arms. And far from being annoyed by the change in his caretakers, the baby issued a gurgle of approval and went readily to the duke.

"There's a good lad, little Joe," Trevor said with approval to the boy. "Now, you must tell me what these women have been getting up to while your papa is off tending the sheep."

If she hadn't seen it with her own two eyes, Isabella would never have believed it if someone had informed her that the Duke of Ormonde would spend the better part of fifteen minutes conversing with an infant. But he certainly did.

Noticing that Isabella could not take her eyes off the duke, Mrs. Jones said in an undertone to her, "He's always been a sweet lad, the duke. Even when he were a young 'un himself. Did whatever it would take to please his papa, learned whatever he could to follow in his footsteps. And then when it came his time to take over duties as the lord of the manor he not only did as his father trained him to do, but did him one better. A kinder, more dedicated master we could not have asked for."

Isabella, unable to remove the image of Trevor as a young boy hanging on his father's every word from her mind's eye, simply nodded.

"He'll make some lady a fine husband one of these days, make no mistake," Mrs. Jones said with a twinkle in her eye.

Stopping in mid-nod, Isabella blanched. "Oh no, Mrs. Jones. There's nothing like that between us. I'm simply here to observe the estate. That is all, I assure you. Indeed, I cannot think of a worse pair in all of . . ."

Realizing that her hostess was still grinning, Isabella paused. "Really, I assure you," she said again.

"If you don't mind my saying so, Lady Wharton," the woman said, "I think you could do a sight worse."

Isabella felt color rise in her cheeks. Trevor, meanwhile, was oblivious to the conversation going on beside him and instead had lowered himself and baby Joe to the floor, where they were playing with a stack of blocks. It was difficult to imagine any other gentleman of her acquaintance risking his breeches by sitting on the floor to play with an infant, much less an infant who belonged to one of his tenant farmers. If Trevor was this open and affectionate with a child to whom he was not related, she could only imagine what he would be like with a child of his own.

Unbidden the image rose in her mind of herself holding a baby, both of them tucked in the circle of this man's arms. Isabella felt her heart clench with longing at the notion. Then, confused by her daydream, she shook her head and recalled her surroundings.

"There is no such bond between the duke and myself," she reiterated to Mrs. Jones. "We are merely relatives by marriage. Only that."

Mrs. Jones looked as if she'd like to argue but did not.

Any further discussion was forestalled by the arrival of the master of the house, who greeted the duke with apparent relief. "Yer Grace, I'm that glad ye're here, for I've just had news from the village that Mary's brother Jacob has been taken up by the bailiff for poaching on Mr. Palmer's land."

The news was met by a gasp from Mrs. Jones. "Oh, Joe! Are you sure it was Jacob? He knows better than to cross Mr. Palmer. Especially since what happened last year with young Robbie Martin."

"What happened to Robbie Martin?" Isabella asked before she could stop herself. Everyone else—even the babe—had quieted as soon as Joe Jones began to speak.

"It was a bad business," Ormonde said, his forehead creased with concern. "Martin was caught poaching on Palmer's land and Palmer chose to swear out the warrant with a magistrate on the other side of the village, who is known by folk hereabout as Hanging Harry for the stiff penalties he metes out."

Isabella had heard that there were some members of the judiciary who saw it as their duty to punish all who came before them as harshly as possible.

"In this instance you might be right that the system in London is superior to that here in the country. It is quite possible for a country magistrate to abuse his authority with little or no consequence for it. And I'm afraid Palmer took advantage of it in that instance."

"Which magistrate has Mr. Palmer chosen to approach with Mrs. Jones's brother?" Isabella asked, though she had a sinking feeling that she knew the answer.

"Mr. Harry Pinchingdale," Mr. Jones said, his face tense with worry. "I wish there was some way to make sure that the bailiff brought young Jacob before a different magistrate."

"I shall look into the matter," Ormonde said, grasping the other man's shoulder in support. "For now, you need to see to Jacob's family. Let my housekeeper know if you need provisions for them."

"Ye're a good man, Yer Grace," Mary said emphatically. "My family thanks you."

"Don't thank me yet," Ormonde said quickly. "I may not be able to do anything at all."

"But ye'll try," Mary said, leaning into her husband's protective arm. "That's more than some would do in the situation."

"We'll leave you to deal with your family, Mrs.

Jones," Isabella said, squeezing the other woman's hand. "I shall keep you all in my thoughts."

The duke and Isabella said their good-byes and were soon on their way to visit the rest of the cottages on the lane.

It was some three hours later that they retraced their steps and headed home.

"I must admit," Isabella told the duke as they approached the last rise before they entered the park surrounding Nettlefield House, "my notions of what your tenant farms must be like were rather more medieval than what I found today. I suppose growing up in town as I did has left me with a rather limited understanding of what it is that the great estates of the landed aristocracy actually do."

"Oh, do not mistake the matter, Isabella," the duke said, expertly steering his mount alongside Dolly as they approached a narrow bit of trail. "Many of the estates hereabouts and elsewhere across England are indeed in medieval conditions. Like Palmer's for instance. It is an unfortunate fact that a great many landowners have about as much interest in caring for their estates as they have in sailing to the Antipodes. They raise rents when they need a bit of extra cash, and they work the land until it is so devoid of nutrients that it can no longer grow the sort of crops that will enable them to pay said rents.

"It is an abomination," he said fiercely. And for a moment Isabella could see past the affable gentleman farmer to the conscientious caretaker of people beneath. It was far more attractive than she could allow herself to admit.

"I wish that there were some way to insist that landowners took better care of their people," he continued.

"But there is not. So I will content myself with ensuring that my own people are well looked after and leave it at that."

Thinking that this might be a means of making the dowager's case, Isabella asked, "What of the tenants of the Ormonde estates? Are they to be left to the wolves simply because your father was treated badly by his parents? That is not the tenants' fault, after all."

Immediately his gaze shuttered and Isabella could see the muscle in his jaw tense with temper. "That has nothing to do with what we were discussing," he said finally. It was easy to see that her words had annoyed him. But Isabella could not allow a bit of anger to keep her from her purpose. She might have found his treatment of his tenants here to be admirable, but she could not allow having seen the duke in a favorable light today to keep her from her purpose.

Just as he cared for his tenants and his sisters, so, too, did she care for her own sister. And after the hell of Perdita's marriage to Gervase, she deserved happiness with Coniston.

"But I do not see the difference," she pressed on as they neared the stables of Nettlefield House. "Surely the tenants of the Ormonde estates are just as deserving of your care as your tenants here are. Surely they, too, have a need for schools and oversight and compassion."

"You know nothing of the matter," the duke said sharply. "Now, let us speak of it no more. I believe you have agreed to accompany me to my magistrate's duty two days hence, have you not?"

"But, Your Grace," she said, her voice high with frustration, "I do not understand how you can say such a—"

"Enough, Lady Wharton," he barked. "Enough. My

responsibilities at the Ormonde estates are my affair and I hope that you will allow me to be the best judge of how to manage them."

Knowing that she had pushed him far enough, Isabella did not speak. She simply nodded and allowed the mare, who had seen that they were close to home, to hurry down the rise to the stables below.

Isabella might have allowed him to silence her now, she thought, staring at the duke's back as he and his mount led the way, but this was not the end of their discussion of the Ormonde estates. She might have become distracted by their visit to the tenant farms today, but no more. She was here to convince him that his place was with the Ormonde estates, and she would not stop until she had gained his agreement.

After a quick change from his riding clothes, Trevor retired to his study to go over some correspondence with his steward. Though he tried to keep his mind on the business at hand, he could not help but remember some amusing tale Lady Isabella had told him on their ride and how easily she'd interacted with his people on their visits with the tenants. Her compassion for the Joneses' situation had touched him. She might seem on the surface to be a selfish beauty, but there was genuine interest in people beneath her veneer of sophistication.

His mother, who had been brought up not terribly far from Nettlefield, would have liked Isabella, he thought. She had always been welcomed by the locals as one of their own, but there had also been just the slightest bit of resentment from the people who thought she'd gotten above herself. Though Isabella was clearly not from the local stock, she had a way about her that set people at ease, just as his mother had. It was an odd thing considering how cold he'd thought Isabella when they first met, but he supposed that might have been chalked up to nerves.

When he'd left off the same column of figures for the third time, Trevor decided it was time to quit for the day. He hadn't been so distracted by a woman in a very long time. Perhaps it was time he took a trip to York on his own to visit the discreet widow he sometimes called upon when the need for female companionship became too pressing. He disliked the notion, but it was a practical enough arrangement and there was no danger that either of them would get emotionally entangled.

He'd just poured himself a much-deserved brandy when a knock sounded on the study door.

"Enter," he called out without turning to see who the person was.

"Your pardon, Your Grace," his head groom said from the doorway. "I wondered if I might have a word."

Wondering if there was some problem with the horses, Trevor gestured the man in and resumed his seat behind the desk.

"Of course, Woods," he said to the man. "What's amiss?"

The groom, who had been with the family for more than twenty years, nodded with the authority that long acquaintance afforded. "Peters found this when he was unsaddling Dolly, and I knew you'd want to hear it right away. Especially what with the damage to Her Ladyship's carriage."

Trevor saw then that Woods held a leather girth strap in his hands, and gestured for the man to bring it forward.

Taking the leather from the man, Trevor saw at once what had bothered the grooms. The thick leather strap that was used to hold the saddle in place had been sliced three-quarters of the way across.

"This is the strap from Dolly's sidesaddle?" Trevor asked curtly. At the groom's affirmative nod Trevor let out a vile curse. If he and Lady Isabella had allowed the horses to gallop that afternoon, Isabella would surely have been unseated. There was no guarantee that she would have been harmed, but the cut strap would certainly have made it likely.

"I'm that sorry Peters didn't notice it this afternoon when he was readying the horses for you to ride out," Woods said with a shake of his head. "I've given the lad a strong talking to, but if you want to dismiss him, Your Grace, I will of course do as ye wish."

But Trevor, too distracted by the mental image of Isabella broken and bleeding on the trail side, dismissed the notion. "I know you run a tight ship, Woods," he told the older man. "And who's to say that the cut wasn't made after Peters saddled them? If he saw nothing amiss when he tightened the girth then it's likely that the blackguard did it while they were waiting for us to come down."

Relief crossed over the groom's face. He bowed his head in obeisance and said, "Thank you, Your Grace. I know Peters is that upset by it and he won't let anything like this happen again."

"I should hope not," Trevor said. Then thanking the man for bringing the matter to his attention, he dismissed the groom.

When the door closed behind the servant, Trevor cursed again. Something was very definitely amiss with Lady Isabella. First the carriage she'd traveled in from

London had been tampered with, which might have resulted in a very dangerous accident for all the passengers on board. Now the saddle of the horse she'd ridden today had been tampered with. It was clear to him that someone was intent upon harming the widow. And he'd be damned if he'd let them succeed while she was a guest in his home.

He drank the rest of his brandy and stood. He had little doubt that the lady would be reluctant to speak to him about the matter. Especially considering their disagreement earlier in the afternoon.

Considering the matter, he decided to leave off discussion of the matter until after dinner, when she was likely to be in a better frame of mind. But he would have answers from her before the day was through.

Of that he was certain.

Striding from the study and toward the stairs, he made his way to his chamber to dress for dinner.

Seven

*T*hough she was not normally one to rest in the afternoon, Isabella found herself agreeing with her maid that she could do with a nap once she returned from visiting the tenants with the duke.

She had never guessed the amount of information a landowner needed to keep at his disposal when it came to maintaining a cordial relationship with his tenants. She had met at least twenty farmers and easily three times as many wives and children in her trip with the duke that afternoon. And to her surprise and admiration, Ormonde not only knew everyone's names, but he also was able to ask after their siblings and parents and children and grandchildren and in some cases great-grandchildren, with an easy manner that indicated he had been doing so for years. He clearly cared for their welfare beyond just ensuring that they were able to produce a good crop yield. He cared about them as people.

She was a little ashamed that she'd never thought beyond the fact that such relationships existed to wondering what differences might exist between one landowner and another. Certainly her father had never revealed the slightest concern for the tenants on his own entailed properties in Kent. And the same held true for her husband, who had visited his country house a grand total of three times during the whole of their marriage.

All of which made it difficult for her to understand how the duke could possibly dismiss the tenants who relied upon him at the Ormonde country estates. It was a disconnect that she found hard to reconcile.

Her mind still teeming with the faces and conversations she'd seen and shared that afternoon, she drifted off to sleep with barely a thought for how unusual it was for her to do so.

She woke up some two hours later feeling refreshed and famished. She pulled the bell for her maid and walked across the plush carpet to the dressing table to brush out her hair.

Propped against the powder jar she noticed a small box wrapped in plain brown paper. Her name was written in a loose scrawl across the top, the hand almost but not quite illegible. Thinking to the note she'd received before, Isabella felt a shiver run down her spine, even as she began to unwrap the package.

She bit back a gasp as she saw that beneath the paper was a beautifully enameled snuffbox.

A snuffbox she'd seen in her husband's hand time and time again over the years of their marriage.

A snuffbox she'd been sure was a gift from his mistress.

A snuffbox she'd destroyed herself out of spite on the day of his funeral.

Her hand shaking, she pressed the mechanism cleverly hidden in the silverwork that allowed the user to open the lid with one hand.

She watched with bated breath as the top of the box sprang open to reveal a small bit of paper. Isabella swallowed, not wanting to look at the paper but needing to know more than she needed her next breath. She turned the box upside down and the paper fell out onto her palm. Carefully she unfolded it and read the words. Written in the hand she had come to know almost as well as her own.

Do you miss me?

By the time her maid, Sanders, came in a few moments later, Isabella was trembling all over. It wasn't so much that someone had gone to great lengths to terrify her. It was the fact that whoever it was knew where she was and had access to her—even if that access was by proxy in the form of servants.

"I've brushed out your crimson silk for tonight, Your Ladyship," said Sanders as she hurried about the room, preparing Isabella's things for the night ahead. "The wine stain came right out once I used the paste recommended by the duke's upstairs maid. I'm quite glad I spoke to her about it."

Unable to stand lest she fall, Isabella gave a noncommittal sound that might have been agreement or dissent. Swallowing, she finally asked, "Sanders, do you know where the small package that was on my dressing table came from?"

The woman paused in her quest for slippers in the wardrobe. Standing, she put her hands on her hips and turned to look fully at Isabella. "Package, my lady?" she asked, her expression puzzled. "I don't know what you mean. I never saw any package."

Isabella turned on the vanity chair and stared at her. "Of course you must have," she said firmly, trying to convince herself that it was the truth. "You must have been the one to put it on my dressing table." She held up the brown paper that had covered the box and proffered it to the other woman. "You see?" she said. "It was covered in this. You probably brought it up here after luncheon and simply forgot about it."

But the maid was steadfast in her denial. "I never saw such a package, my lady. If I had I would tell you about it, naturally." She shook her head with consternation. "You don't mean to say that someone else has been in your bedchamber and left it, surely? Why would someone do such a thing?" Her expression turned sly. "Do you have a secret admirer perhaps?"

Agitated by the woman's denials, Isabella stood up from the table and began to pace. "No, of course not," she said, knowing she sounded as overset as she felt. "An admirer would hardly send me such a thing."

Not bothering to ask her what "such a thing" might be, Sanders crossed to the dressing table and picked up the box, opening it to reveal the snuffbox inside. "Why on earth would someone send you this?" the maid demanded. "It's hardly the way into a lady's heart, that's for sure."

Isabella debated whether to tell Sanders about the note she'd found inside it, but she knew that confiding in the maid would be a bad idea. Though she'd only been in Isabella's employ for a few weeks, she seemed trustworthy enough. However, once Isabella took her into her confidence there was no going back. And she wasn't sure she wanted the maid to know just how much she had feared—and maybe even still feared—her husband. That was something she could only confide to her closest friends.

Forcing herself to calm down, she laughed. "It is an unusual choice, isn't it?" she said, trying to pass off her agitation as lovesickness. "But perhaps the gentleman is unaccustomed to the art of flirtation. It is a pretty little snuffbox, but I am hardly the sort to take up a spittoon!"

She and the maid shared a genuine laugh, and the tension Isabella had been feeling began to dissipate. Someone had intended her to be frightened by the reminder of Ralph's brutality and the suggestion that he could speak to her from beyond the grave, but Isabella knew such an idea was ludicrous. It was troubling, however, to know that whoever it was who wished to make her fearful had followed her from London and into Yorkshire.

Briefly she wondered if she ought to share her fears with the duke. He had the right to know that one of his guests was being terrorized in his home. But to admit such a thing would also mean admitting just how frightened she really was of her husband's memory. Which seemed silly when she thought of it now, but her fear upon opening the package had been very real.

"Whoever it might be," Sanders said, seemingly oblivious to her mistress's troubling thoughts, "he will certainly get an eyeful this evening, for I intend to dress you up finer than fivepence and make no mistake."

And with that Isabella allowed herself to be taken into Sanders's care and be pampered and primped within an inch of her life.

* * *

When Isabella came down for dinner, Trevor was still ruminating over the damaged girth strap. He had instructed Templeton to have the male servants keep a circumspect watch over her while she was a guest in Nettlefield House. Trevor knew if she got wind of such a plan she would object vociferously, but he had to do what he could to ensure her safety while she was under his roof.

He'd tried and failed to determine why anyone would wish to put her in danger. Surely she had been in Yorkshire for too short a period to have drawn the sort of ruthless enemies who would plot her death. She was just what she seemed—an elegant widow who had come to Yorkshire on a commission from her godmother. Hardly the sort of person to attract danger at every turn.

Isabella's arrival in the drawing room put an end to his thoughts on the matter. Or any thoughts at all if it came to that.

Always impeccably dressed, tonight she wore a simple evening gown of crimson silk, the hue of which complemented her creamy skin. Her hair had been elegantly dressed, and the auburn highlights shone in the candlelight as she stepped into the room.

"Good evening, Your Grace," she said, offering him her gloved hand even as he willed the room to stop spinning.

When he was able to rein in his libidinous thoughts, Trevor took her outstretched hand and brought it to his lips, not settling for the air kiss that was customary on such occasions but placing his lips against the cool kid of her gloves. Looking up at her from beneath his lashes, he was rewarded with a blush from her as she took her hand away again.

"You look lovely tonight, Lady Wharton," he said, rising to his full height again. "I'm afraid my sisters are dining in the nursery this evening, since Eleanor refuses to be seen in any of her old gowns and she is saving the other one you gave her for our shopping trip to York tomorrow." He grinned. "She is convinced that Mrs. Renfrew will be so jealous of Madame Celeste's skills that she will work twice as hard on any new gowns Eleanor orders from her tomorrow."

Isabella laughed, and Trevor was captivated by the sound. It was throaty without being wanton, and merry without being frivolous. "You should laugh more often," he said, tucking her arm into his as he led her into the dining room.

"I would endeavor to do so, Your Grace," she said, tilting her head to the side, "if only I could find more things that amused me. I'm afraid the last few years have been less than pleasant for my family and me."

A misstep, that, Ormonde thought to himself. Of course the recent deaths in her family had made her more serious. Certainly he'd had little enough to be pleased with in the years since his parents had died.

"I apologize, my lady," he said quickly. "I am an insensitive clod. Do forgive me."

"I can hardly hold you accountable for the remark, Your Grace," she said, allowing him to hand her into a chair to the left of his own. "You yourself have suffered your own tragedies in these last few years or so, as well. Let us call peace and move beyond it."

Eager to get past it as well, Trevor agreed and turned the subject to one that was only slightly less troublesome. "I'm afraid, Lady Isabella," he began once the footmen had finished serving them their soup course, "that I've a bit of worrisome news to impart, and I'm not quire sure how to go about it."

As he watched her, she stilled and put her soupspoon down. Turning to look at him, she said, "I have often found that bad news is best told quickly, before it has time to fester."

Trevor nodded and said, "Then, I shall do so. I'm afraid that this afternoon following our ride, one of the stable hands found something irregular with your saddle."

Her auburn brows drew together with concern. "What do you mean, 'irregular'?" she asked.

"The girth strap, the bit of leather that helps secure the saddle in place upon the horse's back, was sliced almost through."

Her lips tightened. "Sliced. Do you mean like with a knife?" she asked.

He gave a nod of assent. "Just like that," he said firmly. "I have no way of knowing whether it was done before we left for the tenants' or if someone did it while our horses were idle once we'd reached the village. I only know that for at least part of our ride today you were in immediate danger."

Isabella rested her hands on either side of her soup dish; Trevor could see a fine tremble run through the one closest to his. "Who would do such a thing?" she asked, her voice low and slightly hoarse. "First someone damages the dowager's carriage, then the note, and the snuffbox, and now this! It is too much to be borne!"

She started to stand up, but Trevor stopped her. "Wait, my lady," he said sharply. "What's this about a note and snuffbox? Do you mean to tell me you've received other threats from this blackguard?"

Trevor could see that she was reluctant to tell him,

but she seemed to come to some sort of agreement with herself and told him about the threatening notes and the replica of her husband's snuffbox.

"Why in god's name didn't you tell me?" he demanded, running a hand through his close-cropped hair. "Did you think I was so resentful of your reasons for coming that I would refuse to believe you?"

Isabella looked sheepish. "It wasn't so much that," she admitted, "as my own pride that kept me from speaking. It is hardly a thing to be proud of that someone has seen fit to threaten me in such an outrageous manner. I must have done something to bring this upon myself."

"Don't be absurd," he said fiercely, and when the footmen came to remove his and Isabella's soup bowls and replace them with the next course he gave the men a fright by growling at them in such a way that they removed themselves from the room at once. "Not only are you a guest in my home," he seethed, "but as such you are a lady under my protection and it is an insult to both of us that this person would importune you so."

"Ah yes," Isabella said wryly, "it is an insult to you, of course. Pray do not let me get in the way of your consequence, Your Grace."

Now it was Trevor's turn to feel sheepish. "I didn't mean it that way, of course. I simply am angry that you didn't tell me before so that I might ensure your safety more so than I have done up to this point. My god, the fellow has even managed to get into your bedchamber, it seems, to leave threats."

"Not necessarily," Isabella said thoughtfully. "He might not have delivered the snuffbox himself, but simply paid one of your servants to deliver it."

Trevor stood, grateful to have some clear-cut action he could take to alleviate some of his annoyance. Going to the bellpull, he rang it, and when Templeton arrived Trevor instructed the butler to call all of the servants into the hallway to be addressed by him in fifteen minutes.

"Very good, Your Grace," the butler said, hurrying away to call the servants to order.

"Are you sure this is what you wish to do?" Isabella asked nervously. She was clearly not comfortable with being the reason one of his servants might be sacked. But Trevor was damned if he'd continue to nurse a viper in his bosom, as it were, for one minute longer.

"Of course I'm sure," he said curtly. "The sooner we find out who it was that left the snuffbox in your bed-chamber, the sooner we can ensure your safety."

But when a few minutes later all of the servants were assembled in the hallway, not one of them admitted to taking a package up to Lady Wharton's room. And to his annoyance, Trevor believed them. After he'd dismissed them to return to their own dinner, he went back to the dining room with Isabella, who claimed she was no longer hungry. Even so, he insisted that she try some of the removes Cook had prepared for them. And by the time the last course was served, she'd eaten a few bites at least.

Since it was just the two of them, Trevor didn't leave the room for after-dinner port, but they both retired to the drawing room and the tea tray.

"And you have no notion of who might be doing this to you?" Trevor asked one last time as Isabella stirred sugar into her tea. "It's da . . . er, dashed strange that this coward would decide to accost you now, and not while you are in London. Surely he must have followed you from London into Yorkshire, and that is hardly an easy prospect."

"I know," she agreed. "But whoever it is clearly wishes me to be frightened. I wonder if it could be someone who does not wish for you to take up your responsibilities as the Duke of Ormonde."

"But with all due respect," Trevor said with a half smile, "you haven't been particularly successful at convincing me."

"No," she agreed, smiling back at him, "but you have said that if I give you a chance to show me how important you are around Nettlefield you will at least come to London and give your grandmother a hearing. Perhaps whoever this is wishes for me to leave Yorkshire before I am able to do so."

"It's a thought," Trevor agreed, taking a sip of tea. "Whatever the case, you must know that from now on you are no longer allowed to wander about the house and estate grounds alone."

Though she seemed reluctant to do so, Isabella agreed.

"Now," Trevor said, "tomorrow we will rise early and travel to York. If nothing else you will find the company of my sisters to be a distraction from your worries."

"Indeed yes," Isabella said with a grin, paraphrasing Johnson to say, "A lady who is tired of shopping is tired of life."

"At least you did not say it about London," Trevor said, following her up the stairs to their separate bedchambers. "That is a start."

He was glad to have distracted her from the worry that must certainly be weighing upon her now. Tomorrow they would be away from Nettlefield House and whoever it was who threatened her, and his sisters would surely raise her spirits. But on the day after he would see to it that the search for her tormentor began in earnest.

After a night spent tossing and turning, worrying over who it might be who wished her harm, Isabella awoke the next morning groggy but determined to enjoy her trip to York. She did not tell the girls about what it was that troubled her, though, with the perspicacity of youth, they seemed to guess that something was wrong with her.

Even so, the girls were excited to be traveling into town, and Isabella let herself be swept up in their enthusiasm and did her best to ignore the duke, whose anger on her behalf last evening had left her feeling confused. It was one thing for him to show distant civility to her as a guest in his home, but the way he'd leapt to her defense had felt more than a little comforting. Had she ever been able to depend upon a man to offer her his protection with no questions asked like the duke had last night? She couldn't remember such a time. It was more than a little seductive.

She had hoped he would choose to ride alongside the carriage, as gentlemen often did on such trips, but to her dismay he climbed up into the traveling carriage behind them. It was difficult not to notice that he'd donned more formal attire than what he wore to attend to the home farm and estate. She was displeased to see that he looked even more handsome in town clothes then he did in riding dress. Drat the man.

Fortunately for Isabella, Eleanor and Belinda were more than talkative enough to remove any onus from

Isabella to carry the conversation. She peered out the window at the countryside as the sisters argued over whether the puff sleeve was indeed a fashion statement that would last into next season. As she let the sisters' chatter wash over her, she felt Trevor's gaze on her. But when she dared to look at him from beneath her lashes, he quickly looked away.

Their silence lasted only until they reached York, where they descended from the carriage in what Isabella assumed was the city's main shopping district, which to her surprise was far more sophisticated than she would have expected so far from London.

"Mrs. Renfrew's shop is just down here," Trevor said, taking Isabella's arm, as if they were indeed friends. She would have chided him for his cheek, but she didn't wish to embarrass his sisters. Or so she told herself, trying to ignore the tingling in her belly at the feel of his strong arm beneath her gloved hand.

"I thought you might wish to visit the tobacconist's, or the boot maker's," she said coolly as they followed his sisters to the dressmaker's storefront. "Most gentlemen do not relish a trip to the dressmaker's, I think."

"I can hardly allow you to approve Eleanor's gowns," Trevor said calmly. When Isabella attempted to pull her arm out of his grasp, he held firm. "Don't rip up at me, Lady Wharton. I simply meant that I cannot impose upon you in that way."

"You don't trust my judgment is what you mean," she hissed as they stepped into Mrs. Renfrew's.

"I don't trust Eleanor's judgment," he said in a low voice, turning to look Isabella fully in the eyes. She felt her heart speed up when she saw the sincerity in his gaze. "I know you will try your best to steer her in the right direction," he continued, absently rubbing her arm where he held it. Was he even aware he was doing it? she wondered, feeling a blush creep into her cheeks. "But Eleanor can be quite forceful when she wants her way, and I do not intend for her to appear at the Palmers' ball looking like a lady of the night."

Swallowing her annoyance, Isabella conceded that he had a point. When she was Eleanor's age she'd tried to dampen her petticoats, though her mama had soon put a stop to that. And Isabella had only a few days' acquaintance with the girls, for all that she felt as if she'd known them all their lives. She might indeed need Trevor's backing up her opinion to make Eleanor see reason should she wish to try something more daring than Isabella could allow.

"All right," she said at last. She hadn't forgotten his harsh words of the night before, but she vowed to make a fresh start with him today. If only for the time they were in York.

Though he did not make mention of his title, Mrs. Renfrew was clearly aware that the party that had just strolled into her shop was a ducal one. And she saw to it that they were all treated to her best service. To Isabella's surprise, the woman even seemed to know who she was, though she had never been to York in her life. Clearly the gossip networks of Yorkshire were stronger than she could have guessed.

"Lady Wharton," Mrs. Renfrew said with a deep curtsy, "may I say what a delight it is to have someone as fashionable as you in my shop? I hope you will allow me, if I am not too bold, to make up something for you to wear to the Palmers' ball as well?"

Isabella was under no illusions that Mrs. Renfrew was offering to do so out of generosity of heart. Having a client like Isabella would be a feather in the woman's cap. A feather she would boast about to any and all who came into her shop. Though Isabella would not have minded a new gown, this trip was for Eleanor.

"I thank you, Mrs. Renfrew," she said with a slight inclination of her head, "but I'm afraid I brought far too many gowns with me from London as it is. And today is for Eleanor and Belinda. I will be happy to sing your praises, however, if you please my young friends."

The older woman acknowledged the refusal with grace. "Of course, my lady," she said quickly. "I believe I have just what Miss Eleanor needs to be the belle of the ball."

Mrs. Renfrew took Eleanor and a still-chattering Belinda back to the area where they would be measured within an inch of their lives, leaving Isabella to wait with Trevor for them to return. They chatted amiably for some minutes about nothing of consequence. Isabella could feel yesterday's argument hovering in the wings, but as she was the one owed an apology, she was loathe to bring it up. Unable to endure another moment of tension, she was about to excuse herself to look at ribbons in the front of the shop when Trevor spoke. "Lady Wharton, I apologize if I was unkind yesterday," he began, genuine remorse clouding his blue eyes. "I'm afraid that my grudge against my family sometimes makes—"

He was forestalled from finishing his remarks by a feminine squeal, and Isabella turned to see Mrs. Palmer and Sir Lionel Thistleback hurrying toward them.

Eight

*I*sabella bit back a groan at the sight of Mrs. Palmer accompanied by Lord Wharton's dearest friend. She hadn't seen Sir Lionel in months and, frankly, she was pleased with the arrangement. He had borne witness more than once to Ralph's harsh treatment of her, and ever loyal to him, Lionel had done nothing to help her. Men like Ralph and Lionel, she'd learned, were bound together by their shared interest in anything that took pleasure at the expense of others. And more often than not that pleasure had been at Isabella's expense.

It also sounded as if, from the way Mr. Palmer had allegedly treated the brother of Mrs. Jones, the poacher, Thistleback's host was cut from the same cloth as his guest. Perhaps Isabella should save some of her condolences for the unfortunate Mrs. Palmer.

"My dear Lady Isabella," Sir Lionel crooned after introductions had been made, as he and his hostess joined them in the small sitting room where Mrs. Renfrew kept her pattern books. "It has been an age since I've seen you. Since your husband's funeral, I believe. Such a sad occasion."

Hearing the man mention her husband's funeral so soon after she'd received a physical reminder in the form of his snuffbox sent an involuntary shudder through her. Still, Isabella could hardly mention the matter. She kept her own counsel but tried to be gracious to her husband's friend. "Indeed, I believe you are correct, Sir Lionel. But we must press on. After all, it's what dear Ralph would have wished."

Thistleback's grin indicated that he knew full well that it was not what her late husband would have wished. However, Thistleback did not call her to task for the fib. "My lovely hostess"—he gestured to Mrs. Palmer, who had watched their exchange with avid fascination—"has told me that you are visiting the Duke of Ormonde's home now." Coming from Thistleback, the description sounded as if she were temporarily being kept by the duke while she waited to be claimed by her next lover. Isabella steeled her features not to reveal her disgust.

"Lady Wharton is my guest, Sir Lionel," Trevor said, standing as close to Isabella as propriety allowed. "She has kindly agreed to assist me in planning my younger sister's come-out next spring."

"Oh, how wonderful, Your Grace," Mrs. Palmer gushed, clearly torn between watching the byplay between her guest and Isabella and her desire to know more about the plans for Eleanor's debut. "I cannot tell you how pleased I am to hear you have finally chosen to take up the duties of the dukedom."

If Trevor were the sort of man who kept a quizzing glass, Isabella reflected, Mrs. Palmer would find herself the recipient of the sort of look that had been depressing pretensions for centuries. The lack of such an instrument, however, did not keep Trevor from putting the

grasping woman in her place. "I am so pleased to hear
you approve, Mrs. Palmer," he said coolly, his words
indicating that he felt entirely the opposite. "I will be
sure to consult you the next time I make a decision regarding the dukedom."

But Mrs. Palmer had clearly been at the end of much
sterner snubs. "I would be happy to assist you with
whatever you need, Your Grace." The way she ran a
finger over the pendant resting on her bosom indicated
that her assistance might be more personal in nature
than her words implied. Clearly, Isabella mused, the
unhappy Mr. Humphrey Palmer was failing at his hus-
bandly duties.

An awkward pause fell over the group as Mrs.
Palmer's invitation hovered in the air. Finally, Isabella
spoke. "It is my understanding, Mrs. Palmer, that you
have planned an entertainment in Sir Lionel's honor.
We are here ordering a dress made up so that Eleanor
may attend."

The subject was clearly one that the other woman
relished. "Indeed, Lady Wharton, we are planning a
ball! And I cannot tell you how excited I am that we will
have not one but two distinguished guests from London
at our humble country entertainment."

"Oh, I hardly think that I—" Isabella began, but was
cut off by Thistleback.

"I hope that we will be able to add a bit of town
bronze to your party, Mrs. Palmer," he said with condescension. "Though I hardly think that it will be the
humble affair you predict. Why, you've a bit of town
polish yourself, don't you? And you will have a duke in
attendance as well, won't you?" He raised his eyes in-

quiringly at Trevor, whose face was impassive as he watched the two interlopers.

Still, when he spoke it was mild enough. "Yes, I will be in attendance, Sir Lionel. I will escort my sister and Lady Wharton. I hope that you will remember that they are both under my protection." He said the words in an easy enough tone, but Isabella and no doubt Thistle-back could hear the steel behind them. Even so, Thistle-back, who had never been called a smart man, said, "I hardly think Lady Isabella will like that arrangement, Your Grace. After all, it wasn't so long ago that she was under another man's protection . . ." He paused, letting the insinuation linger in the air, then finished, ". . . her husband's, I mean."

But it was clearly a dig at Isabella's character. Thistle-back had made advances toward her not long after the funeral, but Isabella had sent him away with a flea in his ear. He'd clearly not forgotten the setdown. This ex-plained the whispers that seemed to follow her about London before she left for Yorkshire, however.

"Sir Lionel," she said, managing to keep her voice deadly calm, "I believe you have confused me with some other widow of means. I hope that you will let whoever told you this falsehood know the truth of the matter. I should hate for it to reflect badly on your char-acter. After all, a man's reputation once lost is lost for-ever."

She was pleased to see the man's nostrils flare with annoyance. Even so he said, "I hope you will not take offense at my little joke, Lady Isabella. I was merely making a play on words. Nothing more."

Her eyes avidly watching the interplay between the

two, Mrs. Palmer shook her head, causing her sausage-like ringlets to bounce with the motion. "I cannot keep up with your London intrigues," she said with a small sigh. It was clear that she would like for the back-and-forth between Isabella and Sir Lionel to continue, but her desire to get Isabella's opinion about the fashion overrode it. She was a shallow lady at heart. "Lady Wharton," she said with a wheedling tone, "I hope that you will tell me about the gown Miss Eleanor is having made up. I daresay Mrs. Renfrew is grateful to have someone as distinguished as you come into her shop."

Exchanging a speaking look with Trevor, Isabella allowed herself to be spirited off by the other woman.

Left alone with Lord Thistleback, Trevor returned to his seat in the little parlor area. He was not surprised to find the other man had followed him and taken the seat opposite. He had nothing of importance to discuss with the man. After his insinuations about Isabella, Trevor would rather draw his cork than exchange words with him. The knowledge that he was staying in the neighborhood during the same period that Isabella had been threatened placed the baronet at the very top of Trevor's list of suspects.

Clearly unaware of the direction of Trevor's thoughts, Thistleback made the first conversational foray. "You are quite lucky to have someone like Lady Isabella assisting you with your sisters," the man said, his piggish eyes knowing. "I was great friends with her husband," he said, smoothing the sleeve of his blue coat. "I have known her for many years."

Trevor was curious about Viscount Wharton. How

could he not be when Wharton's shadow seemed to loom so heavily over Isabella? There was the fact that his snuffbox had been used to terrify her. And the note reading *Do you miss me?* A taunt if ever he'd heard one.

She hardly ever mentioned the man, but there was something about the way she tiptoed around his name that let Trevor know her relationship with her husband had not been a happy one. That the man sitting before Trevor had been the fellow's bosom companion only solidified his suspicions. No one who could claim Thistleback as friend could possibly be an honorable man.

"Then you must know that she is an honorable woman," Trevor said at last, his words echoing his thoughts. He could not let the other man's salacious words go without letting him know that Lady Isabella was not without friends. Men like Thistleback sought to belittle the women around them because they could not control them. Trevor would not be surprised if Thistleback had attempted to place Isabella under his own protection and been soundly rejected. His earlier accusations smacked of the fox and the sour grapes.

"I hardly think a social acquaintance is enough for me to make a judgment on the matter," Thistleback retorted. "After all, seeing someone at various *ton* gatherings is hardly tantamount to knowing the contents of another's soul. I do concede, however, that she seems to have behaved honorably despite the whispers surrounding her behavior these last months."

"Perhaps you should tell me about these whispers so that I may judge for myself," Trevor said, attempting to make the other man put his insinuations into more open terms. "After all, I should like to know what kind of person to whom I'm entrusting my sisters' care."

Thistleback's eyes narrowed, as if he was attempting to determine Trevor's sincerity. He was, of course, lying through his teeth. He had no fears at all regarding Isabella's suitability to shepherd his sister through society. Isabella had shown herself to be levelheaded when it came to dealing with them. And she hadn't tried once to seduce him into bending to his will. Given his suspicion that whatever hold the dowager had over her was something of vast importance to her, that alone was enough to convince him of her honor.

"Well, there is nothing overtly scandalous about her," Thistleback said, confirming Trevor's suspicions. "She has attended some rather risqué entertainments, but other than that she hasn't been linked with any one man. And Wharton would not have tolerated her playing him false." He scratched the side of his face. "He kept her on a rather tight leash, if you want to know the truth. He was not a man who would tolerate much in the way of independence from his wife." Thistleback laughed. "Once when she demanded he give up his mistress, he beat her quite severely. I don't think the poor woman could sit for a week."

Trevor said nothing, as he wished fervently that he could go back in time and pummel the late Lord Wharton.

"You won't tell her I told you, though," Thistleback said, his eyes shadowed with worry. "I promised Wharton I wouldn't ever speak of it. It's quite ridiculous when you think of it. Wives aren't supposed to know that mistresses even exist! Let alone demand that their husbands give them up. A man must be able to rule his own roost."

Listening to Thistleback, Trevor was reminded of a long-forgotten incident from his childhood. One of his father's tenants—a brute to begin with—had beaten his wife so badly that the poor woman had lost consciousness. Trevor could still remember how angry his father had been when he'd returned home from the woman's bedside. He'd thrown the husband off the estate with the threat of having him impressed into the navy if he ever returned. It was true enough, Phillip had told Trevor, that the law said a wife was just another possession that a man could do with as he pleased, but a man who ruled his home through violence was not much of a man to begin with.

Neither was Thistleback, Trevor thought as the man continued to justify his friend's abuse of his wife. "And it isn't as if Lady Isabella has suffered for it. In the month after Wharton died, I believe she attended every entertainment society had to offer."

The duke wasn't surprised to learn that Isabella had run wild once her abuser was dead. She was probably starved for freedom and desperate to do all the things she'd been prevented from doing while he was alive. Trevor looked at Thistleback sitting there, looking as if he'd just done something naughty. If it were up to Trevor, he'd make the man pay for his former friend's misdeeds. But that would only hurt Isabella, and she'd been tortured enough. Trevor wanted to know if beatings had been the extent of Wharton's abuse of his wife, but he would have to wait and see if Isabella would tell him.

One thing was certain.

Trevor would be damned before he'd let Isabella anywhere near this man alone again.

Trevor was quiet on the ride back to Nettlefield, but Isabella attributed his silence to his having been forced to pass time with Sir Lionel. The duke wasn't the most gregarious of men at the best of times, and any moments spent with her late husband's friend could not be counted among the best of times.

She had been unhappy to see him approach back in the dressmaker's shop, but she could hardly cut the man dead in front of the Ormondes' neighbors. After all, if she wanted to convince the duke to travel back to London with her she would need to make nice with the people he socialized with here. She doubted Mrs. Palmer had much influence over her host, but every little bit helped.

Besides, Isabella did not wish to call attention to her previous relationship with Sir Lionel in front of Eleanor and Belinda. They were unaware of the vile sorts of things some men got up to, and Isabella would not strip them of their innocence if she could help it. She remembered being just as trusting they were now, and she would do whatever it took to make sure they were able to maintain that outlook for as long as possible.

What troubled her the most about seeing Thistleback, however, was the coincidence between her receiving what must be a replica of Ralph's snuffbox and his bosom friend's appearance in the neighborhood. Could Thistleback be the one who had sent the token? It was just the sort of cowardly taunt a man of his character would find amusing. But surely he was not also responsible for sabotaging the dowager's carriage. After all, Sir Lionel had no notion that Isabella was even expected to travel to Yorkshire. Much less that she'd be doing so in the dowager's carriage.

Something was definitely rotten about the number of coincidences, but she could not tell just what.

Yet.

"I cannot wait for my new gowns to be delivered," Eleanor said, interrupting Isabella's thoughts and all but clapping her hands at the prospect of her new wardrobe. "Thank you again for taking us today, Lady Wharton," she gushed.

"Of course you are welcome," Isabella responded, squeezing the girl's hand. Isabella was surprised to realize it herself, but she enjoyed the girl's company. She was unaffected and enthusiastic and had none of the guile or cunning that marked the demeanor of many young ladies of Isabella's acquaintance. Though she was loath to admit it, Trevor had done a good job raising his sisters, the lack of steady governesses notwithstanding." And you must call me Isabella. Though it is your brother you must thank. I was merely a guest on this trip."

Indeed, even she was thinking of thanking Ormonde for taking them to York. Though there had been the unfortunate meeting with Thistleback, there had been enough other distraction that she was able to stop herself from dwelling upon the fact that someone was trying to frighten her witless.

She let Eleanor's chatter wash over her as she thought about what her next step would be in her quest to convince the duke to come to London. The next day she was supposed to attend the duke's appearance as the local magistrate for the surrounding neighborhood. She'd never thought to find herself at such an event, but she could not help but admit to herself that she was looking forward to it. It was hardly the sort of thing ladies were encouraged to do in the regular course of things, and she was curious about the entire process. Of course, the fact that she'd have a front-row seat at watching the duke mete out justice had nothing to do with it.

Or very little to do with it, she amended.

Or not much to do with it, she amended again.

Really, she told herself, she was entirely neutral about the matter.

She was saved from further argument with herself by the slowing of the carriage before Nettlefield House. And if Isabella blushed a little when the duke handed her down from the carriage, she could blame it on the heat of the afternoon.

"Such chivalry," Isabella teased her host, trying to pass off her breathlessness for mock enthusiasm rather than the real thing. "I might begin to think you wished to charm me, Your Grace."

"Hardly that, Lady Wharton," the duke said, holding her gloved hand for a just a fraction longer than necessary. "I am often given to performing little acts of kindness for my sisters. As you are with them today, you benefit from the habit as well."

But she did not fail to notice that his eyes seemed troubled for the barest moment before he donned his mask of bluff kindness once more. Her heart sank, and all thoughts of flirtation left her. Could Sir Lionel have spoken to him during those few moments they'd been alone at the dressmaker's? Surely not, she told herself, turning away from the duke to follow his sisters into the house.

She had never heard of Sir Lionel speaking out about her relationship with her husband before. Still, now that Wharton had been gone for some time, she would not be surprised to learn that his friend no longer felt quite so secretive about the matter. The idea of Trevor learning anything at all relating to her humiliation at her husband's hands made Isabella's skin crawl. She had endured more than her share of torture at her husband's hands, and knowing that it might become the subject of offhand gossip was chilling in its mundanity. She had no wish for the world at large to know about her past, but even more, she did not wish the knowledge to become so common-place as to be unremarkable.

Do you miss me? And just like that the distractions of the day disappeared and were replaced by fear. She certainly did not miss her husband. And if the reminders of him continued to loom large in her life, she would not be able to even if she wished it.

She was still lost in her thoughts when she stepped into the hall and was greeted by Templeton.

"There is a lady here to see you, Lady Wharton," the butler said, taking her pelisse and bonnet and handing them over to a waiting maid.

When he first spoke, Isabella's heart had leapt at the idea her sister, or perhaps Georgina, might have come to Yorkshire, but his next words shattered her hopes.

"She says she is acquainted with your sister. I have put her in the late mistress's parlor."

It was likely one of the candidates for the governess position, Isabella thought, masking her disappointment.

"I'll see to her, Templeton," she told the man. "Will you please ask Mrs. Templeton to send in a pot of tea and some biscuits?"

Isabella walked down the hallway toward the parlor, only to feel Trevor's presence lurking behind her. She stopped and turned. "Your Grace?" She raised a questioning brow.

She was amused to see him looking sheepish. "I

thought it best I'd ensure the visitor is a welcome one," he said. If he'd had pockets he would have his hands in them.

Somewhat touched by his concern for her, Isabella said, "It is likely someone my sister has sent for the governess job."

Visibly the duke relaxed. "I'd forgotten about that," he admitted. "It seems a very long time since we spoke of the matter, though it's only been a couple of days."

"Time speeds along when you are enjoying yourself," she said wryly.

He laughed. "Something like that, I suppose." He motioned for her to continue and walked beside her toward the parlor. "I will sit with you for your interview with her, if you don't mind. I know I asked you to handle the hiring of someone, but I do not feel comfortable putting someone in charge of my sisters without taking a hand in choosing the woman."

Isabella thought better of him for it. She knew quite a few gentlemen who would rather walk over hot coals than discuss the care and education of the young ladies for whom they acted as guardians. Most would prefer not to set eyes on the young ladies themselves until they were of an age to be seen in company.

"Of course," she told the duke, walking alongside him to the parlor. She couldn't help but feel like they were working as a team in this as in so many other matters. It was nice to know that if something untoward happened she would have someone beside her who would guide her along. Even if it was only for a little while. "I am pleased you are taking an interest," she said aloud. "First a trip to the dressmaker's and now a visit with a governess."

"Do not tell anyone," Trevor said with a crooked grin. "I have a reputation to maintain."

But Isabella knew that the only reputation this man could boast of was that of true gentleman. Definitely not something she could say about most men of her acquaintance.

Nine

The first thing to enter Isabella's mind upon seeing the woman waiting for them in the sitting room was a mental image of a mourning dove.

The card Templeton had given Isabella noted the lady's name as Miss Winifred Nightingale. Dressed from head to toe in gray, the governess whom Perdita had sent was certainly suited to the role. Of Miss Nightingale's surname, however, she was woefully misrepresentative. Unless of course she liked to sing in the evenings.

As Isabella and Trevor entered the room, the woman rose from her perch on the settee and offered them both a very correct, very deep curtsy. And as befitting her station, the lady waited for them to speak first.

"Miss Nightingale," Isabella said, acknowledging the woman's greeting with an inclined head. "I presume you have been sent here by the Duchess of Ormonde."

"Yes, my lady," the governess said with a nod. Her golden hair was pulled quite severely atop her head in a very proper, very serviceable chignon. She had removed her bonnet, which was no doubt just as nondescript as her gown. But there was little she could do to hide the fineness of her features, try as she might to disguise her cornflower blue eyes behind a pair of spectacles. "I believe the duchess said that there are two young ladies here in need of a governess."

Isabella and Trevor stepped farther into the chamber, and while Isabella took a seat on the chair opposite the newcomer Trevor stepped forward to stand with his back to the fire, his arms crossed, as if waiting for the women to begin the discussion.

For all that Miss Nightingale had tried to hide her fine looks, however, it was impossible not to see that in the right gown and the right coiffure the young woman would be stunning. Remembering the governesses who had gone before, Isabella slanted a glance at Trevor to determine whether he was moved by the beauty of the governess, but he did not seem to be affected. Instead he said, "I have two sisters who are in need of your care, ma'am. Eleanor, the eldest, is seventeen and will be making her come-out next year. Belinda, who is thirteen, is still in the schoolroom. I presume you are equally able to instruct them both?"

Showing no signs of infatuation with the duke, Miss Nightingale nodded. "Yes, Your Grace," she said, pulling a letter from her reticule and handing it to him. "Here are my references. One from the Countess of Cornwall and one from Miss Beeton, who was my employer at Miss Beeton's Home for Young Ladies. I believe you will find everything in order."

Isabella noted with approval the mention of Miss Beeton's school. The academy had a good reputation, and Isabella wondered if, like many other of the teachers, Miss Nightingale had once been a student there. "You have the usual abilities to instruct the girls in music and art, I hope. Miss Eleanor in particular is quite gifted artistically and could do with a bit of guidance on that score."

Miss Nightingale turned to Isabella. "Yes, my lady. I am able to instruct the girls in art, music, needlework, geography, and even, if it is desired, the classics and Latin. I can assure you that I am well able to do whatever is necessary to prepare young ladies for their entrance into society. And I am able to do so without succumbing to the charms of the master of the house."

If Isabella had been drinking something she would have showered the room with it. She could not hold back a laugh.

But Trevor did not find the words so amusing. "I am not in the habit of seducing the females in my employ, Miss Nightingale."

"I take it my sister told you of the previous governesses in this household, Miss Nightingale?" Isabella asked, giving Trevor a speaking look. It would not do to frighten their only candidate for governess before she even began the job.

But Miss Nightingale was clearly not one to be scared away by a bit of masculine bluster. "Indeed she did, Lady Wharton," the governess said carefully. "If I may be frank, I am quite capable of keeping to my station. I fear that young women who find themselves needing to seek employment as governesses are often too young and impressionable for the position. Though the master of the house, and at times the sons, do sometimes see the governess as an object of desire and take advantage, other times the governess strays into the unfortunate habit of seeing her employer as a romantic hero. I will not tolerate the former, and I would not stoop to the latter. I am here to do a job, and I will do so to the best of my abilities. And I have no intention of falling in love with anyone in the process."

Isabella could not help but be impressed. It took a great deal of self-possession to speak plainly about such delicate topics, but Miss Nightingale had managed to do so without insulting Trevor or her past employers. Isabella had little doubt that some of those past employers had been so foolish as to see the pretty young woman as a target for their lust. She hoped that Miss Nightingale had put them in their place. Isabella did not like the idea of the proud young woman before her being made to suffer the unwanted attentions of men who saw her as little more than a toy for their amusement. Sometime she despised men.

"I thank you for your frankness," Trevor said, his earlier pique replaced by something that looked like admiration. Isabella felt a pang somewhere in the vicinity of her heart. It was all well and good for her to appreciate Miss Nightingale's strength, but she hadn't counted on Trevor noticing the quality as well. "I can assure you that while you are in my employ you will suffer no untoward advances from me or my male servants."

"I believe my sister explained to you the terms under which the duke is willing to offer you the position?" Isabella asked, suddenly wishing, for reasons she was not ready to examine, for the interview to be at an end.

If Miss Nightingale noticed anything untoward in Lady Isabella's manner, however, she did not say anything about it. "Indeed, Lady Wharton, the duchess was quite clear about the terms and I am prepared to take them. I know that Miss Eleanor is to make her debut next year, so there is no doubt much to be done to prepare her. I presume both girls have had dance lessons?"

Trevor frowned. "I really could not say, Miss Nightingale. I made sure that the other governesses saw to their academic instruction, but as to the social niceties, I have no idea."

Miss Nightingale gave a brisk nod. "I will see to it if they have not. We have a year to prepare for Miss Eleanor's London debut, after all."

"But there is a local ball to which Eleanor will receive an invitation," Isabella said. "Perhaps we could have some sort of instruction in the coming week to ensure that she will not embarrass herself."

Unfazed by the news, the governess simply said, "I believe that will be quite possible." Her tone conveying just the right blend of authority and obedience, Miss Nightingale continued, "If there is nothing further, I would like to be shown to my room, and then meet the young ladies."

Exchanging a look with Trevor, who raised his brows in approbation, Isabella led Miss Nightingale from the room and up to the attics where her room would be.

It was not until they were on the stairs that Isabella realized Trevor had deferred to her in the matter. As if she were the mistress of Nettlefield. It was an unsettling realization, not only because she was in fact an unwelcome houseguest but also because she was confused to realize just how right performing the duty felt. If she weren't careful she'd find herself falling in love with the master of the house just like the previous governesses had done.

And that, she knew, would be far more dangerous than anything her late husband had ever inflicted upon her.

"What the devil is the matter with you?" Blakemore demanded in lieu of greeting the next morning as Trevor rode toward him. "You look as if you wish to throttle someone. And I know it can't be me, because my winning personality does not inspire men to murder."

Any other day, Trevor would have responded to his friend's humor with a good-natured setdown. But the duke had spent the night before trying to forget Thistleback's insidious words about Isabella and failing miserably. That the baronet had considered Trevor might not find his words offensive was disgusting enough, but that he had attempted to poison the duke against Isabella made his blood boil.

He had never understood the sort of man who considered ladies fair game for his casual scorn. To Trevor's mind a gentleman had an obligation to protect not just the ladies in his care but all women from harm of any kind. That Isabella had suffered both emotional and physical harm from her husband was infuriating. But Thistleback compounded the abuse by carrying the tales to whoever would listen. God knew how many other members of the *ton* the fop had told the story. And short of making the fellow leave the country, there was little Trevor could do to stop him from carrying his hateful tales to whomever he met.

"Not in the mood for chatter today, Blakemore,"

Trevor growled, knowing he was being an ass but doing it anyway. "Let's just ride."

If Blakemore thought it odd that his normally good-natured friend was barely civil, he did not make mention of it. Instead he guided his horse after Trevor's, and the two men set off on a cross-country gallop that made conversation impossible.

Grateful for the other man's acceptance, Trevor gave the stallion his head and lost himself in the concentration necessary to ensure neither he nor the horse was injured in the course of their ride. The terrain of the moors and the stark countryside had led more than one man to his death, and Trevor had no plans to become one of them. Even so, he rode harder than he normally did, relishing the way that his body became one with the horse as they tore across the countryside.

Finally, sensing that Beowulf needed a bit of rest, Trevor let the horse slow down and come to a stop near the edge of a rocky hillock.

"Want to tell me what that was about?" Blakemore panted as he brought his own mount to a stop near Trevor's. "You only go full out like that when you are in a temper. And I don't know that I've seen you this overset since you were first summoned to London by the dowager. Has she sent another emissary to lure you back?"

Removing his hat to let the wind ruffle his hair, Trevor allowed his own breathing to return to normal before he spoke. "I took Lady Wharton and my sisters into York yesterday to go dress shopping."

Blakemore blanched. "Ye gods, no wonder you're livid. A shopping trip could make any man go mad."

"It wasn't the shopping trip, you simpleton," Trevor

said with the easy insult of long friendship. "We saw Mrs. Palmer and her houseguest, Sir Lionel Thistleback, there."

"Ah." The other man nodded. "I was unlucky enough to meet the fellow at the tavern on the night he arrived. A more perfect example of 'toadeater' I don't believe I'll ever meet." He shuddered at the memory. "I take it he made much of your title, then?"

"Among other things," Trevor said tersely. He did not like to speak of what Thistleback had said about Isabella. Trevor knew without having spoken to her of the matter that she would die rather than have anyone know what her husband had subjected her to. Even so, he needed for Blakemore to know just how dangerous the man was. Especially given the fact that Isabella's carriage had been tampered with. "I am going to tell you something, Blakemore, but you must swear to me never to repeat it."

All traces of his earlier teasing gone, Blakemore nodded. "Of course."

Quickly Trevor told the other man what Thistleback had said yesterday in the dress shop. Trevor didn't mention the other threats against Isabella. The fact that she was being tormented in his own home was something of which he was not proud, and he could not bring himself to admit as much to his friend.

When Trevor was finished telling Blakemore about Thistleback's insinuations, the other man uttered an oath. "I now do not wonder at your mood. I wonder that you were able to restrain yourself from running him through on the spot."

"Indeed." It felt good to have his own response to Thistleback's remarks confirmed. "I stopped myself only because I knew that Lady Wharton's good name would be further tarnished by the blackguard's death."

"I take it you haven't spoken to the lady about the matter," Blakemore said carefully.

"How can I?" Trevor demanded. " 'Lady Wharton, I thank you for your attention to my sisters; would you mind terribly telling me if your husband beat you?' "

Blakemore scratched a spot between his eyebrows. "No, I don't suppose that would work. It isn't as if you have the right to demand it of her. She's here to lure you back to London, not to have you interrogate her over her past. And it isn't as if the news reflects upon her. Not that the *ton* would see it that way. To their way of thinking all blame falls to the lady, whether she is the one in the wrong or not."

"Exactly," Trevor sighed, closing his eyes in frustration. "Whatever the reason, she is here now, and as such is under my protection. I will do what I can to ensure that the fellow does not spread his rumors, but short of packing him off on the next ship bound for America, I have little recourse."

"I will do what I can to see if the man has spoken to anyone else in the village about the matter," Blakemore said. "I would think that a social climber like that would see his connection to Lady Wharton as something to be nurtured. He risks her good opinion, and therefore her social cachet, by spreading tales about her."

"I hope you are right," Trevor said, grateful to have his friend's ear on the matter. For all that he played at being the idle country gentleman, Blakemore was shrewd at navigating the social waters of the upper classes. More so than Trevor was, that was certain. Which reminded him of another matter. "I almost forgot to tell you. Lady Wharton has engaged a governess for my sisters."

Accepting the change in subject without protest, Blakemore shook his head at the news. "I hope you have found some way to make yourself unpalatable to the woman, Ormonde," he said. "I grow weary of listening to governesses wax poetic over your kind eyes."

"I think this one will be able to remain immune to my charms," Trevor said, turning his horse about for the journey back to Blakemore's estate. "She has quite sensible thoughts on the matter of proper behavior—both for governesses and for their employers."

"What is this paragon of virtue named?" Blakemore asked, guiding his own horse with his knees to follow Beowulf.

"Miss Nightingale, of all things," Trevor said with a laugh.

"Sounds like an alias to me," Blakemore said thoughtfully. "Not nearly as retiring and drab as one normally expects from a governess's name."

"Oh, she's hardly that," Trevor said emphatically. "She's self-possessed, but hardly what I'd call drab."

"Interesting," his friend said. "Perhaps this one will withstand your charms after all."

Trevor rolled his eyes at his friend's jab. He was running out of patience. Which reminded him of another matter requiring patience.

"I almost forgot to tell you what's happened with Palmer!" he said, drawing Blakemore up short again.

"If you tell me that he, too, has engaged a governess with a bird name, I will have to adopt a child so that I can hire one as well," Trevor's friend said glibly.

"Worse," Trevor said, telling the other man what had happened to young Mr. Jacob Carson.

When Trevor had finished, Lord Blakemore whistled. "When it rains on your estate, it pours. And what a coil that Palmer should be involved in this affair as well as hosting that worm Thistleback."

"Men like Palmer will always be the sort to attract dirty dealings," Trevor said with a scowl. "The only question now is whether I will be able to convince Moneypenny to bring Carson before me tomorrow rather than Hanging Harry."

"I should think the man would be willing to sell his sister if enough silver crossed his palm," Blakemore said cynically. "It's a nasty business, but you'd be doing it out of pure reasons."

"Aye," Trevor agreed. "I suppose I'll have to send someone out to find Moneypenny when I get back so that he can bring Carson before me. I've got the Joneses hiding him while Palmer's men are looking for him."

"And I always thought you lived a dull existence," Blakemore said with a shake of his head. "The past week at your house makes mine look like the pump room at Bath."

To Isabella's surprise, the magistrate's court for the village of Nettledean took place not in the local tavern or public rooms but in the drawing room of Nettlefield House. She wasn't quite sure she was comfortable with that.

"It is at the discretion of the magistrate where these things are held," the duke informed her as they made their way to the designated spot after breakfast. "And as my father always held them here, I decided to keep up the tradition."

"Do you not feel a bit . . ." Isabella struggled to find the words for what she was trying to say. "I mean . . . that is to say, is it not, uncomfortable to have accused men in and out of your home like this? What of your sisters?"

She was in a particularly tetchy mood after yet another sleepless night worrying about the anonymous threats being made against her. And now she had the added burden of Thistleback's presence in the neighborhood to inflate her worries. She knew she was being short with Ormonde, but she found she was unable to stop herself.

She had chosen to wear her most demure day dress, an exquisitely cut wool gown in deep forest green, for the occasion. The neckline was more modest than most of her other gowns and she did not want to draw attention to herself. Even so, she had not missed Ormonde's intense gaze quickly masked when she entered the breakfast room.

Now, however, he gave her a sharp look and she feared the amity they'd shared the day before had been shattered by her ill temper. And who could blame him?

"I would hardly allow the proceedings to be held here if I thought it were possible that my sisters would be endangered by them, Lady Wharton." His lips were pursed with annoyance. "The men who come before me are hardly hardened criminals. The most we get are petty thefts and poachers. We are not London, after all."

"Of course not," Isabella said, trying to keep a tight rein on her temper, "but even so, these are not the sort of men you would in the general scheme of things invite into your drawing room, are they? I much prefer the way these things are handled in town, with the courts meeting in their own rooms."

Good lord, she thought. She had turned into one of those insufferable ladies who did nothing but compare whatever vicinity they found themselves in unfavorably to London: "Oh la, London is ever so much more cosmopolitan than Manchester, Sir Thingummy."

Just as they stopped outside the drawing room, Ormonde turned to face her, his annoyance evident. "I asked you to come here today, my lady, so that you could see that I have responsibilities here at Nettlefield House that affect not only the people on my land, but the people of the surrounding community as well." His face was stern and Isabella could not help but feel a bit like a schoolgirl being taken to task. Not that she didn't deserve it. "I take my duties quite seriously, and I do not undertake them lightly or without a certain understanding that by doing so I am doing my part to keep this county safe. If you cannot attend these proceedings without constantly comparing them to the ones in London, which I venture to guess you know very little about as well, then I shall have to ask you to leave off and return to my grandmother with the news that you have failed in your mission."

Isabella flinched at his tone. Not only had she insulted him, but she'd also endangered the very reason she'd come to Yorkshire in the first place. She mentally cursed her sharp tongue and said, "I am sorry, Your Grace. You are quite right. I am afraid that I can only blame my worry over my own situation for my ill temper. Please do let me see how you conduct your duties as magistrate and I promise that I will keep my tongue firmly between my teeth."

Twin wrinkles appeared just between the duke's brows. "You apologize?" he asked, almost as if he suspected her of some trick or other malfeasance.

"I do indeed," she said sincerely. "I hope that you will—"

She left off speaking when she realized that while they were arguing Templeton, having decided that it was time to begin the proceedings, had instructed the footmen to open the double doors leading into the drawing room.

"His Grace, the Duke of Ormonde, and Lady Wharton," the butler intoned, for all the world as if he were announcing new arrivals at a ball.

Feeling a flush burgeoning in her cheeks, Isabella took the duke's arm, which he had offered almost as soon as his butler began to speak, and allowed him to lead her into the chamber.

So much for keeping to the background, she thought wryly as she held her head high and walked toward the farthest corner chair in the room. Once she was settled there, she allowed herself to glance around the room at the people in attendance—only to realize that they were the only ones there.

From his seat beside a low trestle table Ormonde said, "You may bring in the parties in the first matter, Templeton."

Wanting to comment but determined to keep quiet lest she further annoy the duke, Isabella watched as the doors were opened yet again to admit a dough-faced older gentleman attired in the lace and silks of the previous century, complete with a periwig. And beside him

walked Sir Lionel Thistleback, his own attire more up-
to-date but just as eye-catching with his brightly em-
broidered lavender waistcoat and ostentatious fobs and
cravat pins.

"Sir Lionel Thistleback and Mr. Humphrey Palmer,"
said Templeton as the two men entered the chamber and
stepped forward to stand before the duke.

The two men greeted the duke, who inclined his head
and showed no sign that he'd expected them this morning. Fortunately, to Isabella's mind, Sir Lionel didn't notice her perched in the rear of the chamber, and she meant
to keep it that way. If she could have made herself disappear, she would have done so. Ormonde, she was pleased
to notice, looked none too pleased to see the men before
him. If she wasn't mistaken he looked even angrier now
than he had earlier when they'd argued.

"Mr. Josiah Moneypenny, constable, and his prisoner, Mr. Jacob Carson," Templeton announced as a man
who was clearly some sort of merchant entered the room
leading a very large, wild-eyed young man who topped
his captor by several inches.

This must be Mrs. Jones's brother, Isabella thought.
There was some resemblance between the prisoner
and the housewife Isabella had met two days ago,
though the prisoner was rather more unkempt than Mrs.
Jones had been.

"Yes, thank you, Templeton," the duke said with a
grimace at his butler's treatment of the proceedings. "I
will ring for you if I have further need."

Turning to Palmer, Trevor asked, "Is Sir Lionel a solicitor, that you have brought him along with you today, sir?"

The bewigged man raised a jeweled quizzing glass to

his eye and said, "My dear duke, I have brought Sir Lionel along as a witness to the crime, of course. Any fellow can see he has more presence than a lowly solicitor, surely."

"A witness, eh?" Ormonde asked, turning his gaze to the baronet. "How can you have witnessed a crime in Yorkshire a few days ago when to my knowledge you were not yet in the county?"

Thistleback smiled with the same oily condescension that had always made Isabella feel slightly ill. "Why, Your Grace, you are correct in your knowledge of my whereabouts. But I received news of the crime in a letter from Mr. Palmer, and as such I believe that makes me a witness. Does it not?"

The look of incredulity on Ormonde's face said that it most certainly did not. But rather than telling Thistleback to leave, Trevor shrugged and said, "I believe you swore out a warrant for Mr. Carson last week, Mr. Palmer, and it would appear that Mr. Moneypenny has arrested the fellow. What offense do you claim against Mr. Carson?"

Mr. Palmer inclined his head and smiled, revealing a mouthful of yellowed teeth. "Why, my gamekeeper caught Mr. Carson on my land with a dead rabbit in his hands and the very trap that killed the creature only feet away from him. I cannot hold with poachers on my land, sir. Stealing the very meat from my family's mouths."

Isabella felt ill watching the oily man claiming such a crime against himself. Poaching was a problem, but surely if the man took better care of his tenants it would not be necessary. She had seen how worn and dirty the prisoner's clothing was.

"Mr. Carson," the duke said, turning to the man still being held fast by Moneypenny. "Is there anything you wish to say in your defense?"

"Answer His Grace, you great looby," Moneypenny said, shaking the man by the arm despite his greater height and breadth. "Tell him what ye told me afore."

"Begging your pardon, Yer Grace," the prisoner said with a surprisingly soft voice, "I were that desperate. It's been a hard winter and my Sarah was just brought to bed again. Iffen there was work hereabouts or if Mr. Palmer would stop raising the rents, then mebbe—"

"Do not try to blame this on my friend Palmer, you thieving rascal," Thistleback interrupted before the man could finish his statement. "If you were to exercise some self-control and weren't constantly breeding them perhaps—"

"That will do, Thistleback," Ormonde said sharply. "There are ladies present."

"The devil you say," Thistleback burst out, scanning the room until he saw Isabella in the back and stopping, his mouth agape. Turning back to Ormonde, he demanded, "What is she doing here, Ormonde? This is no place for a lady. Surely you can see that!"

"She is here because she wishes to be here, Sir Lionel," Isabella said, standing and walking toward the front. "I will thank you to keep your opinions to yourself. And stop interrupting the proceedings. I am quite confident that you are not even a proper witness as these things go."

"Thank you for that, Lady Wharton," the duke said dryly. "Now, if you will return to your seat, perhaps we may continue?"

Stopping halfway from the front of the room where the men were gathered, Isabella saw that the duke was saying something to her with his eyes. Just what it was he was saying she could not discern. But it was enough to convince her that perhaps she had best keep out of the matter. It would not do to let her dislike for Sir Lionel and Mr. Palmer color whatever Trev—the duke, she corrected herself—was going to decide about Mr. Carson.

Once she was seated, the duke continued, "Mr. Carson, I can well imagine that you have had a difficult year on Mr. Palmer's estate. However, that does not give you leave to steal game from his land whenever you wish."

"But, Yer Grace," the man objected, his hangdog expression growing even more morose, "I cannot leave Sarah and me bairns to take care o'themselves. Please, Yer Grace—"

Ormonde raised his hand to forestall any further protest. "I have seen the affidavits from Mr. Palmer's gamekeeper. It would seem that by your own admission you are guilty."

To Isabella's dismay the prisoner seemed to diminish before her eyes, his shoulders sagging, all the fight gone out of him. Surely the duke would not sentence the man to jail or, worse, to hanging for one stolen rabbit. She watched with a sinking stomach as Sir Lionel patted Mr. Palmer on the back at his apparent victory.

"However," the duke said, and Isabella felt her breath catch in her throat, "since you have been held in gaol for the past week while we were waiting for the affidavits to be sworn, I will consider your punishment to have already taken place and I will request that at this time Mr. Moneypenny free you to go about your business. But if I hear any word of you or your sons poaching again, I will see to it that you are punished much more harshly."

While Ormonde had continued speaking Isabella had

felt her eyes fill with tears and to her surprise she found her hands clasped before her in some sort of silent supplication. She realized now what he had meant when he talked about his duties as a magistrate being important to the surrounding community. What if Mr. Carson had found himself before someone like her father had been or, worse, like Wharton had been? It was horrific to imagine that in someone else's hands the man might have found himself transported or, worse, hanged.

"This is absurd!" Mr. Palmer said, his face turning nearly the color of his puce waistcoat. "The man was poaching on my land and I expect you to mete out the justice he deserves, Ormode."

"I have done so, Mr. Palmer," the duke said curtly, rising from his seat before them. "I suggest you reconsider the manner in which you decide to raise your rents and refuse to make repairs on the cottages on your estates. I realize that poaching is a crime, but I cannot fault a man for doing so when he has been driven to desperation by the mismanagement of your estates. I would suggest that you look into getting a more competent bailiff if you wish to keep this same thing from happening again."

Trevor stood his ground while Palmer and Thistleback fumed before turning to stalk from the room and out of the house.

"I canna thank ye enough, Yer Grace," Mr. Carson said, shaking the duke's hand like a pump handle.

"Thank me by never poaching on Palmer's land again, Carson," the duke said. "And if you are looking for honest work, come back next week and have a talk with my head groom. I've heard from Moneypenny here that you are a dab hand with a horse."

With another barrage of thanks, Carson, followed by a grinning Moneypenny, stepped out of the chamber and into the hallway beyond.

"Now do you understand?" Ormonde asked as he waited for Isabella to cross the room to stand at his side. "I cannot abandon these people simply because my cousin had the misfortune to get himself killed before he could have a son. I won't do it."

"I understand that you are tied to the people here, certainly. But I begin to wonder if some sort of compromise might be worked out."

"What do you mean by that?" Ormonde asked, his auburn brows rising in question.

"I'm not sure yet," Isabella said, unwilling to voice her idea just yet. For now it was enough that she was almost finished fulfilling his requirements so that he would accompany her to London. She did care about what happened to the people here and the people of the duchy of Ormonde, but for now she was content with the knowledge that her sister's engagement was well on its way to being preserved from the dowager's interference.

For now, that was enough.

Ten

"No, Ellie, turn your foot like this." Belinda demonstrated the step for her sister. Much to everyone's surprise, the girl who had little use for fashion or social graces had taken to dancing like a cat to cream.

The duke had been co-opted into the dance lessons, as had his friend Sir Lucien Blakemore.

Miss Nightingale had taken up a position at the pianoforte.

Now Isabella was watching as Ormonde, partnering Belinda, stood back as she demonstrated the step for her sister.

"That's what I'm doing, Belinda." Eleanor was, sadly, not quite as adept at dancing as her younger sister, and her frustration with the activity was beginning to show. "We may as well stop. I'm never going to be able to do this properly before the Palmers' ball."

"Do not give up so soon, Miss Eleanor," coaxed Sir Lucien. "I have it on very good authority that the young men of the county are quite looking forward to dancing every set with you."

The duke looked as if he wished to hunt down these

young men and thrash them, but the other man's words seemed to do the trick with Eleanor. She blushed prettily and asked, "Really? You aren't just saying that?"

The baronet placed his hand over his heart. "On my honor, it's the truth."

"Don't be so missish, Ellie," her sister said with a roll of her eyes. "Of course they'll want to dance with you. You're prettier than either of the Green sisters and you won't see them sitting out any of the dances."

Sensing that a sisterly spat was imminent, Isabella interrupted. "I think you have mastered the polonaise for now, Eleanor. Why don't we try the waltz?"

"Isn't that a bit fast for the country?" Ormonde asked with a frown. He was clearly having some issues with his baby sister moving into the adult world.

Before Isabella could speak, Miss Nightingale said, "Your Grace, it is perfectly acceptable for a young lady to dance the waltz at a country ball. When she goes to London, of course, she will need permission from the patronesses of Almack's, but here it will be quite unremarkable."

"Miss Nightingale," Isabella instructed, "will you please play a waltz? Sir Lucien and I will demonstrate."

If either the duke or the governess objected to the notion, neither of them said it aloud. Miss Nightingale simply nodded, and the duke folded his arms across his chest, his mouth pursed in a grim line as he watched the couple.

Blakemore was an excellent dancer, and Isabella had to admit that it was not unpleasant to be held in such a handsome man's arms. They twirled through the drawing room, where earlier the footmen had been asked to roll up the carpets for the impromptu lessons.

Isabella knew the precise moment when the baronet lost his concentration and missed a step. It was when Miss Nightingale coughed. It was discreet and barely audible over the sound of the pianoforte, but as soon as the noise pierced the air Isabella felt her partner stiffen and stumble.

He caught himself at once, but not before Ormonde stepped forward and said, "I think you've demonstrated enough, Luce; let me show them how it's done."

Isabella was startled by the duke's intrusion, not least because she had not thought him able to perform the steps of the waltz. But, for all that his parents had kept him buried in the country, the duke danced beautifully. And Isabella could not deny that the feeling of his strong hand at her waist and the other in her hand was intoxicating. She had been unwilling to admit it, but she could no longer deny that she found the Duke of Ormonde to be devilishly attractive. In part because she sensed that his regard, once won, was worth far more than the easily dismissed charms of the men she was accustomed to back in London.

Once, twice, she and Trevor whirled through the room, the music of the pianoforte weaving a spell around them, almost as if they were alone in the room. The duke's intense blue gaze sending coils of heat from her chest to her belly, and lower. What would it be like to have that gaze on her in a more intimate setting? A shiver ran through her at the thought.

"Cold?" Trevor asked, pulling her ever so slightly closer. They were still perfectly respectable, but Isabella was now close enough to inhale the sandalwood and clove scent of him. She could feel the warmth of his skin through the fabric of his coat and gloves where her hands held on for dear life.

"I just felt a little chill, that's all," Isabella said, sounding breathy to her own ears. She could tell by the way his eyes narrowed that he knew the real reason for her shiver, and she could not, for love or money, look away. It was as if some invisible force kept their eyes locked together across the scant space between them.

In that moment, Isabella felt all of her cares fall away. The threats, the worries over her sister, the danger Thistleback posed to Isabella's reputation. None of it mattered but this man, with his strong arms clasping her waist and hand, leading her through a dance that felt more intimate than any of the moments she'd spent in Ralph's bed. There was something about this man, this dance, that rang with truth in a way that threatened her very soul.

As if sensing how close she was to tears, Trevor said in a voice so low that only she could hear it, "Easy. Easy there."

At last, the final strains of the music died out, and Trevor and Isabella came slowly to a stop. She was pleased to note that he, too, was a little out of breath. And was it her imagination, or was he taking his time letting her go?

"Now that is how a waltz should be performed," Belinda said with a sigh.

But Eleanor would have none of it, "You have never even seen a waltz before today. How would you know?"

"I've seen pictures," the younger girl retorted. "And I think Trevor and Isabella make a lovely couple."

Sir Lucien disguised his guffaw behind a cough. To Isabella's relief, the duke did not say anything at all.

"Do you think you'll be able to dance the waltz, Eleanor?" she asked, careful not to make eye contact with any of the adults in the room. It was one thing to get lost in the dance while it was going on but quite another to reveal just how transported she had been.

"I think so," Eleanor replied. "But I would rather dance with Sir Lucien, I think. I love you, Trevor, but I'd rather not dance the waltz with my brother if I can help it."

Now it was Trevor's turn to roll his eyes. "I suppose it's to be expected. But remember I'll be watching, Luce."

The other man threw up his hands in innocence. "You have nothing to fear from me, Your Grace. I've known Eleanor since she was in the cradle." He turned to the young lady. "No offense intended, my dear."

"None taken," Eleanor said with a laugh. "You are hardly my notion of love's young dream, you know."

Miss Nightingale coughed. Whether it was to cover up a laugh Isabella could not say. But it caught Sir Lucien's notice. "Are you ill, Miss Nightingale?" he inquired sweetly.

"Not at all, my lord," she responded, her lovely face impassive. "I simply had a tickle in my throat. Pray forgive me for calling attention to myself."

Eleanor and Sir Lucien had just begun to dance the steps of the waltz when Isabella heard a slight throat-clearing sound behind her. Turning, she saw Templeton. Not wishing to disturb the lesson, she gestured for the butler to follow her into the hall. She felt Trevor's gaze on her the whole time, but he made no move to follow them.

"What is it?" she asked the older man once they were out of the drawing room.

"This came for you just now, my lady," he said. "It is

marked 'Urgent,' so I thought you would wish to see it at once."

He handed her a neatly folded missive, her name scrawled in a firm, masculine hand on the front. There was no direction on the letter, so it could not have come by post.

"Who brought this, Templeton?" she asked, trying to decipher the crest on the wax seal.

"A footman from the Palmers' household, my lady," he said. "The fellow said that he would not wait for a reply."

Isabella felt her heart drop. "Oh, it is doubtless the recipe I requested from Mrs. Palmer yesterday," she said with what she hoped was a carefree laugh. "I'll just take this up to my room and put it with my things."

She was halfway up the stairs when she heard a voice call her name. Turning, she saw Trevor at the landing below her.

"Is aught amiss?" he asked. "Templeton said you'd received a letter."

She tried to discern from Trevor's tone and expression whether he knew who had sent the letter, but it was impossible to judge from this distance. Deciding to brazen the thing out, she said, "Oh, it is just a note from Mrs. Palmer about a freckle remedy we discussed at the dress shop in York. I tend to freckle quite badly when I spend any time in the sun and she was kind enough to offer me the recipe for her own remedy."

Even from this distance, Isabella could see that the duke didn't believe her one bit. Even so, he did not press her.

"I rather like freckles," he said with a half smile. "I hope you won't get rid of them all."

He spoke as if he would have a chance to see her freckles up close, but Isabella knew that he would not. It was regrettable since she felt the pull of attraction between them, even now when she was annoyed at his curiosity.

"I'm afraid you are the only gentleman of my acquaintance who does," she said wryly. "Most men seem to see them as a sign of a low nature."

"I suspect I am the only gentleman of your acquaintance who does many things, Lady Isabella." The duke paused at the foot of the stairs, his hand resting on the banister as if he were debating whether to follow her up.

And suddenly Isabella knew that they weren't talking about freckles anymore.

Not wishing him to see the doubt in her eyes, she hastily excused herself and hurried up to her room.

After the dance lesson, the girls and Miss Nightingale had returned to the schoolroom and Lucien had gone home. Since Isabella had not returned, Trevor decided to do a bit of sleuthing.

It had been easy enough to ask Templeton whether her letter had indeed come from the Palmer house. When the butler affirmed that it had, there was little doubt in Trevor's mind that it had come not from the lady of the house but from either her husband or her guest. The only question was, what could either Palmer or Thistleback need to correspond with Lady Isabella about?

Though he had no idea what the letter said, the duke knew in his gut that it was not a friendly missive. Though Thistleback had tried to give the appearance of a fond former acquaintance, there had been something in the man's manner the other day in York—something lurking just beneath the surface—that set every protective instinct in Trevor's body on high alert.

As for Palmer, the only reason Trevor could imagine his neighbor could have for contacting Isabella would be in an attempt to have her influence his own decision in the matter of Mr. Carson. Though Trevor had a hard time imagining Palmer would go out of his way for something like that. He seemed like the sort who would send a minion in his stead.

Isabella had taken a tray in her room for dinner, so Trevor had been unable to ask her any further questions about the letter. And, left to his own devices, he had retired to his study to brood. He had grown accustomed to having his orders obeyed, both as the head of his household and as a landowner. And part of him wanted to simply climb the stairs up to Isabella's bedchamber and demand that she tell him who had sent the letter and what they wanted of her. But as she was a guest in his home and not one of his tenants or even a blood relation, he could do nothing of the sort.

It was a damned coil.

The mantle clock had just marked the hour of midnight, and he was ready to declare himself a suspicious fool and go to bed when he heard the squeak of the door leading from the drawing room to the garden. Grateful he'd let the candles burn themselves out, in the glow of the firelight he rose and stepped out into the darkness.

As his eyes adjusted to the dark, he saw a female figure, doubtless Isabella, creep along the flagstone path toward the summerhouse.

It was simply too coincidental to imagine that she had been unable to sleep and decided to take a midnight stroll.

Isabella's slippers made no sound as she moved across the garden path toward the small outbuilding, and Trevor was careful to tread softly as well. He had no intention of embarrassing her. He only wished to ensure that whoever she was meeting did nothing to physically harm her.

"You came," Trevor heard a man say as Isabella neared the entrance. In the dim light, Trevor could see the man looming in the doorway, the white of his cravat gleaming in the darkness, though it was impossible to see his face.

"You gave me little choice," Isabella said coolly from the bottom of the steps. "I could hardly ignore your summons when you hold such a revelation over my head."

As Trevor watched, the figure bowed and gestured for his quarry to enter the summerhouse. Trevor was reminded of the spider and the fly.

"Come now, Lady Isabella," the man said. "We are old friends, are we not? We've shared such *intimate* times together. You know that I would never do anything that would truly harm you." The fellow's tone made Trevor's skin crawl.

"I know nothing of the sort," Isabella said as Trevor, making sure to keep out of their lines of sight, slipped forward and crouched beneath the open window of the little retreat.

"We are not friends, Thistleback. Nor have we ever been such." Trevor heard the note of revulsion in her voice and wanted more than anything to comfort her. But he had to hear the swine's demands first. "You were my husband's crony and were witness to some of the most humiliating scenes of my existence. I do not mind telling you that I had hoped never to see you again."

"Tsk-tsk, Lady," the baronet chided. "There's no need for harsh words. I feel sure that you and I can come to some sort of understanding. After all, I would not wish for you, the widow of my dear friend, to come to any harm."

Trevor had little doubt that as a boy Thistleback had plucked the wings from flies just to watch them suffer. But to Trevor's great admiration, Isabella was not cowed. Or if she was, she didn't let it show. "Cut line," she snapped. "I wish to spend as little time in your company as possible. Tell me what you want so that I may get back to my bed."

"Ah yes." Thistleback's tone was ugly. "I have little doubt that he is wondering where you've wandered off to. Poor old Ralph is barely cold in his grave and you've already found a replacement for him. But then, I suppose you consider the duke a reward for enduring all those years with your husband. I wonder if he realized you were simply biding your time, waiting for him to die. Certainly he must have guessed as much while he was employing the lash."

When she did not respond, Thistleback sighed and said, "Very well, if you are going to be like that, I suppose that I will get to the point. You, my lady, are like the proverbial cat, always landing on your feet. And as your old friend, I think that you would be willing to share that good fortune with me. As you know, my father is a tightfisted old fool and I could do with a bit of the ready to keep me afloat. You understand, do you not?"

But Isabella had clearly decided that the least she said to the blackmailing worm the better. "How much?"

The flatness of her tone made Trevor curse the darkness. There was something frightening about the degree

to which she'd removed all emotion from her tone. Thistleback clearly did not notice the change, however, or he
didn't care, because he responded in a pleasant tone, "I
think five hundred should cover things." He sounded like
a dinner companion settling a small wager.

"Pounds?" Isabella demanded, aghast. "You do know
that Wharton left me with only my widow's portion, do
you not? It is hardly enough to keep my household running. And certainly not so great as to allow me to give
you five hundred pounds."

Thistleback, it seemed, did not give a hang. "I also
know that you are very close to your dear sister, Ormonde's widow, who is rich as Croesus. She would not
have let you come away on your little adventure in the
north without plenty of pin money."

"I hardly expected to need five hundred pounds for
the journey," she pointed out. "It's Yorkshire, not Paris."

"How much do you have then?" Thistleback's voice
sounded peevish.

"I will give you fifty pounds and you'll be happy to
have it." Trevor was pleased to hear the finality in her tone.

"I suppose I can live with that," Thistleback agreed
grudgingly.

"And I expect you to be gone from here as soon as you
receive the money," Isabella continued, her voice hard.

Thistleback's laugh was ugly. "Fifty pounds is not
nearly enough to buy my departure, my dear." Gone was
the friendly, forced joviality. "I rather like it here in
Yorkshire. So many old friends."

"I'll get the fifty pounds to you tomorrow," Isabella
said brusquely. "I will try to get more from my sister,
but I warn you that if you cause harm to me or to the
members of this household, I will not pay you a cent."

"Excellent," Thistleback agreed. "Such a pleasure doing business with you, Lady Isabella. I hope you won't let this sour our previous acquaintance. After all, we share such happy memories."

Though he longed to beat the man to a bloody pulp, Trevor held back while Thistleback bounded down the stairs, whistling quietly as he went.

Trevor listened to the sounds of the night birds and the wind in the trees, thinking that Isabella would come out and go back into the house. But when he heard a muffled gasp, followed by a soft sob, he realized that she was weeping.

Damn it.

He was angry as hell with her for not telling him about this nonsense. What if Thistleback had decided to assault her? Or worse? All of this raced through Trevor's mind, even as he stepped loudly up the summerhouse stairs and walked in to see her huddled alone on the banquette seat.

He wanted to scold her, but what he wanted more was to take her in his arms and offer comfort.

The sound of boots on the stairs gave Isabella a start. Worried that Thistleback had returned, she stood, her back ramrod straight, but realized almost at once that the man who entered the summerhouse was Trevor.

Which, to her horror, made her feel worse.

"Your Grace," she said, her voice hoarse from tears. She cleared her throat and tried to sound normal. "I'm afraid I could not sleep."

But he was not so easily duped. Pressing his handkerchief, still warm from where it had been in his coat pocket, into her hand, he led her back to the bench. "Do not dissemble," he said curtly. "I heard it all."

Oh god. He'd heard it all.

To Isabella's surprise, however, she was not quite as mortified as she'd once thought she'd be.

There was no doubt that she hated for Trevor, who seemed to be so utterly decent, to know how her husband had humiliated her. But mixed in with the distress was relief. She had kept this secret so close to her for so long that finally having someone else—someone besides her sister—know the truth lessened her burden somehow.

"Then you know what my husband did to me," she said aloud, needing to hear the words. "You know that he beat me. What you don't know is that he sometimes did worse. And sometimes he did it in front of his good friend Thistleback."

Her voice was oddly calm. She would have thought saying these things—to Trevor of all people—would be painful, but all she felt was numb.

She felt the bench sink a little as he took a seat beside her. She was grateful, but also worried, that he didn't sit too close.

"If there were a way to bring your husband back to life so that I might kill him again, I would do it," he said quietly. "I'm of half a mind to kill Thistleback in his stead. Certainly he deserves it for what he said to you tonight."

Isabella had expected anger but not the threat of violence. Trevor was the last man she'd expect would resort to violence on her behalf. But she'd misjudged men before. Why not this one as well?

Hoping to lighten the mood, she said, "If such a thing were possible—resurrection, I mean—you'd be forced to wait your turn in the queue. I fear that Wharton was not as well loved as he thought he was."

But Trevor did not laugh. Instead anger seemed to radiate from him. "Why didn't you tell me Thistleback was threatening you?" he demanded, his hands clenched into fists at his sides. "Damn it, Isabella, how can you have been so foolish?"

"Because it is none of your affair," she said, feeling cornered. "The more attention we pay him, the better he likes it. And that's just what he wants."

"He wants more than attention, Isabella," Trevor said curtly. "He wants your fear as well. He enjoys seeing you flinch at his every word, never knowing if this will be the day that he reveals your secret to the world. He's a sick bastard who should not be allowed to walk freely about the countryside."

"How do *you* know what a man like that feels?" she demanded angrily. "You, who have lived here in Yorkshire all these years with your loving family and lovely, supportive neighborhood. You don't know what sort of things a man like that thrives on. You are too decent to know. Too noble."

"You make me sound like a cross between a milksop and a simpleton, madam," Trevor said, affronted. "Just because I have lived for most of my life in the country does not mean that I have no notion of how men behave. I have been to university; I am not as wet behind the ears as you seem to think me. And unfortunately, evil is the same no matter where it lives."

Isabella bit her lip. He was right. She did make him sound like less than a man. But she'd been so accustomed to thinking men were either all good or all bad that she'd forgotten that there were any number of men who were a bit of both. Who were aware that evil existed but weren't drawn into its cloying web.

"Perhaps that is true," she acceded, "but you cannot deny that the Thistlebacks of the world seem to thrive in the city."

"Do they, Isabella?" he asked. "Or is that simply where *you* have encountered them?"

"Yes," she admitted. "But all of this is beside the point. I know just what sort of man Thistleback is and I know how to deal with him."

"I suppose that paying him what he asks is your way of dealing with him?" Trevor demanded, frustration evident in his tone. "If you go about this your way then you'll simply be paying the man fifty pounds a week for the rest of your days."

Unable to remain seated, Isabella began to pace the summerhouse floor. "I cannot let him tell the polite world what I suffered at my husband's hands," she countered. "The *ton* might think me a bit wild now, but I will lose every bit of self-respect I have if it's known by all and sundry just how Ralph degraded me. I cannot let Thistleback do that to me. I will not."

"And I will not allow him to remain in Nettledean for one more day while he holds this threat over your head," Trevor said hotly. "In fact, I will ride over to the Palmers' first thing in the morning and demand that the blackguard leave at once."

"You will do no such thing," Isabella hissed, frustrated beyond all caring. "This is not your battle to fight. It is mine."

"Yes," he said, leaping up from the bench, "I see how you fight. By paying the bastard off."

"Keep your voice down!" Isabella said through clenched teeth. "Do you wish to rouse the household? I cannot think that you wish to be discovered with me in the summerhouse in the middle of the night."

"Do not tell me to lower my voice!" Trevor said, though he did speak in a quieter tone.

"And," he added, taking her by the upper arms, "I will be discovered in the summerhouse with whomever I please."

And on that nonsensical note he kissed her.

Eleven

$\mathcal{D}$espite the fact that she'd been longing for his kiss for days, Isabella was taken off guard.

It was the only explanation she could find for her utter devastation when Trevor took her in his arms. His lips were soft, and as they moved over hers Isabella found it difficult to believe that finally, finally, they were touching. Though she would have denied it if anyone had asked her if she desired such a thing even minutes before now, she knew now that she had been longing to feel his hands, his lips, his body, against hers from the beginning. And when he pulled her closer, opening his mouth over hers, she felt every last resistance melt away into nothingness, leaving in its place acceptance and an eagerness that Isabella could no longer deny.

She reveled in the feel of him against her, from the bristle of his unshaven cheeks to the solid strength of his shoulders and back beneath her hands. Everywhere their bodies touched, she felt the heat of their connection.

More than just physical, theirs was a meeting of two wounded souls. Isabella couldn't have said how she knew it, but deep within her she knew that Trevor had been damaged somewhere along the way. Perhaps not in the same way that Isabella had been, but there were different types and degrees of hurt. And she knew that Trevor had experienced it.

Giving in to the mix of desperation and desire that threatened to consume her, Isabella let her hands roam, slipping one into the open collar of his shirt, stroking against the hot skin of his throat and chest. When he slid one hand up to cup her breast, she gasped and slipped her other arm up to tangle in the soft curls at his neck.

In a silence punctuated only by occasional gasps of pleasure, they explored each other with the tactile curiosity of new lovers. And it wasn't long before restlessness had her shifting in his lap, trying to soothe the ache between her thighs. With a groan part pleasure, part pain, Trevor moved his hips beneath her. "Ah, god, Isabella, stop. For pity's sake."

Biting her lip against the feel of his hardness pressed against her softness, Isabella brought her mouth to his ear and whispered, "You do not seem to wish it." As if to prove her point, she rubbed herself against the bulge in his breeches.

Panting, he leaned his forehead against hers and said in a strained voice, "I do not want to take you here. It's not fitting."

And just like that, she remembered just where they were. And why they were here. The pulse of desire that had felt so desperate seconds before was replaced with embarrassment.

Making as if to scramble off of him, Isabella tried to shift away but found herself in a hard grasp. Trevor kissed her gently and ran a finger down over the slope of her nose. "You deserve better," he said softly. "You deserve the best. And the best is not a lumpy bench seat in a summerhouse where anyone might stumble upon us."

She had not thought him capable of surprising her more, but Isabella felt her mouth fall open at his declaration. She'd never considered herself an overly sentimental sort, but Trevor's words brought forth a lump of emotion in her chest that no amount of common sense could dispel. When had a man ever thought so much of her that he chose to defer his own needs in order to satisfy hers?

"You are right," she said, afraid that he would hear the tremor in her voice. She realized just how close she'd been to giving herself to a man she had known for less than a week. It was slightly shocking. She had vowed when Ralph died that she would never put herself in a man's power without first learning all she could about him. And yet here she was placing herself in danger all because of a handsome face.

Did the duke even like her, she wondered, much less hold her in the sort of esteem she would need to ever submit to the sort of relationship they'd been about to embark upon? She knew that he was a good man. She'd seen that time and again in his dealings with his sisters. But it was his dealings with her that she needed to know more about.

"Come with me and we'll discuss it further," he said roughly, pulling her by the hand out of the summerhouse and up the path into the house through the French doors of the study.

They'd just crossed the threshold of the room when a gasp from the bookshelves made them both stop, startled like children caught out in a misdeed.

"Trevor!" Belinda gasped. "Lady Wharton! Whatever were you doing out in the garden at this hour?"

To Isabella's amusement, Trevor's fair skin betrayed him, a flush creeping up his neck, his cheeks, and finally to the tips of his ears. "What are you doing awake at this hour, Bel?" he countered. It was the purview of elder brothers the world round to dodge questions from their sisters, it would seem.

"I couldn't sleep," she said with a frown, her blue eyes narrowed. Isabella felt a flush creep into her own cheeks. "Where were you?" Belinda repeated.

Before Trevor could evade his sister's question again, Isabella jumped in. "We were admiring the stars," she said easily. "One doesn't get to see them nearly as well in London. I was afraid I'd be set upon by wandering cattle, so I had your brother accompany me. For protection of course."

Isabella felt both Carey siblings stare at her. "Are there cows or sheep loose on the moors?" Belinda asked with a frown. "I'd heard that one of Mr. Palmer's tenants had a cow get out, but I think the farthest she got was Mr. Davies' pasture."

Trevor's lips twitched. "No, I don't think it's a big problem for us at Nettlefield," he said. "But one can never be too cautious."

He and Belinda exchanged a look that Isabella read to mean "look how foolish the lady from London is." She was more than happy to sacrifice her pride for the sake of Belinda's innocence. Good lord, what if the child had come out to the summerhouse? They wouldn't have been able to explain that away.

"I had never thought that you might be as frightened at being in the country as Eleanor and I might be in the city," Belinda said kindly. It was obvious, though, that she thought Isabella's fears of wild cattle were bordering on insanity.

"Hadn't you better get back to bed, Bel?" Trevor said briskly. "If you've found a book for yourself, that is."

"Oh yes," his sister responded, clasping a book to her chest. "Just a novel that Eleanor discarded ages ago. Will you walk up with me, Lady Isabella?"

Isabella risked a glance at Trevor, who shrugged behind his sister's back. With a sigh of disappointment, she followed Belinda up the stairs to the family wing, and they paused outside the girl's bedroom door.

Trevor, who had come up after them, said good night as he walked down the hall toward his own bedchamber. Isabella watched him go, and then turning to say her good nights to the girl, she found Belinda watching her curiously.

"What?" she asked, feeling the blush rise in her cheeks again. The child had the most intense way of pinning one down with her gaze. She would make a remarkable parent one day, Isabella mused. She already had the scolding look down pat.

Belinda was silent for a beat but then shrugged and shook her head. "Nothing, I suppose. I just got the oddest feeling that you and Trevor were up to something. You had the same look about you that Ellie and I have when we're trying to get away with some mischief." Isabella was trying to decide how best to respond when the girl laughed. "But that's silly, isn't it? Grown people like you and Trevor don't get up to mischief, do they?"

If she only knew, thought Isabella as she bid Belinda good night and shut her bedchamber door behind her.

If she only knew.

*   *   *

The next morning, the day of the Palmer ball, Isabella woke with a start to find Belinda sitting on the edge of the bed.

"Finally," the girl said, shaking her head in exasperation. "I thought you'd never awaken. Do you always sleep this late?"

Isabella was unaccustomed to children as a general rule, but she was even more unaccustomed to them waking her at dawn. Still, she gave a yawn and sat up. Just in time for her maid to come bustling in.

"I'm sorry, Lady Wharton," Sanders said. She didn't specify what she was sorry about, but Isabella could guess. "I'll just got get your hot water."

Coward, Isabella thought, turning back to Belinda. Isabella was suddenly grateful that Trevor hadn't slipped back into her bedroom as she'd hoped he would last night. It would be quite difficult to explain his presence to his all-too-knowing little sister.

"What brings you here, Belinda? We did not have plans to go look at kittens or examine baby birds in their nests or some such animal adventure, did we? Besides, you were up quite late. Did you not feel the slightest bit of a need to linger in your bed this morning?"

"I never sleep in. There is always too much to see and do." Belinda's blue eyes, so like her brother's, rolled in that particular way that only children and teens could manage. As if she found Isabella's human frailty a bore. "It's the day of the Palmers' ball and we must prepare for it. There is so much to be done. So wake up and come help me."

Since Belinda was too young to even attend the ball, Isabella was somewhat perplexed. "What is there to do?" she asked, not bothering to stifle a yawn. "You aren't even going to the ball, if you don't mind my saying so. What on earth have you to do for it?"

"It's Eleanor," the girl said with vehemence. "It is her first ball and I mean to ensure that she is the most popular young lady there."

Somewhat bewildered by the girl's demands, Isabella asked carefully, "And what is it we are meant to be doing to help her?"

"First of all," Belinda explained in a manner that might better be employed in explaining the rules of cribbage to a toddler, "we must help her choose a gown. I know that Mrs. Renfrew was meant to send her one, but we need to see that it fits properly and if it doesn't we need to find an alternative.

"Then we must ensure that her hair is styled perfectly," she continued. "Then we should help her choose which reticule to bring. And so on and so forth."

"But it is"—Isabella consulted the clock on the mantle across her bedchamber—"only nine fifteen in the morning. Surely, we should wait and do those things later in the day, when we are closer to leaving for the ball."

"Oh, I know," Belinda said with a shrug. "I just wanted to be sure that you knew we'd be needing your assistance later in the day."

Biting back a sigh, Isabella simply nodded. On the one hand, the girl's enthusiasm for her sister was endearing. On the other hand, Isabella had been up quite late and, since she hadn't spent it being thoroughly ravished by the girl's elder brother, she'd hoped to at least sleep a bit later than usual.

It was, however, not to be.

Her mission completed, Belinda got up from the bed. "I will just leave you to dress for the day." Her eyes turned serious. "You won't forget about Eleanor tonight, will you?"

Suddenly reminded that both girls had lost their mother and were desperately in need of guidance from a woman, Isabella nodded. Impulsively she hugged the girl. Isabella was not, as a general rule, a demonstrative person, but some situations simply cried out for a show of affection. And to her pleasure, Belinda hugged her back. "I won't forget her," Isabella told her.

Stepping back, Belinda smiled brightly. "I knew you wouldn't let us down."

As the girl left the bedchamber, Isabella wondered what would happen to the girls when she left to go back to London. She had genuinely grown fond of them and didn't like to imagine them here in the country without any guidance from a woman of their own social standing. What would happen when Eleanor began attending more social functions? What if one of the neighborhood boys attempted to persuade her into more than just a few kisses? Who would she go to with questions? Trevor was a conscientious brother, but a girl could hardly confide the details of her personal life to her brother.

Still ruminating on the situation, Isabella flung off the bedclothes. If she was awake, she might as well go down to breakfast.

Her ablutions made, she donned a pretty blue morning gown and allowed her maid to dress her hair.

"Mr. Templeton asked me to tell you that the paintings you did with the young ladies the other day are dry now," Sanders said as she patted one last curl into place. Isabella surveyed herself in the mirror and reflected once again just how lucky she was to have found the woman so soon after her previous maid had left to return to her family in the country. Sanders might not have the most entertaining personality, but she was a wonder with hair. "He's put them in the blue salon if you wish to see them."

"Excellent," she said, rising from her dressing table. "I'll just go have a look at them before breakfast."

Slipping from the room, she went down to the first floor and hummed a waltz as she made her way to the blue salon. Now that she was awake, she may as well make the most of it.

The paintings were set up on the easels that they'd used that day when they'd painted. Eleanor's and Belinda's were facing the door while Isabella's faced out the window. Smiling, she stepped closer to see both girls' work side by side. The paintings themselves were expressions of their artists. Belinda's painting was marked by her large and expressive brushstrokes, while Eleanor's reflected the young lady's contained attention to detail.

Wanting to see her own work as well, Isabella walked around to the other side to see it. As she turned the corner, however, the flash of red on the canvas told her something was wrong. None of them had needed to use the vermillion pigment at all. Yet someone had.

The careful work she'd put into the painting was obliterated by red paint dripping down the canvas like blood.

I know what you did, BITCH!

Her scream was unintentional but heartfelt.

* * *

Trevor tried and failed to keep his mind on the estate books in front of him. But all he could think of was Isabella.

It had taken all of his willpower to stop himself from slipping into her bedchamber in the night. He'd even had his hand on the doorknob to do just that when his conscience got the better of him. What sort of example did it set for his sisters if he took advantage of a houseguest while they were in the house as well? Not that they would know about it, of course, but he would know it. And something about it just didn't sit right with his conscience. A gentleman did not take advantage of a lady in distress. And she must be upset after her encounter with Thistleback the night before.

No, it was for the best that he hadn't succumbed to passion last night. Or so he tried to tell his aching body, which he was not sure would ever forgive him. Trevor was not in the habit of keeping a mistress, though he did, on occasion, conduct a discreet liaison from time to time. But he could not recall a time in recent memory when he'd burned with passion for someone like he burned for Isabella. It was inconvenient as hell that she happened to be his houseguest—no matter how unwelcome she'd been at first—and his sisters' friend. He liked to think that she was his friend now as well, though the complications of such a friendship had not gone unnoticed by him. But so long as she remained under his roof, and in danger to boot, he would simply have to keep his trousers fastened.

He was in the middle of calculating a column of numbers when he heard what sounded like a shriek from down the hall. Mindful of Thistleback's threats the night before, Trevor raced down the hallway to the blue salon, where he found a pale Isabella lifting a canvas down from its perch against an easel.

"What is it?" he demanded, hurrying to her side to take the heavy painting from her. "What's the—"

Trevor stopped in mid-sentence when he caught sight of the red paint marring her landscape scene. "Who did this?" he asked, wrenching the canvas from her hands, fighting the urge to throw it bodily across the room. Instead he set it down near the fireplace, facing the wall so that Isabella couldn't see its foul message. "Was it Thistleback?"

Collapsing onto a nearby chair, Isabella shook her head. "I don't know. I don't think so. He has no way of knowing about—" She paused, and Trevor was angered to see tears well in her eyes.

He went to her. He didn't care if she was as strong as hell and wanted her space. He knelt beside her chair and handed her his handkerchief. "What does he have no way of knowing about?" Trevor asked, trying to keep his voice gentle.

Thanking him for the handkerchief, she dabbed at her eyes and swallowed. There was obviously something she wanted to hide from him. He could see it in her troubled eyes.

"Tell me, Isabella," he demanded, taking her hand in his. "Tell me what he's talking about. He says he knows what you did. What did you do?"

She gave a strangled laugh. "Nothing. That's just it. I did nothing and he's punishing me for it."

"Does this have something to do with your husband?" Trevor asked, clenching his jaw at the thought. "Talk to me, Isabella."

"No, nothing like that," she said, visibly composing

herself and taking a deep breath. "I actually can't think that this has anything to do with Thistleback. It has to be someone else."

Rising, Trevor began to pace, stopping before the mantle to turn the painting out again to see the hateful words again. "What does this person think you did?" Trevor asked after a minute of studying the red paint.

"I don't suppose you'd be content to simply forget this happened?"

Had the woman not spent the past week in his company? "Not remotely."

She sighed. "I thought not." Rising from her chair, she went to peer out the window. He was unsure whether she was looking for something in particular or just trying to collect her thoughts.

Finally, she turned and stepped over to the bellpull and tugged. "I, for one, would like to have some tea before I begin my story."

Twelve

*O*nce the tea tray had been brought and Isabella was alone again with Trevor, she busied herself with pouring for them both, the ritual of the tea table giving her some solace while her mind raced.

To his credit, Trevor did not press her to speak before she was ready. Though she could see well enough that he was chomping at the bit for an explanation. That patience was one of the things that she most admired about him. He would sooner gnaw off his own arm than make her talk before she was ready.

Finally, realizing that she must say something or risk their tentative friendship, she said, "I do not think that this threat came from Thistleback. Though I would just as soon ascribe it to him if it meant that I was only being terrorized by one person instead of two."

"So you have received other threats?" Trevor asked, settling his teacup into its saucer.

Isabella nodded. "I had hoped that the other notes I received were from Thistleback, but it occurred to me this morning that he has no way of knowing what happened the night that Gervase died."

"And that was?"

In an expressionless voice, Isabella told Trevor about what had happened that night at Ormonde House. How Gervase had put his knife to Perdita's throat and how he'd ended up with both a gunshot and a knife wound. When Isabella was finished, the room was quiet, except for the sound of her heartbeat, which she knew Trevor must be able to hear as well.

"And you think that someone knows the truth about what happened and is using it to punish you?" Trevor leaned forward, his forearms resting on his knees.

"I can think of no other reason for the notes and the carriage accident—you yourself said that the carriage must have been tampered with. And there is no possible way for Thistleback to know of any of this. He was not there that night, and if I recall correctly he wasn't even in London on the night Gervase died. Unless he has a spy in Ormonde House there is no way for him to know of it, or my presence there that night."

"It does seem unlikely," Trevor agreed. "But what are the chances that you could have attracted not one but two blackmailers?"

"Three if you count the dowager," Isabella muttered, knowing it sounded ridiculous even as she spoke the words. "I am not such an unpleasant person," she said. "Am I? Do I truly deserve to be so persecuted?"

"Of course you don't," he said. "And the dowager doesn't count because she is a bane to everyone. Not just you. As for Thistleback, the blame for him may be laid firmly at your late husband's door."

"But who is it?" she asked, frustrated beyond all care.

"Someone with entry into this house," Trevor said with a frown. "I will instruct Templeton to make sure that the doors and windows are all locked. In fact, I'll have him see to it this afternoon."

The notion that someone had simply walked into the house and defaced Isabella's painting had not occurred to her. Because she had only been thinking of what the bloodred paint had made her feel. But now, knowing that someone had been in the same house as Eleanor and Belinda and Trevor, Isabella felt a tremor run through her body.

"Oh god," she whispered. "What if he tried to come to my bedchamber while Belinda was there this morning? What if she were harmed because of my presence here? I have to leave at once. Go back to London."

Returning to London would ruin Perdita's chances of a happy match with Lord Coniston, but Isabella would have to do what she could to ensure that the dowager's campaign against her did not work. She knew that Perdita would agree with her that the safety of her young cousins would matter more.

"You will do no such thing," Trevor said, standing and taking her hands in his. "Whoever this is wants you to give up and to leave. And I for one have no intention of giving him what he wants."

"Why aren't you jumping for joy?" Isabella demanded. "From the moment I first arrived you've dreamed of nothing but putting me on the first stage back to London. Now that I finally declare myself willing to do just that, you're against the notion?"

Twin flags of color appeared on Trevor's cheeks. "If you haven't noticed, I have not said anything of the sort for at least three days now."

"Oh yes," she said wryly. "And what has wrought this change in your wishes, Your Grace?"

He said nothing, but the single raised brow he directed at her spoke volumes.

Isabella felt her own blush rising. "Well, I suppose there is that," she said, not willing to make eye contact.

"There is also the fact that my sisters adore you," he replied, pulling her toward him. "And that if I were to send you back to London before you are able to witness Eleanor's success tonight at the Palmer ball, I would find myself drummed out of my own home."

Remembering Belinda's enthusiasm that morning over her sister's mini-debut, Isabella nodded. "That is very likely true," she said gravely, allowing him to pull her up against his strong chest.

"Stay," he whispered against her ear, even as he slipped his arms around her waist. "Come to the ball tonight. I'll keep Thistleback away from you and tomorrow he'll be on his way back to town. And I'll do some digging to figure out who is trying to frighten you over Gervase's death."

"*You* will?" she asked, leaning her head against his shoulder and allowing herself just the briefest moment to experience the comfort of leaning on someone else.

"*We* will," he amended, kissing the top of her head. "Though I will be eternally grateful if you will still perform the heavy lifting when it comes to assisting Eleanor in her preparations for the ball tonight."

At the mention of the ball Isabella pulled back from him. "I almost forgot! I promised Belinda that I would help her make this afternoon special for Eleanor."

Isabella patted at her hair and stepped over to the pier glass to examine her eyes for puffiness. "Do I look as if

I've been crying?" she asked, turning back to look at Trevor.

"Not at all," he assured her. "Go help Belinda. I will see you this evening."

Before she stepped out the door, Isabella turned back one last time. "Trevor, thank you. For your help. I . . ." She tried to find the words to tell him just what it meant to have a man on her side that she could rely on. It was a far cry from what she'd come to expect from Wharton. "Just," she said, finally, "thank you. For everything."

Not wanting to linger lest she began to weep again, Isabella stepped out into the hall and closed the salon door firmly behind her.

That evening found Trevor in his dressing room under the not-so-tender ministrations of his valet, Jennings, who was thrilled at the opportunity to finally use his not-inconsiderable skills to dress his master as his station demanded.

Standing before the glass while Jennings put the finishing touches on his pristine white cravat, Trevor could not help but admit that he'd done well to hire the fellow. Not only was Trevor's hair arranged in what could only be called a stylish fashion, but also his evening attire was bang up to the mark, if he said so himself.

"There, Your Grace," Jennings pronounced, stepping aside so that his master could see his stylishly tied cravat, a sapphire winking from its folds. "You look every inch the duke, if I do say so myself."

Trevor couldn't argue with that. Though he still had no wish to take up the title he'd never wanted. Even so,

Isabella had made a convincing case for his taking up his duty to his family. Not his grandmother, whom he still held in contempt for her treatment of his parents, but certainly for his late cousin's wife—Isabella's sister—and the army of other cousins, aunts, uncles, and various other relatives who had had no hand in his father's banishment. Trevor had done his best to keep the estates running and the tenants well cared for, but from his experience at Nettlefield he'd seen how some estate matters could only be properly attended to by the master of the house. And though the estate manager at the Ormonde country estate seemed competent enough in his correspondence, who was to say the fellow was equally as reliable in person?

Trevor was not quite certain when his mind had begun to change on the matter, but he was slowly but surely beginning to see that by refusing to take the reins of the dukedom he'd done a disservice to all the servants and tenants and distant relatives who relied upon the estate for their keep.

"Thank you, Jennings," Trevor told the other man. "You've done an excellent job of turning this sow's ear into a silk purse."

To Trevor's amusement, the valet puffed out his chest like a bantam rooster. Inclining his head, Jennings said, "It is my pleasure, Your Grace. And may I say that I do not believe you to be so much of a sow's ear as a diamond in the rough, so to speak."

His lips twitching in amusement, Trevor nodded, dismissing the man.

Now Trevor had another errand to attend to. He crossed the dressing room and into his bedchamber to the small desk by the window. Picking up the velvet bag there, he opened the strings to make sure that the contents were undisturbed and made his way to his sister Eleanor's bedchamber.

To his surprise, his knock was answered not by his sister's maid but by Lady Isabella, whose crimson gown was a sight to behold. Her breasts were cupped by the bodice in a manner that all but invited a man to bury his face between them. And the skirt skimmed her curvaceous figure like a second skin. It was quite his favorite of her gowns he'd seen thus far. And he rather liked them all.

"Are you finished ogling, Your Grace?" Isabella asked tartly, startling him from his reverie. He was pleased to note a slight flush creeping up her chest into her cheeks.

Trevor cleared his throat. "I was merely admiring, Lady Isabella," he lied. He had been ogling and was not sorry for it. "You are looking quite well this evening." It was an understatement, but he could hardly be expected to divulge all he was thinking while his sisters stood on the other side of the room..

"Thank you," she said inclining her head in a way that revealed more of her slender neck, tempting him to bite it. Seemingly unaware of his inner turmoil, Isabella said, "Eleanor is nearly ready. My maid is just putting the finishing touches on her coiffure."

Isabella leaned forward to whisper confidentially, "She's quite nervous, so anything you can do to reassure her when we come down will be greatly appreciated."

Grateful that she was here to deal with his sister's nerves, Trevor nodded. "Of course. I suppose it is quite a—" He lost his train of thought as he noticed the curl dipping down to kiss her shoulder.

"Quite," Isabella replied with a quirk of her lips. "Now, what can I help you with?"

Her low voice coupled with that gown sent several lascivious notions of how she could help him running through his mind, but he shook his head to clear it. His sister was in the next room for God's sake.

Looking down at the floor, he realized he was still holding the jewel bag. He handed it to Isabella. "I thought Eleanor might wish to wear some of Mama's jewelry tonight," he said. "I trust you'll be able to choose something that is appropriate to the occasion and her age."

Isabella's eyes softened as she took the bag. "What a sweet brother you are," she said, a genuine smile lighting up her face. "Eleanor will be ecstatic. We were just wondering what she might wear to set her apart from the other girls."

Under the influence of that smile, Trevor thought, a man might be inspired to move mountains. Giving in to temptation, he leaned forward and kissed her softly on the lips. It was just a kiss. Though the jolt of desire it sent through him was not easy to ignore, he held it back. "Thank you for helping her," he told Isabella. "I know she appreciates it."

Her cheeks pink, Isabella still managed to raise a questioning brow. "And you?" she asked.

"I am quite grateful," he replied. "I'm not quite sure how I'll ever repay you."

Her eyes darkened. "I can think of a few things," she said. The aborted seduction of last evening hung in the air between them for a moment.

Then the moment passed.

Trevor squared his shoulders and gave her a brisk nod. "I will see you downstairs."

It had been years since Isabella attended a country ball, and she found she'd forgotten that sense of unrestrained enthusiasm that separated them from their London counterparts. It was quite refreshing, she thought as she, Trevor, and Eleanor were announced by the Palmers' very stuffy butler. Isabella much preferred the pleasant assurance of Trevor's own majordomo.

Mr. and Mrs. Palmer had greeted them with an unbalanced sense of welcome. Mr. Palmer, though quite polite, seemed less than pleased to be in attendance at his own ball. Isabella could well imagine him enjoying a visit to the tooth drawer with more enthusiasm. Mrs. Palmer, however, made up for her husband's dourness with her own brand of effusive welcome.

"We are ever so pleased to welcome you, Your Grace, Lady Wharton," she gushed. "And of course, Miss Eleanor, what a delight to see you here. I am quite sure that you will find yourself in excellent company for this, your first foray into the social whirl. May I say that you look quite pretty? That gown is quite fetching, isn't it?"

Greeted by this onslaught of chatter, Eleanor simply nodded and looked every inch the girl on the verge of making her debut. Isabella was pleased by the girl's neat manners. And in her gown of palest pink, which was set off perfectly by her mother's pearls, Eleanor was indeed very pretty. Isabella had little doubt that whatever local swain saw her first would be instantly smitten.

"My guest Lord Thistleback has already joined the dancing," Mrs. Palmer said. "I'm sure you will wish to have a long chat with him about your mutual London friends."

Before she could respond, Trevor said, "I feel sure Lady Wharton will be far too busy dancing for a long conversation."

"Indeed," Isabella said to the other woman, not wishing her to sense the tension that had descended upon them at the mention of Thistleback. She could only imagine Mrs. Palmer's glee at learning her houseguest had a secret to hold over Isabella's head. While their hostess was openly courteous to her, Isabella knew quite well that Mrs. Palmer was the sort of woman who would be jealous of anyone who might steal the spotlight from herself. She saw every other woman as a potential rival. And she would delight in seeing her rival brought low by scandal. It was simply the sort of woman she was.

"It has only been a week since I left London, Mrs. Palmer," Isabella told the other woman with a smile that did not reach her eyes. "I feel sure that we are both up-to-date on whichever town gossip there is to be had."

Oblivious to the tension between the two women, Mr. Palmer said, "I don't see why you'd want to speak to the fellow. He's as silly a man as I've ever met."

Cheerful in the face of her husband's rudeness, Mrs. Palmer tittered, "Oh, Mr. Palmer, you do say the drollest things." Turning back to Trevor, Isabella, and Eleanor, Mrs. Palmer waved them on. "We do not wish to keep you here. Go, and enjoy yourselves."

Taking their hostess at her word, Trevor ushered Isabella and Eleanor into the ballroom, where they saw that indeed the dancing had already begun.

"I see the Misses Green over there," Eleanor said. "May I go speak with them, Trevor?"

The duke nodded. "Go, enjoy yourself. But do not, under any circumstances, accept any invitations to walk out on the terrace, or any other such nonsense."

Like any girl of her age, Isabella sighed. "I am not a simpleton, Trevor."

Then she turned and hurried over to chatter with her friends.

"Well done," Isabella said with a laugh. "I don't believe I've heard that particular admonishment since I was around Eleanor's age."

"As a man," he replied with almost a growl, "I know how persuasive we can be. And I have no wish to see my sister ruined before she even makes it to London to make her debut."

Isabella couldn't argue with that logic. But it was the second part of his statement that caught her attention. "Then you are considering allowing her to come to London for a season? That's wonderful!"

"It wouldn't just be Eleanor," he said firmly. "It would be all of us. If I am to accompany her to London, I would bring Belinda with us as well."

He looked at Isabella intently. "Your words have not fallen on deaf ears, you know. I have been thinking quite a bit about duty and what I owe to—"

"Good god, Ormonde," Sir Lucien interrupted, "you look as if you are talking serious business. And everyone and his cat knows that a ball is not the place for such chats. Lady Wharton, allow me to solicit you for the set that is forming before you expire from boredom."

Wishing to hear more about Trevor's change of heart but also knowing that it was a matter better discussed someplace less public than a ballroom, Isabella took a deep breath and smiled at Sir Lucien. He was an amiable man, and she had little doubt that he had stood friend to Trevor in the worst of times as well as the best of times. And she did love to dance. "I would be delighted, Sir Lucien," she said, taking his outstretched hand.

Before they could step onto the ballroom floor, however, Trevor touched her on the arm. It was just a touch, but she felt it down to her toes. It was going to be so difficult to stop herself from succumbing to her own desire for the man, she thought with something like panic. She was careful not to let any of her inner turmoil show on her face, however.

"Save the first waltz for me," Trevor told her simply. As invitations to dance went, it was hardly the most elegant. Even so, she could not stop herself from saying, "All right," just before Sir Lucien led her onto the floor for the set that was forming.

"Careful," Sir Lucien said as walked with her. "Don't let the other women here see what I just saw. Else you'll find yourself the object of gossip and a great deal of feminine ire."

"I'm sure I don't know what you mean," she said, mentally cursing herself for not hiding her feelings better.

As the strains of the song began to play, Sir Lucien merely raised his brows. He clearly did not believe her.

"Believe what you wish," Isabella said, stepping forward to take his hand as the dance began. "I shall simply attribute your suspicions to your own feelings of a romantic nature."

"Touché, my dear!" Sir Lucien said with a laugh. "A very nice deflection of the focus from you to me."

"Thank you," Isabella said with relief. Perhaps now he would drop the subject.

But she was not so lucky.

"Perhaps it is not so much something to hide," the baronet continued when the dance brought them together again, "as something to be a bit more discreet about. I have little hope for Ormonde on that score, you know. He has never been very good at dissembling. Honest to a fault, is our Trevor."

"Then what good would it do for me to dissemble?" Isabella asked, grateful that the music was loud enough to hide their conversation but not so loud as to prevent them from hearing each other. "If I were indeed dissembling, which I have not yet admitted is the case."

Sir Lucien's eyes lit with mirth. "Far be it from me to accuse a lady of untruth, Lady Wharton. Even so, I fear your partner in crime has given the game away. Trevor cannot hide his feelings to save his life. And I very much fear he's smitten."

At the other man's assessment Isabella felt her heart unclench, and instead a bubble of happiness rose up in her chest, threatening to burst out from her in giddy laughter. Clamping down on her emotions, she regained her composure and blinked at Sir Lucien. "You exaggerate, surely," she said, trying to sound skeptical.

"Perhaps," the man said, "and perhaps not. I can only say that I've known him my whole life and I've never seen him look at another woman like he looks at you."

Before she could question Sir Lucien further, they had to change partners and Isabella was startled to find her new partner was none other than Thistleback. Who, unfortunately, appeared to be his usual loathsome self.

"Lady Isabella," he said, clearly not cowed in the least by their quite public location. "I hope you have reconsidered my offer of last evening."

The man spoke as if he'd offered to purchase a horse from her instead of trying to blackmail her for something she had no control over.

"If by 'reconsidered' you mean 'decided to ignore completely,'" she said coolly, "then yes, my lord."

She saw, with some degree of amusement, his lips tighten. "I could destroy your reputation," he said through clenched teeth. "Utterly."

"You could," Isabella agreed, "but you would in turn find yourself facing some serious questions about your own role in Ralph's schemes. I have little doubt that there are some gentlemen in town who would be quite interested to know that you both made it a regular practice to use weighted dice in your gambling pursuits."

"You wouldn't dare," Thistleback hissed as the movement of the dance brought them closer together.

"Try me," she said, her voice low and hard. She had spent a great deal of the night—the part where she wasn't regretting Trevor's scruples over summerhouse seductions—thinking about how to rout Lord Thistleback, and what she'd finally decided was that any show of weakness would simply play into his hands. Bullies would only be routed by another bully. So she was prepared to combat his insinuations with a show of force.

Fortunately, the dance returned them to their original partners at that point, and it was with some relief that Isabella took Sir Lucien's arm again.

"What was that about?" he asked, his eyes narrowed on the back of Thistleback's head as they promenaded. "He looks as if you just told him to go jump in the nearest lake."

Her own gaze on Trevor as he stood chatting with a

group of gentlemen, Isabella said, "Something very like. I'm afraid that Lord Thistleback is not a man who enjoys being denied."

And determined not to let her husband's crony ruin her evening, Isabella gave herself over to the movements of the dance.

Thirteen

$\mathcal{F}$rom the side of the ballroom Trevor kept a watchful eye on both Eleanor and Isabella. He did his duty by dancing with a few of the wallflowers, but for the most part, he was unable to keep from watching the ladies of his own party.

Thistleback's presence was troubling, especially considering his threats against Isabella, but there was nothing Trevor could do to make the fellow leave. He was the Palmers' guest, and Trevor could hardly approach the man in an open ballroom and demand that he hie himself back to London. Or, better yet, to the Americas. Trevor would just need to ensure that the man didn't harm Isabella any further.

He was waiting impatiently for the waltz Isabella had promised him when Lucien approached. His usual lighthearted countenance was marred by a troubled expression.

"I don't suppose you saw that Thistleback approached Lady Wharton during our dance?" Lucien asked, his tone low to keep from drawing the attention of the other guests.

Trevor's jaw clenched. From where he stood he could see Isabella performing the steps of a quadrille with Mr. Palmer. "I did not," Trevor said, his voice equally low. "What happened?"

"I'm not sure exactly," Lucien responded. "I only know that the dance steps required her to link arms with him and when she came back to me she looked troubled and he looked smug."

"Damnation," Trevor muttered. "I told the bastard to leave her alone."

"What's going on, Trevor?" Lucien asked. "You told me before that the fellow had been a crony of Wharton's, but this seems more serious than that."

"He's blackmailing her," Trevor said in a low voice. "He forced her to meet him last night in the garden, not knowing I'd followed her. I mean to see to it that he leaves her alone for good."

His back straight, he looked across the ballroom where Thistleback was holding court with several of the local ladies. His type was manipulative enough to charm those who had no suspicions of his true nature. And unless Trevor wished to ruin Isabella's reputation, he could say nothing publicly about the fellow.

"He looks as if butter wouldn't melt in his mouth," Lucien muttered. "I've always hated a bully. Especially one who preys on females. Just say the word and we'll ensure that he doesn't try it again."

Trevor was grateful for his friend's support but said, "I would if I didn't think it would harm Isabella's reputation more than his. We'll just keep a careful eye on the bastard and if he hasn't left the neighborhood tomorrow morning we'll ensure he's on the next mail coach back to London."

The current dance ended then, and Trevor looked across to where Isabella's partner bowed low over her hand. "If you'll excuse me," he said. "I must go waltz with Isabella."

"Lucky bastard," he heard Lucien mutter as he walked away.

As he approached her, he saw Isabella's eyes soften as she spotted him. When he reached her side, he greeted her partner, Mr. Fellowes, a local gentleman who had made his fortune with several cotton mills. "Fellowes, haven't seen much of you this spring."

The other man bowed. "Ormonde. I've been in London. Business, don't you know?"

Trevor had always been impressed by the other man's plain speaking when it came to his business dealings. He wished that more people would be so open. "Understood," he said. "I believe I'll be making a trip south before too much time has passed. Also on a matter of business."

Trevor felt Isabella's gaze on him but did not betray his awareness as he chatted a little with Fellowes about local matters. Finally when the strains of the waltz began, the other man bowed, thanked Isabella for the dance, and took himself off.

"So," she said as Trevor took her in his arms, holding her slightly closer than was allowed, "you weren't joking about your plans to go to London."

"I've only just decided it tonight," he said as they began to dance. "I've decided that it's time for me to visit the dowager, and to make my bows at court."

"What brought about this change?" she asked, her eyes narrowed, as if she suspected him of some trick. He couldn't blame her, given the men she'd been accustomed to. "I thought you were still thinking matters over."

"I thought it might encourage a certain gentleman to leave you be," he said firmly.

She colored at the mention of Thistleback. "I hardly think he'll be dissuaded from pestering me by your decision to go to London. He knows London. He'll have little trouble finding somewhere to run to ground."

"I will simply have to be persuasive," Trevor said with a flash of teeth. "I can be, you know."

"I have little doubt of that," she said lowering her lashes.

They'd neared the doors leading to a side terrace, and with ease Trevor swept them both through the doors and out onto the flagstones.

Most of the guests had chosen to take the air on the main terrace. This was a smaller, more intimate garden that was formed around a large fountain with the god Pan very prettily spitting water back into the pool below.

"What are we doing here?" she asked as she walked around to the back of the fountain, where they wouldn't be seen from the doorway. Her face was flushed from the dancing, and Trevor was having the devil of a time keeping his eyes from the creamy skin exposed by her gown. In answer to his question, he merely raised a brow. If possible, she blushed even more. "Oh," she said as he stepped closer, unable to keep his hands to himself anymore.

He'd expected some sort of protest from her, but she said nothing as he slid his hands up her arms and touched her gently on the face. "Isabella," he said, even as his mouth descended upon hers and took her lips in a surprisingly gentle kiss.

She made a soft sound of acquiescence as she opened her lips beneath his. Trevor nearly growled with approval as she slipped her hands beneath his coat and pulled him to her.

"Ah, god," he whispered as he took her bottom lip between his teeth and sucked. She was intoxicating. There was no other way to describe the effect she had on him, he mused as he kissed his way down her chin, over the soft skin of her neck, and down, down to her cleavage, where he dipped his tongue before tugging down her bodice for a glimpse of her bare breast. "This gown has been begging me to do this all evening."

Her fingers threaded through his hair, Isabella sighed with pleasure as his lips closed over her peaked nipple. "We shouldn't be doing this," she exhaled. "Eleanor—"

"Is being watched by Lucien," Trevor said, moving to Isabella's other breast. "God, Isabella," he said, moving back up her body to take her mouth in a fierce kiss. "You make me lose all semblance of civilized behavior," he muttered. "I want to carry you off to bed and keep you there until neither of us is able to walk."

"Trevor," she whispered, kissing him with flattering abandon. "I stayed awake for hours last night thinking of you. Of this."

"Me, too," he said, thrusting his tongue against hers. The heat of her mouth made his erection, if possible, even harder. "God, me, too." He let his hands wander down to grasp her bottom, pulling her body against his.

With one hand he slid the sleeve of her gown down over her shoulder, and allowed his mouth to follow a path down her neck and lower. She was beginning to grind her pelvis against him when a voice called from the terrace doorway, "Perhaps they are out here, Miss Eleanor."

At the sound Trevor froze and pulled back from Isabella. They both stood panting for a moment. There was no disguising the fact that Isabella had just been thoroughly kissed. He helped her pull up the bodice of her gown and smoothed her hair, though it had escaped enough pins to look wanton. Allowing her to smooth his own hair a bit, he pulled his coat back into place, took her hand, and led her around the fountain to face their search party.

"Ah, here you are, Your Grace," Mrs. Palmer crooned, her face alight with excitement as she took in their disarray. "And Lady Wharton."

"Mrs. Palmer," Trevor said, his coolness revealing that he had no doubt that their hostess had deliberately sought them out. He saw Eleanor slightly behind the older woman, looking apologetic.

"I only asked if she'd seen you," his sister said. "I did not ask her to go looking for you."

"It's all right, Eleanor," Isabella said with a smile. "You did nothing wrong." Her voice implied that Mrs. Palmer was not so innocent.

A silence descended upon them before Trevor made a split-second decision that would affect all of them. But he had to do something to save Isabella's reputation. He was the idiot who'd risked it by taking her into the garden, and he was the one who must make it right. "Mrs. Palmer," he said, his voice sounding hoarse to his own ears. "You and Eleanor may be the first to wish me happy. Lady Wharton has just consented to be my wife."

Isabella felt every muscle in her body tense. She turned to stare at Trevor. "What did you . . . ?"

"Darling," he said, squeezing her hand. "I know we said we'd wait to make the announcement, but we've just been caught out. And I, for one, cannot wait to inform the world that you have accepted me."

Trust me, his eyes said. And Isabella found herself unable to contradict him. He clearly had some sort of plan, and he had thus far proved to be an honorable man, so she would let his announcement stand. For now.

"I know, sweetheart," she said, squeezing his hand more tightly than absolutely necessary. "I merely wished for a bit of time. To inform my own family, you know. How surprised they will be."

Mrs. Palmer looked from Trevor to Isabella, then back again. It was clear she found the timing of the announcement to be suspicious, but she was hardly one to look a gift horse in the mouth. "My dears," she gushed. "I am so happy for you both!"

She rushed forward to step between them, taking them each by the hand and leading them into the ballroom, where, conveniently, the current dance was just ending. "Everyone!" she cried. "Attention! Please!"

The guests in the ballroom turned to face their hostess, looking expectant.

"I have just had the most wonderful news! The Duke of Ormonde and Lady Isabella Wharton have just informed me that they are engaged to be married!"

The room erupted in chatter as the assembled guests took in the news.

Sir Lucien stepped forward to grip Trevor's hand. "Congratulations, you old devil," he said. "You are a complete hand! I never guessed for a moment that you'd planned to announce this tonight."

At a speaking glance from Trevor Sir Lucien's eyes

sharpened and he nodded. Not betraying his suspicions, he turned to Isabella and kissed her on the cheek. "Congratulations, Lady Wharton," he said.

Still unable to reconcile herself with what had just happened, Isabella accepted Sir Lucien's congratulations and was soon engulfed by ball guests eager to offer her their felicitations. It was a far cry from her first engagement announcement, which had been a private affair among her, Wharton, and her parents, who had been less than enthusiastic at the match.

When Eleanor stepped forward, Isabella was surprised to see tears in the girl's eyes. "I am so sorry, Isabella," Eleanor said quietly. "I had no idea Mrs. Palmer would go looking for the two of you like that. I merely inquired if she'd seen you and before I knew it she was scouring the terraces for you."

"There's nothing to be sorry for," Isabella soothed the girl. She had enough to worry about without adding guilt over trapping her brother into marriage. "Mrs. Palmer is a force to be reckoned with and I have little doubt that she'd have gone on a search sooner or later without any prompting from you. I am only glad that it was your brother I went outside with and not someone else."

Eleanor frowned. "You wouldn't have, though?" she asked. "Gone out on the terrace with anyone else, I mean?"

"Of course not," Isabella assured her, though she was not quite ready to forgive Trevor for his announcement.

The girl relaxed a bit. "Good. Because I think you will make him a splendid wife. He is so serious, you know. And I know the duty of the dukedom weighs upon him no matter how he might pretend that it doesn't.

He's seemed much happier since you came to stay. Though I know he protested at first."

Isabella filed the girl's words away for further examination later. Now she said, "Thank you, Eleanor. No matter what happens between your brother and me, I wish you to know that you can always come to me if you have need of advice or just a sympathetic ear."

Eleanor didn't seem to like the implication that this business between Isabella and Trevor might not last, but she did not say so. She simply embraced Isabella and turned to wish her brother congratulations.

The next well-wisher was as unwelcome as his hostess had been.

"I see that you have once more landed on your feet, Lady Isabella," Sir Lionel Thistleback said, his smile wide so that if anyone was to see them talking they would assume he was merely offering his congratulations to an old friend. "I hope that His Grace realizes what sort of woman he is getting entangled with. I wonder if he knows just how Wharton used to—"

Before the man could continue, Isabella felt Trevor step close to her, slipping his arm about her waist. "Thistleback," he said, his mouth smiling but his eyes deadly serious. "I am well aware of how you spent last evening, and I would advise you to quit this neighborhood before your health becomes, shall we say, endangered."

Thistleback's eyes narrowed with hatred, but he did not betray any trace of his true feelings in the rest of his posture. "I was just telling my hosts that I will be heading back to London tomorrow, Your Grace," he said jovially. "I was merely saying my good-byes to Lady Isabella. Her late husband would be quite pleased to know she was being so well looked after."

Perhaps realizing that he did himself no favors by continuing to press his attentions on Isabella, he turned and walked away, leaving Trevor and Isabella to themselves.

"If he approaches you again," Trevor said quietly, "you are to let me know at once. I will not have him threatening you again."

She knew well enough that Thistleback had only left the field for now. But to Trevor she simply said, "Of course."

Thistleback, she was afraid, would need to be routed by Isabella, and Isabella alone.

There was no time for further discussion with Isabella at the Palmer ball, and in the carriage on the way home, accompanied as they were by Eleanor, was hardly the place either.

When they arrived back at Nettlefield, it was to find that Belinda—against Miss Nightingale's orders—had snuck back downstairs after bedtime to wait for her sister.

Before Isabella or Trevor could stop her, Eleanor burst out with the news. "Bel, you'll never guess it! Trevor and Lady Wharton are going to be married!"

Since the girl had been quiet beyond a brief congratulations in the carriage, Isabella found her enthusiasm over the match when she shared the news with her sister to be a bit surprising, but it seemed genuine enough. Belinda, however, was the one who was truly impressed with the news.

"That's so wonderful!" she screeched, throwing herself into Isabella's arms to give her a huge hug. "I knew that Trevor wasn't so foolish as we thought him to be!"

"Thanks indeed," her brother said with mock enthusiasm. "I'm glad I finally meet with your approval."

"Oh, you know what I mean, Trevor," his younger sister said with a grin. "It's just that you haven't done a very good job of choosing a wife. And we'd quite given up hope."

"Belinda, dearest," Isabella told the girl, "you musn't be so outspoken. You'll hurt your brother's feelings."

With laughter and more teasing the party retired to the drawing room, where Trevor allowed his sisters to sip champagne along with the adults, and before very long everyone was headed upstairs for bed.

Stopping outside Isabella's bedchamber door, Trevor took her hand in his and kissed it. Isabella was about to speak when he put a finger over her lips.

"I know we have much to discuss," he said. "And I thank you for allowing me to handle my sisters tonight without insisting that we talk first. I promise you that we'll talk tomorrow morning."

Isabella knew that for better or worse, their engagement was a real thing now, so she nodded and said, "All right. But I'll hold you to that promise. For we do have much to discuss. Not the least of which is how you maneuvered me into this engagement."

And with a quick kiss on his cheek she turned and went into her bedchamber, closing the door firmly behind her.

But it was not until well after breakfast the next morning, when Trevor was in his office dealing with estate business, that Isabella finally ran him to ground.

* * *

It wasn't that he didn't wish to discuss matters with her. It was more that he wasn't quite sure what to say. At the time, his announcement had seemed the most logical thing in the world. After all, he was in need of a wife, his sisters were in need of female guidance, and Isabella was currently unattached. Only after he'd gone to bed the night before had he started to think better of his impetuous decision.

He was not normally given to doing things on impulse. It was one of the things that made him such a good steward of his father's estate. One couldn't take impulsive risks and expect to remain successful as a farmer. And yet, ever since Lady Isabella Wharton had come into Trevor's life he'd found himself doing things that he would never have done as a general rule. He'd followed her to the summerhouse—something he would never have done to a guest under his roof before her arrival. He'd allowed himself to take advantage of her physically. True, he'd stopped before they'd taken the next, irrevocable step, but that was only because Belinda had caught them sneaking back into the house like a couple of young lovers involved in a tryst.

But intuition and gut feelings were something his father had told him again and again were not to be ignored. Yes, one's instincts might sometimes be wrong, but for the most part, there was a reason why we felt the need to turn left when everyone around us was turning right. And from the moment Trevor had met Isabella he'd been drawn to her.

She was smart and strong and had, as far as he could tell, managed to survive marriage to a man—if his association with Thistleback was any indication—who had treated her as little more than a pawn in his sick games. Any other woman in her situation would have emerged from such a marriage damaged beyond hope. But not Isabella. She was as emotionally strong as anyone Trevor had ever met. And there was a sweetness to her, which she only showed when no one was looking, that he longed to bring out into the light.

He hadn't consulted her before he'd made his announcement the night before, but he was determined to convince her that it was the right thing for them to do.

So, when she finally hunted him down in his study, he greeted her warmly. And indicated that she should sit down.

"May I offer you some brandy?" he asked, moving toward the sideboard. "Or I could ring for tea, if you wish it."

Isabella's brow lifted. "I have no wish for any sort of refreshment, Your Grace," she said. "You know quite well why I am here. And I don't need refreshment to do it."

"You're angry," he said, sitting down behind his desk.

"Of course I'm angry," she said with a toss of her head. "You announced our engagement last night before a ballroomful of your neighbors without consulting me about it."

"So, you would have been all right with my announcement if I had consulted you first?" he asked, leaning back in his chair.

"You'll never know, will you?" she demanded. "How could you, Your Grace?"

He watched the emotions play across her face, saw the hurt behind her eyes. "You're not just angry," he said, understanding dawning. "You're hurt as well. Whyever for?"

She looked away. Her profile was proud. Strong. And

lovely. "My first marriage was entirely out of my control," she said quietly. "My father agreed to the match
before consulting me. My betrothal announcement was
published in the *Times* before I could even consent to
the match. And of course, my husband spent the entirety
of our marriage making every decision for me. From
what I was to wear to whom I was to socialize with"—
she turned to look Trevor fully in the eye—"and when
and how he would use my body.

"For you to take control from my hands once again in
such a high-handed manner was not only inconsiderate; it
was no better than what Lord Wharton would have done,"
she continued. "And I had thought better of you."

Silence fell upon the room as Trevor watched her. His
gut twisted as he realized the truth of what she said. He
had not considered just what a betrayal it was for him to
so thoroughly take the reins away from her like he had
done. He had only thought to take advantage of the moment afforded by Mrs. Palmer's ill-timed intrusion. He
saw Isabella bite her lip and wanted more than anything
to go to her. To wrap her in his arms and reassure her in
a way that would let her know that he had not meant to
hurt her.

But he knew that the last thing she wanted from him
now was physical affection.

"You are right," he said at last, raising his hands as if
in surrender. "It was wrong of me. I saw a means of turning the tables on Mrs. Palmer, and of salvaging your
reputation, and I took it. I should not have done so without consulting you first."

Her surprise at his apology was like a punch in the gut.
Clearly she was unaccustomed to being vindicated.

"I . . . ," she began, her throat hoarse as she tried to get the words out. "I thank you, Your Grace," she finally finished. "It means a great deal to me to hear you say so."

"I had no intention of hurting you, Isabella," he said softly, his eyes never leaving hers. To his shock, he saw tears there. That he had brought such a strong woman to this point filled him with self-loathing. "Truly," he continued. "I would not have done if it I'd considered how wresting control of our . . . whatever it is between us would look to you. Especially given your relationship with your late husband."

She nodded and, breaking eye contact, looked at her hands in her lap.

Unable to stay away any longer, Trevor stood and walked around to perch on the edge of the desk before her. Leaning down, he slid a finger beneath her chin and lifted her face so that he could see her eyes. He stroked a thumb under her eye, wiping a single tear away. Softly, slowly, giving her every opportunity to push him away, Trevor kissed her. To his surprise and delight, she slipped her arms around his neck and held him to her. Opening her mouth beneath his to draw him in.

After a moment, he pulled back.

"Does this mean that you will consider marrying me after all?" he asked. Her eyes were luminous with unshed tears but also sharp.

"I will," she said, stroking his face. "Though I hope that you will never do such a high-handed thing again."

He shook his head. "I can only promise to try. There might be times when for your own safety or the safety of my sisters or, if we are so fortunate, our children I am forced to make decisions that affect us all. I will promise, however, to consult with you if at all possible if I need to make such a choice. And I will never, ever, take away your will as your late husband did."

She nodded.

Trevor continued, "What he did you to, Isabella, was monstrous. And I trust you know me well enough to know that I would never use you in the manner that he did."

"I do," she said with a rueful smile. "I would not consent to marry you otherwise, no matter how compromised my reputation might be given our interlude in the Palmers' garden last evening."

He dropped his hand from her face and took hers, pulling her to her feet. "Would you prefer to be married in Scotland, which is not very far from here, or in London by special license? Scotland would allow us to get away for a bit by ourselves, while London will take a bit of planning, since I have every intention of taking my sisters with us."

She smiled. "I've never been to Scotland. I should like to take a quick jaunt north before we must travel to London and deal with the dowager and no doubt her long list of duties she expects you to fulfill for her as soon as you reach the ducal town house."

"Excellent," he said, grinning back at her, his heart light now that they'd gotten past the tangle of last night's actions. "I will set about planning our trip north."

"And I will find your sisters and explain to them that we will be traveling to London sometime in the next few weeks," she said.

Her cheeks turning pink, she added, "Thank you, Trevor."

His brows drew together. "Whatever for?"

"For understanding. About my objections to last

night." She cleared her throat. "I will endeavor to make you a good wife. I know that my time with Ralph has made me . . . difficult, in some ways. But I will do my best not to let my first marriage color my marriage to you."

Unable to stop himself, Trevor gathered her against him and kissed her again. "Never," he said. "Never for a moment think that I hold anyone but Ralph to blame for what he did to you."

With a hesitant nod Isabella pulled away and was gone.

Fourteen

*O*f course I'll look after your sisters and Miss Nightingale while you are on your wedding trip," Lucien said with a frown. "I am shocked you even feel the need to ask."

Trevor had ridden over to his friend's estate the morning after the ball. The weather had turned cold, as sometimes happened in early spring when winter seemed reluctant to release its hold. The chill suited Trevor's somber mood as he pulled up his collar against the wind. He had much to consider and was grateful for the glass of brandy before the fire in Lucien's study.

"Isabella has told me that I should not take too much for granted," he said wryly, savoring the fiery warmth of the brandy. "She's right, of course. But it does make a man dashed nervous. Though I suppose she has had more reason to be wary than most."

"True enough," Lucien said, stretching his long legs out before him and crossing them at the ankles. "Did I ever tell you that I was at Eton with Wharton?"

Trevor frowned. "No. Why are you just now informing me of it?"

His friend shrugged. "I don't know. It didn't really occur to me, to be honest. He was several years ahead of me. And I didn't catch his notice, thank god."

"He was one of *those* boys, was he?" Trevor asked, not surprised. "Something tells me I won't like what you're about to tell me."

"Oh, I have little enough to tell about the man," Lucien assured him. "He was simply one of the older boys who enjoyed every bit of authority being older and stronger gave him. He thought nothing of requiring his underlings to wait on him hand and foot. Do his lessons. Polish his boots. If there was an unpleasant task that needed doing, he was sure to find a way to get out of it. Preferably by making some other poor creature do it for him."

"That sounds about right," Trevor said morosely. "A bastard through and through. Or so I would imagine from what little Isabella has told me of him."

"I tell you this not so that you will feel sorry for her, Trev," Lucien said seriously. "I tell you so that you will know just how much strength of will she must have to have survived years of marriage to the bastard with her spirit intact. A woman like that is stronger than you or I can possibly fathom."

"She is that," Trevor said with a smile. "She's managed to endure marriage to Wharton in addition to interference from the dowager. If she were any stronger she'd be a general."

"Or a duchess," Lucien said with a grin. "I am happy for you, old fellow."

"Don't get all maudlin on me, Luce. You look awful when you cry."

The other man rolled his eyes. "I am serious. Or am

trying to be." He thrust a hand through his already-tousled hair. "Marry your Isabella and be happy. And don't let the dowager do anything to separate you once the knot is tied."

"It's not like you to be so melodramatic," Trevor said, his brows drawn.

"It's just good to see you happy for a change," Lucien said with vehemence. "I don't think I've seen you smile this much since both your parents were alive."

Startled, Trevor realized that his friend was likely right. He hadn't meant to become so serious, but he was saddled with a great degree of responsibility when his father died. It had necessitated him becoming much more focused than he had been before.

"Have I really changed that much?" he asked his friend.

"Only to those who know you as well as I do," Lucien said with a smile. "Now, go to Scotland and leave me to look after your sisters and their governess."

Relieved but not quite knowing why, Trevor thanked his friend and headed back to Nettlefield.

As Trevor had said, the trip to Scotland was brief.

To Isabella's surprise, he chose to ride with her in the carriage. The conversation he initiated after a few moments of trivialities, however, was far from lover-like.

"I want you to think of who might wish to frighten you or get revenge against you for my cousin's death," Trevor said, sprawled easily on the opposite seat, as if he were asking her opinion on the latest opera in Covent Garden.

She had hoped the journey north would give her a bit

of respite from worries over the person trying to frighten her. And her expression must have communicated as much.

Taking her hand, Trevor gave her a crooked smile. "I know this is tiresome for you, but I wish to keep you safe. The more I know about the situation, the more I can do to ensure that this person is stopped."

Isabella sighed with resignation. She supposed she would have to discuss the matter sooner or later. And Trevor deserved to begin their marriage knowing as much as she did about the situation. "You are right," she said, appreciating his willingness to be gentle with her. "I suppose I've grown so accustomed to dealing with this—and every other trouble that befalls me—on my own. And to be honest, it stings a bit to reveal the gory details to anyone. Even you."

"I know," he said. As he shifted to take the seat beside her, Isabella felt a moment of panic. Which he must have sensed, because he was careful to keep some distance between them. "But you must learn to share the burden," he said, reaching down to where their hands were joined. "I, too, have grown too used to being in control of things. But the devil of it is, Isabella, that we are none of us in control of things. It simply isn't possible."

"I am in control of myself," Isabella said quietly, looking down at their hands rather than at the man beside her.

"You are," he said, bringing her hand closer, and slowly, carefully, finger by finger removing the kid glove that covered it.

She took in a breath and held it as they both watched him work the leather over her hand, unclothing her hand with as much care and finesse as if he were removing her gown.

"No fair," she said softly, raising her eyes to meet his. "Your hand is still covered."

He raised one auburn brow. "So it is," he said with that crooked grin. "I suppose you'd better remove my glove. For fairness's sake, of course."

"Of course," she agreed, quaking inside despite her outward stillness. As he had done, she took his hand in both of hers and finger by finger removed the glove until his left hand was as naked as her right one. Tossing his glove to join hers on the opposite seat, she examined his hand. It was not the hand of a pampered gentleman. Though his nails were neatly trimmed, there were calluses where he'd held farm tools, or repaired bridges, or done whatever else the village of Nettledean had asked of him. It was the hand of a man who was not afraid of hard work. A strong hand.

Wordlessly he entwined their fingers and held her hand against his. Palm to palm.

There was something about the feel of his naked hand against hers that was more intoxicating than a kiss, more intimate than sex.

"Our hands fit well together," Trevor said quietly. Isabella noted absently the tiny lines radiating from the corners of his blue eyes. They were the eyes of a man who laughed, who showed compassion, who labored alongside his tenants when necessary in the warm sun.

He was everything her late husband was not.

She wanted to look away, suddenly frightened at being the focus of such a good and honorable man. But she did not have the strength to do it. For all his virtue, he also commanded a degree of power over her.

"We fit well together," she agreed. "For now."

At last she managed to break the spell and look away.

And it may have been her imagination, but she could have sworn she felt his disappointment.

"For as long as you'll have me," he said, after a moment. He lifted their joined hands to kiss the back of hers. "I'm not Wharton, Isabella. I won't hold you captive or try to bend you to my will. I don't want that kind of marriage."

In spite of herself, she was curious. "What kind of marriage do you want?" It had never actually occurred to her that he would have any sort of expectations about their marriage. Foolish, she realized now, but she'd been so busy wrestling with her own fears and expectations about marrying again that she'd not considered he might have some sort of fears over the match. He was a man after all. And men, as she well knew from past experience, held all the power in marriage.

"I would very much like a marriage like my parents had," he said without a trace of bashfulness. It was one of the qualities she most appreciated in Trevor—his matter-of-fact way of explaining things. "Theirs was a love match, of course, so we've already missed the mark there, of course. But what I would like, very much, for us is to have the sort of partnership they shared."

"I do not know that I've ever seen a marriage such as that," Isabella said truthfully. She had hoped for such a match with Wharton, or at least something amicable. But he'd been too unwilling to allow her any sort of free will for that sort of marriage to develop between them. "I should like to try it, though."

"I think we've already proved we work well together," Trevor said, stroking the back of her hand with his thumb. "We managed well enough with Eleanor and Belinda."

"When you weren't ripping up at Eleanor over her

gown," Isabella said with a grin. "I thought the talk about redheads and their tempers was an old wives' tale."

"She's my little sister," he said with mock affront. "I am not ready to think of her as able to wear a gown like that. If it were up to me she'd wear pinafores and her hair in braids for the rest of her days."

"Which is why it's a good thing I was there to smooth the waters," Isabella said. "I suppose you are right. We do work well together."

"An excellent start for a marriage partnership, I think," he said. "But now you must allow me my male pride and let me slay this dragon for you."

"Which one?" Isabella asked without irony. "There are several chasing me at the present time.

"Not," she added, "that I acknowledge you alone will be the one to find this person, mind you. I still believe that I should have a hand in ferreting them out and making them pay."

"That bit of stubbornness aside," Trevor said seriously, "I think we should work on the unknown dragon first. Thistleback is likely on his way back to London now. And my grandmother is there are as well. We will deal with her when we travel there in a week or so."

Isabella couldn't stop the gasp of surprise she felt at his announcement. "Do you mean it?" She was so relieved that she felt tears well in her eyes. She hadn't known how much her worries over the dowager's threats against Perdita's match had been preying on her mind.

At his nod she threw her arms about his shoulders and hugged him close. "Thank you, Trevor. Thank you so much. I know you did not wish it, but I will be so relieved to have this particular worry removed from my mind. You cannot even imagine."

"I did promise you that I would go there with you if you agreed to spend time with me doing some estate business. And with the Palmers' ball out of the way, you have attended all of them."

"I know," she said, pulling back from him and hastily wiping the tears from her eyes. "But, as you know, I am not accustomed to gentlemen who keep their word."

He handed her his handkerchief, which she took with a sheepish grin. "I hope you will learn to expect it, my dear," he said, squeezing her hand. "You deserve it."

She wasn't so sure about that, but she could hardly argue with him when he was being so incredibly good about everything. Still, she was feeling a bit uncomfortable with the degree of emotion she'd just shown, so she turned the subject back to the one he'd begun with. "I cannot think of who might wish to frighten me. Only a few people know the true circumstances of Gervase's death. My sister, Georgina Mowbray, the dowager, and your personal secretary, Lord Archer. To everyone else we put it about that Gervase's death was a terrible accident."

"I didn't realize Lord Archer was aware of what had happened," Trevor said thoughtfully. "He has seemed to be quite reliable in our correspondence over Ormonde estate business."

Isabella frowned. "You have been in correspondence with Lord Archer?" she demanded. "For how long? And why didn't you tell me earlier? That might have gone a long way toward appeasing the dowager!"

Trevor had the good grace to look abashed. "I have handled much of the estate business at Ormonde House since my cousin's death." He thrust a hand through his russet hair, revealing his agitation. "You know me well enough by now to know that I could not allow the people of the ducal estate to suffer because I do not wish to bow to my grandmother's wishes. I knew Lord Archer's brother at university and he always seemed to be a level-headed fellow. So I allowed Archer to guide me. He likely did most of the work for my cousin in any case."

Isabella shook her head, dumbfounded. "I should have known it," she said finally. "It did seem rather out of character for someone as conscientious as you to abandon the estate just because you were unhappy with the dowager."

"So," Trevor continued, once more taking her hand in his. "If you have allowed Lord Archer in on your secret, I suppose that means you trust him?"

"Implicitly," Isabella said. "Which is why I do not think he can have anything to do with the threats against me. If it comes to it, I should think it more likely that the dowager was behind the plot than I would believe it of Lord Archer."

"But what motive would she have for frightening you?" Trevor extended his long legs before him in the cramped interior of the carriage. "If she truly wished to frighten you, wouldn't she keep you in London so that she could watch the results of her handiwork?"

"She was devastated by Gervase's loss," Isabella said, thinking back to the days just after the duke's death. There had been some speculation that the dowager would go into a decline. Of course that had come from her own maid, who was loyal to a fault and given to dramatics. "Even so, I believe you are right. If she blamed Gervase's death on me, which she may well do, she would have kept me close to her so that she could see me suffering through her torments. She would hardly send me into the country where it would be more difficult to manage her little surprises."

"Whoever it is," Trevor said, "they must have either followed you to Yorkshire or traveled with you. Have you noticed anyone who seems familiar lurking around? A servant who takes too much interest in you, perhaps? Or a face on the streets of York who looked like someone you'd seen before?"

Isabella shook her head. "No," she said with a weary sigh. "I've racked my brain trying to think of who it might have been that sent the letters or the snuffbox or ruined my painting, but I can think of no one. I trust all of the servants who came with me from London and I haven't seen anyone in our trips to York or out and about in the village who looked familiar."

To her dismay, she felt tears well in her eyes again. For someone who prided herself on her self-possession, Isabella was losing control of her emotions with disturbing frequency. She turned her head so that Trevor wouldn't see, but he missed nothing.

"There now," he said, gathering her up as if she weighed nothing and pulling her into his lap. "I know you're frustrated with this business. I am, too, if you want to know the truth. In fact, I might burst into tears at any minute. I can be quite the watering pot actually. You are in for a long and tearful marriage with me, I'm afraid."

She laughed at this absurdity, even as he took his handkerchief from her hand and dabbed at her eyes. They both grinned at each other like fools until something changed between them. He kissed the end of her nose. And said, his voice barely a whisper, "Let me share your burdens, Isabella. My shoulders are broad. I can carry them."

She might have resisted, but confronted with this man who seemed willing and able to give her shelter, she found she no longer wanted to. Slanting her head, she leaned forward and took his mouth in a sure, strong kiss. Saying with her body everything she was unwilling to say with her voice.

To her awe, she felt him tremble against her for just the barest moment before he slipped his arms around her and kissed her back. Perhaps he was not so laconic about this match as he pretended. His easygoing manner was, she realized, just as much of a disguise as her own iciness. Donned to protect the tender soul beneath.

He allowed her to take the lead in the kiss, opening his lips only when she licked softly at the seam between them. Surprised and excited by the novelty of being the one to do the pursuing, she tentatively stroked her tongue into his mouth. She could feel the tension in his muscles, the way that he held himself back. She knew with certainty that he was giving her this power. And it overwhelmed her as no degree of seduction on his part could have.

Breathing in his scent of sandalwood mixed with something innately Trevor, she unleashed her own burgeoning passion and kissed him with all the pent-up desire she'd felt since that first night on the roadside in Nettledean. Clumsily she tugged off her other glove and stroked her hands over his chest, frustrated by the clothes that prevented her from feeling his bare skin.

He must have sensed her annoyance, because he pulled off his own glove and unbuttoned his coat and waistcoat, all the while allowing her to take the lead at their joined mouths. Taking her hand, he guided it to his side, slipping it beneath his opened coat and waistcoat.

She felt the warmth of his skin through the fine lawn of his shirt but was distracted by the feel of his erection straining against her bottom.

Gathering her skirts in her other hand, before he could protest she came up on one knee and lifted the other to straddle his lap. "There," she said against his mouth. "That's much better."

With one hand she stroked him through his breeches, from base to tip. It was something her husband had demanded of her from the time they were first wed, but she knew instinctively that Trevor was allowing her to do this. There was no demanding hand covering hers, telling her how to stroke him. Only a hand at her breast, stroking her in tandem with her own hand on him, robbing her of breath even as she felt him gasp against her mouth.

"Sweeting," he whispered, "this is lovely, but . . ."— he paused as she stilled her hand and squeezed lightly— "god in heaven, we have to stop or I will forget myself."

"What's wrong with that?" Isabella asked, against his mouth. "I want to see you forget yourself, Trevor. I am not the only one who needs to lose control."

He gripped her hand and removed it from his erection, regret shining in his eyes. "That may be true," he said, kissing her wrist lightly and lifting her hand to rest on his shoulder. "But I choose not to do so in a carriage on the road to Gretna. There will be time enough for you to test me tonight."

Isabella sighed. "I suppose you are right. It would not be seemly for the Duke of Ormonde to take his wife in a carriage."

Trevor laughed. "It has nothing to do with seemliness or the dukedom." His eyes darkened as he kissed her lightly. "I simply know that once I get started discovering every inch of your body"—he pulled back and stroked his thumb over her lower lip—"I will not want any interruptions."

At the predatory look in his eyes Isabella felt herself give an involuntary shiver. Perhaps her betrothed was not so easygoing as she had at first thought.

Fifteen

*W*hen they arrived in the village of Gretna they set out at once to the nearest blacksmith, where they were married in a brief ceremony that was a far cry from the pomp and circumstance that had accompanied Isabella's first marriage. Instead she stood up with Trevor before the anvil priest with a nosegay of violets and calmly recited her vows. Trevor's kiss was brief and not nearly as passionate as the one they'd shared the night before, and she could not decide whether she felt relief or disappointment.

"I've had the driver arrange rooms for us at the local inn," he told her as they stepped out into the drizzle of the afternoon. "I hope that is agreeable to you. It is rather late to head back to Nettlefield, and after your lost wheel on the way up from London I did not think you would wish to travel at night."

She shuddered at the memory of the accident. "You are quite right," she said. "I thank you for considering it. I would much rather travel during the day."

He offered her his arm and they made their way to

the inn. Once there, he left her to rest in their room while he went to see to the horses.

When she reached their room, however, she realized that one of her cases was missing. As it contained her jewelry box, Isabella was perturbed to find it had not reached her room.

"I'll go down and see what's become of it, my lady," Sanders, her maid, said as she picked up Isabella's slippers. The maid had arrived in a separate coach with Trevor's valet earlier in the day.

But restless and not really wishing to nap, Isabella waved her off. "It's no matter, Sanders," she said. "I'll go down and see to it. I wish to find out if the duke has requested a private dining parlor at any rate."

So it was that Isabella found herself hurrying down the stairs in search of Trevor or their driver or both. As she neared the first-floor landing, however, a rather short man brushed past her.

"I beg your pardon, my lady," the man said, bowing slightly. Then, as if only now looking at her fully, he paused. "Oh, Lady Wharton," he said, a calculating gleam in his eye. "What a delightful surprise."

Realizing that she was looking at Sir Sidney Phillips, she cringed inwardly. If she and Trevor wished to keep their marriage a secret, then she would need to think quickly.

"Sir Sidney," she said, adopting her most chilly aristocratic pose. "If you will just excuse me." She continued past him down the stairs.

"But Lady Wharton," he protested, following after her. "I hope we will be able to chat. You are the last person I thought to encounter here in the wilds of Scotland, after all. Whatever can you being doing here?"

Isabella shut her eyes in frustration. If she told him to mind his own affairs, he would know at once that she had some sort of secret to keep. Then again, if she engaged him in mindless conversation he would do his utmost to winkle the truth from her anyway.

Before she could reply, however, she spied Trevor striding toward the stairs.

She raised her brows to warn him from coming closer, but her new husband was apparently unable to read eyebrow messages.

"Hello, my dear," he said, stepping closer and taking her arm proprietarily, "I thought you were resting."

"I was," she said though clenched teeth, "but I chanced upon Sir Sidney here."

As if he'd just noticed the little man who stood before them, gazing back and forth between them like a mongrel spying a juicy bone, Trevor turned to Sir Sidney in surprise. "Ah, I don't believe we've met," he said with a slight bow. "Ormonde at your service."

At his words Sir Sidney's eyes widened. "Lady Wharton," he gushed, "I had no idea you were acquainted with the duke."

Trevor laughed. "I should say we're acquainted," he said, pulling Isabella closer to his side. "Lady Wharton has just done me the honor of becoming my wife."

Sir Sidney's mouth opened and closed, not unlike a hungry trout, Isabella thought nastily. Finally he recovered his powers of speech. "Your wife? My goodness me," he said, his eyes glowing with glee at being privy to such a prime bit of gossip. "May I offer you both my heartfelt felicitations, Your Graces."

His eyes twinkling, Trevor leaned forward to the other man, "I'd appreciate it if you wouldn't tell anyone you saw us, old man." To Isabella's shock, he actually winked. "We don't want word to get out just yet. We haven't told my grandmother yet, don't ye know?"

Though he could not possibly mean to keep his promise, Sir Sidney nodded. "Of course, of course. Think nothing of it. I perfectly understand family obligations and the like," he said. "And the course of true love and all that . . . what?"

"Precisely," Trevor said, smiling beatifically at the other man. "Now, my dear, shall we retire to our chambers? I fear that my wife is quite fatigued after our trip here. You'll excuse us, won't you, dear boy?"

Silent, Isabella allowed herself to be escorted up to her chamber, where Trevor dismissed her maid at once.

Once Sanders was gone, Isabella turned to him, frustrated despite their earlier amity. "Why on earth did you tell Sir Sidney about our marriage?" she demanded. "He is one of the worst gossips I know. I would not be at all surprised if he weren't composing a letter for the post to London right this minute."

"I am not a fool, Isabella," Trevor told her patiently. "I am well aware of what Sir Sidney will do. And I told him for precisely that reason."

"Why?" she asked, her frustration rising. She knew that Trevor was well-intentioned, but she had spent years in London battling the Sir Sidney Phillipses of the world and she was annoyed that her new husband hadn't bothered to consult her on the matter. "I know the dowager will likely have heard of our engagement from someone who attended the Palmers' ball, but I had hoped to keep the news of our marriage to ourselves. At least for the time being."

But Trevor was clearly not as overset about this as

she was. Turning to the sideboard where a decanter of brandy had been thoughtfully provided by their host, Trevor poured both himself and Isabella a drink. "I know that's what we discussed, but I think this will suit our plans just as well."

He turned and handed her a glass, which she took and sipped. The brandy burned a path down her throat, warming her.

"It is a tactical maneuver," he said, propping himself up against the sideboard. "I want whoever it is that is trying to terrify you to know that you are under my protection now. That you are no longer dealing with his schemes on your own."

"It's not that I do not appreciate your protection," she began; then catching his skeptical gaze, she shrugged. "Perhaps I do not appreciate it as I should, but I do appreciate it. I simply do not like the notion that I will be seen as hiding behind your coronet."

"Why the devil not?" Trevor demanded. "I am sure plenty of people will suggest that I am hiding behind your skirts to escape my grandmother's ire."

"Surely not," Isabella said with a gasp; then she realized that he was perfectly right. People would assume that he'd married her as a way of getting back at the dowager. Perhaps even to beat her to the punch when it came to choosing a wife. "I suppose you are right," she admitted.

"What's good for the goose is good for the gander," Trevor said, raising his glass to her. "And as I said before, we are partners in this. I will offer you my shoulders for part of your burden and you will offer me yours—slim though your shoulders may be—for part of mine."

"What if this person strikes out at both of us?" she

asked. It hadn't occurred to her that she might need to fear for Trevor's safety, but the thought now sent a stab of fear through her. She would not be able to stand it if he was harmed simply because of his proximity to her.

He seemed to realize what she was thinking and crossed to touch her cheek. "We will deal with the consequences no matter what happens," he said to her, his eyes serious. "Whatever the blackguard tries, we'll deal with it together."

Isabella gave a brisk nod, still worried about what might happen to him as a result of their union, though she supposed it was too late to worry about such a thing now. After all, they were well and truly married now.

"I've asked the innkeeper to serve supper up here," Trevor said, taking the seat opposite and stretching his legs out before him. "I hope you don't mind. Though I suppose we could go down and search out your friend Sir Sidney as a dinner companion if you wish it."

His eyes lit with mischief and she couldn't suppress a laugh, grateful for the gentle teasing. "I assure you that I am quite content to have dinner alone without our gossiping friend. I find that I'm quite famished and do not wish for my appetite to give rise to untoward gossip."

Realizing how those words might be construed, she felt a blush rise. But if Trevor noticed he didn't say anything.

Excusing himself to change out of his travel dirt, he left her alone to do the same. Isabella felt a frisson of excitement at the thought of what might happen between them once dinner was over. It had been a long time since she'd been to bed with a man. And she guessed that Trevor would be as energetic and thoughtful in bed as he was out of it.

She gave a shiver at the thought and gave herself over to her maid to ensure that she was as ready as she could be for whatever might happen between her and Trevor tonight.

Trevor couldn't stop watching her.

It was hardly odd, given that she was the only other person in the room. And he was conversing with her. But a small part of his brain was watching her as she talked. Cataloging every contour, every curve. Reveling in the knowledge that the woman sitting opposite him was his wife.

His wife. He hadn't even known her last week, and now he was tied to her for the rest of their natural lives. It was insane.

But even as he listened to her recount a funny story about the antics of a clown at Astley's Amphitheatre when she was a child, his body was aware of her. Wondering what it would feel like when all those delicious curves were uncovered and pressed against him.

He felt like a beast, but there it was. He was looking forward to bedding his wife.

"Your Grace," she said, interrupting his thoughts, "is there something amiss?"

He sat up straighter. "Why would you ask?" he said, though he knew good and well why.

Up went that questioning dark brow. "You have been watching me with all the tenderness of a butcher eying a suckling pig."

That startled him into a laugh. "I can assure you that butchery is as far from my thoughts as it could possibly be."

She raised a hand to her throat and fingered the garnet cross there. "Then why do you stare?" she asked. "If you are having second thoughts about the marriage, then you might have considered that before you broadcast our marriage to Sir Sidney."

"You worry too much," he said, hoping his smile took the sting from the words. "I am having no second thoughts about you or the marriage, and Sir Sidney Phillips is the last thing on my mind."

"Then what?" she demanded, her cheeks growing pink, as if she had begun to guess the tenor of his thoughts.

"What, indeed," he said, standing and reaching for her hand to pull her up with him.

The servants had long ago cleared the dishes from their supper, and Isabella had dismissed her maid for the night.

"Isabella," Trevor said, bringing her closer to him. "I would like very much to make love to you."

She looked down, and he saw her cheeks grow pinker.

When she didn't respond he bent his knees so that he could look into her downturned face. "What's amiss?" he asked quietly. "Bridal nerves?"

But she shushed him. "It's not that," she whispered, her voice thready, a far cry from her usual confident tones. "I . . . that is to say . . . my . . ."

He longed to fill in the words for her, but he had no notion of what she was trying to say. So, painful as it was, he waited.

". . . my husband," she began, taking a deep breath and turning her face up to meet Trevor's gaze. "My husband said that I wasn't very good at it," she said quickly. "Bedsport, I mean. So I am willing, but I hope you won't be disappointed if I am not quite as good at it as you would wish."

Trevor was silent as he took in her words and fumed over the impossibility of throttling a dead man. He would never have guessed that a woman of Isabella's confidence and beauty could feel so utterly vulnerable about her ability to please a man in bed. Her very presence there would be enough to satisfy many. However, he admitted to himself that he would like very much to see all of that self-possession dissolve under the application of relentless pleasure.

Even so, he could disabuse her of one notion at least. "There is no possible way that I could ever be disappointed in you, Isabella," he said, making sure to look her squarely in the eye. Her gaze was worried but steady. "No possible way," he repeated. "You are a lovely, passionate woman. And I expect nothing more tonight than for you to be honest with me. If you dislike something, tell me. If you like something, tell me that as well. But don't ever think that I come to our bed with expectations of you. This isn't a schoolroom test that you can pass or fail."

He was frustrated to see that there was still doubt in her eyes, but he could hardly expect for her to simply slough off the years with that bastard she'd been married to in the space of an hour. He would simply have to work at winning her trust.

"Do you understand?" he asked, his voice sharp with frustration—not at her but at the situation. "Isabella?"

She nodded. "I suppose," she said her lips pursed. "But don't say I didn't warn you."

That surprised a laugh from him. Pulling her closer to him, he kissed her, willing her to relax against him, even as his own heartbeat accelerated. Slipping an arm around her waist, he pressed into her softness. Nibbling at her lower lip, he was pleased when she opened her mouth and let him in, welcoming his tongue into the heat of her mouth. Once, twice, he stroked into her, sliding his hands down to grasp her bottom, pulling her against his erection.

Her arms twined around his neck, and her fingers thrust into his hair, pulling his mouth closer as she began to stroke back.

"Don't ever think," he breathed out, kissing a path down her throat, "that I don't find this . . . you . . . maddeningly attractive."

As he wended his way toward her breast, he felt her hand pulling him against her and gave a silent cheer. "This, Isabella," he said, thumbing the nipple of one breast while he lightly bit the peak of the other through her gown, "this is us together. No past lovers, no past husbands, just us two together."

She gasped and clenched his shoulders. "Trevor," she exhaled. "Just us."

He took her hand and pressed it against the front of his breeches. "Feel what you do to me, Izzy," he said. "This is how you excite me."

She looked at him, then, her eyes wide with the knowledge that he could want her that much.

Cursing, he pulled her hand away and gathered her up into his arms and crossed on unsteady feet to the door to his bedchamber. It was probably not up to the usual standards of the Duke of Ormonde, but he bloody well didn't give a damn at the moment. Like an ancient chieftain claiming his mate, he lowered her to the sheets, pleased at the mix of excitement and hesitation in her eyes.

Silently he tugged her to her feet, turned her about, and began unbuttoning the seemingly endless line of buttons down her back. Finally she stepped out of her gown, her corset was dispensed with, and she wore nothing but her shift and stockings.

Turning in his arms, she still managed to look regal in her undress. He could see her hands twitch, perhaps anxious to cover her breasts, but she kept them by her sides. He looked. He could not help himself. Gazing hungrily at her nipples dark through the thin material of her chemise and the dark triangle between her legs. It was erotic as hell and he was incapable of looking away.

"Your turn," she said huskily, that questioning brow quirking again. And he quickly dispensed with his coats, cravat, and shirt. Sitting on the side of the bed, he set about removing his boots but stopped at her staying hand.

"Let me help," she said, going to her knees before him and grasping the heel of his right boot and tugging. After a bit of a fight, the boot gave up, and she removed the other one. He thought wistfully of the possibilities of her on her knees before him and then berated himself for being a selfish oaf. Taking her hand, he pulled her to her feet, and lifting her again, he deposited her onto the cool sheets.

Reclining like a royal concubine on the bed, she raised her arms to him. "Come," she said, licking her lips that were already reddened from his kisses. "Come to me."

Shucking his breeches, he did just that, stretching out on his side next to her. He felt his face redden when she looked down at the evidence of his desire for her, her eyes widening with surprise and just a little hesitation.

"It will fit," he said hastily. "I assure you."

She gurgled with laughter. "I wasn't thinking that, you oaf."

"Then what?" he demanded with a mock growl, flipping her onto her back and pressing that very impressive erection against her.

"If you must know," she said primly, "I was thinking of Lucifer."

He paused. "You mean the dark lord? Satan? Old Scratch? Beelzebub?"

"Technically he is the fallen angel from *Paradise Lost*," she corrected. "But no, that is not who I am referring to. Lucifer was a stallion on my father's country farm."

"Ah," Trevor said with a grin. "So you are comparing me to a stallion. I can approve of that, I think. But what precisely were you thinking of about Lucifer?"

She bit her lip. "Well, he was a stallion, as I said. So he spent a great deal of time . . . er . . ."

"Doing what stallions do?" Trevor asked politely, looking with fascination at the tiny freckles covering her nose. He hadn't taken her for a country girl, but it would seem that his new bride contained many facets he had yet to uncover.

"Yes." She nodded. "And he was quite fond of me. And he would do anything to be near me. I wasn't allowed to ride him, but he opened every gate, got past every restraint, to simply be near me."

"And you fear that I'll be like Lucifer?"

She smiled, reaching up to touch a lock of auburn hair that had fallen onto his brow. "No," she said softly. "I was thinking of how constant he was to me, but how inconstant he was with the mares. He had a veritable harem. And he was loyal to none of them."

"Ah." Damn. It was back to her husband then. "Isabella," Trevor said, leaning in to kiss her. "I am no saint, but nor am I the man your former husband was."

"But you are a man," she said, her eyes sad.

"Yes," he said, his eyes never leaving hers. "And I promise you that I will not play you false. We might not have married in a traditional ceremony, but I intend to keep all the vows of the Church of England marriage ceremony."

He lifted her left hand and kissed the fourth finger where his ring rested. "With this ring," he said against her palm, "I thee wed."

A single tear beaded up at the corner of her eye, which he kissed away. "With my body," he whispered, grasping the bottom of her shift and sliding it up and over her head, "I thee worship." He gasped at the feel of skin on skin and was gratified to feel her swift intake of breath. "With all my worldy goods," he said, sliding down over her body, scraping the beginnings of his beard over the softness of her skin, breathing in the scent of her, gathering her knees in his hands, and opening her body wide to his gaze, "I thee endow." He caressed the soft skin of her thighs as he kissed the heart of her.

Isabella stared in disbelief at the glint of candlelight in Trevor's dark russet hair as he kissed a trail from one inner thigh to the other. "Your Grace," she said, closing her eyes as she felt his teeth graze a particularly sensitive spot, "you need not . . . that is to say . . . it's not necessary for you to— Oh! God, do that again!"

"Liked that, did you?" She could imagine his expression as he said the words, but was too overcome with sensation to comment. Her first husband had never been particularly interested in her pleasure during their bed-chamber sessions, as she thought of them. But Trevor, it would seem, was determined to ensure that she felt as much as he did.

He teased her relentlessly with his mouth, then, when she rocked against him, with his fingers. Unable to control her response, Isabella heard herself whimper, but by that point she didn't care. Once, twice, he thrust into her while at the same time he teased that sensitive place with just the right degree of pressure. Never in her life had she felt so out of control, so lost to all sense of restraint. Under his hands she felt savage and desperate. And before she could stop herself, Isabella found herself bucking against his hand like a madwoman. Over and over again until she splintered into a million fragments. Like a fireworks display she'd once seen at Vauxhall.

Spent, she lay there, her legs splayed like a common strumpet, breathing hard, waiting to come back to herself. She felt her new husband kiss her once on the belly, then crawl up the bed to recline next to her, his head propped up on one arm.

"I can feel you looking at me," she said, not opening her eyes. She could also feel his very impressive erection pressing against her hip.

"I am admiring you," he corrected, kissing her on the nose. "Who would have thought all that passion was lurking beneath your cool, collected surface?"

She peeked out at him from between her lashes. "Passion or wantonness?" she asked softly.

"Either," he said, caressing her breast. "It's an asset certainly. No matter what you call it."

She looked up at him. "What manner of man are you?" she asked, her mouth twisting in a wry approximation of a smile. "You bed me at the first opportunity, but then you delay your own pleasure in order to give me mine. I think you must be attempting to become a saint."

He laughed, and for the first time she noticed that perhaps his easy demeanor wasn't as easy as she'd previously thought. "I'm no saint, Izzy," he said, sliding over to cover her body with hers. In a pantomime of savagery, he scraped his teeth over her neck, stroking his hands down her arms to grasp her hands and in one swift motion bringing them above her head and holding them there with one hand. "Not at all," he continued, pinching the peak of her breast lightly while he kissed his way up her neck to her mouth, where he took her lips in a deep kiss. Isabella could taste her own essence and was aroused. "I'm a man, that's all," he whispered against her mouth while he pulled her knee up and poised himself at her entrance. She bent her other knee to open herself more fully, and in one swift thrust he seated himself fully within her. The attention he'd paid to her earlier had ensured that her own moisture eased his way, but even so, he was indeed a big man and it had been over a year since Isabella had been with a man. She welcomed the intrusion, however. Welcomed the act that joined her with this man as his wife.

"Izzy," he said against her neck as they reveled in their joining. "Sweet. So sweet."

Isabella would have stroked him, but her hands were still imprisoned above her head. But something about the position intrigued her. She'd been dominated by a man before, but this she knew was just a game. Unable to touch him with her hands, then, she widened her knees and dug in her heels, allowing him to sink farther into her. And when she thought she'd go mad from wanting, he began to move.

Lifting herself, she met him thrust for thrust, and once again Isabella felt her excitement build. She reveled in every sensation: the scent of Trevor's sandalwood soap, of his skin, of his sweat mingling with hers. Through her lowered lashes she watched the play of his muscles beneath his skin as he braced himself over her, even in his passion careful not to overwhelm her. And over the sound of her own small murmurs and gasps she heard the slap of skin against skin, of the slide of their flesh against each other. But before long, she lost all grasp on the world around her and all of her concentration centered on one sensation only: the drive toward pleasure. Trevor's stroke became erratic, and so, too, did Isabella's movements, and as if by prearrangement their slow lovemaking became desperate. Until at last, Isabella lost her battle for control and she felt her consciousness splinter. As if from far away she felt Trevor press one last time into her, heard him groan, and for a moment felt him collapse onto her.

If she'd been herself, she might have teased him for the lapse in gentlemanly behavior. But she was in no condition to speak, let alone tease. As it was, he recovered himself soon enough and with a whispered "sorry" he turned to his side. Unaccountably, Isabella felt bereft to feel him leave her, but when he gathered her close to his side she sighed and tucked herself against his chest.

She heard the thrum of his heartbeat beneath her ear as he idly stroked her naked back.

It seemed as if a conversation was in order, but before she could speak she heard a soft snore and realized that her bridegroom of a few hours had fallen asleep.

And though she would not have thought it possible, soon so did she.

Sixteen

The trip back to Nettlefield was uneventful. Trevor chose to ride in the carriage along with his wife rather than on horseback. He found her to be an entertaining traveling companion once again, and her tales of life in London often left him chuckling. Though his first impression of her had been that she was a society flirt with little interest in anything or anyone besides herself, the real Isabella was far more complex than he'd given her credit for. True, she did have an almost encyclopedic knowledge of fashion, but she also knew much about the current political situation and could argue quite passionately about the plight of the poor and even, to his surprise, the Irish.

"I'll bet you had no notion that a flibbertigibbet like me even knew that Ireland existed, let alone that our government treated its people so abominably," she said after a particularly impassioned speech.

"I would hardly have called you a flibbertigibbet," he said wryly, kissing the back of her hand, which was currently clasped in his own. "Perhaps a lady of leisure," he offered.

"Come now, Your Grace," she countered. "I have little doubt that when you found me on the side of the road in that overturned carriage you would have liked nothing more than to leave me to my fate. I am eternally grateful that you did not."

"Well, I am a gentleman, my dear," he said. "And even when I was annoyed at your high-handed manners, I could not help but notice that you were possessed of a pair of the most delectable breasts it has ever been my good fortune to set eyes on."

Isabella gave him a playful swat. "Villain! I might as well have been rescued by an ogling farmer with roaming hands."

But Trevor could tell there was no real outrage in her protests. "I am quite pleased with our arrangement," he said, pulling her closer to his side. "I am not normally given to praising the dowager, but she did a good thing in sending you to Yorkshire to fetch me. However unpleasant she might be."

"Oh, she is much more than simply unpleasant," Isabella said with vehemence. "She is quite devious. And cares little for how her behavior is perceived by anyone else. I suppose that's what comes of being a duchess for thirty years. All that unchecked power goes to one's head."

"I certainly hope that you do not mean to follow in her footsteps," Trevor said teasingly.

"Hardly," Isabella returned. "And not only because I have learned from my sister's mistakes on that score. When she was first married Perdita tried to include the dowager in the running of the ducal household and the social obligations. But she soon learned that no house can serve two masters—or in this case mistresses.

At every possible turn the dowager undermined her to the point that Perdita finally withdrew from the field altogether. And unfortunately, the duke did little to make his grandmother back down. After all, she had run roughshod over his mother in the same way that she did so over his wife. Instead he saw his wife's role diminished while his grandmother's was elevated. Before long the servants went back to their old ways of deferring to the dowager when it came to household matters."

Trevor heard all of this with an air of frustration. "I will have no compunction about telling the dowager just how unwelcome her interference will be," he said. "Though," he continued, "it might be better for your own peace of mind, as well as for your reputation among the staff, if you rout her yourself first."

"Oh," Isabella said with a smile, "have no fear of that. My first action upon arriving in London will be to have a very long chat with her about just what her role in the household will be. I have little doubt that in my absence she has moved back into Ormonde House and has begun bullying Perdita about the arrangement of the furniture and all that nonsense."

"Why does your sister allow the dowager to bully her so?" Trevor asked, puzzled. "I have a difficult time imagining a sister of yours being bullied by anyone, much less another woman."

"You are kind to say it," Isabella said with a shake of her head, "but you cannot know what it is like until you've been there yourself. Perdita and I grew up in a very disjointed sort of household. And unfortunately, we married quite young. We were neither of us very lucky in the men our father chose for us to marry. And though Perdita was thought at the time to have made the better match—after all, a duke outranks a viscount—it turned out that despite his elevated status, the late duke was hardly the catch society thought him to be."

"In what way?" Trevor pressed. There was something about his cousin that Isabella was not telling him. He knew that her own husband had been physically abusive. Could it be that Perdita's husband had been so as well? Or was there something else?

"I do not like to tell my sister's story without her consent, Your Grace," Isabella said with a frown. "Suffice it to say that he and Ralph were quite good friends. And in some respects, the late duke outpaced his friend by a great deal."

"I am sorry to press you, my dear," Trevor told her, squeezing her hand. "I know this must be difficult for you to speak of. I simply wish to know as much as possible about what went on in the Ormonde family before I go trampling in like a bull in a china shop. I cannot know how best to handle the dowager unless I know how her son managed the dukedom. And I most definitely wish to know as much as I can about the dowager before I meet her. Forewarned is forearmed."

"As to managing the dukedom, that was mostly up to the duke's personal secretary, Lord Archer. I don't know how Ormonde managed to keep him from leaving and going to work for someone who was more amiable. I certainly would have done."

Trevor was grateful that Lord Archer Lisle hadn't left, too. Though he knew himself perfectly capable of handling the affairs of the dukedom, he would be a fool to think that he would be able to simply step into the role without any previous training and excel at it from day one. His correspondence thus far with the secretary in-

dicated that Lord Archer was a levelheaded and orga-
nized man who was knowledgeable about every aspect of
the estate. And Trevor was damned grateful to have him.

Trevor's new wife, however, was more perceptive
than he'd given her credit for. "You have nothing to fear on
that score, Your Grace," she told him firmly. "I have
seen how marvelously you run Nettlefield. And I have
little doubt that you'll do just as well with the Ormonde
estates. Once you've managed one estate much of it car-
ries over. Or so I would assume."

"You are no doubt right," he told her, kissing her on
the nose. "Now, I believe I requested that when we are
alone you call me Trevor. I do not care for the idea that
we will one day be in our dotage and you will continue
to refer to me as 'Your Grace.' It simply will not do."

"But I thought you only meant for me to address you
as Trevor when we are—" She broke off, blushing. "That
is to say, in private-private." She whispered the last two
words lest he think she referred to some other more
open sort of privacy.

"I should prefer that as well," he said into her ear.
"Now," he said, grasping her by the waist and pulling
her into his lap, "do you consider this to be private-
private? Or are we both wearing too many clothes?"

Isabella's response was muffled by his mouth.

They arrived at Nettlefield just after the dinner hour.
They were greeted on the stairs by Belinda and Eleanor,
who had heard the approach of the carriage and hurried
downstairs to meet the newlyweds.

"What was Gretna like?" Belinda asked, tugging on

Isabella's left hand, while Eleanor slipped her own arm through the right.

"Was it very romantic?" Eleanor asked with a sigh. "It must have been, for how could a place so devoted to marriage not be romantic?"

"Did you actually marry over an anvil? Was he a real blacksmith? I can't imagine Mr. Fawkes from the village simply stopping in the middle of some smithing task to marry people. For one thing, he gets quite sweaty while he's working." Belinda's nose wrinkled at the thought.

"Give us a moment to adjust to being out of the carriage, girls," Trevor told his sisters from his position behind them on the stairs. "I don't think you've let Isabella get a word in since we entered the house."

But Isabella didn't mind. She was surprised to realize just how much she'd missed the chatter of the Carey sisters. She remembered all too well the excitement of welcoming her parents home after they'd been on some journey or other and how she and Perdita had often peppered them with questions. Or the girls had peppered their mother with questions, Isabella amended. Her father would disappear into his study as soon as he returned.

She was pleased to note that Belinda and Eleanor harbored none of the fear for their brother that she and her sister had felt for their father.

"Oh, pooh, Trevor," Belinda scoffed. "Isabella can tell us herself if she's overwhelmed. And clearly she is not."

"How can you tell that?" he asked wryly, following them into the hallway that led to the family chambers.

"She hasn't told us to be quiet for one thing," Eleanor said with a grin. "Have you, Isabella?"

Noting Trevor's raised brow, Isabella grinned back. "It's true. I haven't."

Shaking his head at them, Trevor surrendered. "Don't say I didn't try to save you," he said, stopping before his bedchamber door. "Now, if you ladies will excuse me, I intend to wash off the dirt of the road." His lingering look indicated that he would very much like Isabella to join him, but she studiously ignored him. There would be plenty of time for that when she'd spent a bit of time with his sisters.

"Come, girls," she told them, heading for the door to the mistress's chamber, which was just down the hall from Trevor's. "I brought you both gifts."

Her ears smarting from the squeals of delight, she stepped into her rooms and found her maid unpacking her bags.

"Sanders, did you unpack the gifts I brought for the girls?" she asked.

"They're on the desk by the window, Your Grace," Sanders said. "Shall I ring for a bath to be brought up?"

"Yes," Isabella said absently as she led her sisters-in-law to the window. "Thank you."

The girls had already descended upon the desk where their gifts sat.

"The one in the blue paper is yours, Eleanor," Isabella said with a smile. "And yours is the pink, Belinda."

Though she and Trevor had only been in Gretna overnight, Isabella had insisted upon visiting one of the local shops to pick up baubles for the girls. She was very aware of the responsibility of her new role as their brother's wife. And she had grown quite fond of them in her short time at Nettlefield. She knew just how hungry they were for feminine guidance, and she wanted to prove to them that she was as eager to provide it as they were to receive it.

"I love it," Belinda said, removing the cameo pendant from its box. Isabella could still recall her very first piece of jewelry—a pin not unlike the one she'd chosen for Belinda. She'd gazed upon it for hours after her mother brought it to her from some trip she'd taken with her own sisters. To Isabella's surprise and delight, Belinda threw her arms around her and gave her an enormous hug. "I cannot wait to show it to Flossie." Clearly the cat was a greater admirer of jewelry than Isabella had given her credit for.

"Open yours, Ellie," the younger girl prodded her sister. "I want to see!"

Carefully, Eleanor unwrapped the paper from a larger box than Belinda's. Inside lay a pair of elegantly crafted ivory hair combs.

"Oh," Eleanor gasped. "They are lovely." She turned to Isabella with a sweet smile. "I love them. Thank you!"

"You must be sure to thank your brother as well," Isabella said. "He spent a great deal of time poring over every item in that particular shop. He wanted just the right thing for you two."

"He did?" Belinda asked, her mouth agape. "I cannot imagine it."

"He loves you both very much," Isabella told them, recalling his insistence that he and Isabella visit just one more shop. "I know he seems to spend a great deal of time working on the estate and whatnot, but he does think a great deal about whether he is making the right decisions where you two are concerned."

"We'll thank him," Eleanor assured her. "And thank

you again." She hugged Isabella, before leading Belinda to the door.

"We are very glad you're our sister now," Belinda said before they left.

Isabella stood for a moment, then wiped her eyes and told herself not to be a goose.

Now that she was alone, the fatigue of the journey settled upon her at once. She'd heard the footmen delivering the hot water to her dressing room while the girls had opened their gifts. Eager to soak away the aches in her body, she crossed the room into the dressing room and found Sanders putting her favorite scent into the steaming bath.

"Excellent," she said, stepping farther into the chamber. "I haven't looked forward to a bath in quite some time."

"Before you get in," Sanders said, "it seems you received a package while you were gone. I assume it was a wedding or betrothal gift, since Templeton says it was hand delivered. I was going to let it wait until morning, but to be honest, Your Grace, it's begun to smell a bit. So I think it might be cheese or something edible. You know how country folk are."

Isabella bit back a smile. "I know we are far from London, Sanders, but you really mustn't be such a snob."

"Hmph," Sanders responded. "There's a reason I stayed in London instead of taking a position in the country, Your Grace. These country folk aren't civilized, if you don't mind my saying so."

Isabella had thought the same thing when she'd first arrived in Yorkshire, but her opinion of the people here had changed not long after she'd become acquainted with them. Of course Sanders's acquaintance thus far had been with the servants, who, for all Isabella knew, were savages. So she forbore from chastising her.

Taking the box from Sanders, she noted that it did indeed smell. If it was cheese she would simply have to send a thank-you note and pretend that it had been delicious to whoever had sent it. "There was no card with it?" she asked the other woman.

"No, Your Grace," Sanders replied, not even bothering to pretend she wasn't desperate to know what the box held.

Carefully, Isabella untied the ribbons holding the lid on. "Well, here we go," she said, lifting the lid with a laugh.

But all laughter fled when she saw what was inside.

She heard a scream and realized with shock that the sound was coming from her own throat.

Trevor had finished his own bath and was submitting to his second shave of the day when he heard Isabella's shriek. Despite wearing a dressing gown with nothing underneath, he sprinted toward the door that separated their two dressing rooms and threw it open.

He found both Isabella and her maid staring with shock and horror at an open box. The lid had been cast aside, along with a pretty grosgrain ribbon that had clearly held the package closed.

"What is it?" he demanded, stepping forward and looking inside.

Neither woman responded as Trevor stared in repugnance at the dead rabbit in the box.

"Poor little creature," Isabella said with a shudder. "I hope it didn't suffer overmuch."

Trevor wrapped his arms around her, livid to feel her trembling beneath his arms. "Take it downstairs," he instructed his valet, who had followed him and was hovering in the doorway between the two rooms.

Jennings stepped forward and lifted the box. "I'll take care of it, Your Grace."

He was stepping away when he stopped. "Your Grace, there's a note inside."

Trevor paused, his hand resting between Isabella's shoulder blades. He watched as Jennings gingerly reached into the box and withdrew a folded sheet of foolscap. Silently he handed the note to his master. Isabella's maid, exchanging a look with Trevor, followed the valet from the dressing room, leaving Trevor and Isabella alone.

"I'm all right," Isabella said, pulling away from Trevor in reluctance. "I want to know what it says."

Wordlessly Trevor unfolded the paper and held it out so that they could both see what it said.

I had to get the evil out

Isabella gasped, covering her mouth with her hand to keep herself from crying out.

Trevor was at her side in an instant. "What is it? Do you recognize the handwriting?"

Wordlessly she shook her head and buried her face in his neck, needing more than ever the feel of his strong body holding her. "N-no," she managed to say. "But the words, they are familiar." Her body began to shake uncontrollably.

"Easy," Trevor said, gathering her up in his arms and carrying her bodily into his bedchamber. As if she were a child, she felt him lower her to the bed and climb up beside her, never letting her go.

After a few minutes of him stroking her back, calming her, she stopped shaking and was able to speak. "I am sorry," she said softly.

"For what?" he asked, not letting her out of his arms. "For being human?"

"I hadn't expected it," she said simply. "I thought no one knew about what Mama had done, you see. So, it came as a shock."

"I think you'd better tell me," Trevor said, kissing the top of her head. "I can't protect you if I don't know the whole story. If you're up to it, that is."

She allowed herself to relish the feel of his strong arms around her for a few moments, drawing strength from his nearness.

Swallowing, she began, proud that her voice was steady as she spoke the words: "When I was a small child, four years old, my mother went mad."

Trevor didn't say anything and Isabella was grateful for his silence. She'd only told one other person in her life this story, and Wharton's reaction had been to backhand her.

"She suffered a great deal with each pregnancy," Isabella said, fumbling with the buttons on Trevor's waistcoat so that she'd have something to do with her hands. "After Perdita, the doctors warned Papa that she should not conceive again. But he didn't heed them. And when Perdita was two years old, she became with child again. Only this time, she had no troubles until after the child, a boy, was born."

"What happened?" Trevor asked.

"At first nothing. She seemed pleased to have given Father a son at last. But within a week or so she became tearful. She wept constantly. Perdita and I were not allowed to see her. But I could hear her, shrieking, crying, railing. Papa hired a nurse to watch over her full-time. And I believe there was talk of sending her to Bedlam. But at the time I didn't know about that. I was simply a child who wanted her mother.

"One night, a few weeks after my brother's birth, she left her chamber while her nurse was sleeping and stole into the nursery." Isabella spoke, but it felt as if someone else were telling the tale. "I later learned that she'd been having visions of the devil telling her that my brother, her baby, was his child and that she had to kill him or he would destroy the world. So, my mother, in her madness, smothered the baby. Then drank a bottle of laudanum."

"Christ," Trevor said vehemently. Isabella tried to pull away, but he would not let her. "You were only a child. How did you come to find about it? I cannot think your father told you."

"Hardly," she said, grateful for Trevor's protective arms. "My godmother told me when I'd been married for a year or so. Papa managed to hide the truth of things. He put it about that Mama and my brother both died from a fever."

"I am sorry, Isabella," Trevor said, stroking her back. "More sorry than I can say."

"I will consent to an annulment if you wish it," Isabella said softly. "Wharton was livid when he learned of it, and rightly so. Madness does run in some families."

"You can hardly control what traits your parents give you," Trevor said, ever reasonable. Isabella was beginning to wonder if he possessed a temper at all. "Besides, our marriage was a matter of honor. I could hardly have compromised you and refused to marry you. That would be the behavior of a blackguard."

"Not many men would see it that way," Isabella said, unable to look at him. "Wharton certainly wouldn't have done so."

"I believe I have made my opinion about your first husband known," Trevor said, his voice clipped. "I suppose he beat you when he learned of it."

Her face buried in Trevor's chest, Isabella nodded. Knowing she had to tell the whole story while they were speaking of it, she said, "I was with child, and . . . I lost the baby."

Trevor cursed and got up from the bed to go stand by the window.

Isabella felt bereft, but she could hardly blame him for wishing to have some space after hearing such a tale. She had known she'd have to tell him the story sooner or later but had cravenly hoped that it could wait until they'd been married for longer.

"It was wrong of me to wait," she said, pulling her knees up to her chest so that she could hug them to her. "I waited until I was with child to tell Wharton and he was understandably angry. I wanted a baby so much, but I knew I had to warn him, in case . . ."

"In case you went mad like your mother did after you gave birth?" Trevor asked, not turning away from the window.

"Yes," Isabella said. "I will do whatever you wish, Trevor. I will consent to an annulment or I will return to London. Whatever you wish to do."

He turned from the window to stare at her. "I do not want an annulment. I have already said that marrying you was a matter of honor and I meant it. You will be no less compromised by me if we annul the marriage."

She tried to read his expression, but it was unusually blank. "All right," she said.

"Whoever sent that package knew about your mother," Trevor said, sitting on the edge of the bed.

Isabella nodded, and moved slightly back so he would have room. "Yes, they had to have known the story."

Turning onto his side to lie facing her, Trevor watched her, his gaze intent. "Then we need to determine who might have known. Have you told anyone other than Wharton?"

"Only Perdita," she said, watching Trevor with wary eyes as he reached out to her. "What are you doing?" she demanded, no longer concentrating on the mystery of who was trying to frighten her.

"I am comforting my wife," Trevor said, pulling her against him again.

"I thought you were angry with me," she said, unable to resist the lure of his comforting arms.

"Not with you," he said, leaning back so that he could look her in the eye. "With Wharton. For what he did to you. Your child."

The tears came, and this time Isabella allowed them to run down her face unchecked. "You are such a good man," she said, lifting a hand up to caress his cheek. "I should have known you'd react to the tale by reiterating your reasons for marrying me in the first place."

He took her hand and kissed the palm. "You have had little enough experience with decent men," he said. "I hope that you will begin to expect goodness rather than dishonor. Not all men are as your father and your husband were."

"Once we find the person who is trying to frighten me," she said, tucking her head under Trevor's chin, "perhaps then I will be able to expect more from the men around me."

"And in the meantime," Trevor said, kissing her, "I will endeavor to raise your expectations on my own."

Seventeen

"You know that I'll do whatever you need me to while you're gone," Lucien said, his affable countenance tight with unaccustomed gravity.

Trevor had ridden over to the other man's estate as soon as he awakened. Long after Isabella had fallen into a restless sleep, Trevor had lain awake pondering what his next move must be in the cat-and-mouse game that her mysterious correspondent was playing. Trevor had little doubt that while he and Isabella were in Yorkshire whoever the person was would continue to become more and more dangerous. Though there were not as many people in the countryside as there were in London, the sheer vastness of the moors made it easy for whoever this was to remain hidden. Not long before he'd thrown off the bedclothes and dressed for the day, Trevor had decided that what might be called for was a change of scenery. Clearly this bastard had little enough trouble terrorizing Isabella at Nettlefield. Perhaps a return to London, where the incident that had set all of this chaos in motion had occurred, would bring matters to a head.

"I know you will," Trevor said to Lucien. "Though I do apologize it comes so close on the heels of our trip to Scotland." He smiled despite his somber mood. "I had not thought to turn you into a nursemaid."

"You are a font of hilarity," Lucien said with a scowl. "You needn't worry about me, however. That Miss Nightingale of yours is as efficient as any I've seen."

"That she is," Trevor agreed. "And I don't mind telling you how relieved I am to finally have a governess for my sisters who spends more time thinking of them than she does of me."

"For what it's worth," Lucien continued, turning the conversation firmly back to Trevor's problem, "I think you're doing the right thing. I'm just as fond of the countryside as you are, but there is something very unprotected about it. There's nowhere to hide. And for all that this fellow might be able to blend into the crowd better in London, I have little doubt that Ormonde House is like a bloody fortress."

"That's it exactly," Trevor said. "Here I feel like we're simply waiting for him to make the next move. And security is hardly something that I've spent a great deal of time emphasizing at Nettlefield. There's never been a need for it. But Ormonde House is as tight as a tick."

"You speak of it as if you've been there," Lucien remarked, his face impassive but his eyes revealing his suspicions.

Trevor shrugged. "I might have paid a visit to it on a trip to London once or twice. Though I made damned sure to keep it a secret from my family there."

"While your father was alive?" Lucien asked, brows raised. "I cannot imagine that he would have been pleased by that."

"God no," Trevor said with a grin. "He would have skinned me alive.

"But," he continued, "there was a time, not too long after he died, that I found myself curious about what it was he'd been cut out of. I have to admit to being astonished by the sheer power of the place. It's huge, Lucien. It rivals St. James Palace in size. And I have little doubt that the dowager rules over all of it with an iron fist."

"What do you think she'll do when you descend upon her, wed to the woman she sent to lure you back, and seeking shelter from a madman?"

Trevor was blunt. "I don't give a hang what she'll do. It's my house, and though I know it's been her greatest wish that I go to London and allow her to turn me into her pawn, she's going to be greatly disappointed to find that I haven't the first intention of allowing that to happen."

"That's the spirit, old boy." Lucien grinned. "Just don't be surprised if she proves to be reluctant to go quietly."

"I have little doubt that she'll fight me at every turn." Trevor grinned back. "But if she pushes me too far, I'll simply have her installed in the dower house. It is my prerogative as the duke, after all."

His grandmother, he thought, should have been careful what she wished for.

"So soon? But what about your sisters?" Isabella demanded once Trevor had finished telling her of his plan. "I thought you weren't planning to leave for another week at the earliest. And surely London will be a much easier place for this person to escape detection."

"My sisters will be well looked after by Miss Nightingale and Lucien," Trevor said, taking her hand in his.

They were in the morning room that Isabella had taken as her personal study. He had leaned back against the mantle while he explained the gist of his plan, but as soon as Isabella began her objections he'd taken the seat next to her on the settee. Once she'd have felt crowded by his closeness, but now she only felt comforted by his presence.

"And I see no reason for us to delay our departure," he continued. "It seems arbitrary to wait simply for the sake of waiting."

Isabella bit back a sigh. She supposed he was right. It was a surprise to her just how quickly she, who had spent her entire life in the city, could become accustomed to the slower pace of country life. She missed London, of course, but she would miss Nettlefield when they left it. "You don't think we should bring Eleanor and Belinda with us?" she asked. "I should like to show them the sights. I think Belinda would adore it."

He rubbed his thumb over the back of Isabella's hand. "Not this time, my dear. For one thing, if the dowager proves to be more of a handful than I expect then I don't wish for them to be caught in the cross fire. I have yet to meet her in person, but from what you've told me, she can be quite ruthless. And I do not wish for them to be harmed."

"I wish there were something I could do," Isabella said, standing up and pacing the small space between the settee and the fireplace. "It is infuriating to know that this person knows so much about me, but I know so little about them."

"We will fix that," Trevor said, his blue eyes focused on her face. "I promise you that once we are safely ensconced in the Ormonde town house I will make it impossible for this bastard to get to you. And I will find out who they are."

But Isabella had difficulty believing him. "Have you even been to London before?"

If he was stung by her question, he didn't show it. "As a matter of fact, I have. It's true that I am not acquainted with my family there, but I spent a little time there when I was at university. I went home with school friends and even attended a few *ton* functions."

Isabella tried and failed to hide her surprise. "But you made it sound as if . . . I had assumed that—"

"I know what you assumed," he said with a slight smile. "And I might have allowed you to think it without correcting your misapprehension. Especially when you first arrived at Nettlefield. But the fact remains that I am quite familiar with London and I am not entirely ignorant about Ormonde House. I have, after all, been corresponding with the duke's—I suppose my—personal secretary about the place for the past year or so."

"I did know that, actually," she said with a sharp nod. "But it sounds as if you have no need of me for this trip at all," she said, knowing she sounded hurt and frustrated but unable to keep her emotions from her voice.

But before she could say more, Trevor was up and at her side. "I need you because you are my wife," he said, slipping his arms around her. "Surely the fact that I've been handling the Ormonde estate business doesn't erase the fact that you know the dowager and all the rest of the Ormonde family far better than I do. And I didn't marry you because you are some sort of golden ticket that will open the doors of London society for me."

"No, you married me to preserve my reputation," she

said with a frown. "And because you needed someone
to help you with your sisters."

She focused on the knot of his cravat. She had been
married for all those years to Ralph, who had tormented
her in every possible way, but she'd never felt as vulnerable with him as she did now with Trevor. If this was
what it meant to give your he— She stopped herself before she could complete the thought. Better not to travel
down that road.

"I married you," Trevor said, bending his knees so
that he could look into her downcast eyes, "because I
wished to. Not because either of our reputations was compromised. And certainly not just to have someone around
who could deal with my sisters. Though I will admit that
to be an added bonus.

"Come now," he continued, lifting her chin with his
finger and kissing her. "Are you going to come with me
to London so that we can rout the dowager and catch this
person who is hell-bent on terrifying you?" He said the
last with a crooked grin.

Isabella shook her head. It was impossible to stay
away from this man. Especially when he was at his
charming best. Damn him.

"You are absurd," she said, unable to stop the smile
from turning up the corners of her mouth. "I will come
with you to London. But you must know that I will want
to be as involved as possible when we capture this fellow."

"Absolutely," Trevor said with a smile. "I'll need
someone to hide behind, after all."

Isabella couldn't help it. She laughed.

*   *   *

The trip from Yorkshire to London took four days. Because they were traveling without the girls, Trevor made the decision to go as fast as they could given the circumstances. The dowager's carriage, which had finally been repaired, was following behind Trevor and Isabella's vehicle and carried their baggage and Isabella's maid.

He chose not to send a letter ahead of them informing his grandmother of their impending arrival. Surprise was, after all, a tactical advantage, and he was damned if he'd give it up just to make her more comfortable. They stayed at an inn just outside of London on the night before they descended upon Ormonde House. And as he made love to Isabella that night he couldn't help but feel that tomorrow might bring changes to their relationship that he wasn't able to foresee. For all that he felt he knew what sort of person she was at her core, there were still aspects of her personality and past that he had yet to learn. And despite what she'd told him about the night his cousin had died, he knew in his gut that there was more to the story than she was telling him.

As the carriage rolled to a stop outside the door of Ormonde House, he pulled her close for a kiss. "Head high," he told her. "We must approach her as a team, or she'll try to play us against each other."

He was not surprised to see Isabella raise one dark brow. "Are you sure you've never met your grandmother before?" she asked. "Because that's just what she's going to try to do. And I was about to warn you of the fact."

"I know how manipulative women work," he said with a shrug. "You've met the ladies of Nettledean, haven't you?"

She grinned and allowed him to hand her down from the carriage.

Pulling her to his side, Trevor straightened his hat and offered his wife his arm. When they reached the top of the steps, the door opened to reveal the dour-faced butler, Timms. "Lady Wharton," he said, inclining his head. "Whom may I say accompanies you?"

Not letting her respond, Trevor handed the fellow his hat and gloves. "The Duke of Ormonde."

If the man was surprised by the announcement, he didn't show it. He merely handed Trevor's things to a waiting footman, who betrayed his surprise only by a slight widening of his eyes. The servants were well trained, at least, Trevor thought.

"Very good, Your Grace," Timms said, his stoic expression revealing nothing. "May I say how good it is to welcome you to Ormonde House? We have kept your rooms ready in the event of just such a happy occasion."

"Excellent. And I trust that you will ensure that my wife's rooms will be made ready as well," Trevor told the man, taking Isabella's hand in his own, lest the butler assume he had some other wife waiting in the wings.

"Of course," the butler said, inclining his head at another footman. "I'll have word sent to Mrs. Timms at once."

He turned his attention to Isabella. "May I be so forward as to wish you happy, Lady . . . that is, Your Grace?"

"Of course, Timms," Isabella said with a smile. "I thank you. Now, can you tell us if the dowager is at home this afternoon?"

"She is indeed, Your Grace," the older man said with a smile. If Trevor wasn't mistaken, the old fellow looked positively gleeful. In as reserved and restrained a manner as possible, of course. "Shall I have tea sent up to her sitting room?"

Isabella turned to Trevor. "What do you think, darling? Shall we go up?" Trevor knew that what she was really asking was a tactical question. Would they go to the dowager in her own territory, or would they choose some neutral location for their first meeting?

Deciding to let her make the decision, he shrugged. "It's up to you, my dear."

She nodded. "Then we'll have the tea tray in the duchess's sitting room, Timms."

"I trust you'll be able to find your way to the sitting room, Your Grace?"

"Of course," she said. Then, before he could walk away, she asked, "Timms, can you tell me if the young dowager is in this afternoon?"

"I believe she has gone to pay afternoon calls, Your Grace," Timms said. "But I feel sure that she will be quite pleased to learn of your return."

Trevor watched as Isabella stared after the departing butler for a moment. If the man thought it odd that the sister of the previous mistress of the house had now taken her place, he didn't say it. If Trevor read the situation aright, he would say that the old man was fond of both of them. And not fond of the dowager. Yet another ally, he thought to himself.

"Shall we go up?" Isabella asked him, linking her arm in his. "I must confess that I'm quite famished. Cook makes the most delicious little cakes. I think you'll like them."

Somewhat bemused by the entire situation, Trevor allowed himself to be led up the stairs and toward the family rooms.

Eighteen

What is the meaning of this?" the Dowager Duchess of Ormonde asked, stepping into the sitting room that had once been hers. The new duchess was pleased to see that the knowledge smarted for her godmother, though Isabella did feel a pang of guilt over it. She had chosen to have the dowager's first meeting with Trevor in these rooms because it had been one of the things she most resented when Perdita married Gervase. Now the dowager would be annoyed by the fact that they'd been passed on to Isabella. Be careful what you wish for, Isabella thought."You cannot simply order me about like a servant."

"I hardly call issuing an invitation to tea the equivalent of ordering you about," Trevor said, rising from his position next to Isabella on the sofa. "And you are hardly the one to complain about being ordered about. I believe it was not so very long ago that you sent Isabella up to Yorkshire to fetch me to London like a recalcitrant schoolboy."

"Hmmph," the dowager retorted, lowering herself to the chair on the other side of the tea table with some difficulty. "It was high time for you to take up your duties as the duke. What nonsense for you to bury yourself away in Yorkshire holding on to a grudge that wasn't even yours to begin with. I was merely reminding you that your duty is to the family."

If Trevor was expecting to be welcomed with open arms by his grandmother, Isabella thought, he was to be sorely disappointed. Her godmother had never been a demonstrative person, but now faced with the very situation she'd done her utmost to make happen she was still positively glacial.

"And I thought it was to my family that I was showing loyalty by refusing to come to heel," Trevor said, resuming his seat. "But that's neither here nor there. I am here now and quite ready to take up the duties of the dukedom."

"Excellent," the dowager said with a nod. Not even pausing to take a breath, she went on, "I have a list of excellent ladies who will make the perfect duchess for you. I believe that Lady Marianna—"

If Isabella weren't so amused, she'd have been shocked. Though she supposed she should have stopped being shocked by the dowager's behavior long ago.

Trevor cut her off. "I have no need of such a list. I already have a wife."

The dowager's eyes hardened. Isabella had seen the very same look precede some of her most heated quarrels with the dowager. Clearly Timms had not told her about Isabella's marriage to Trevor, which was at once hilarious and terrifying. The dowager on a good day was not altogether pleasant. But the dowager on the day that she realized her greatest wishes had been thwarted was positively catastrophic. Even so, Isabella wouldn't give up what she was about to witness for love or money.

"Isabella," the dowager barked, "you may leave us. I am grateful that you were able to persuade my grandson to give up his sheep and come to London to do his duty, but we have much to discuss now." She inclined her head in the manner of a god granting a prayer. "I will keep your sacrifice in mind when it comes to your sister, have no fear."

But Trevor found nothing funny about the situation, apparently. "Isabella will remain here with me. As is only right."

"Well," the dowager conceded, "I do think it magnanimous of you to allow her to see the fruits of her labor, but there are things we should discuss that only family should be privy to."

"Yes," Trevor said patiently. "And Isabella is family."

"This is foolish," the dowager said, her patience wearing thin. "Yes, she is the sister-in-law of the former duke, but that hardly makes her—"

Isabella could almost feel sorry for the old woman. If she hadn't brought the whole business down upon herself, that was.

"No, I mean she is my wife," Trevor said firmly. "Surely that is enough to earn her a place in this conversation."

The room grew eerily quiet as the dowager took in Trevor's words. Isabella could hear the clock on the mantle tick. A costermonger calling out the price of his wares on the street outside. A door creaking in some other part of the house. Silently she slipped her hand into Trevor's as the dowager opened and closed her mouth like a fish.

"Your," she began, her voice increasing in volume as the words left her mouth, "your . . . what?"

To Isabella's horror, the dowager's face turned an un-natural shade of purple. "You married him?" she de-manded, leaping up from her chair and approaching Isabella with menace. "You were supposed to bring him back to London! Not marry him! Do you know what you've done? You foolish, foolish girl!"

Trevor rose as if to stop the dowager from striking Isabella, but to Isabella's surprise, instead of launching herself at her new granddaughter-in-law, the Dowager Duchess of Ormonde collapsed.

"She's sleeping," Perdita said, quietly closing the door to the old dowager's bedchamber. Perdita didn't have her sister's dark hair and brows. Instead her hair was a lighter shade of brown. They had the same blue eyes, however, and there was something about the arch of their brows and the slant of their cheeks that marked them as sib-lings. "Dr. Henderson says that she should be kept quiet for the next few days to ensure she doesn't suffer an-other attack."

"How long has she been hiding this?" Isabella asked from her place on the settee. She had been shaken by the dowager's fit, and Trevor had been surprised and pleased by her quick assessment of the situation. Like most men, he had little knowledge of what to do when someone fell ill, and since he was not acquainted with the dowager, he had no way of knowing if the collapse was due to something she often suffered from or if it was a new oc-currence. Resuming his seat beside Isabella, he watched as Perdita tried to frame a response to her sister's ques-tion, perching on a chair opposite them.

"I believe she has been having little spells for some

time now," Perdita admitted, pouring herself a cup of tea from the pot on the table between them. "You know how proud she is, Isa," she said with a shake of her head. "I would not be surprised if this was something she's been hiding from us for a year or more."

"Since your husband's death, you mean?" Trevor asked. He was not surprised to see both women blanch, considering the way that the late duke had died, but Trevor was beginning to understand why his grandmother had been so adamant about him coming to London to assume the role of the duke.

If she was cowed by the question, Perdita didn't allow it to enter her voice, however. "Yes," she continued, "I suspect that the shock of his death was likely the incident that caused her to suffer her first spell. She took his death quite hard. Even knowing what a . . ." She paused, obviously trying to come up with some delicate way to describe her late husband.

"He knows, Perdy," Isabella told her with a glance at Trevor. "I told him everything. About that night."

Perdita looked from Trevor to Isabella, her creamy complexion turning paler. She swallowed before saying, "I suppose you had to."

"He is my husband," Isabella said, lacing her fingers through Trevor's. He felt a lump form in his chest. But her next words made it dissolve. "And he is the duke, so if there is any danger of our being prosecuted he will stand up for us." Suddenly their hasty marriage—despite his own insistence upon it—took on a different complexion altogether.

"Quite," he drawled. "I will certainly ensure that you do not hang for murder. At the very least."

He felt a fool for not seeing the possibility sooner. It

had simply never occurred to him that Isabella might have orchestrated their reasons for marrying. She'd seemed so resistant to marrying again. Could that have truly been an act?

Now was hardly the time to consider the matter, however. There were other things to consider.

Beside him, Isabella had the grace to blush. Whether it was guilty or not he could no longer trust himself to decide. "I didn't mean it like—"

But he cut her off, not wishing to hear excuses now, asking Perdita, "If the dowager has been ill all this time, who has really been running the Ormonde estates?"

"She has, for the most part," Perdita said, though she looked a bit uncomfortable at the byplay between Isabella and Trevor. "And you, I suppose. Also, I believe a great deal of the estate business has been handled by Archer."

"The duke's—rather my—secretary." It wasn't a question. He'd found, through their correspondence, that Lord Archer was a competent and at times brilliant secretary, maintaining both the estates and the at-times-complicated management of the various dependents on the dukedom with a light but firm hand. "He resides here, does he not?"

"Yes, Your Grace," Perdita said with a slight blush. "I believe he is currently in his—I mean your study."

Trevor didn't miss her corrected mistake. Was he going to have to put the fellow in his place as well as ensure that the dowager relinquished her control of the dukedom?

Trevor stood, deciding to leave the sisters to the conversation. "I'll just go pay him a visit then," he said. He turned to Isabella. "I trust I'll see you at dinner?"

Perhaps still regretting her earlier slight, Isabella

smiled up at him. "Yes, of course." Giving in to impulse, Trevor leaned down and kissed her full on the lips. Before either sister could comment, he left the room and went in search of the duke's . . . his . . . study.

"That certainly doesn't look like a marriage of convenience," Perdita told her sister with a grin.

Isabella knew her face flamed with color but tried to pass it off. "He just wanted to prove a point, or some such nonsensical masculine thing. I can hardly blame him given what I just said about possible prosecution."

"Yes," her sister agreed, leaning back in her seat to survey Isabella. "He wanted to prove that you are his wife and that he's in love with you."

Perdita had always been the more romantic of them. Even before they made their debuts, she'd waxed philosophical about the handsome young beaux who would come and sweep them both off their feet. She'd been sorely disappointed when the opposite happened. Now Isabella wondered how her sister had survived marriage to someone like Gervase yet still believed in happy ever after.

"It truly is a marriage of convenience, Perdy," she said, feeling like a clod for crushing her sister's romantic notions but unable to let her continue to think of Isabella's marriage as anything but what it was. "We were caught in a compromising position at a country ball. Trevor needed someone to look after his sisters and I agreed to it." She didn't mention the fact that Trevor seemed to be the only person who believed that she wasn't going stark raving mad.

"Isa," her sister said with a look of reproach. "You might gammon everyone else in Christendom about the circumstances behind your match, but I know you. And there is no way on earth you'd have consented to marry again unless you were head over ears in love."

The situation was far more complicated than Isabella was willing to reveal to her sister at this point. Aside from the fact that Isabella did, indeed, fear that she was falling in love with her own husband, the knowledge that someone was trying to discredit her made her current relationship with him one in which she relied upon him for far more help than she would have liked. Now that they were finally back in London, where she was in her preferred milieu, she hoped that the balance of power would shift a bit and she would be able to repay Trevor for the support he'd given her when they were in Yorkshire.

Aloud, however, she merely said, "We are fond of one another, and that's the end of it. Besides, we've only known one another for a few weeks. That's hardly the basis for true love."

But Perdita remained unconvinced. "Say what you will, Sister, but I know what I see before me."

Deciding to get a bit of her own back, Isabella asked her sister, "What of you and the Earl of Coniston? Are we to see an announcement in the papers before too long?"

To Isabella's surprise, however, her sister did not break into a bashful grin as she'd expected; instead Perdita looked troubled. "I'm afraid I have some bad news on that front. Lord Coniston and I have decided that we should not suit after all."

Isabella could not keep from gaping at her sister. "What do you mean you 'should not suit'? I thought you had all but accepted the man! At least that is how things were before I left for Yorkshire. Did the dowager perhaps put some sort of spoke in the wheel there? For if she did I will have no compunction about—"

"No, no, nothing like that," Perdita said quickly, her tone placating. "This was between Coniston and myself. I must ask you to keep this solely between us, but the truth of the matter, Isa, is that I simply do not love him."

Isabella took her hand. "But when did this happen? How? I thought you had decided that what you felt for Lord Coniston was far more real than your feelings for Gervase."

"I can't really say when or how it happened," Perdita admitted. "I simply knew one day while we were having a rather stilted conversation over the luncheon table. It really should not be difficult to carry on a conversation with the man you are supposed to love. And we were always arriving at some sort of conversational impasse."

"No, you are right about that," Isabella said thoughtfully. Even when she and Trevor were arguing, they never had difficulty finding things to say to each other. It was one of the things she loved about him.

Startled at the turn of phrase, she nevertheless chose not to overanalyze the thought. After all, it was simply a way of speaking. It didn't mean she loved him, for pity's sake.

But Perdita's next words gave Isabella pause.

"I know you are surprised, but I must say that your arrival just now has only reinforced my certainty that we have made the right decision in breaking off our prebetrothal, I suppose you'd call it."

"What do you mean by that?" Isabella asked with suspicion.

"Only that seeing you with your Trevor has reminded

me of what true love looks like," Perdita said with a laugh. "And I can tell already that the two of you are madly in love."

Impulsively Perdita hugged her sister, and though Isabella wasn't quite sure she agreed with her sister's assessment of her marriage to Trevor, she hugged her back.

"You're quite mad," Isabella told her, "but I do love you. And I hope that one of these days you will find a husband who loves you to distraction."

"I love you, too," Perdita said with a grin. "Even if you have stolen a march on every other lady in London by marrying Trevor before the rest of us even had a chance to meet him."

Eager to change the subject, Isabella asked, "What has really been going on with the dowager since I left?"

Perdita shrugged. "Once she convinced you to leave for Yorkshire, she seemed to . . . deflate." Her eyes darkened with worry. "I know that she blackmailed you into going," she said, "and I do hate that in choosing not to marry Coniston I made your trip to Yorkshire utterly unnecessary—aside from your marriage to Trevor of course. But I just don't think the dowager had it in her to stop my engagement if I'd wanted to go through with it."

"She's a sour old woman," Isabella retorted. "If I didn't believe her capable of doing those very things I wouldn't have left town." She reached across to take her sister's hand. "I know you hold her in some affection, dearest, but she truly believes that we were responsible for Gervase's death. And she's never for a moment believed him capable of the things he did to you."

"You just don't know her as I do, Isa," the younger woman said with a sigh. "I know you don't trust her. You have every reason not to, considering how she returned you to Ralph that time you tried to run away. But she thought she was doing the right thing. She's from a different generation. The Duchess of Devonshire put up with all sorts of outrages from her husband and never really left him. I believe the dowager thought that you were simply being headstrong or overreacting."

"I was not overreacting," Isabella said through clenched teeth, remembering again just how betrayed she'd felt when her own godmother had told her husband where she was hiding from him. "He killed the child I was carrying, Perdita. If I'd remained with him he would have killed me as well. As it was, he nearly did so when I was returned to him."

"She didn't know, Isa. I promise you," Perdita said, tears forming in her eyes. It was an old argument between them, and one that Isabella knew her sister took to heart. Maybe if Isabella had spent as much time with the dowager as her sister had she'd understand the old woman's behavior like Perdita did. But Isabella still couldn't understand how her sister could defend the woman who had accused her of intentionally killing her husband. "She stayed with the old duke, so she didn't understand why we shouldn't stay with Ralph and Gervase."

"Let's not argue over her, Perdita," Isabella said, a sudden weariness coming over her as she recalled all of the heartache and drama that had surrounded her first marriage. "There is something I must tell you."

At Perdita's squeal of delight Isabella realized that she'd perhaps phrased that wrong. "No," she said with a nervous laugh, "I assure you it is not that I am with child." It was far too soon for such a thing. Besides which, she had enough on her plate at the present time without the addition of a pregnancy to the mix.

"It is something else entirely," she said firmly. "Something much more sinister." Quickly she explained to her sister everything that had happened to her while she was in Yorkshire, beginning with the intentionally broken carriage and ending with the dead rabbit.

"Who would do such a thing?" Perdita demanded. She could be quite fierce when her loved ones were endangered.

"I don't know," Isabella said with a lift of her shoulders. "At first I thought it might be someone who knew about how Gervase died, but this last note is almost eerily similar to Mama's last words. Who knows about that but us? Papa is dead, after all. And I only told Wharton."

"No one that I can think of," Perdita said. "I was always quite careful not to say anything to Gervase about it. Especially after I saw how Wharton used it against you."

"That's what I thought," Isabella said. "But god knows who Ralph told. He was quite angry about it when I told him." An understatement if ever there was one.

"Someone obviously knows now," Perdita said, her light brows drawn. "What would someone have to gain by making you think you're going mad?"

"I'm not sure," Isabella said truthfully. "There's no reason I can think of for someone to persecute me in this way. I thought at first that it might be the dowager, but her illness makes that a slim possibility."

"There is the fact that you were there when Gervase died," Perdita said carefully. "The dowager might not be capable of perpetrating such a scheme, but Gervase left any number of friends and associates with reason to hate you."

"But what of you, and Georgina?" Isabella asked, not

liking to think of her sister and her friend being subjected to the sort of games that this villain had put her
through.

Perdita looked down.

"Perdita?" Isabella asked, her stomach tightening.
"What is it that you aren't telling me?"

"I didn't tell you because I thought you were in Yorkshire falling in love. . . ." She looked sheepish at her
own foolishness. "But both Georgie and I have received
notes in the past week or so."

"What did they say?" Isabella asked, though she
knew what her sister would say.

" 'I know what you did last season.' "

Nineteen

Trevor found the personal secretary to the Duke of Ormonde in the massive study, just where Perdita had said he would find him.

He didn't bother knocking, preferring to simply walk in like he owned the room, since he did. And he wanted to gauge how the man responded to such a tactic. Trevor wasn't sure who was terrorizing Isabella, but as the man who ran the Ormonde estates, Lord Archer, younger son of the Duke of Pemberton, was in as good a position as anyone to orchestrate such a campaign of mental attacks.

The man himself was seated not at the largest desk in the room, which was piled with newspapers, mail, estate books, and any number of documents that went into keeping the House of Ormonde running smoothly, but instead hunched over a smaller desk to the side, where he wrote feverishly in a large ledger. The piles were neat, clearly ordered by someone who knew that tidiness was a must when dealing with some twenty properties, farms, estates, and various other holdings.

His boots soundless on the thick carpeting, Trevor stepped closer, not speaking until the younger man, as if sensing his presence, looked up. As soon as Lord Archer realized who it was he'd been interrupted by, he leapt to his feet and offered a deep bow.

"Your Grace," he said, his voice cultured and smooth, and as urbane as Trevor's was blunt. "It is a pleasure to finally make your acquaintance. Welcome to Ormonde House."

Lord Archer stepped out from behind the desk and bowed again.

"Lord Archer," Trevor said with more gruffness than he'd intended. "It is good to finally meet the man who runs the Ormonde estates."

If the fellow showed the merest hint of resentment, that might be a clue that he was vulnerable to being used as a means of getting at Isabella. But there was no sign of anger or frustration at being taken for granted in Lord Archer's manner. Far from it.

"I would hardly say that, Your Grace," the young lord said with a good-natured laugh. "I am merely the man who keeps things in order so that the big decisions can be made by you. And that's the way I like it."

Gesturing for the other man to take a seat before the fire, Trevor followed him and took a seat himself. "So you have no ambitions to run a household of your own one day?"

Lord Archer rubbed his forehead, causing a dark curl to tumble over his brow. "I won't say that I don't wish for a home of my own one day," he admitted, "but I am quite content for now to act as your personal secretary. Though I will admit that I hope your arrival in London might mean that you are ready to take up your seat in the Lords."

Taken by surprise, Trevor laughed. "I hadn't really

thought of it, to be honest. Politics has never been an ambition of mine, though I do understand the need for those in power to do what's needed to keep the nation running."

"I hope while you're in town that I might be able to persuade you to take a more active role, Your Grace."

Trevor was pleased by the other man's plain speaking. He did not betray a hint of shyness about the matter, for which Trevor was grateful. It showed him that Lord Archer Lisle was a man who knew his own mind. "I will look forward to hearing your argument, Lord Archer," he said with a smile. "What role have my predecessors played in the government?"

He leaned back and listened attentively to his secretary outline what Gervase, his father, and the dowager's late husband had done in their own time in the House of Lords. It was clear that Lord Archer was an acute observer of politics, the government, and all that those subjects entailed. When he was finished, Trevor knew that the House of Ormonde was generally considered to have Tory leanings but that from time to time, when politically expedient, they voted with the Whigs. And he realized that he could do far worse than to allow his secretary to steer him through the shark-infested waters of the English political system.

"Why have you not stood for a seat in the Commons yourself?" he asked when Lord Archer had finished. "It's clear that you know everything there is to know about the political situation."

Lord Archer leaned back in his chair, relaxing for the first time since Trevor had entered the room. "To be honest, Your Grace, while I am well versed in the matter, it is not my passion. My greatest pleasure comes from running the estates. I have—have always had—an affinity for numbers and I'm never happier than when I'm managing the estate books and making the numbers balance."

Despite himself, Trevor was surprised. "But you spoke just now as if you thought about nothing but politics morning, noon, and night."

The other man shrugged. "It is my job to be informed. And I am interested in it. Just not to the point of wishing to make it my life's work."

"You are the younger son of the Duke of Pemberton, correct?"

"Yes," Lord Archer said, flicking a nonexistent bit of fluff from his coat sleeve. "As a younger son, I was given the options of the army, the church, or being a personal secretary. Having no affinity for war and no special calling for the church, I chose the last. If there is one thing I know intimately, it's how a ducal household runs."

If that was the case, then Trevor would find the fellow a font of necessary information. But what Trevor truly wished to know was something he wasn't sure the young man would be willing to tell him. "What can you tell me about the late duke?" Trevor asked abruptly. He had decided that if he was going to ask the question he may as well be blunt about it.

If Lord Archer was surprised, he didn't show it. "What do you wish to know?" Trevor noticed a slight sharpening of his companion's gaze. There was dislike in his eyes, but not for Trevor.

"You may as well tell me what you know about his death."

The secretary's jaw tightened. "His death was an accident," Lord Archer said tightly. Gone was the affable young man of before, and in his place was a man who harbored a secret.

"You needn't look at me like I'm the enemy," Trevor said matter-of-factly. "I know what a bastard my cousin was. And I have no doubt that he deserved what happened to him."

"Lady Wharton . . . I mean Her Grace," Lord Archer corrected himself, "she told you? About that night?"

"Ah, so you've heard our news?" Trevor should not have been surprised that the word of their marriage had reached Lord Archer's ears. But he was.

"It is my job to be informed, Your Grace," Lord Archer said with a rueful grin. "And I happened to be in an alcove of the hallway when you informed the butler. Allow me to wish you both every happiness."

Trevor inclined his head. "My thanks. And I should think it would be no surprise that my wife would share the circumstances of my predecessor's death with me."

Lord Archer reddened slightly. "I did not mean to sound so shocked. It's just that none of the ladies is comfortable speaking about that night. Perdi—uh, I mean the young duchess"—to Trevor's amusement the man lost his cool composure and thrust a hand through his thick dark hair—"does not speak of it at all. Even to . . . friends."

Trevor had little doubt who the man meant by "friends." He wondered how long the other man had been in love with his former employer's wife. He also wondered if she knew. Of course this was hardly the stuff that he had come to the study to concern himself with. Steering the conversation back to the late duke, he said, "I know what happened that night. And I believe that someone is trying to frighten Isabella into confessing the truth of the matter to the authorities."

He hadn't intended to reveal all of this to Lord Archer when he'd first come into the study, but he was convinced that the man's affection for the young dowager cleared him from the list of people who had reason to reveal the truth about the duke's death. Trevor would eat his hat before he believed Lord Archer Lisle capable of betraying Perdita like that. Indeed, if Trevor was not mistaken, far from wishing to avenge Gervase's death, the secretary wished he'd killed Trevor's late cousin himself.

Even so, Trevor thought long and hard before responding when Lord Archer demanded, "Tell me everything from the beginning."

Deciding to go with his gut and hoping he would not have cause to regret the decision, Trevor did.

"My dear Lady Wharton—oh no, I mean Your Grace, of course!"

It was the third time the Dowager Countess of Humphries had "slipped" and called Isabella by her old title. None of the old biddies who filled the drawing room at Ormonde House had forgotten for a minute that Isabella was now the Duchess of Ormonde. But they played at forgetting just to call attention to the fact that she'd married without their knowledge or approval. Not that the latter was necessary, but they certainly seemed to think it was.

Added to the surprise nature of her marriage was the fact that she'd married the Duke of Ormonde, stealing a march on their own daughters and granddaughters and in effect keeping the Ormonde title in the family. They would be loath to admit it, but as soon as an eligible titled gentleman surfaced on the marriage mart they all began to think of him as theirs until they declared otherwise. Such was the nature of marriage among the titled set.

"Of course, Lady Humphries," Isabella said wryly, taking a sip of her tea. She scouted the room for someone, anyone, who might relieve her from this boring prattle, but alas, there was only Perdita, who was similarly engaged on the opposite side of the room.

"How long do you think the dowager will be confined to her bed?" Mrs. Selfridge, a kind, if abrupt, lady with whom the dowager had been friends for decades, asked. "I cannot think she is at all comfortable being cooped up in there." The two had made their come-outs together and were known as much for their youthful exploits as for their standing in the *ton*. "She has always been a restless sort of person."

"A week at the very least," Isabella replied, not wishing to think of the dowager's restlessness at the moment. Isabella had enough to deal with considering the attempts to drive her mad. "But I will be sure to tell her that you are thinking of her," she said, not unkindly. "I know that she will appreciate your kind thoughts."

"If you ask me," Lady Humphries said with a raised brow, "rest is just what Louisa needs. She's been at sixes and sevens ever since Gervase died as he did." Her expression indicated that she had her doubts about the circumstances of that death. "It has been such a burden for her, to be left in charge of things in the absence of the new duke." At this she sent a not-so-veiled glare Isabella's way. A glare that Isabella returned gladly, considering that far from feeling burdened by her duties, the dowager had loved every minute of being in charge of the dukedom. "Some people"—again she glared at

Isabella—"might have considered that while they were off sulking in the country."

Before Isabella could retort, Trevor himself stepped into the drawing room, bringing all conversation to a halt.

"My apologies, ladies," he said, at his most charming, Isabella noted with approval. It would take all that and more to make these old cats treat him with any sort of respect. "I hate to disturb your chat, but I was wondering if I might borrow my wife for a moment?"

She really should take a moment and introduce him to their guests, but Isabella was eager to escape them herself, so she excused herself to the company at large and followed him out into the hallway.

Once the door had closed behind them, Trevor pulled her wordlessly into a nearby parlor.

"What was that about?" she asked breathlessly. "Not that I'm not gratefu—"

He kissed her before she could finish. It was quick, and devastating. And ended far too soon.

"There," he said, pulling away. "Had to get that out of the way first."

Unable to respond, Isabella just touched her lips and looked up at him. Really, he had found the perfect way to silence her.

"Now," he went on, annoyingly unaffected by the kiss. "I need you to tell me something."

Bracing herself for a question relating to her previous marriage or perhaps about Perdita and Gervase's relationship, she held her breath.

"What do you think of my coat?" he asked. Isabella thought he was joking at first, but his expression revealed that he was deadly serious. "Is it terribly out of fashion? I mean, it's almost brand-new, yet Lord Archer informs me that I'll have to have a whole new wardrobe made up if I'm to be taken seriously as the duke. I thought the whole point of being a duke was not having to bother with all of this nonsense."

At the very real frustration in his gaze Isabella fought back the impulse to give him a hug. Instead she told him the truth. "While I'm sure that coat is very acceptable by Nettledean standards, it is quite out of fashion for London. Especially for someone of your standing. In fact, I think you will need to have new boots, new coats, new breeches. New everything. Just leave the details of it to Lord Archer. He knows exactly what a man of your standing will need to cut a dash. And if you don't wish to be too much the dandy, he can at least ensure that you are dressed appropriately."

Trevor frowned. "I was afraid you'd say that."

He looked like a pouting little boy, and Isabella gave in to impulse and smoothed the hair from his brow. "It might appease you somewhat to know that because you are a duke, you can have the boot maker, the tailor, the haberdasher all in to take your measurements here. So there's no need to go out on a shopping expedition or to make a big show of it."

But that didn't seem to make him any happier. "It's such a waste of time and effort," he said with a sigh. "I know that these people depend upon my business to pay their own bills, but it does grate to know that I could completely rebuild the tenant cottages at Nettlefield for what a coat by Weston will cost me."

Isabella did understand. Though she had grown up in a privileged household, her time working with charities had caused her to realize just how much money the people of the *ton* spent simply dressing themselves. "I know, dearest," she said, blushing as the endearment escaped her lips before she could stop it. "That is to say, I do know what you mean. But think of it as another expense of maintaining the dukedom. Like paying the underbutler or ensuring that the carriages are well sprung."

"I like that," he said with a grin. "You just compared the ducal corpus to a well-sprung carriage."

Seeing the glint in his eye, she moved closer. "If I recall correctly, Your Grace, you are quite well sprung as it is."

Growling, Trevor pulled her against him.

"Oh, I do apologize," Perdita squeaked from the doorway, hurriedly pulling the door closed again. "Only," she called softly from the hallway, "there is a situation that I think you both should be apprised of."

Leaning her head against her husband's strong chest, Isabella sighed. "I miss Nettlefield already."

"Yes, because being interrupted by my sisters is so much more agreeable than being interrupted by yours," Trevor said, pulling back from her and tucking a strand of hair that had worked loose from its pins behind Isabella's ear.

She turned and opened the door. "What is it, Perdy?"

"I'm afraid you've received a package," Perdita said, making no attempt to hide her curious glances between Isabella and Trevor. "It's in your sitting room. And it sounds quite odd."

"What do you mean, 'odd'?" Trevor asked, stepping up to slip his arm about Isabella's waist.

"It rattles," the young duchess said with a frown.

"I don't understand," Isabella said, her trepidation replaced with puzzlement. "Why should that be odd? It's probably just a wedding gift that broke or something."

"Not that kind of rattle," Perdita said firmly. "It sounds like a . . ."

What other kind of rattle could there . . . ?" Isabella froze.

"Oh my god," she said, a chill running up her spine. "Like a baby's rattle?"

At Perdita's nod she knew with a start that her tormentor had followed her.

The package looked quite similar to the one with the rabbit in it, Trevor thought as he, Isabella, Perdita, and Lord Archer hovered around the gaily beribboned box.

"Shall I do the honors?" Lord Archer asked, removing a penknife from his pocket.

At Trevor's nod the other man slipped the knife under the ribbons and cut them, leaving the lid of the box ready to be opened. Carefully, he put the knife down and removed the top from the box. All four of them leaned forward to peer into the bandbox.

Nestled within a carefully arranged froth of cloth was a tarnished silver baby's rattle.

Exchanging a look with Isabella, Trevor reached in and removed the rattle, turning it about in his hands. Lord Archer, meanwhile, removed the cloth from the bandbox and shook it out. It was a dressing gown. A man's dressing gown.

"What on earth?" Perdita asked, looking from the rattle to the gown. "Does this mean anything—?"

"It's Wharton's!" Isabella interrupted, stepping back from the gown as if it contained the body of the man himself. "And the rattle is one that I purchased before—" She broke off, dropping into a nearby chair.

"We bought it together," Perdita said, moving to stand beside her sister. "The rattle. We bought it the week after Isabella found out she was to have a child."

"There's a note," Lord Archer said, reaching into the box. He proffered the folded letter to Trevor, who took it warily.

I know what you did last season. And the season before. And I will make you pay.

"So this person is laying the blame on Isa for not only Gervase's death, but also Wharton's and her child's?" Perdita asked, aghast. "Clearly this person is delusional."

"Madmen often are," Trevor said without a trace of irony. "This person, whoever they may be, seems to hold Isabella responsible for all the bad things that have ever befallen her. I wonder that they haven't lodged a complaint against her for your mother's death as well."

"But who is it?" Isabella asked, jumping up from her seat to pace the chamber. "I cannot think of anyone who would mourn both Gervase and Wharton in the same breath. They were neither of them particularly well loved. Except by their mistresses. But as far as I know they never shared one."

"Who would have access to these things?" Trevor asked, indicating to Lord Archer that he should put the items back in the bandbox and remove them. "Did you have them stored somewhere in particular?"

"I don't really recall what became of Wharton's clothing and personal belongings." Isabella said, pausing in her tracks. "I dimly recall telling his valet that he should do something with them, but that time is a bit of a blur for me. I engaged a house of my own later that month and left the rest of the house for his heir, a distant cousin."

"And the rattle?" Trevor asked gently. "Did you have it packed away somewhere?"

Isabella nodded. "I keep it in a box in my bedchamber. But I haven't actually looked in the box for a long time. I couldn't bear to give it away, but it's hardly something I wish to look at every day."

"Lord Archer," Trevor said to the other man, who had returned from disposing of the box. "I should like for you to pay a visit to the new Lord Wharton and see if he knows what became of his predecessor's belongings."

With a brisk nod Lord Archer left to see to it.

"Isabella," Trevor said, "what became of your husband's mistress?"

"Mrs. Savery?" she asked, puzzled. "I have no idea. I never met the woman. And after he died, I had no ties to her. As far as I was concerned she was out of my life."

"Do you think that Wharton might have told her about your mother? And your miscarriage?"

Isabella paled. "I don't know. He wasn't in the habit of confiding in me, but I have no notion of how he interacted with her."

"How would she have learned about what happened with Gervase?" Perdita asked, her brow furrowed. "Wharton was dead by the time that happened."

"It is not all that unusual for the demimondaine to associate with each other, is it?" Trevor asked. "They can hardly mix with the ladies of the *ton,* after all."

"He's right," Isabella said to her sister. "Perhaps Mrs. Savery and Gervase's mistress were on speaking terms."

"But the dowager was adamant about keeping the circumstances of Gervase's death secret." Perdita's expression was grim. "Could someone have disobeyed her?"

"She's hardly the sort of person to inspire undying loyalty," Trevor said wryly.

"It's true, Perdy," Isabella said, moving to offer a comforting hand to her sister. "And was not Gervase's valet incensed about the whole affair?"

"He never did care for me," Perdita said with a frown. "I can see Kingston divulging the tale to his mistress."

"It simply remains for us to track down Mrs. Savery and her compatriot Mrs. . . . ?" Trevor began.

"Pringle," Perdita supplied. "I believe the late Mr. Pringle was a tailor."

"I'll come with you," Isabella said, stepping forward toward Trevor.

But he stopped her, taking her shoulders in his hands. "I dislike holding you here like a hostage, my dear," he said, "but until this person is caught, I do not wish for you to leave Ormonde House."

He could see from the mulish set of her jaw that she did not care for this plan one whit.

"I am hardly a child, Trevor," Isabella said with a frown. "I can be of some help to you in finding Mrs. Savery. The butler at my town house was the underbutler at the home Wharton and I shared. I have little doubt that he remembers her."

"Be that as it may," Trevor said firmly, "I wish you to remain here. Now, give me the direction of your town house."

She was angry, but Isabella told him the address of her house. "When you learn nothing," she said, "be sure to come back and get me. I will be more than happy to assist you."

Standing with her arms crossed over her chest, in the universal stance of annoyed wife, she allowed him to kiss her. Trevor was almost persuaded to take her with him. Then he remembered just how dangerous this person might be. "I will be home in time for dinner," he said, kissing her on the cheek.

He wasn't sure, but he thought she uttered a very bad word as he left the room.

Twenty

*A*s it happened, neither Trevor nor Lord Archer was back in time for dinner. Isabella had shared a quiet meal with Perdita and all the while wondered where her husband was and what he had discovered.

After dinner, she'd pleaded a headache and retired to listen furtively for the sound of Trevor returning to the room adjoining hers.

Before long she fell into an uneasy sleep punctuated by dreams in which she ran through a nameless castle, chased by some faceless entity that taunted her from the shadows. She awoke hours later, still fully dressed, to find the fire burned down and the candle beside her bed guttered. A glance at the clock revealed that she'd been asleep for hours.

Worried that she'd missed hearing Trevor's return, she rose from the bed and padded on bare feet toward the door of the dressing room. She'd almost reached the other side of the chamber when an unearthly wail made her gasp and clutch a hand to her throat.

What the devil was that? It sounded like a wounded

animal. She was unable to tell where the sound had come from, only that it terrified her.

She waited to see if it would happen again, but she was met with only silence. Hugging herself with her arms, she finally took another step and was startled again when another cry sounded. This time it was louder.

And somehow she knew that the sound wasn't being made by an animal but by something all too human. A baby.

Was this what it had been like for her mother? she wondered. Had it been the inability to stop the unearthly cries of her infant son that drove her to kill first him and then herself? Though Isabella knew in her gut that this was yet another ploy by the person who had been tormenting her, she could not halt the feelings of terror that coursed through her as she listened to the disembodied cries echoing around her.

"No," she said to herself. "No. This is not real. It's a trick. It's a trick."

Drawing on some inner core of strength, she pushed past her fear and forced herself to concentrate not on the fear the cries inspired but instead upon who might be controlling them. Straightening her spine, she flung open the door leading to the dressing room and hurried to open the door leading into Trevor's bedchamber.

Inside, things seemed much as they should be, with one exception. His bed was turned down, but there was no sign that he'd returned yet.

Where is he? She felt a stab of fear as she realized that he might have met with some misfortune while searching for Mrs. Savery. Isabella wished for the fiftieth time that she'd insisted upon accompanying him. She could hardly protect him from every sort of threat, but at least they'd be together. And she'd know whether he was safe or not.

Another wail from the disembodied child, however, reminded Isabella that she herself might be in danger now. It was likely that her tormentor knew of Trevor's absence and that was why she was being subjected to the current spate of terrors.

Turning slowly in place, she tried to determine where the crying, which was constant now, was coming from. Moving toward the door that led into the hallway, she thought it was coming from there. Stepping out into the hall, she followed the wails, which almost sounded as if they were coming from within the walls.

She had gone about thirty feet down the darkened passageway when she saw a door ajar up ahead. Could it have been left open for her benefit? As she got closer, she realized that it was an "invisible" door leading into the servants' passageway, a system of halls running parallel to the main hall. It was a way for servants to remain out of sight so that the wellborn ladies and gentlemen of the house would not need to see them. The practice had always seemed a bit hypocritical to Isabella, as if she and her peers were in denial about the fact that their every whim was accommodated by an entire class of people.

She paused on the threshold, knowing that she should fetch Lord Archer or Perdita, but she was tired of hiding behind others and letting them fight her battles for her. The baby's cry grew louder, and Isabella knew that whatever the case, she also needed to rescue the child from whoever was using it as part of this cruel game. And she was convinced now that it was a real child and not just an illusion or an adult playacting. A person who would use a real child to further their schemes would have no compunction about harming an innocent in the process. Which meant that Isabella needed to find the baby soon or something more terrible than her own torment would happen.

Stepping into the servants' passageway, Isabella noted even in the dim light that it was far less ostentatious than the main hall. There was no intricate wallpaper here, no shining brass wall sconces. Only unadorned cream-colored walls trimmed in a dull greenish gray color. The contrast was telling, and reminded Isabella that whoever it was threatening her might be someone who resented the differences between these two worlds.

Finally, she came to another open door, this one leading into the nursery, which to her surprise was lit up like Vauxhall during a fireworks display. Isabella blinked against the brightness of the candles and stepped inside.

Scanning the room, she saw her maid, Sanders, seated in a large rocking chair near the fireplace. Puzzled, Isabella found herself reluctant to step toward the maid. "Sanders, what on earth are you doing here? I thought you would have been abed long ago."

But the child in Sanders's arms told Isabella that her lady's maid had a reason for remaining awake long into the night that had nothing to do with her duties and everything to do with tormenting her mistress.

Sanders's words only confirmed Isabella's suspicions. "Come, my lady," Sanders said, never pausing in her rocking. "Let's not pretend that you don't know why I'm here. You may have taken a long while to figure it out, but surely by now you have done so."

Faced with the betrayal of someone she'd considered a trusted ally, Isabella shivered but tried not to show the fear or revulsion she felt. Her first priority must be the safety of the babe in Sanders's arms.

"I was beginning to wonder if you were as foolish as Ralph always said you were," the maid said with a shake of her head. "Even now you didn't figure it out until I led you here. It's a right shame. *My Lady.*" This last was said with a degree of sarcasm that revealed just how hateful it must have been for the woman to speak to Isabella with such deference for the time she'd served her.

And as she listened, several pieces of the puzzle clicked into place for Isabella. How the letters had reached her in Yorkshire. How her painting had been defaced when it was clear that the house had been locked up tight. How the replica of Ralph's snuffbox had arrived at just the right moment. And, most frightening of all, she recalled how Sanders had been the one to bring her attention to the box with the dead rabbit in it.

It had been Sanders all along. Thinking back to just how intimately the woman had been involved in her life over the past few months, Isabella was hit with a wave of disgust that made it difficult for her to remain standing. How could she possibly have been so blind to the woman's perfidy? It was terrifying just how much Sanders had been able to deceive her.

Now, not wanting to disturb the maid lest she harm the child, Isabella shut the door behind her and stood motionless just inside the room.

"I must give you credit for your guile," she said calmly. "But I'm afraid I still don't understand things fully. Why would you do such a thing to me, Sanders?

What possible harm can I have done you that would inspire you to such hatred? Did I even know you before you came into my employ?"

Never pausing in her rocking, the maid shook her head at Isabella's lack of comprehension. "You still don't understand it, do you, Isabella?" she asked. "I suppose I shall have to spell it out for you as I've had to do with every other detail."

Her eyes cold, she sneered at Isabella, her hatred for her mistress transparent at last. "I was your dear husband Ralph's mistress!" Sanders shouted, making the baby cry harder.

"Hush, you little brat," she hissed, shaking the child, who settled back down with a pitiful cry.

Turning back to Isabella, Sanders went on, "You didn't remember me because I was beneath the notice of the likes of Lady Isabella Wharton. Ladies all pretend that women like me don't exist. They get to live in the fancy house with the titles and the jewels. While the rest of us, the ones whot do the real work, live hidden away so that you don't have to see us."

Her face contorted into a mask of hatred. "The same is true for our babies. Yours get the benefit of your husband's good name, while ours are called bastards. And when they die?" Her voice broke as she seemed to relive a particularly difficult memory. "When our babies die they're not even good enough to rest in the same ground as your perfect little angels! I ask you what can be more innocent than a newborn babe taken from this world before its time? What harm could it do for a child of mine to be laid to rest in the same hallowed ground as a child of yours?"

Isabella gasped as Sanders removed a pistol from its

hiding place on the chair beside her and trained it at Isabella. Her mind racing, she tried to think of something—anything—that would somehow convince her husband's former mistress to put down the pistol and give the baby to Isabella.

Perhaps that was the answer, she realized. Perhaps she should appeal to Sanders as another mother who had lost a child. She took the seat opposite the madwoman. Schooling her voice to a calm she didn't feel, she asked, "When did your baby die, Charity?" Now she knew that the woman she had called Sanders was in reality Mrs. Charity Savery, her husband's longtime mistress, whose own baby by Ralph had died.

But to whom did the baby she held in her arms now belong? Had Charity kidnapped the child solely in her quest to torment Isabella? Surely it was not Charity's child, for she'd been in Isabella's employ for too long to have given birth to a child this young.

"He died a week or so after yours," Charity responded sullenly to Isabella's query. "Bet you didn't know Ralph had gotten us both with child at the same time. He was proud of it. Thought it meant he was a powerful man, that he could do anything."

Isabella remembered with disgust her husband's glee when she had informed him that she was with child. She'd thought it was because at long last he would have an heir, thus proving himself to be as virile as he claimed to be. But now she understood that there had been another reason for his enthusiasm. Ralph would have thought himself something close to omnipotent for achieving such a feat as getting both his wife and his mistress with child in such quick succession.

Of course, his joy had turned into contempt when he

learned the circumstances behind the deaths of Isabella's mother and brother. Then he treated her like a prisoner, always on the lookout for some sign of impending madness.

"Of course, when you miscarried and I lost my baby so soon after he was born," Charity continued, "Ralph showed just where his loyalties lay," the other woman said bitterly. "He didn't even shed a tear over my little Charlie, but he carried on for weeks over the loss of your whelp. If I'd had any doubts over who he valued more, he set me straight then. When I asked him for the funds for a proper burial he told me to pay for my own bastard's grave. As if he didn't have a hand in fathering the boy."

Isabella thought back to the weeks following her miscarriage. It was not a time she remembered well, simply because she'd been in such despair and had taken so much laudanum to numb her pain that she'd spent much of the time sleeping. How much worse would she have felt if she'd carried the child to term and lost him then? she wondered. It was hardly surprising that Mrs. Savery was so angry now. Especially if Ralph had behaved as she said he did.

"He was a detestable man," Isabella said, not bothering to hide her vehemence. "He used you and dismissed you. He took out his frustrations on me with his fists, and worse. He deserves neither one of our pity."

But if she had thought the other woman would agree with her, Isabella was in for a surprise. Instead of chiming in with her own contempt for the man who had hurt them both, Charity began to laugh. Not a joyous sound, but a maniacal one.

"Of course he beat you," she said with a shake of her

mobcapped head. "You kept him from doing what he really wished and marrying me. He might not have treated me like a queen," she continued, "but he loved me. We loved each other. And no amount of money from your father or threats from the dowager could change that. He was weak, it's true. Otherwise he never would have married you in the first place. But his father had his rules. And Ralph was nothing if not an obedient son. So he married you to make his father happy. And he kept me in our little house to make himself happy."

It was a common enough tale, Isabella supposed. Plenty of gentlemen lived double lives, keeping a wife and children in one, respectable, residence, and a mistress in another. But Isabella hadn't considered that Ralph would have defied his father in such a way. Of course, she was the embodiment of his obedience to the older man. She wondered suddenly if her father-in-law had known about her husband's arrangement with Mrs. Savery. Isabella somehow thought he might have.

"I see," she said aloud. If she could perhaps keep the woman talking, Trevor would discover she'd left her bed and would come looking for her. "Why did you wait so long to punish me? It's been nearly four years since Ralph died, after all."

"I was approached by a certain person," the other woman said casually, "a person who wanted to pay me to make your life a living nightmare." She shrugged. "What can I say? I needed the money. And I know enough about you from Ralph's stories that I knew just what to do to frighten you."

Isabella was surprised to hear that the woman had been hired by another person to frighten her. Who would do such a thing? And why? She thought back to the first note she'd received. *I know what you did last season.*

Could the person who hired Mrs. Savery be doing this as a means of revenge for Gervase's death? It seemed so far-fetched. And yet it made a diabolical kind of sense.

Though she knew the other woman had little reason to tell her, Isabella asked, "Who was it that hired you to frighten me, Mrs. Savery? Will you tell me?"

The baby stirred in the other woman's arms and began to fret. It was disturbing to watch Charity soothe the baby even as she kept the gun trained on Isabella. "There, there, little mite," Charity crooned. "There's nothing to be frightened of. Nothing at all."

To Isabella she said coldly, "I wouldn't tell you who hired me, even if I could. Because that would give you some satisfaction. And I'll be damned before I see you relax ever again, Your Grace." She said the courtesy with contempt, as if the very words tasted terrible in her mouth.

It was worth a try, Isabella thought, even as the woman's words sent a shiver down her spine. She wished suddenly that she'd waited for Trevor to return before charging up here. If only because together they'd have an easier time rescuing the baby.

"I'm not quite sure why you hate me so much," Isabella tried again. "Clearly Ralph was far more fond of you than he was of me. I was little more than an obligation to him. You were the one he wanted to be with. Even though I didn't know you were there waiting for him across town, I knew that his heart belonged to someone else." She was improvising now, but she decided if she could convince the other woman that Ralph had truly loved her perhaps she would let down her guard a little.

"You lie," Charity said, her eyes narrowed. But there was a hint of something there, hope, perhaps, that told Isabella she was making progress.

"No, not at all," she said, leaning forward in her chair a bit, as if they were two acquaintances chatting over the tea table. "In fact, I once found a note that I thought was written to me but I now suspect was written to you."

The promise of a letter from her dead lover proved to be just the right sort of lure to spark the woman's interest. "Why do you say that?" she asked, her eyes a bit less narrow, her lip between her teeth.

"It was addressed to 'Darling' for one thing," Isabella said, hoping that Ralph had been as careless with his endearments with the other woman as he was with her. "Does that sound familiar?"

When the other woman's eyes lit up, Isabella knew it did. Grateful for her late husband's laziness, she went on, "If you'll just let me go back up to my bedchamber, I'll retrieve it for you."

But that would have been too easy. Charity's gaze hardened and she shook her head. "I don't think so, Your Grace. I don't think I trust you not to go running for help. No, I'll come with you, just to keep you company, you understand."

Careless of the baby in her arms, Mrs. Savery rose from the chair and in the process woke the sleeping baby, who began to wail. "Shut up. Shut up." Jerking her head at Isabella, Charity indicated that she should take the baby from her arms.

"You hold the little one," she said coldly, "and I'll

follow you to your bedchamber. I still don't trust you not
to run, but at least with the baby in your arms you'll be
hampered a bit."

Taking the child, Isabella was disturbed to see a red
mark on the baby's cheek as if she'd been struck. "What's
her name?" Isabella asked the other woman.

"Doesn't have one so's I can tell," Charity said. "I got
her from a woman in Whitechapel whot runs a nursery
of sorts."

Isabella could guess what sort of nursery Charity spoke
of. Ladies of the *ton* weren't supposed to know such places
existed, but Isabella had heard about them from Georgina, who in turn had learned about them through her
charitable work. They were horrible places where babies were kept and drugged with laudanum until they
were too weak to survive. Isabella cuddled the child to
her even as she vowed that they would both escape this
ordeal. And holding her head high, she led the other
woman out of the nursery and into the hallway.

"Let me see the note again," Trevor said to Lord Archer
from their table at the Goose and Pickle.

Wordlessly the man handed Trevor the folded missive. They'd been approached by an urchin with the note
just as they were leaving the Wharton town house.

It had been two hours since the appointed meeting
time, and Trevor was feeling hoodwinked. He scanned
the words on the page once more to see if they'd missed
something. But the message was simple enough. They
were to meet this person and in exchange for fifty pounds
he would tell them who was responsible for tormenting
Isabella. But there was something about the words. The

paper. Something that triggered a memory. If only he could remember what.

"Is there anything odd about this note, Archer?"

Trevor's companion frowned. "You mean besides the fact that it's a blackmail note? Not particularly."

"There's something here," Trevor said with a shake of his head. As if the shaking would dislodge whatever was making him feel uneasy.

"'If you want to know who's teasing yer lady wife, bring fifty pound and I'll tell yer,'" Archer recited the note from memory. "Is it something about the phrasing?" he asked. "The grammar?"

Trevor thought through the wording of the note again. "It's 'lady wife,'" he said. "Someone has used that precise phrase with me recently." He'd met so many new people since his and Isabella's arrival in London it was difficult to remember all of them. But someone had used the phrase. It was common enough, but not one that was used all that frequently in his hearing.

Archer shook his head. "I haven't heard it recently. But who has been speaking to you of Isabella? Perhaps we can narrow it that way."

"Since the majority of conversation I've had since I got to town has been about my hasty marriage, that will hardly make a difference."

"Good point." Archer took the note from Trevor and looked at it. "It's the sort of phrase a person uses when issuing an invitation, like 'and will your lady wife be joining you this evening?' or when asking after her, 'And how is your lady wife?'"

Trevor nodded. "Yes, but those sound like inquiries from our peers. For some reason I think this came from someone with a lower accent."

Archer tipped his head to the side, rather like an inquiring spaniel. "It would be highly irregular for a servant to use the phrase with you. It's overfamiliar. And I cannot imagine Timms allowing such a thing in Ormonde House. Or Mrs. Timms for that matter."

"Yes," Trevor said. "That's why it feels so out of place. But I'd swear it was someone in Ormonde House. Not that there isn't an army of servants to go through there."

"But not that many who would have reason to speak to you," Archer pointed out. "With whom do you have conversations among the servants? Your valet, and I believe you'd remember him saying such a thing. The maids? The footmen? Isabella's m—"

"That's it!" Trevor interrupted. "It was Isabella's maid, Sanders." He felt a chill run down his spine. "I stepped into Isabella's bedchamber to . . . uh, speak to her, and Sanders made a point of telling me that she'd leave me alone with my 'lady wife,' as if she were doing me a favor by leaving."

"She would certainly have the kind of access necessary to blackmail you. And if she knows whoever it is that has been frightening Isabella—"

"But that's just it," Trevor said. "I've had the feeling all evening that this was a diversionary tactic. What if it's Sanders who has been doing all of this to Isabella? She knows everything about Isabella's daily life. She knows her likes and dislikes. Just what it will take to push her over the edge." Sanders even knew, though he didn't say it aloud, when he and Isabella made love. When they quarreled. When they made up.

"If this was a ploy to get us away from Isabella,"

Archer said, "then we'd better get back to the house at once. Because she's had two hours alone with her."

But Trevor was already out of his seat and rushing out of the tavern.

"Just tell me where the letter is," Charity said sharply once they'd reached the sitting room attached to Isabella's bedchamber. The hand holding the gun hadn't wavered once as they'd made their way to the mistress's suite. And with her prize in sight, the maid had nearly begun to vibrate with anticipation of reading her former lover's words to her. She was obsessed, Isabella knew now. Obsessed with a man who had treated her like a used handkerchief. To be cast aside once he'd finished with her. But clearly whatever bond the other woman had shared with Ralph, it had been different from her own. Perhaps to Charity's disordered mind that had been love.

"It's hidden inside a book of poetry," Isabella said, hoping that Charity's anger when she discovered that Isabella was lying would be distraction enough to let her escape. She moved toward the small shelf of books near her writing desk. "It's Shakespeare's sonnets."

The book was one she kept with her whenever she traveled. She only hoped that Charity had never looked inside it before. Otherwise Isabella was in danger of having the woman catch her out in the lie.

Isabella hoisted the baby onto her shoulder, relieved to feel the child's shallow breaths on her neck. "Here," she said, reaching out a hand to grasp the book before Charity could. Isabella flipped open the volume where she'd absently slipped a bill from Madame Celeste to use as a bookmark and hoped that it looked enough like a personal letter to fool the other woman.

Unfolding it, Isabella improvised, pretending to read aloud:

"'Darling, As I write this my wife sleeps. And all I can think of is you and the child you carry. If only our child could inherit the title instead of the accursed child of this loveless union I'm trapped in. It is you I love. Only you. And no amount of whinging from Isabella can change that. You are the wife of my heart. And I will do whatever it takes to make sure we can be together. Yours, Ralph.'"

As Isabella said the words, she feared that she was overdoing it. Ralph had never been particularly demonstrative with her. But she hoped that Charity's wishful thinking was enough to make her believe that for the space of this one letter he'd unburdened his heart, such as it was.

"Again," Charity said, tears streaming down her face. "Read it again."

To Isabella's astonishment, Charity had taken a seat in the desk chair and was looking to Isabella like a child requesting a story. Charity had even rested the gun in her lap for a moment.

"I—" Isabella froze. She had improvised the letter. She wasn't sure she could say the words again just as she'd said them the first time. "Why don't I give it to you?" she said. "That way you can read it yourself."

"Read it," Charity said, lifting the gun again. "I want to hear it again. And I want to hear it in your voice."

There was something in the other woman's voice that made Isabella's skin crawl. It was true that Charity likely could not read the letter for herself. But she also enjoyed, in some twisted way, having her former lover's wife read his words of love to her, his mistress.

"Please," Isabella said, her voice soothing. "May I put the baby down so that I can read it properly?"

The maid's eyes narrowed. As if assessing Isabella's request for the trap it was. To Isabella's relief, however, Charity seemed to find the request innocent enough. More fool her. "All right. Put it in the window seat."

Carefully, Isabella stepped over to the window seat. Not turning her back on the pistol-wielding woman, Isabella lowered the baby onto the cushion and then stood up straight. The letter was clasped in her left hand, while the right, which had been holding the baby, now held a pillow from the window seat concealed behind Isabella's back. Not wishing the child to be in the line of fire, Isabella stepped quickly away from the window and toward the other side of the desk.

" 'Darling,' " she began to recite the letter again, " 'As I write this . . . ,' " she went on, saying the words as best as she could remember, watching to see if, as before, Charity dropped her guard as she listened to Ralph's supposed words. To Isabella's relief, she did. Once more the pistol lowered to rest in Charity's lap while she lost herself in the letter.

In her head, Isabella counted down. Three. Two. One.

Still reciting the fictitious letter, she lifted the pillow and rushed at Charity with it.

Twenty-one

Ormonde House was quiet when Trevor and Archer arrived. Timms was waiting for them at the door, however.

"Where is the duchess?" Trevor asked before Timms could welcome them home.

If Timms was startled by his master's sharp tone, he didn't show it. "I believe she is in her bedchamber, Your Grace. Is something amiss?"

Trevor ignored the question and bounded for the stairs. He could hear Archer behind him, shouting for the butler to send for the watch.

When Trevor and Archer got to the door of Isabella's suite, Trevor could hear voices. But before he could turn the knob, Archer stopped him.

"You don't know what's happening in there. This woman has spent the past few weeks terrorizing your wife. And she clearly had some grand finale in mind for tonight. You don't want to rush in too quickly and startle her into doing something that will harm Isabella."

"Then what?" Trevor asked through clenched teeth. "She's got my wife in there. What am I supposed to do?"

"Come with me," Archer said, leading him down the

hallway a bit to a seemingly bare bit of paneled wall. To Trevor's astonishment, when the other man pressed a portion of the trim the door opened out to reveal a hidden passageway. "It's for the servants," he said, quickly taking a torch from the wall. "These passages run between the family rooms and behind the fireplaces, so that they can go about their business without danger of being seen by the family."

Trevor would marvel at the architecture later. Right now he wanted to know what was happening in Isabella's rooms. He followed Archer down the dark hallway and, sure enough, they could hear voices coming from Isabella's sitting room. They stopped just beside what was clearly the back of a fireplace.

"May I put the baby down so that I can read it properly?" Trevor heard Isabella ask.

"Baby?" he asked. "Where the devil did a baby come from?"

"Come look," Archer whispered, showing Trevor a peephole that looked into Isabella's sitting room. When this was over he was going to go through all of these rooms himself and make sure that no one would ever be able to spy on him and Isabella again. "She's got a pistol. You don't want to startle her while she's got that pointed at your wife."

Trevor watched silently as Isabella carefully laid the baby down in the window seat. What he could see that her captor could not was that Isabella had picked up a pillow while she was depositing her precious bundle. Isabella, he was proud to see, had a plan.

"'Darling, as I write this . . . ,'" she said, seemingly reading from a letter in her outstretched hand. As he watched she seemed to tap the pillow out in beats. One.

Two. And on three she charged the woman in the chair, pressing the pillow against her face.

"Come on," Archer shouted, bursting into the bed-chamber, followed by Trevor.

The two women were rolling on the floor while Isabella tried to get control of the pistol. The two men rushed at them, and while Trevor helped Isabella up from the floor Archer dragged Charity to her feet and pinned her arms behind her back.

"Let me go!" she shouted. "Damn you! Get your hands off of me!"

"Thank god," Isabella said, collapsing against Trevor's chest. "Thank god you came. I was afraid she'd kill us both. She's been the one threatening me. All this time. My own maid. What a fool I've been."

"Easy," Trevor said, holding her close. "It's all right. I've got you. You're safe now."

"I'll just take Sanders downstairs and see if the watch has arrived yet," Archer said, tucking the pistol into the back of his breeches. "I'm glad you're safe, Your Grace."

But neither Isabella nor Trevor heard him leave.

"So all this time it was Sanders who was trying to frighten you?" Perdita said with a shake of her head. "It's extraordinary. I never for a moment considered that it might be her who was doing it."

The sisters, Trevor, and Archer were gathered in Isabella's sitting room, a pastry-laden tea tray before them on the table. Isabella sat in the shelter of Trevor's arms. Since they'd seen Sanders, or Mrs. Savery, taken away by the watch, he hadn't been willing to let Isabella out of his sight. And she was all right with that.

"Nor did I," she said, taking a sip of her own tea. "But the true villain of the piece is as yet uncaught."

"Can you really think that she was telling the truth when she spoke of being hired by someone else to torment you, Your Grace?" Archer asked, his handsome face creased with worry. "I mean, Mrs. Savery can hardly be considered a reliable source of information in any matter, let alone this one."

"She seemed perfectly convinced of the matter when she spoke of it to me," Isabella said with a shiver. "Though I suppose it is possible that she deluded herself into thinking she'd been hired by someone just so that she would not bear the guilt for it herself."

"I mean to take no chances," Trevor said, his arms tightening around Isabella. "We will depart London at the end of the week for Yorkshire."

"But we only just arrived," Isabella said in a weak protest. If the truth of the matter were known, the glitter of town had lost much of its allure for her. "Though I do miss Eleanor and Belinda." She turned to her sister. "You must come with us, Perdy. You will adore the girls. And I know they'll adore you. And you may help me plan Eleanor's come-out ball next year."

"I think that's an excellent notion," Archer opined. "If you don't mind my saying so, Your Grace." Isabella watched as her sister blushed under the secretary's gaze. Interesting, she thought. Perhaps she needed to have a talk with Perdita. Sooner rather than later.

"I will think about it," Perdita said, rising. "Now, if you don't mind, I am exhausted. When I heard those shrieks all I could think was that you were being murdered in your bed." She bent to hug Isabella.

"I'll take myself off as well," Archer said, rising to

follow Perdita from the room. "Good night, Your Graces." He offered a slight bow before he left the room.

Alone now with Trevor, Isabella turned to snuggle up in his arms. "I wonder if Perdita knows he's in love with her," she said idly. "I don't know how I never noticed it before now. But I suppose I never felt the state myself, so I had no way of recognizing it."

"Does that mean what I think it means?" Trevor asked, holding her back from him so that he could look into her eyes.

"I don't know," Isabella said playfully. "What do you think it means?"

"Do not tease me, woman," Trevor said with a mock growl. "Are you in love with me, or are you not?"

"I cannot be the first one to admit such a thing," she said primly. "After all, it is hardly seemly for a lady to confess her love to a gentleman before he has done so to her."

"You and your rules," he said, kissing her soundly. "Very well, I love you. In fact, if the truth be known, I adore you and have done since you first mistook me for a common laborer weeks ago in Nettledean."

She kissed him back for a long while before she said, "Did you really adore me way back then? I was rather horrid to you, if memory serves."

"You are horrid to me now," he said against her mouth. "Refusing to admit you love me. I don't know what I've done to deserve such a thing."

Isabella sighed and leaned her cheek against his shoulder. "All right," she said, stroking his chest. "I love you. Happy now?"

His response was silent but heartfelt.

Epilogue

The next afternoon, Isabella, Perdita, and Georgina, who had been away in Bath when Isabella first returned to London, sat comfortably ensconced in Isabella's sitting room over the tea tray, catching up with one another and going over the details of Isabella's ordeal first in Yorkshire and then in London.

"What became of the baby Mrs. Savery used to frighten you?" Georgina asked. "Poor wee mite."

"She's being cared for by the sister of one of the kitchen maids who just had a baby of her own," Isabella said with a smile. "Timms thought of her almost as soon as he heard about the child. He has a soft heart."

"That's quite true," Perdita agreed. "And a hard one when it comes to Mrs. Savery's sort. I don't think I've ever seen him as angry as he was when he learned what she'd done to you, Isa."

"What I find hard to believe is how one woman was able to create such a furor," Georgina said with a shake of her blond curls. "Even if she was being assisted by some unknown mastermind from afar."

"She did manage to make my life quite difficult for a

few weeks there," Isabella agreed. "But I suppose the degree of assistance she received rather depends upon who it was helping her. And unfortunately, we still don't know who that was."

Perdita poured each of them another cup of tea and added another biscuit to her plate. "Whoever it is behind the whole operation, I wish he would decide once and for all to be finished with the business. I have little choice but to look over my shoulder constantly."

"I agree," Georgina said firmly. Reaching into her reticule, she retrieved a folded bit of foolscap and handed it to Isabella. "I received this just this morning. And I do not think that your Mrs. Savery could possibly have smuggled the notice out of Coldbath Fields Prison."

"'I know what you did last season,'" Isabella read from the note. "I had so hoped that all this would be over now. Especially because I have not received another note."

"Do not fret, dearest," Perdita said, squeezing her sister's hand. "Georgie and I will be quite all right. I'll be in Yorkshire with you and Trevor after all. And with Mrs. Savery out of the picture, and all the rest of the servants examined with a fine-tooth comb, there is little chance that he'll get to me. And Georgie plans to remove to Bath, where all will be well."

"Do you mean to tell your new employer about the threats, Georgie?" Isabella asked their friend as she blew on her too-hot tea.

"Good lord, no!" Georgina said with an unrepentant grin. "I need this position and I do not mean to give Lady Throckmorton reason to dismiss me even before I start."

"I do wish you would accept Trevor's offer to have

you come live with us," Isabella said with a frown. "I'm quite sure my sisters-in-law would adore you!"

"You are too good, Isabella," the widow replied, "but I could not possibly impose upon your charity like that. Besides which, I have already accepted the position with Lady Throckmorton. She and I were quite close when we were following the drum together and I think looking after her as she sets tongues wagging in Bath will be quite amusing for me."

"You've simply got too much pride for your own good, Georgie," Perdita said with a grin. "Not that we can blame you. Also, I should think it will be a trial after a while to spend too much time in company with the lovebirds."

"I resent that!" Isabella said with a blush. "We are not a trial. We are simply blissfully happy, and if you cannot manage to endure it for the next few weeks then perhaps you should stay in London."

"Oh, don't be so sensitive. I was merely teasing you a little." Perdita said with a laugh. "Besides, you promised me that I should be able to attend a sheepshearing at the very least!"

A soft knock on the door preceded Trevor, who said from the doorway, "I hope I'm not disturbing you ladies, but I have a bit of news for Isabella."

"Come in, darling," Isabella said with a bland expression. "Perdita was just telling me how much she's looking forward to seeing the splendors of Yorkshire. She has a particular fondness for sheep, I believe."

"Oh, we've plenty of those, Duchess," Trevor said to his sister-in-law before lowering himself into a wing chair beside Isabella's.

"So, what is this news?" Isabella asked. She was curious since he'd only been headed for White's when he'd left the mansion earlier in the day.

"Well, I have it on good authority that a certain Sir Lionel Thistleback has just left for the first packet bound for the Americas."

"No!" Isabella said with a gasp. "What happened to him? And who made it happen, so that I can thank them properly?"

"He's as nasty a man as I've ever met," Georgina said with a shudder. "If he'd been in the military he'd have been court-martialed and hanged long ago."

"Well, I am quite content to have him on the other side of the world," Trevor said with feeling. "Apparently he was found to be blackmailing a certain cabinet minister's wife over her gambling debts. Little did he know, however, that the minister knew all about the debts and had agreed to pay them without complaint. When he learned of the scheme, he told Thistleback he was too dishonorable to duel with and threatened Thistleback with imprisonment if he didn't leave for America immediately."

"And Thistleback simply left?" Isabella asked with astonishment. "I can hardly believe it!"

"Well, he did take a little persuading from what I hear," Trevor said. "He was escorted to the docks with just the clothes on his back, forced to drink laudanum, then deposited on the ship into a locked cabin lest he try to escape. I do not think he will have a very happy crossing."

"Good riddance," Perdita said. "After what he tried to do to you, Isabella, I hope he never comes back."

"Thank you for telling me, my dear," Isabella told Trevor, leaning over to kiss him quickly on the cheek.

But he turned and kissed her in earnest, much to the mock disgust of Perdita and Georgina.

"What did I tell you, Georgie?" Isabella heard her sister complain to their friend. "Lovebirds. I don't know how I shall manage to keep from becoming ill every day while I am in Yorkshire with them."

"Oh, I think they're sweet," Isabella heard Georgina croon.

"Do you think we're sweet?" Trevor asked, pulling back a little from Isabella to look into her eyes.

"I don't think we're sweet," she said, gathering him closer so that she could whisper into his ear. "I know we are, because we are in love."

Don't miss the next book by Manda Collins

Why Earls Fall in Love

Coming soon from St. Martin's Paperbacks!